A ROSE IN NO MAN'S
LAND

A ROSE IN NO MAN'S LAND

John C. Kerr

Book Guild Publishing
Sussex, England

First published in Great Britain in 2011 by
The Book Guild Ltd
Pavilion View
19 New Road
Brighton, BN1 1UF

Typesetting in Baskerville by
Keyboard Services, Luton, Bedfordshire

Printed in Great Britain by
CPI Group (UK) Ltd, Croydon, CR0 4YY

A catalogue record for this book is available from
The British Library

ISBN 978 1 84624 628 9

For Susan

Preface

In the early months of the First World War, a group of Americans who ardently supported the Allied war effort organized the American Field Service as a unique means of assisting the French and British without violating America's strict neutrality laws. The AFS recruited young men, primarily from college campuses in New England, to travel to France at their own expense and serve as volunteer ambulance drivers in sections attached to the French, and to a much lesser extent, the British armies. The ambulances were converted Model T Fords, purchased from the factory with funds donated to the AFS, shipped to France and there fitted out with hardboard siding and racks to support stretchers.

Thousands of young Americans answered the AFS appeal and served in France and Belgium from early 1915 until America finally entered the war in April of 1917. A disproportionate number came from the elite Ivy League universities, with Harvard alone supplying over 300 volunteers. Each section was assigned to a particular French or British unit, the unpaid drivers wearing army uniforms without insignias, driving the manoeuverable little Model Ts with a red cross and the words American Field Service painted on the siding. Driving at night without lights near the front lines, the work was hazardous, with over 100 AFS volunteers losing their lives. But perhaps as important as the service the American volunteers rendered to the French and British wounded, is the part they played in swaying public opinion in the US to enter the war on the side of the Allies. Theodore Roosevelt, speaking at an AFS gathering in New York in 1916, said:

> There is not an American worth calling such, who is not under a heavy debt of obligation to these boys for what they have done. We are under an even greater debt to them than the French and Belgians are... The most important thing that a nation can possibly save is its soul, and these young men have been helping this nation to save its soul.

1

The driver stared into the darkness, swerving to avoid a tree that suddenly appeared against the black. He swore under his breath as he clutched the wheel and tightly gripped the gearshift.

'Damn!'

'Maybe it would help if you hang your head out,' suggested the man on the seat next to him, visible only by the orange tip of his cigarette.

The driver craned his head out of the open-air cab, maintaining a speed of no more than ten miles an hour.

'I saw a sign for Zillebeke back there,' said the passenger, who flicked his lighter and studied the hand-drawn map in his lap. 'We should be coming up on Hill 62.'

Brilliant flashes like giant fireflies blinked on the horizon, momentarily illuminating the snub-nosed hood of the Model T. A rocket raced into the sky, trailing sparks in a graceful parabola before bursting into a star-shell in the low clouds, spreading faint light across the country-side.

'That's better,' said the driver, a young American named Frank Harrington, now able to see the road ahead. 'You didn't warn me we'd be making these runs without headlamps.'

'Oh, Jesus,' said Bill Larrabee, tossing out his cigarette. 'Speed it up, Frank.'

As the guns thundered and the horizon flashed, Harrington was conscious of a different sound, whining, growing louder, coming ... and then an ear-splitting concussion that rocked the car and almost caused him to lose control as he jammed his boot on the gas pedal.

'Whiz-bang,' said Larrabee calmly. He audibly exhaled as the star-shell winked out.

'That was close,' said Harrington. 'It's almost like they were...'

'...Aiming at us?' said Larrabee. 'They were.'

'You mean to tell me,' said Harrington as he slowed to a crawl, 'that even with that red cross painted on the side, the lousy Boche would shoot at an ambulance...?'

'The gunners see somethin' movin' on the road,' said Larrabee. 'They see it, they fire. For all they know, it's an ammo truck. Hell, it's dark out there,' he added incongruously.

As they slowly made their way along the shell-pocked road, Harrington grew more confident in his ability to discern the ghostly trunks of the few trees along the verge, as if he'd acquired a sixth sense. He realized that he was thankful it was such a dark and moonless night. He noticed, too, that the reverberations of the guns were much louder. 'How much further?' he asked.

Larrabee stared ahead in the darkness. 'We ought to be coming up on the checkpoint. Unless we made a wrong turn back there. The *poste* is next to one of their batteries, according to this map.'

'Post?' said Harrington, swerving to avoid another tree.

'*Poste de secours*,' said Larrabee. 'The aid station. I'm still learning the Brits' system. They haul 'em into the aid stations on stretchers,' he explained, 'the *blessés* – wounded – and we take 'em out to the field hospital. What the Brits call a Casualty Clearing Station.'

Harrington flinched as the heavy British guns roared, the muzzle flashes briefly lighting the low clouds. 'And then what?' he asked.

'And then we go home. To our sweet, little billet. Unless

2

we pick up another load, that is, to take to one of the hospitals on the Channel.'

Harrington nodded and concentrated on working the gear-lever of the Model T. Two British sentries suddenly loomed in the darkness. Slamming on the brakes, Harrington leaned out. A tall infantryman, rifle slung on his shoulder, ignored Harrington as he curiously examined the ambulance.

'What the bloody hell...?' he said, stooping to peer inside.

'American Field Service,' said Larrabee. 'Here for a pick-up.'

After a quick glance at the red cross stencilled on the siding, the sentry jerked a thumb toward a muddy track. 'Turn right at the sign for Hill 62,' he said. 'The aid station's a hundred yards down that lane.'

But for the almost continuous flashing, they would have never seen the hand-lettered sign by the dirt track. Harrington strained to keep the tyres in the ruts while conscious of the massive bombardment to his right, to the rear of the British lines.

'Ypres,' commented Larrabee as he studied the fires glowing against the night sky. 'They're pounding the hell out of it.'

Harrington braked as a volley erupted from a battery of British howitzers fifty yards in front of them, partially obscured by a copse of trees. He thought he saw a small group of men, some standing, others prone. Down-shifting, he steered for the men and said, 'That must be the aid station.'

'OK, Frank,' said Larrabee, sitting up straight. 'Let's make quick work of it.'

He reached for a flashlight as Harrington brought the ambulance up to a British officer who was standing beside a row of stretchers.

'Leave it running,' instructed Larrabee, 'so we don't have

3

to fool with cranking it.' He threw open the door and jumped out.

As Harrington climbed out, another volley from the nearby battery deafened him, and the shock wave knocked him to the side.

In the glare the British officer had an opportunity to inspect the vehicle, with its American Indian-head insignia painted on the hardboard siding beside the red cross and block letters SSA, for *Section Sanitaire Américaine*. Harrington and Larrabee were wearing the khaki uniform of the British Army, though unadorned with badges of rank or regimental patches. Larrabee casually walked up to the officer.

'Who in the hell are you?' asked the officer. 'And where's *our* bloody ambulance?'

While Harrington opened the doors at the back of the Model T, Larrabee quickly assessed the situation, counting three men lying on stretchers and two others, injured but standing. 'American Field Service,' he replied, noting the bars of a captain on the officer's collar. 'And *we're* your bloody ambulance.'

'Americans,' said the officer dismissively. 'And where, may I ask, are the RAMC?'

'Look, Captain,' said Larrabee as he knelt down to examine one of the wounded, 'we're here to pick up these men. Somebody decided to send us over to help out with your army, though I'd prefer the French any day...'

'Now see here,' said the captain.

'Let's go, Frank,' said Larrabee, grasping the handles at the foot of the nearest stretcher.

As the wounded man cried out, Harrington took the other end and they hoisted the stretcher and slid it onto a rack at the rear of the ambulance. As they were loading the second stretcher, Harrington and Larrabee could hear the man fighting for breath above the roar of the guns.

4

'Gas,' said the captain, who watched with a grim smile. Larrabee secured the stretcher and returned for the third man. As he bent down to grasp the handles, he paused and then reached down to examine the large bandage swaddling the man's thigh. He switched on his flashlight and shone it on the wound, revealing a bright scarlet mass of gauze.

'Put out that torch, for heaven's sake!' barked the captain.

'Come here, Frank,' said Larrabee, kneeling over the stretcher. 'Give me a hand.' He reached into his pocket for a penknife and began cutting away the man's trouser above the bandage.

'What in God's name are you doing?' demanded the captain.

'He's bleeding to death,' said Larrabee as Harrington stood helplessly to the side. 'The femoral artery's severed. Run get me some rubber tubing, Frank, from the toolbox on the passenger side.'

'Unhand the man,' said the captain, aware that the two wounded men standing beside him were observing the scene with great interest.

'OK, Frank,' said Larrabee as Harrington scrambled back from the Ford with a three-foot length of tubing. 'Reach in – here – and put some pressure on the wound while I get a tourniquet on him.'

Harrington reluctantly reached for the man's thigh. His hands were immediately covered with warm, sticky blood that flowed freely from a deep gash despite the heavy bandage. In a quick, expert motion, Larrabee drew the tubing around the man's groin and fashioned a knot, which he tightened with a small stick.

'There,' said Larrabee. 'Can you feel it, Frank?'

Breathing heavily, nauseated by the blood covering his hands, Harrington was aware of the abrupt diminishment of the flow. 'Yeah,' he muttered. 'It's stopping.'

'Let's go,' said Larrabee, jumping to his feet and bending down to take the handles.

Wiping his hands on his trousers, Harrington reached for the other end and they carefully carried the stretcher to the ambulance and slid it onto the rack.

'There's room for one more in the back,' said Larrabee, motioning to the two standing wounded. 'The other fellow will have to sit up front.'

Harrington helped one of the men, who was using his rifle as a crutch, to squeeze into the space between the stretchers, while Larrabee opened the door for the other man. The captain approached him.

'What's your name?' he asked with a scowl. 'I'm writing you up.'

'Larrabee. Bill Larrabee, Captain. What's yours?'

'Bastard,' said the officer under his breath as Larrabee climbed in and swung the door shut. 'I'm Captain Nigel Owen and these are my men. See that they're well taken care of.'

'Let's go, Frank,' said Larrabee, looking over the pale face of the man sitting between them, frozen in a mask of pain.

As Harrington pumped the accelerator and shifted into gear, he was aware that he'd been strangely indifferent to the thunder of the cannons. Turning the Ford in a tight circle, he steered for the ruts, taking care to jostle the wounded men as little as possible. Once they were back on the paved road, the sentries retreating in the rear-view mirrors, he turned to Larrabee and said, 'That was quick thinking back there. Where did you learn...'

'I spent my summers at Yale working as an orderly at New Haven General. I'm headed for medical school when this is all over.'

'I see,' said Harrington, wincing as the Ford bounced over a pothole.

6

'There's no way that fella could have made it to the Clearing Station without a tourniquet. He should be OK if we hurry.'

Harrington nodded and gunned the engine.

'It's the gas case that worries me,' added Larrabee. 'Sorry German bastards!'

'Bloody masks are more trouble than they're worth,' spoke up the young British soldier sitting between them.

'Let's have a look at that arm,' said Larrabee. Carefully untying the bandage, he shone his light on the bullet wound through the forearm. He reached for a bottle and liberally splashed iodine on the wound. 'Disinfectant,' he explained to the grimacing soldier.

'Nice piece of work back there,' said the soldier through gritted teeth. 'On Freddie's leg.'

'Yes, well, your captain certainly appreciated it.'

'Captain's a tough old boot,' said the soldier in a more relaxed voice. 'But he looks after the lads. Not many officers would've come with us to the aid station under fire like that.' Harrington turned and smiled at the boy, relieved that the booming was receding.

'Look up ahead, Frank,' said Larrabee. Harrington squinted, just able to make out the outline of a vehicle in front of them. 'Pull up closer,' said Larrabee, 'and flash your lights. It may be one of ours.'

When Harrington flicked the headlights, he was surprised that there were only a few yards separating the two vehicles. Easing up on the gas, he read aloud the identification stencilled on the fender: 'AFS-8-12.'

'Number 12,' said Larrabee. 'That's Deac. He'll know the way. We'll convoy in with him.'

* * *

'Fall in, ladies.' The Sister's unsmiling face disappeared from the opening in the tent flap.

'Umm,' groaned Kit Stanley, rolling over on her side, clinging to the fragment of a dream and the last, precious moments of sleep. She was vaguely aware of a match being struck and the flickering light of a candle.

'C'mon, Kit,' said the petite nurse on the cot beside her in the cramped space of the bell-tent. 'Time to wake up.'

'Um hmm.' Kit propped herself up on an elbow and rubbed her eyes. 'So sleepy.' She brushed back her hair and swung her white-stocking-clad feet over the side. 'What time is it?'

'Two? Three? What difference does it make?'

Both nurses had been sleeping on top of the covers in their long, blue–grey dresses and white bibs and aprons, their polished black shoes left at the foot of their cots. With the single candle casting eerie shadows on the canvas, Kit slipped on her shoes and wearily stood up, suppressing a yawn with a sigh. With only the slightest concern for her appearance, she buttoned her collar, secured a white cap atop her thick, brown hair, and followed her tent mate into the night air.

They paused to listen to the rumble of an approaching convoy. As they crossed the courtyard to the main building of the old monastery – which had been hastily converted to a Casualty Clearing Station – Kit wondered where they would find room for the new arrivals. The last batch had filled the cots, with the overflow left to manage as best as they could on their bloody stretchers, while the walking cases had been told to make themselves comfortable on the floor, outside in the courtyard, or wherever else they could find a decent resting place.

Kit walked from the darkness of the courtyard into the glare of the bulbs suspended from the vaulted ceiling of the chapel. As she hurried between the tightly packed cots, Kit's nose twitched at the carbolic and ether mingling with the odours of filthy, unwashed men.

'All right, ladies.' The Ward Sister, a senior nurse in the Royal Army Medical Corps, looked sternly at the young women standing in a semi-circle around her – all of them 'VADs,' shorthand for 'volunteer aid detachments'. 'We shall have to make the best of it,' said the Sister, 'nursing these men on their stretchers until more beds are available.'

The nurses turned toward the commotion on the far side of the chapel, where a tall, broad-shouldered soldier was half-carrying, half-dragging a wounded man through the entrance, followed by orderlies bearing a stretcher.

'Miss Stanley, Miss Tisdale, lend a hand there,' instructed the Sister. 'You other girls stay with me.'

By the time Kit reached the tall soldier, a sergeant, he had lowered his badly wounded comrade onto one of the few available cots. An orderly carefully parted the wounded man's jacket to expose a large, bloody bandage covering his chest. Kit turned from the unconscious man on the cot to the sergeant. Besides deep concern, she could see pain in his hooded eyes. Blood dripped from the hand he held to his side.

'Let's have a look at that,' she said, carefully pulling open his muddy tunic. 'Oh, my,' she said with a sharp intake of breath. 'You've got a nasty wound.' As the man stood stoically still, she peeled away the blood-soaked bandage from a jagged shrapnel wound in his ribcage. 'You shouldn't have carried that man,' she admonished him, looking up at his dirty, unshaven face. 'You belong on a stretcher yourself.' She glanced at the regimental patch on his shoulder. KRRC. The King's Royal Rifle Corps.

'Jane,' she said. 'Look after the lying case while I see to the sergeant.'

The crowded chapel was filling with orderlies searching for space for their stretchers amid the cries of the wounded and shouts of the medical officers. Helping the sergeant to sit, Kit found a large pair of scissors, cut away his

9

bandage, and splashed disinfectant on a sponge. At the contact of the cold sponge on the wound, the colour drained from the sergeant's face, his head snapped back, and he fainted dead away. Loss of blood, thought Kit, as she reached for his shoulder to keep him from falling from the chair. After a moment he came to, intensely embarrassed.

'We must find you a cot,' said Kit, 'and an orderly will help you out of those clothes.' She grimaced at the thought of the grey-back lice no doubt crawling beneath his filthy uniform.

'Thank you, Sister,' he said with a weary smile.

Amid the arriving stretchers and walking wounded, Kit was aware of the voice of the medical officer attending to the soldier the sergeant had carried in. As she turned to look, the soldier's eyes fluttered open and a smile lit up his boyish face at the sight of the pretty young nurse standing over him.

'Surgical case, nurse,' said the MO, scribbling a note. 'See to it that an orderly gets him ready.'

'Yes, sir.'

The Ward Sister walked over to Kit. 'Miss Stanley,' she said. 'Report to the operating theatre. They've been at it all night and need a relief.'

As the orderlies lifted the stretcher, the wounded boy lightly touched Kit's apron and said, 'Thanks, Sister,' eliciting a glare of disapproval from the *real* Sister. Smiling inwardly, Kit responded with a short, obsequious bow, and turned to make her way out between the crowded rows of stretchers.

* * *

With the shelling fading in the distance, the drivers determined it was safe to switch on their headlamps for the final leg of the drive to No. 8 Casualty Clearing Station at Bailleul, ten miles south-west of the Flemish market town of Ypres.

'How are you feeling?' Bill Larrabee asked the young Tommy on the seat beside him.

'Oh, I'm all right, sir.'

'Not sir,' corrected Larrabee. 'Anyhow, we're coming up on the Clearing Station. Before long, you'll be getting your ticket to Blighty.' In the dim light of the dash he detected a faint smile on the soldier's face.

'Blighty?' said Harrington.

'England,' explained Larrabee. 'Every Tommy's dream.' The young soldier nodded.

The convoy turned into the gravel drive at the monastery and came to a stop in the courtyard. Within moments, British orderlies emerged and began unloading the wounded. Larrabee climbed out, stretched, and said, 'Let's get these *blessés* out of the back, Frank. At least the *couchés*. They were pretty bad off.'

As they opened the rear doors, they could hear the man on the upper stretcher desperately struggling to breathe, wheezing with an awful sound.

'Christ,' said Larrabee, grasping the handles and sliding back the stretcher. As they lowered the stretcher, they could see the terror in the man's eyes and yellow frothing from his nostrils and bubbling at his lips. Harrington looked away and tried not to listen as they carried the man across the courtyard to the entrance to the Clearing Station.

'Poison gas case,' Larrabee explained to the orderly as they lowered the stretcher to the ground. 'He's in a bad way.'

They stared at the man, who seemed to be trying to speak when his eyes rolled back and a final, gurgling cry escaped his lips. Harrington turned away into the darkness, unable to watch.

'C'mon, Frank,' said Larrabee bitterly. 'Let's get the next one.'

*   *   *

11

After washing up at the nurses' station, Kit hurried from the noise and chaos of the chapel to the relative calm of the operating theatre, where the surgeons had been working without let-up since afternoon. As she entered the canvas marquee, the only sound was the faint hiss of the acetylene that brightly illuminated the operating tables with white light. The surgeons were covered with blood up to the elbows. They paid her no notice as she silently took the place of one of the exhausted VADs.

'Look after the sterilization tray,' instructed the Sister, whose tired, grey eyes were all that could be seen between her mask and snug white cap.

As Kit arranged a tray of stainless steel instruments in the bubbling bath, orderlies wheeled in another gurney.

'All right, we're done with this man,' said one of the surgeons.

The orderlies stood patiently to one side as the nurses finished bandaging the unconscious man's abdomen. During the brief respite, the doctors pulled down their masks, stripped off their bloody gloves and slumped into chairs at the side of the tent. Donning rubber gloves, Kit laid an array of sterilized instruments on a tray under the watchful eye of the RAMC Sister. As soon as the gurney was rolled away, the new patient was transferred to the operating table. The anaesthetist spoke softly to the man and secured a mask over his face. The surgeon, wearing fresh gloves and his mask in place, briefly studied the note pinned to the sheet.

'Shrapnel wound to the left thigh,' he commented. 'Severed femoral artery. We'll have to be quick about it. He's in shock from the loss of blood.'

'Nurse,' said the Sister through her mask. 'Step forward.'

Kit walked up to the table, steadily holding the tray of instruments. Parting the sheets that draped the soldier, the surgeon glanced at the anaesthetist and then said, 'Scalpel.'

Kit handed the instrument to the surgeon, who accepted

it without looking up. She forced herself to stare straight ahead at the canvas, concentrating on the hiss of the lamps. With a quick flick of his wrist, the surgeon sliced the tubing wound tightly around the man's groin. A fountain of bright-red blood spurted from the wound, spraying Kit's bib and chin.

'Clamp,' said the surgeon calmly as the Sister held a cotton-wool compress over the wound.

Her knees shaking, Kit exchanged the clamp for the scalpel, receiving another jet of blood on her apron before the surgeon was able to clamp off the artery. The flow of blood stanched, the moment of panic fled, and she mechanically passed the instruments from the tray as the surgeon made quick work of dislodging the shard of steel, stitching the artery, and closing the wound.

Unconscious of the passage of time, listening to the hiss of acetylene, the murmured instructions, avoiding the ether fumes, she concentrated only on her simple tasks, admiring the skill of the surgeons as one patient after another passed under the glare of the lamps.

'Fifteen minutes,' said the Sister as the surgeons wearily filed out of the tent.

Overwhelmingly tired, Kit stripped off her gloves. Leaving the tent, she passed through a small chamber in the adjoining building where the medicines and analgesics were stored. Seeing that she was alone, she opened a locker and removed a small bottle of medicinal brandy. Patting it in her pocket under her apron, she wandered outside, taking a deep breath of cool night air, looking for a quiet place to sit. With the stars shining through a break in the clouds, she slumped on a bench by the garden wall. Unbuttoning her collar, she reached for her cigarettes and matches, and after lighting one and taking a deep drag, pulled out the small bottle and helped herself to a tot. With the kick from the nicotine and alcohol, she felt suddenly wide awake. Aware of the presence of another form in the shadows, she said, 'Hello, there.'

'Hullo.' A man stepped into the starlight and said, 'I hope I didn't startle you.'

'Hah,' said Kit with a shortish laugh. 'I'm too knackered to startle...'

'Knackered?'

Kit stared in the dim light. 'Who are you?' she asked.

'I'm Frank.' He peered at her. 'I'm learning to see in the dark.'

'Are you? You sound like an American.'

'I am.'

'What are you doing here?'

'I was just asking myself the same question. No, actually, I'm an ambulance driver.'

'An American? How queer.'

'What about you?' he asked. He stared at her uniform, unable to make out the red cross sewn on her bloodied bib. 'You're covered with blood.'

'Yes.' She could see the dark-red stains on his trousers and cuffs. 'So are you.' She tipped back her head and had another sip. 'Here,' she said, offering him the bottle. 'Have some.'

'What is it?'

'Brandy. Aqua vitae.'

Harrington smiled in the darkness as he accepted the bottle. 'I could use some *vitae*,' he said, taking a swallow, savouring the pleasurable sensation. 'What do you do here?' he asked.

'I'm a mere, lowly VAD.'

'A what?'

'You *are* new,' she said with a laugh. 'A V-A-D. Volunteer nurse. There're droves of us.'

'I see.' Harrington took another sip and passed her the bottle.

14

Taking another drag on her cigarette, she said, 'What in heaven is an American doing driving an ambulance in Flanders?'

'I'm with the American Field Service. This is my first night.'

'American Field Service ... Oh, yes, I've heard something about that. Helping out with the Frogs.'

'Yes, and with the British, too. At least my section. I'm Frank Harrington,' he added pleasantly, extending his hand.

'And I'm Kit,' she said, giving his hand a quick shake. 'Kit Stanley. Oh, my.' She quickly jumped up. 'Sorry, Frank, I've got to get back. Sister will skin me alive.'

'Goodbye, Kit.' He watched as she hurried off into the building. 'Thanks for the drink,' he called to her. 'Maybe I'll see you around.'

2

Despite the cool air rushing through the open cab and the raindrops pelting his face, Frank Harrington struggled to stay awake. He studied the ravaged landscape in the grey dawn: splintered trees jutting grotesquely from muddy, shell-pocked fields that, a year before, had been filled with ripening corn; abandoned farm buildings, partially demolished by shelling; the bloated corpses of horses and cattle along the roadside. Somehow, a windmill was still standing in the distance, its wide, canvas sails slowly turning in the breeze, an image from a Low Countries guidebook. Weak daylight extinguished the flashes on the horizon, the thunder of cannonade receding like a summer storm, with only an occasional, dull *whump* in the distance. Frowning, Harrington peered ahead through the light rain, concerned that he had lost his way but unwilling to disturb Bill Larrabee, who was sleeping on the seat beside him.

Larrabee suddenly sat up and studied the indistinct horizon. 'Whoa,' he said. 'You missed the turn.'

'How in the heck can you tell?'

'See that spire over there?' Larrabee pointed to Harrington's left.

'Barely,' said Harrington, squinting at the dim outline of a church.

'That's Poperinge. We're two miles back the other way.'

Harrington slowed almost to a stop and fought to turn the Ford around, momentarily spinning the tyres in the muck. Once they were moving again, he slowly exhaled.

'Whew,' he muttered. 'Why don't you take over, Bill? I've about had it.'

'Sorry,' said Larrabee, leaning back on the seat. 'Your turn to drive. And besides, you need to learn your way around.'

Five minutes later, without a word between the two exhausted men, Harrington spotted a road on his left, the ruts barely visible in the tall grass, and impulsively made the turn. A mile or so in the distance he could discern a clump of trees on a gentle rise and the silhouette of buildings that struck him as vaguely familiar. As they approached the tiny village, Harrington pulled over to allow a column of soldiers to pass. Not marching, but slogging along in twos and threes; scattered over several hundred yards, they strained forward under the weight of packs and rifles, soaked by the rain. The men were wearing kilts above their mud-spattered puttees, a tartan Harrington couldn't name, and glengarry caps, rather than the usual khaki.

'Would you look at that,' he said. 'I wonder where the bagpipes are?'

'Gordon Highlanders,' commented Larrabee. 'Coming out of the line.'

A burly sergeant at the head of the column turned to his men. 'Are we down-hearted?' he called out in a thick brogue.

'No!' shouted more than a hundred men in unison. Weak smiles flashed across their boyish faces, and the cheer seemed to infuse them with renewed energy.

When the last of the stragglers had passed, Harrington pumped the accelerator and steered back onto the ruts, certain they were within a half-mile of their billet, a bite of food, and sleep. Passing a crumbling brick wall, the track intersected a paved road, where a small sign announced their arrival at La Clytte, a Flemish village of perhaps 200 souls before the arrival of the German Army in August

17

1914, now inhabited by the British Expeditionary Force. Harrington stopped to allow a young woman to cross the road, wearing wooden sabots and a long, shapeless dress, pushing a handcart crammed with pots and pans, with a dirty, barefoot boy at her side. Both woman and child wore vacant expressions, oblivious to the ambulance.

'OK, Bill,' said Harrington with a yawn. 'Where to?'

'Turn right. It's about a quarter-mile.'

Part of the red-tiled roof of the sturdy brick farmhouse had been blown in by an unexploded shell – a *loupé*, or dud, Larrabee had explained – but most of the structure was intact, providing shelter from the elements and, more importantly, a habitable cellar.

Harrington turned off the road and parked next to another Model T ambulance with the same Indian-head insignia on the hardboard siding.

'Looks like Deac beat us home,' said Larrabee as he opened the door and sprang out. 'Borden must be out on a pick-up.'

Harrington climbed out and stood stretching for a moment, staring absently at the dull sky in the lightly falling rain. 'I could sure use something to eat,' he said, massaging his stomach.

'Breakfast's on the stove,' said a tall young man as he ducked out of the low doorway, holding a ceramic bowl and a piece of crusty bread.

'Mornin', Deac,' said Larrabee. 'Any coffee?'

'Larrabee's cowboy coffee,' replied Herman 'Deacon' Caruth, so named for his ascetic appearance and the tiny Bible he kept in his breast pocket. 'Pot's on the stove.'

Harrington stooped as he entered the dim living room whose beamed ceiling and plaster walls were begrimed with smoke and ash. The 'stove' was a rusted grate over a bed of glowing embers in the fireplace. Reaching for a bowl on the rough-hewn mantel, he helped himself to a serving of porridge from a saucepan over the fire. The five-room structure was devoid of furniture. Stacks of biscuit boxes served as tables amid the pallets the men had fashioned from bedrolls and army blankets. Harrington slumped on the floor with his back against the wall and dipped his fingers into the warm, sticky porridge, feeling a cool breeze on his face from the window whose panes had long since disappeared. With a bit of food in his stomach, he felt suddenly, overwhelmingly sleepy, his eyelids drooping.

'How'd it go', enquired Deac, standing over him, 'on your first night out?'

Harrington glanced up and smiled, dipping his fingers for another bite.

'Frankie did all right,' said Larrabee as he knelt by the fire and poured a mug of coffee from a spatter-wear pot. 'That damned aid station was right at Hill 62, under pretty heavy shelling.'

'You're telling me,' said Deac, slumping down on the floor next to Frank. 'The Boche are really pouring it into the Salient. What did you have?'

'The usual,' said Larrabee. 'Except for this one gas case. The poor s.o.b. was a goner by the time we got him to the Clearing Station. Wasn't he, Frank?'

Harrington nodded, remembering the look of abject terror in the man's eyes and the disgusting foam at his lips and nostrils. Listening to the repartee, he felt he was becoming one of the men. 'Yeah,' he said. 'Poor bastard.'

'Anything else exciting on your maiden voyage?'

'Not exciting, exactly,' said Harrington, placing his bowl on the rough floor and sucking his fingers. 'But interesting.' Both men looked at him expectantly. 'I met this good-looking British nurse at the CCS,' he explained. 'She gave me a drink.'

'Oh, really?' said Larrabee with a quick arch of his eyebrows. 'Said she was a V-A-D. What's that?'

'Volunteer nurse,' said Larrabee between sips of coffee. 'There're scads of them. Stands for "victim always dies".'

Harrington laughed out loud while Deac looked on with a bemused expression.

'Are they trained nurses?' asked Harrington.

'Naw,' said Larrabee. ''Bout all they're trained to do is mop the floors and empty the bedpans. Know as much about nursing as your kid sister. You got a sister, Frank?'

'Yeah, Bill,' said Harrington, stifling a yawn. 'I got a sister.'

Curled up under the blanket, Harrington slept the deep, dreamless sleep of the truly exhausted, out as soon as his head hit the rolled-up jacket that served as a pillow, oblivious to the snoring from the forms huddled beside him. At first the shaft of daylight from the open door and the commotion didn't penetrate the fog, but then he was dimly conscious of someone saying his name. 'Cut it out,' he murmured, rolling over.

'Get up, Frank,' said Bill Larrabee, kneeling beside him and shaking him by the shoulder. 'Let's go.'

Raising himself up on an elbow, Harrington blinked and looked around the small room as two men darted out the door. Peering at Larrabee, he said, 'What the heck...'

'Air raid. Hurry it up. We need to get down to the *cave*.'

Throwing back the blanket, Harrington jumped up and stumbled after Larrabee toward the bright daylight, vaguely aware of a droning airplane engine. Wooden doors on the side of the farmhouse opened to what at home he would have called a storm cellar. Harrington scrambled after Larrabee down the steps into the musty enclosure, swinging the doors shut behind him. In the darkness he could see only the whites of the eyes of the three men huddled on the floor. They listened to the approaching airplane, the engine growing louder, alternating pitch, as it sharply descended.

'Taube,' said one of the men.

'Yep,' agreed another.

'What?' said Harrington.

'Lousy German plane,' explained Deac. 'They send 'em over in the daylight to bomb the rear areas.'

'Here he comes,' said Larrabee as the droning grew louder.

Harrington visualized the plane flying low over the flat, treeless landscape, conscious that his throat was dry, his heart racing. Something about waiting for a bomb to fall while sheltering in a cramped, dark cellar was far more terrible than facing shellfire on the open ground.

'Oh, Jesus,' moaned the man next to him. The engine cut out for a moment, coughed, sounded directly overhead and died away. In the next instant, the tiny cellar shook with a tremendous blast that deafened the men and filled the air with choking dust. The man next to Frank, coughing, jumped to his feet and started for the steps before Larrabee grabbed him and pulled him back.

'Sit down, Borden, for God's sake!' said Larrabee. 'The sonofabitch may be coming back.'

The men anxiously listened as the engine noise receded. After waiting a full three minutes, Larrabee said, 'OK, boys, let's take a look.' He stood part way up, threw open the cellar doors and clambered up the steps.

Harrington waited for the others and then trooped up after them. When he emerged, blinking in the bright sunshine, Larrabee was standing with his hands at his hips examining what was left of one of the Fords. The vehicle was parked between the farmhouse and a smoking crater. The blast had smashed the hardboard siding into matchsticks, crumpled the chassis, and left the front end a twisted mass of steel. The men searched the pale-blue sky, listening.

'There he is,' said Deac, shading his eyes and pointing toward the horizon. 'He's going after that *saucisse*.'

Harrington could hear the droning of the engine and then saw the wings dip as the Taube banked away from the sun toward one of the fat, sausage-shaped barrage balloons suspended over the nearby town of Poperinge. The men watched with fascination as the German pilot executed his attack, waiting until the last minute to fire his machine gun at the oversize target, which popped like a giant party balloon before tumbling toward the ground. The men turned and looked up at the sound of another plane, flying low and fast overhead.

'One of ours,' said the compact man standing next to Larrabee, another veteran of the AFS named Henry Borden. 'Sopwith.' The tan British biplane gave chase, forcing the Taube to retreat toward the German lines.

'He's probably out of bombs anyway,' said Borden with a shrug as the remains of the balloon disappeared from the sky.

Harrington turned back to the smashed-up ambulance. Larrabee was standing with one hand on the undamaged door and a foot on the running board, staring inside with a rueful expression.

'That was my car,' he said as Harrington walked up. 'I'll have to ride with you until they can get me another one.' Harrington merely nodded, wondering what the bomb might have done to the farmhouse if the Ford hadn't taken most of the blast.

'What the hell,' said Larrabee. '*C'est la guerre*. Let's go inside and get some shut-eye.'

Despite their exhaustion, the men, with nerves on razor edge, couldn't sleep. Harrington sat on the floor, his back against the wall with his arms clasped around his knees, wearing his khaki uniform with his boots on, unlaced.

'So you were telling me,' he said to Bill Larrabee, who

was sitting next to him smoking a cigarette, 'after you got to Neuilly...'

'Right. In April. They assigned me to Section 1 and sent us up to Dunkirk to help out with the BEF. Been there ever since.'

'Mm hmm.'

'So why did you join up, Frank?'

Harrington glanced briefly at Larrabee, wondering whether he was serious or just joking around. 'Me?' he said. 'Probably the same reasons as you and the others.'

'Most of 'em were spoiling to get into the war,' said Larrabee. 'Come to the rescue of France and all that. I was just bored.'

'Oh, really?'

'Well, I went home to Wyoming after graduation, and my dad wanted me to stay and help out on the ranch. The next thing you know there's a war on, and I figured, what the hell, sounds like fun.'

'Fun,' said Harrington glumly. He looked around the squalid room.

'Listen, Frank, I'm not one of those who's rarin' for the US to get in this fight. Not after what I've seen.' Larrabee studied Harrington and then asked, 'So why *did* you join?'

'Well, Bill, I happen to think you're wrong. I think Wilson's wrong. We *should* go in. And after they sank the *Lusitania*, I figured as soon as I graduated I'd volunteer. So I signed up, they put me on a boat, and here I am.'

'Yep,' said Larrabee, tossing his cigarette butt into the cold fireplace, 'here you are.'

* * *

If someone had suggested to Kit Stanley six months earlier that she would be looking forward to the daily routine at No. 4 General Hospital, she would have thought them mad. But after a week at the Casualty Clearing Station at

Bailleul, stretched to the limits of endurance by the endless tide of wounded and dying, she was positively delighted to return to the neat rows of tents and tidy wooden structures at the military hospital outside the French seaside village of Camiers.

The red cross sewn on Kit's bib had faded to carnation-pink from repeated scrubbings with bleach, and her long-sleeved cotton dress, belted at the waist, was a pale blue–grey. Tall and trim, she wore her light-brown hair pinned up, in the fashion of the day, and even without a touch of make-up, her oval face and hourglass figure would turn the head of any man she encountered among the complex of tents and huts of the military hospital, one of dozens of such facilities hastily erected along the Channel coastline to care for the flood of wounded from Flanders. Following the furious fighting in the autumn of 1914, the British lines formed a salient in German-held territory east of Ypres, a projection the British were determined to consolidate and the Germans equally determined to dislodge. It was a fine July morning as she hurried along the duckboards from her bell-tent to the ward, the air cool and fresh with a hint of sea salt and the sky a pale blue. She paused to gaze at a steamship on the horizon, undoubtedly evacuating the more serious cases to auxiliary hospitals in Kent or East Sussex or the great hospitals in London. The others, she reflected, would remain in the temporary hospitals like hers at Camiers until they could rejoin their units – or until the bugle sounded The Last Post at a lonely, wind-swept funeral behind the dunes.

She noted the time on the clock – just 7:00 a.m. – as she opened the screen at the entrance to the marquee. Apart from the daylight filtering through the canvas, the only illumination inside the large, A-line tent was a single hurricane lamp. As she passed between twin rows of iron beds, covered in dark-brown army blankets, most of the men were awake, propped up on pillows, with smiles of recognition on their young faces.

'Where've you been lately, Sister,' called out one lad as she walked past. 'Off on holiday?'

'Hush!' commanded the Ward Sister, an RAMC nurse in her mid-forties seated at the spare wooden table at the centre of the marquee. 'Good morning, Miss Stanley,' she said, slipping off her stool.

'Morning, Sister,' replied Kit. She smiled at the orderly, a kindly gentleman from Shropshire who'd volunteered for the medical service after his son was killed in the battle of Mons at the outbreak of the war. He looked up from an article he was reading about Lord Kitchener's grandiose plans for his New Army of Territorials, hundreds of thousands of volunteers that had swelled the ranks of the modest professional British Army since the autumn of 1914. 'Hullo, Kit,' he said. He put the paper aside and transferred a stack of fresh bandages from a cabinet fashioned out of sugar boxes to the dressing trolley. On the wide table next to the cabinet was a large pitcher of water, the sterilization bath, and a demijohn filled with clear disinfectant.

'Are we ready to begin?' asked the Sister, turning to the orderly, who replied with a deferential nod.

She led the way to the end of the marquee, where a badly wounded soldier was obscured behind a cloth screen. Kit followed behind the orderly pushing the trolley. Pausing to inspect a note fastened to the foot-rail, the Sister commented, 'Dangerously Ill List.' The large man propped up on pillows was a sergeant with the Princess Patricia's Canadian Light Infantry, better known as the Princess Pats, a brigade of volunteers that had suffered terrible losses in the recent fighting for Bellewaerde Ridge in the Salient.

The Sister drew back his covers to reveal a large bandage that covered his chest. 'Good morning, Sergeant,' said the Sister. 'Feeling better today?'

Without waiting for a reply, she reached for the adhesive and stripped away the bandage in a quick motion, exposing an irregular, gaping wound from the shoulder blade to the nipple, the flesh bright red and filled with oozing pus. As the poor man winced in pain, Kit raised a hand to her nose and mouth, trying to block out the odour from the suppurating wound.

'Gas bacillus,' said the Sister impassively, as if the patient weren't listening. 'We shall have to irrigate.' She turned to the orderly and said, 'The Carrel and Dakin solution, if you please, Mr Maxwell.'

He reached for the demijohn of clear liquid, a solution of boiled water and ¼ per-cent hypochlorous acid. Faced with an alarming rate of amputations, two British doctors had devised the mixture, which had proved somewhat effective in halting the spread of the deadly bacterial infection.

When the orderly had screwed off the lid, Kit reached in and filled a large glass syringe with the solution, whose powerful disinfectant odour battled with the awful smell of the gangrenous wound. Handing the syringe to the Sister, Kit studied the man's face, his eyes squeezed shut in an expressionless mask, as the cold liquid was liberally poured over the open wound. Tears formed at the corners of his eyes and slipped down his pallid cheeks. After sponging the jagged edges of the wound, the Sister instructed the orderly to pour more of the solution on a fresh bandage, which, with Kit's help, she carefully secured over the wound.

'There we are,' she said with a prim smile. Kit thought for a moment the man had fainted, but he acknowledged the comment with a weak smile.

'Keep an eye on his temperature,' said the Sister in an

26

aside to Kit as they moved to the next bed, where a young man was lying in peaceful repose. A note affixed to the foot-rail indicated that he too had been placed on the Dangerously Ill List. Kit looked mournfully at the young soldier, whose cheeks had a tinge of pale blue. His eyes were puffy and shut, and though he was sleeping, his breathing was shallow and irregular. The Sister reached for his wrist and struggled to detect a faint pulse. Turning away from the soldier, the Sister briefly made eye contact with Kit, a look of deep sadness in her usually expressionless eyes. 'Nothing to be done,' she whispered. 'Asphyxia.'

'Chlorine gas?' said Kit. She thought back to the description of the ghastly new weapon in the last letter from Nigel, a captain in the infantry to whom she was more or less engaged but from whom she hadn't heard in weeks.

'Yes,' said the Sister. 'You can tell by his bluish pallor. The next twenty-four hours should tell the tale.'

By the time they reached the end of the marquee, changing dressings, irrigating septic wounds, and dosing the men with what few medicines were available, the nature of the wounds were far less serious, the prospects brighter for a 'ticket to dear old Blighty' or alternatively to convalescent camp and a return to the front. The freckled-faced boy in the last cot, no more than eighteen, gave Kit an expectant look as the Sister examined the bullet wound on his forearm.

'Healing nicely,' she said. 'No sign of infection.'

'But, Sister,' he said, 'it's giving me the devil of a time. I can scarcely...' He stopped at the sound of the screen door swinging shut behind a tall major, one of the regimental MOs.

'Good morning, Sister,' the major said pleasantly. 'Miss Stanley,' he added, looking Kit in the eye.

'Good morning, Doctor,' said both women in unison.

27

'Now, we shall have to clear as many men from this ward as possible,' he said in a businesslike tone. 'There's been more ghastly fighting around Ypres and we're expecting some very heavy convoys.' He glanced down at the young soldier who responded with an encouraging smile. 'Mark him for convalescent camp,' he quietly instructed the Sister as the boy's smile melted into despair. Moving to the next cot, the doctor quickly assessed the situation, a shrapnel wound to the thigh. 'Mark him BL,' he said with a frown. The soldier's face lit up as the Sister reached for a red tag with the letters 'BL' for 'boat lying' – evacuation by hospital ship across the Channel to England – to Blighty.

It was almost noon when the MO completed his rounds, and Kit was restive, uncomfortably warm in the uniform dress that reached from her throat to her ankles, and dying for a smoke. More than half the cots had been marked either for evacuation to England or convalescent camp, leaving only the desperate cases who, in all probability, would never see home or return to their units.

When her replacement arrived, Kit politely excused herself and made her way along the duckboards to the camp post office, where, as she hoped, a letter was waiting for her. Tucking the army envelope, with 'Capt. Nigel Owen' scrawled on the back flap, in her apron pocket, she threaded her way through the maze of marquees to the bell-tent she shared with Jane Tisdale, another VAD she'd known in London before the war. She slumped on her cot with a heavy sigh, kicked off her shoes and reached for the pack of cigarettes on the campaign table.

After lighting one, which she'd only dare in the privacy of her tent, she took a drag and studied the military envelope. Though she was immensely relieved by the letter, signifying that Nigel was alive, part of her dreaded it. With the cigarette between her lips, she extracted two sheets of onionskin. 'Darling Kit,' he began, 'how I have longed to

be with you during the miserable days and nights of these
past weeks.' Taking another drag, she lay back on her cot
and read:

Please excuse my penmanship as I am writing in the
dim light of a single candle in our dugout under
intermittent German shelling. As you'll no doubt read
in the papers, we've been in the thick of the fighting
at a wretched place known as Hooge Château, where
our engineers succeeded in detonating a tremendous
mine under the Huns' trenches...

Huns, considered Kit. That's how Nigel usually referred to
the Germans. Never as the *Boche* like everyone else. Perhaps
his disdain for the French matched his dislike of the
Germans. After describing the valour of his men and the
terrible casualties they had suffered from constant shelling
and poison gas attacks, he got to the point she'd been
waiting for:

...as soon as we're relieved, which hopefully will be
soon, I've put in for a pass. Oh darling, we could meet
in Paris even if just for a few blissful days. I dream
of holding you in my arms, it's driving me mad. If
only I could see you, touch you, I know I could
persuade you to be mine. We're so right for each
other, we could pick a date, or who knows – we might
simply find a padre and tie the knot then and there!...

She couldn't read on. Carefully refolding the pages in the
envelope, she took a final drag on her cigarette and stubbed
it out in the ceramic ashtray. Dear God, she considered
with a sigh, what could she do?

29

3

The lieutenant paused to listen, arm on the parapet and head just an inch below the rim. The dark, moonless night was eerily quiet, with only the occasional crack of a sniper's rifle or the boom of artillery in the distance. Further along was his objective: a sandbagged length of corrugated tin arching over a sharp bend in the trench – Suicide Corner, home to C Company, 7th Battalion, the King's Royal Rifle Corps. The battalion held the British line at Hooge Château, a lovely estate before the war, with a wooded park and man-made lake, situated two miles east of Ypres on the Menin Road at the very tip of the Salient. The lieutenant slowly approached the sentry, who stood with his back against the sandbags, cradling his rifle, sound asleep. After studying the man for a moment, the lieutenant jabbed a finger at his chest.

'What the bloody hell...?' cried the young private, his eyes wide open, almost dropping his rifle. The lieutenant glared at him in the darkness. 'Sorry, sir,' he added, coming to attention.

'Get up on the fire-step, Wilson,' commanded the lieutenant, 'where you can see. Like this.' Reaching for the sandbags, he climbed up on the dirt ledge and stood up straight, affording him a clear view of No Man's Land beyond the British wire. It was the new men, he considered, thinking they were playing it safe, who usually had their heads blown off.

'But, sir,' whispered the private, 'can't they see us?'

'Good God, man,' muttered the tall officer, 'how do you expect to do your duty?'

The private carefully climbed up next to him and peered out into the darkness. 'The Germans site their machine guns', explained the lieutenant in a quiet voice, 'to fire here, right at the top of the parapet. And at night, the fire's un-aimed, of course.'

The private nodded.

'So you're better off standing up here like this, where you can see, than popping up to steal a look over the top, where a stray round would hit you right between the eyes.'

'Yes, sir,' said the private doubtfully. 'But what about snipers?'

'Snipers have to have something to aim at. There's no way they can see us on a night like this, even with a telescopic sight. And besides, this is the only way you could spot a German patrol coming over on a raid.'

'Yes, sir.' The private stared out into the blackness beyond the double line of barbed wire.

'Been quiet like this all night?' asked the lieutenant.

'Yes, sir. Hardly any shelling at all, just a shot every so often down in the crater.' He pointed to their left.

'Hmm,' said the lieutenant. 'I don't like it.' He glanced down as another soldier made his way along the narrow trench.

'Lieutenant Barnes?' said the soldier, a burly sergeant. The lieutenant nodded. 'The captain sends his compliments, sir, and asks to see you right away.'

'Very well,' said the lieutenant, jumping down from the fire-step. 'Keep a sharp lookout,' he instructed the private as he started after the sergeant.

Barnes could make out the flickering light of a candle in the concrete reinforced dugout some ten feet below the surface of the Flemish farmland. Ducking through the blanket draped over the entrance, he stood before the company Commanding Officer. Captain Nigel Owen was seated on a campstool with a tin cup, smoking a cigarette.

'Come in, Barnes. Have a seat.' He motioned to an empty ammunition case.

Barnes glanced briefly around the smoky dugout, noting that both cots were empty. Owen reached for a whisky bottle and offered it to Barnes. 'Have a drink?'

'No thanks,' said Barnes, squatting on the ammo case.

'Quiet night,' said Owen, expelling smoke from his nostrils and stubbing out the cigarette in an ashtray shaped like a miniature frying pan.

'Too quiet.'

'Think the Huns are planning something?'

'I shouldn't be surprised, after the Rifle Brigade blew them to smithereens with that mine.'

'Well,' said Owen, leaning forward and stroking his carefully trimmed moustache, 'that's why I sent for you. I want you to take out a patrol. I fancy the Germans could be preparing to retake the crater.'

'Yes, sir.'

As he stood up, Barnes noticed the captain's finely polished cavalry boots and wondered how he kept them free of mud. 'I'll take along Sergeant-Major Pearson and a few others.'

'Suit yourself. Just pass the word to Parker that you're going out.'

'Right.'

Barnes touched a hand to the bill of his cap before ducking through the blanket and starting up the steps. He expected to find the sergeant-major sleeping in the dugout twenty yards down the trench. But as he walked up to the entrance he could overhear the hardened veteran speaking to two of the new men, explaining the science of survival.

'Trench fighting's no good,' said the sergeant. 'If you're lookin' for a cushy one, a real Blighty – say a bit o' shrapnel to the arms or legs – wot's needed is a fight out in the open, a regular battle.'

Barnes smiled as he listened to the murmurs of comprehension.

'All you're likely to get in the bloody trenches', said the sergeant, 'is a bullet in the head or a mortar that'll do you in...'

'Perhaps,' said Barnes, stepping into the dugout, 'your chances for a cushy one, as you put it, Sergeant, would be a bit better out in No Man's Land.'

'Well, that's true enough, Lieutenant,' said Sergeant-Major Pearson with a grin that revealed his white teeth in the darkness.

'I'm taking out a patrol,' said Barnes in a serious tone, 'and I'll need you to come along. Bring your revolver and two men. Tell them to grab a few bombs. We're pushing off from Petticoat Lane in ten minutes.'

Lieutenant Barnes and the men of his patrol crouched on the fire-step at the point where a shallow communications trench disappeared into the darkness – 'Petticoat Lane'. Suicide Corner, Petticoat Lane, Old Bond Street and The Arch – names given to features of the maze of trenches by the Tommies who'd dug them in the Belgian clay and held them for over six months.

The sergeant-major steadied the ladder as the lieutenant, unburdened by rifle or pack, dashed up the rungs and disappeared over the top. After a moment he was followed by the sergeant and two enlisted men. Hugging the rutted earth, the men peered across No Man's Land toward the German lines, invisible some 200 yards in the distance.

'Let's get cracking,' whispered Barnes, crawling flat on his belly through a gap in the barbed wire. 'We'll take it nice and easy.'

After ten minutes snaking across the shell-pocked earth under the dark sky, the moon and stars obscured by a thick layer of cloud, Barnes halted and raised himself up on his elbows.

'Listen,' he whispered to Pearson, who had crawled up next to him. 'Hear anything?' Faint music from a gramophone drifted across No Man's Land in the still night air, a scratchy recording of 'Mademoiselle from Armentières'.

'Cheeky buggers,' whispered the sergeant.

The music abruptly stopped, and the muffled sound of men's voices was barely audible. Barnes stared into the whites of Pearson's eyes, and both men nodded.

'Let's go a bit closer,' whispered Barnes, 'and see what we can hear. Pass the word.'

Barnes started forward, moving more quickly. Reaching out as he crawled along, searching the ground in the darkness for the German wire, he suddenly grabbed a fistful of decomposing flesh and fabric – what remained of a partially buried corpse. 'Damn,' he muttered, wiping his hand. He paused and peered straight ahead, unable to see much of anything from his vantage point flat on the ground.

He heard a soft *pop* and watched as a rocket shot up into the black sky in a shower of sparks, blossoming into a star-shell that painted the blasted landscape in silvery light. Barnes contorted his body in an attitude of sudden, violent death as a German Maxim, not thirty yards in front of him, fired a long burst, the bullets whining over his head toward the British trenches. In the silence that followed, the star-shell winked out.

Barnes listened carefully, never moving a muscle. He could distinctly hear voices, the German gunners, and then others and the jangle of gear, the sound of dozens, perhaps hundreds, of men. Glancing to his left, he saw that one of his men had crawled ahead of him. Just as Barnes was debating going after him, the man abruptly rose and hurled a bomb toward the German trench.

It was a good toss, well aimed, exploding directly over the nearest section beyond the coiled wire. The Germans immediately answered with a burst of machine-gun fire that struck the foolhardy private in the shoulder, knocking him backward. Unholstering their revolvers, Barnes and Pearson jumped to their feet, firing wildly at the German position before grabbing the wounded man under his arms and hauling him back toward the British lines.

'Thank God they can't see us,' said the sergeant between clenched teeth as bullets sang all around them. 'Get the hell back to our line,' he called to the other private, who was lying flat on his belly, immobilized with fear.

Barnes and Pearson managed to drag their comrade back to the British wire as desultory German fire slapped at the tops of the parapets, thanking God the Boche hadn't sent up another flare.

'Coming over,' called out Barnes as they shoved the wounded man over the top into the waiting hands of the men in the trench. Just as Barnes vaulted over the top, a rifle round struck the sandbag, grazing his knuckle. He dropped to one knee and reached into his pocket for a bandana, wrapping it around his bloody hand. The sergeant-major knelt over the wounded private, helping to fasten a field dressing over his shoulder.

'How is he?' asked Barnes.

Looking up, the sergeant said, 'He should be all right. Bloody sod.'

With a quick glance at the boy's pale face, the lieutenant turned and started down the trench for the captain's dugout. Hurrying down the steps, he pulled aside the blanket and entered the dark, fetid enclosure.

'Captain Owen,' he said softly. A form stirred on one of the cots.

'What is it?' murmured Owen.

'It's Barnes. I've come to report.'

35

'Barnes.' Owen threw back his blanket and sat up. With a yawn he struck a match, lit a candle on the biscuit tin beside the cot, and reached for his cigarettes. In the dim light, Barnes unwrapped the bandana and briefly examined his injured hand.

'Well?' said Owen after lighting a cigarette with the candle.

'Something's up, all right,' said Barnes as he retied the bandana. Owen eyed him expectantly, taking a deep drag. 'The German trench was full of men. Up, moving about, talking.'

'You're certain?'

'Yes, Pearson and I could both hear them. They're coming over.'

'Well,' said Owen with a yawn, 'I suppose I should alert the officers. Double the sentries.'

'Sir.'

Owen gave the lieutenant a narrow look, irked by his rigid adherence to military etiquette. 'Well, Barnes, what is it?'

'Sir, I would suggest sending a runner to the CO of the Rifle Brigade.'

'Oh, you would.'

'Yes, sir. Advising him to expect an attack in force by daylight.'

'Good God, Barnes, you don't know that. That's rank speculation.'

'They're attacking. That much is *not* speculation. Why else would they have mustered an entire company at three in the morning? The only question is where. I'd lay ten-to-one it's the Rifle Brigade, to pay them back for that bloody mine.'

'Well, I'll think about it. In the meantime, wake up Parker and Timmons and order the men to stand to.'

'Yes, sir.' Barnes turned to go.

'Oh, and Barnes.' The lieutenant stopped and looked back. Owen smiled. 'For your sake, I hope this isn't a drill.'

*   *   *

Kit stared at the small square of sky through the hospital marquee window; it was almost black, but tinged the faintest grey ... or was that just her imagination? She closed her eyes and listened, unable to detect any sound of breathing, let alone groaning, from the bed closest to the stool where she was sitting with her arms folded across her chest. The sergeant was sleeping peacefully now, after the long hours thrashing in febrile delirium, murmuring nonsense. She opened her eyes and looked again at the sky, certain now it was growing lighter, if imperceptibly. It was darkest, she reflected, just before dawn, and it would be light before the orderly came on duty. Please, dear God, she prayed, let the sergeant live till morning.

But it was not to be. After listening to the silence for another ten minutes, Kit stood up and walked to his bedside. She looked at his still face, eyes peacefully closed as if he were dreaming a pleasant dream after the hours of fever-induced nightmares. She reached down and lightly touched his forehead – cool and dry. Nor was there the slightest movement of his chest beneath the covers. She felt for a pulse at his wrist. The sergeant was dead.

Kit hurried to the centre of the marquee where the Night Super was perched on a stool, reading by the light of a hooded hurricane lamp. Glancing up at Kit's anguished face, she knew without asking that the vigil had ended. She closed her book and stood up.

'Miss Stanley,' she said. 'The sergeant...'

'Yes, Sister,' said Kit as she brushed away a tear. 'He's gone.'

'We'll have to see to him.'

'Can't it wait for Mr Maxwell?' Kit looked imploringly into the older woman's tired eyes.

'No,' she said quietly, trying not to wake the other men. 'It will be daylight soon. We can't afford for the others to see...'

'No,' said Kit, her eyes downcast. 'I suppose not.'

They carefully folded the sergeant's cold arms across his chest and drew the sheet over his head. Quietly rolling a trolley to the end of the marquee as first light glowed in the windows, they considered the problem of moving the body.

'He's such a large man,' whispered the Sister with a grimace.

Kit looked at her expectantly.

'We shall have to roll him over,' said the Sister. 'Here, help me with his shoulders.'

The two women grasped the corpse, growing stiff, and heaved him over on one side, exposing his bare legs and buttocks under the thin cotton gown. Kit modestly wrapped the body with the sheet and then helped the nurse to roll him from the bed onto the trolley.

'There,' said the Sister with an audible sigh. 'Take one end, Miss Stanley, and I'll take the other.'

They quietly rolled the trolley outside. The sky was the palest blue, with a lavender nimbus, and the still air was fresh and cool. Taking a deep breath, Kit looked up at the sky, feeling irrational joy at merely being alive.

'You've had a long night,' said the Sister, standing at the screen door. 'Take a turn in the fresh air.'

Once she was alone, Kit reached under her apron for her cigarettes and matches. With so few souls about she might as well hazard a smoke. She strolled between the marquees, watching the shore birds wheel and turn high over the dunes. Slumping onto a bench, she lit a cigarette and took a drag, understanding why the wounded soldiers always craved a cigarette when they arrived at the CCS. After a few minutes she was aware of the sounds of an approaching convoy, the cough of exhaust, the tyres crunching the gravel drive. Tossing her cigarette into the modest flower bed, she stood up and stretched, summoning the strength to face the next wave of gassed and shattered bodies.

The marquee had been emptied of all but the most serious cases, leaving fully half of the beds empty, to make room for the wounded from the latest vicious fighting in the Salient. Kit stood beside the Sister at the centre of the tent, watching as the orderlies transferred the men from stretchers to the cots and began cutting away their filthy, blood-stained uniforms in preparation for bathing them and changing their dressings. Kit breathed a sigh when another VAD entered the marquee, relieving her after her long stint on night duty.

'You're excused, Miss Stanley,' said the Sister, 'though I may need to summon you if we're falling behind.'

'Yes, ma'am,' said Kit with a slight bow. 'I'll be in my tent.' She smiled at her replacement and hurried outside. She slipped off her cap and shook out her hair as she walked along the duckboards, debating whether to stop at the canteen for a cup of tea and a pastry. As she rounded the bathing hut, she almost collided with a tall young man who was examining the lettering over the door.

'Hullo,' he said with a grin. 'We meet again. And this time I can see you.'

Kit briefly studied his face and then broke into a smile. 'Why, it's the American,' she said.

'Frank,' he said. 'And you're Kit, if I remember correctly.'

'Very good.' She was puzzled by the absence of a badge of rank or insignia on his uniform. 'What are you doing here?' she asked.

'The usual. Delivering a load of *blessés* from the station.

My first run to this particular hospital. You must work here.'

Kit nodded and continued walking. 'You appear to be lost,' she said as he fell in beside her.

'Well, I was hoping to grab a cup of coffee, and I ...'

'I'll show you the way. I was thinking of stopping in myself.'

After stirring sugar and milk into his mug, Frank Harrington walked over to the side of the hut where a Red Cross volunteer was dispensing tea and biscuits to the off-duty nurses, orderlies, and doctors.

'Care to sit down?' he asked Kit as she accepted a cup from the volunteer. He motioned to an empty table.

'Thanks,' she said with a smile, 'but I shouldn't. We're not allowed to fraternize with the officers.'

Harrington looked briefly into her pale blue eyes. 'Well,' he said, 'I'm not an officer. Heck, I'm not even a soldier.'

She gave him a curious look. 'You're not?'

'No, just a volunteer driver. That's the only thing our government would allow, seeing as we're neutral.'

'Oh, yes...'

'But they make us wear these darn uniforms. Anyway, I thought fraternizing was something that went on between men.'

Kit laughed softly. 'Well,' she said, 'as you're not in the army, I suppose it's all right.'

He pulled back a chair for Kit and then sat down opposite her. 'Sorry,' he said, suppressing a yawn with his hand. 'It's been a long night.'

'It certainly has.'

'You look pretty worn out.'

She wearily ran a hand through her hair and a troubled look briefly crossed her face. 'Yes,' she said, 'I was up with a ... well, a difficult case.' With a brighter expression she said, 'Tell me about yourself, Frank.'

'Me? Let's see, I hail from Quincy, Massachusetts, and I signed on with the AFS just as soon as I graduated from college.'

'Which college?'

'Harvard. Heard of it?'

'Why, of course. Harvard, Yale...'

'And what about you?' Harrington gave her an encouraging smile and took a sip of coffee, feeling more awake.

'We live in London. I volunteered as a VAD last October, though father forbade it. I've been here at No. 4 since January.'

As she raised her cup to take a sip, Harrington glanced at her delicate fingers. 'That's it?' he asked.

She was taken aback by his peculiar Yankee directness but somehow didn't mind. 'Well,' she said, 'I live at home – the oldest of three ... all girls. You have siblings?'

'A sister. And she's an army nurse like you, in training down in Texas.'

'I'm not a real nurse,' said Kit, pushing aside her tea. 'But I might as well be, with the things I've had to do. Where are you staying?'

'Up the road in Dunkirk. That's where our section's stationed, though I just came in from a billet.'

'Hey, Frank!'

Both of them turned to look at a young man on the far side of the room, a comic sight in high, laced boots, a regulation uniform with a Sam Browne belt, and a wide-brimmed cowboy hat tilted back on his head. With a wave, he called out, 'C'mon, Frank. Time to saddle up.'

'Well,' said Harrington as he pushed back from the table. 'I'd better be going. It's been a pleasure.'

'Yes,' she said. 'I enjoyed the visit.'

He stood up and straightened his tunic. 'By the way,' he said. 'I owe you a drink.'

She smiled at the memory of the contraband brandy they'd shared on that miserable night at Bailleul. 'Yes, Frank,' she said. 'You do.'

'I'll take you up on that. Goodbye, Kit.'

'Goodbye.' She watched, feeling strangely happy, as he turned and walked away.

4

Lieutenant Albert Barnes stood to his full height on the fire-step and rested his arms on the top of the sandbag parapet. Raising binoculars to his eyes, he peered at the black horizon. No moon, he considered, and an eerie silence over what was usually the most heavily shelled half-mile of the entire British front stretching across Flanders from the Channel to the French border. There wasn't even the sound of that bloody gramophone.

Days earlier the British had succeeded in detonating a massive mine under the German trenches facing Hooge Château. Teams of Welsh coal miners, working under constant shelling, tunnelled 150 yards across No Man's Land, packing the firing chamber with 3,000 pounds of ammonal, an explosive three times more powerful than gunpowder. The spectacular blast flung a thick column of dirt, concrete and body parts hundreds of feet into the air, half-burying British troops waiting to storm the German line. The Boche had angrily retaliated with almost constant shellfire. High explosive from their batteries of howitzers, 'whiz-bang' shrapnel rounds, and the trench mortars lobbed by their deadly Minnenwerfers. But on this dark, midsummer night, silence prevailed over the German lines ringing the gaping mine crater, filled with mud and rainwater and held by a thin battalion of the Rifle Brigade.

Barnes, twenty-two years old and a graduate of Exeter College, Oxford, eased down from the fire-step and peered into the darkness beyond Suicide Corner. After a moment he identified Sergeant-Major Pearson carefully picking his way among the men curled up along the narrow trench, stealing a few hours' sleep on the quiet night.

'Pearson,' whispered Barnes. 'Over here.'

'Yes, sir.' The sergeant approached Barnes and gave him a perfunctory salute.

'Did the captain send a runner?' asked Barnes. 'To the Rifle Brigade?'

'Yes, sir. I happened to be standing nearby when he reported in.'

'And what did he say?'

The sergeant glanced to his left at a rifle report that echoed in the still air. 'It seems, sir,' he said, 'that the RB are being relieved. By a battalion of the 14th Division. Kitchener men,' he said dismissively.

'I see.' Kitchener men, thought Barnes wearily. Newly minted soldiers with none of the experience of the Old Contemptibles, the professional army whose ranks had been decimated in the constant fighting since October of 1914. 'And when is this relief expected?' he asked quietly.

'According to the runner, the new men should be in place by daybreak.'

The lieutenant grimaced, aware of the Germans' penchant for launching an attack at dawn when a unit holding a section of the line was being relieved. Due to the wretchedness of trench conditions in the saturated Belgian soil, the troops manning the front lines were relieved at regular 48-hour intervals. 'All right, Pearson,' said Barnes. 'I don't like it. I think these Germans are planning a show. Pass word to the other sergeants for the men to stand to at 0430, Captain's orders. Forty-five minutes hence.'

'Yes, sir.' The sergeant touched a hand to his cap and disappeared down the trench into the darkness.

After quickly checking the time, Barnes climbed back up on the fire-step and peered out into No Man's Land. Squinting, he tried to discern the outline of the crater, where the green troops of the 14th Division would be relieving the exhausted men of the Rifle Brigade – the troops to the immediate left of his own battalion: the 7th King's Royal Rifle Corps – the KRRC. Resting his head on his arm, he lightly dozed for a quarter-hour, all the while alert for the slightest activity from the German lines.

He opened his eyes at the sound of the men of C Company filling the trench and the metallic snap of bayonets sliding into place. Barnes jumped down and hurried past the sleepy men to the company CO's dugout. Throwing back the ragged blanket, Barnes came to attention and said, 'Beg pardon, sir.'

'What is it, Barnes?'

Captain Owen, seated at his sagging camp table, frowned and looked down at his notebook, a pencil clenched in his teeth.

'I understand the Rifle Brigade are being relieved...'

'Yes. What of it?' Owen shot Barnes a look of annoyance.

'The relief are Kitchener's men.'

'Look, Barnes...'

'If the Germans are planning a show...'

'Yes...'

'I would think it prudent, sir, to prepare the men to counter-attack. In the event the crater is overrun.'

Owen yawned and carefully extracted a cigarette from the pack on the table, which he thoughtfully tamped against the face of his watch. 'Perhaps,' he said at length, 'you've learned to read the Germans' minds, Barnes. Or ... perhaps you've lost your nerve. Now, as I've got a report to finish, why don't you take your position with the men, who've been ordered to stand to...'

A tremendous crash rattled the dugout, and bright orange glowed through the blanket over the doorway. Owen dropped both his pencil and unlit cigarette. Abandoning military etiquette, Barnes turned and dashed up the steps.

The sky to the left glowed a lurid red-orange, and a strange hissing sound could be heard amid the thunder of cannon fire. Leaping up on the fire-step, Barnes watched in disbelief as long tongues of flame arced across the sky, pouring into the crater.

'What the bloody hell...?' muttered the man next to Barnes, the streaming jets of fire reflecting in his eyes.

'Jesus,' said Barnes, conscious of the screams of the men in the crater, unlike anything he'd heard in months of fighting. In the next instant, the trench was engulfed in shellfire, forcing the men down from the parapet, sheltering from the storm of steel splinters. A disgusting odour assailed their nostrils – burning flesh. Barnes moved in a crouch down the trench, searching for the sergeant-major.

'Pearson,' he said loudly, taking him by the shoulder.

'Yes, sir.' The veteran soldier's face betrayed no emotion as he ducked at a nearby explosion.

'Get the men in some kind of order and return fire.' Barnes made his way down to Suicide Corner, past men firing over the parapet with bayonets fixed and others who lay where they'd fallen, to the bend where the KRRC lines joined the old Rifle Brigade position. The screams grew louder and the stench more nauseating. As Barnes stood up to glance over the parapet, rifle fire burst from his left – *from their own trench* – striking the man beside him, followed by a German grenade that bounced on the parapet and exploded a few yards beyond.

They've taken the crater, Barnes reasoned in the same moment that he turned and fired point-blank with his revolver. Hastily retreating a few yards, he crouched just as a diminutive Welshman lobbed a couple of bombs down the trench, temporarily halting the Germans.

'Barnes!'

The lieutenant looked up to see Captain Owen standing erect, his eyes ablaze in the glare of the burning crater.

'They're flanking us, Barnes,' said the captain. 'They're in our rear.'

'Yes, sir. They've burnt out the crater.'

'Assemble a squad to hold them off,' ordered the captain. 'And then take the company over the top to counter-attack. We've got to drive them back.'

Both men dropped to their knees as three German infantrymen appeared out of the darkness, firing wildly before being savagely beaten with rifle butts and bayoneted by the British troops.

'Go on, Barnes!' yelled Owen.

Aware of fire coming from both directions, Barnes scrambled down the trench, clogged with fallen men, searching for Sergeant-Major Pearson. He found him on the fire-step, a bloody bandage on his forehead, exhorting the men to keep up their fire.

After hastily conveying the orders, and passing word down the line, Barnes led the hundred or so survivors over the top, plunging wildly into the crater, heedless of the Germans' rifle and machine-gun fire and of the smoking charred bodies of the men of the Rifle Brigade, victims of the first use of flame throwers in modern warfare.

Within minutes the counter-attack was over; the German assault halted if not repulsed. In the hand-to-hand fighting in the mud and bloodied pools of the mine crater, a thousand men were lost. In the end, falling back from the withering German fire, Barnes was flung to the earth by a mighty, invisible hand; a fragment of shrapnel that entered his back and pierced his lung.

*   *   *

The almost constant flashes of cannon fire on the eastern horizon illuminated the shell-torn landscape – a flickering chiaroscuro revealing the road ahead, enabling Frank Harrington to keep the Model T from veering into the splintered trees and ditches along the verge. The convoy was approaching Hellfire Corner, the deadly intersection on the Menin Road, a mile to the east of the ruins of Ypres. He floored the accelerator, involuntarily ducking as a German round shrieked overhead.

Harrington and his comrades had been rousted from their farmhouse billet with an urgent summons for every available ambulance. Now that Bill Larrabee had a replacement for the vehicle destroyed in the air raid, Harrington was accustomed to going out alone, having overcome his fear of driving at night without headlamps. Flinching at another exploding shell, he tightened his grip on the wheel and stared at the dim outline of the road, anxious to find the aid station before daylight.

The constant, thundering barrage was unlike anything he'd witnessed in four weeks of duty with the AFS. Maybe it was the Boche, he wondered, as the cool air poured through the open windscreen, or maybe it was the British on the attack. He vainly searched for the ambulance in front of him. They'd set out in convoy, with Deac Caruth taking the lead, followed by Henry Borden, Harrington and Bill Larrabee bringing up the rear. The roar of the guns was much louder now, the horizon an almost constant flash. The fender of Borden's Ford loomed so suddenly that Harrington, with a squeal of brakes, narrowly avoided a collision.

In the next flash he caught a glimpse of a British sentry directing the Americans to turn to the right. With a jerk of the gear-lever, Harrington nosed forward, following Borden onto a bumpy, dirt track that seemed to run parallel with the British lines. After pulling over to allow a convoy of the bulky RAMC ambulances to get by, they slowly made their way across the shell-pocked, treeless ground to the regimental aid station a quarter-mile to the rear of the front, arriving just as the first rays of the sun streamed through the thick smoke.

48

As he waited, Harrington studied the surreal scene, fascination winning out over the impulse to duck below the dash. Death was all around them, horses and mules lying grotesquely amid the fallen men and detritus of battle. Abandoned rifles and packs were strewn among the corpses, illuminated by the muzzle flashes of the guns and the faint dawn. Dense, acrid smoke billowed across the orange sky. The wounded were lined up in neat rows as dozens more appeared out of the shadows, some hobbling but mostly on litters borne by exhausted men wearing red armbands with the letters 'SB'. A glimpse of the Inferno, thought Harrington as a shell struck a hundred yards to their rear.

'Hey, Frank!'

Harrington could see Henry Borden waving his arms. He threw open the door and jumped out.

'Give me a hand, Frank,' called out Borden, who was swinging open the doors at the rear of his ambulance.

Harrington hurried over to Borden, who was standing between two stretchers. Noticing a peculiar odour, Harrington looked down. He was shocked by the sight: the whites of the men's eyes standing out against their blackened faces, like players in a minstrel show, their hair and eyebrows burned away, uniforms charred.

'Good God,' said Harrington.

'Let's get them loaded,' said Borden, grasping the handles of a stretcher with a grunt.

After loading the two badly burned soldiers, Harrington hurried after Borden to the centre of the aid station, where an RAMC officer was supervising the triage.

'Drive these burned men straight away to No. 4 GH at Camiers,' the officer instructed Deac Caruth.

'Not to the CCS at Ballieul?'

'No. To Camiers. And any other serious cases you've got room for.'

'Yes, sir.'

Harrington leaned over to Borden and asked, 'What happened to these men?'

'Some sort of liquid fire,' said Borden, 'according to a stretcher-bearer. The Boche turned hoses on Hooge Crater and burned 'em alive.'

Harrington looked away as another horribly burned boy was carried past. After loading the ambulances, Harrington was about to climb behind the wheel when four muddy and dishevelled soldiers arrived with another stretcher. Glancing at the wounded man in the faint light, Harrington was relieved to see that he wasn't burned, though from his ashen pallor it was clear that he'd been badly wounded.

'Room for one more?' asked a diminutive stretcher-bearer in a thick Cockney accent.

Harrington nodded and said, 'Sure.'

'Poor old Barnsey,' said the soldier as he helped his comrades hoist the stretcher onto the upper rack. 'Looks like 'e's bought it this time.'

Harrington swung the doors shut and secured the latch.

Deac Caruth craned his head out, his hand on the steering wheel, and yelled, 'Ready, Frank?'

'Hang on a minute. I've got to give her a crank.'

Harrington jammed a steel crank through the hole in the grill and gave it a hard, clockwise turn. With a backfire that was drowned by the roar of the guns, the engine clattered to life. Tossing the crank in the toolbox, Harrington jumped in, shifted into gear, and hit the accelerator, anxiously following Borden's Model T back on the bumpy track toward the rear. The trip across the rutted, shell-pocked terrain thankfully lasted no more than five minutes, and Harrington heaved a great sigh of relief as the convoy turned back onto the Menin Road toward Ypres. He focused on the fender in front of him, trying to rid his mind of images of the burned soldiers' faces and the look in their eyes. Liquid fire. First it was poison gas, and now liquid fire...

Though Ypres was no more than two miles from the British lines, the road was badly congested with supply trucks and horse-drawn artillery, and a good fifteen minutes passed before the convoy rumbled through the Menin Gate into the ruins of the medieval market town. It was a cool morning, the sky washed free of smoke, and the sun shining brightly on the shattered remains of the once magnificent Cloth Hall. As they waited for a column of troops to cross the heap of rubble and bricks that had once been the town square, Harrington stole a quick glance into the rear compartment, relieved that the three severely wounded men were lying quietly, motionless. But as he eased off the clutch, a long groan penetrated the thin panel. Harrington had no idea how long it would take to reach Camiers, but he was sure it would be too long. The usual routine was to take the wounded to the Clearing Station at the old monastery, less than ten miles away, but now their route would take them through the British supply depot at Poperinge, on to St-Omer, and many miles beyond to the Channel coast.

Leaving the Salient behind, the gently rolling Flanders fields, lush green and bright with scarlet poppies from the summer rains, bore no trace of the war's devastation. By the time the convoy turned at last into the gravel drive at the seaside complex of tents and wooden huts, three hours had passed. The sun beat down from the cloudless sky, leaving a sheen of perspiration on Harrington's brow despite the open-air cab.

As they rumbled up to the large hut with the 'Administration' sign over the door, a senior RAMC medical officer stood waiting on the steps, arms crossed, flanked by a team of orderlies. From the look on the MO's face, Harrington deduced that word of the terrible new German weapon had been passed from the front. Killing the engine, he wearily climbed out, hurried around to the rear, and swung open the doors. For a moment Harrington closed his eyes, afraid to look inside the hot, fetid compartment.

'See to the burn cases first,' called out the MO as the orderlies began unloading the stretchers. 'Take them to marquee 12.'

Opening his eyes, Harrington gazed at the blackened boots of the soldier on the bottom rack. Even the laces were burned away. Grasping the wooden handles, he yelled, 'Somebody give me a hand!'

Bill Larrabee silently appeared beside him and took the other end of the stretcher. With one glance at the man's face, he looked up at Harrington and said, 'It's no use, Frank. He's gone.'

Harrington allowed himself a quick look at the dead soldier. 'OK,' he muttered, fighting back nausea as they lowered the stretcher to the ground.

As they eased the next stretcher from the ambulance, Harrington fully expected that the boy, too, would have expired during the long journey, but, to his surprise, his eyes flickered open and he managed to whisper, 'Water,' from his cracked and blistered lips.

After helping the RAMC orderlies transfer the burn cases, only five of whom had survived the ordeal, to the large marquee that had been made ready for them, the exhausted Americans returned to their Model Ts. Harrington suddenly remembered the last soldier they'd loaded before speeding away from the aid station. Oh my God, he thought, as he looked up at the soles of the man's boots on the upper rack, detecting no movement or sound.

'Hey, Bill,' he called. 'Come over here!'

Larrabee, slumped on the fender of his Ford smoking a cigarette, tossed it aside and walked over to help Harrington slide the stretcher out.

'Is he burned?' asked Larrabee.

'No.' They carefully lowered the stretcher to the ground. The soldier's eyes were closed and his face ghostly white, without the slightest colour at his lips.

Larrabee knelt down and felt for a pulse.

'He's alive,' said Larrabee after a moment. 'Barely.'

He carefully parted the khaki tunic and examined the bloody bandage on his chest. 'OK, Frank,' he said, standing up. 'Let's take him inside.'

As they hauled the stretcher along the duckboards, Harrington could tell that the man was breathing by the tiny red bubbles that appeared at his lips with each slow exhalation. It must be his lungs, he thought, fighting another wave of nausea.

Number 12 marquee was chaos, attendants rushing from bed to bed under the supervision of the RAMC doctors who'd been summoned to deal with the badly burned soldiers who'd survived the harrowing ride from the front. The hitherto somnolent men were screaming in agony as the nurses and orderlies peeled away their uniforms and began to apply their dressings.

Larrabee looked over his shoulder. 'Way in the back, Frank. I can see an empty cot.' They slowly manoeuvred past the doctors and nurses and carefully laid the man – a young lieutenant of the King's Royal Rifles – on the single empty bed in the corner of the tent. Without a word, Larrabee found a pair of scissors and quickly cut away the lieutenant's uniform, exposing his bare torso swathed in the crude dressing, as Harrington stood helplessly to the side. Removing the dressing with a quick slice of the scissors, Larrabee inspected the jagged gash below the right nipple.

'Exit wound,' he commented. 'Shrapnel. Must have pierced his lung.' Looking up, he said, 'Find me some alcohol, Frank, and a fresh bandage.'

As Harrington turned back toward the centre of the

marquee he almost collided with the Ward Sister as she strode quickly toward them. 'What's this?' she demanded, walking up to the bedside. Gazing at the patient, she said, 'This man's not burned. He doesn't belong here.'

'Maybe not,' said Larrabee, leaning over the unconscious lieutenant. 'But he's damned near dead.'

'Well, he'll have to be moved,' said the Sister. 'Orderly!'

'Too risky,' said Larrabee, standing erect and looking the nurse in the eye. 'His lung's haemorrhaged. He needs to lie still.'

'Come along now,' said an orderly, placing a hand on Larrabee's arm.

'Now wait a minute,' said Larrabee hotly, shoving the orderly's hand aside.

'Listen, Sister,' said Harrington, stepping forward. 'We're not trying to make trouble, but...'

'What's this?' An RAMC doctor walked up to the bedside and looked down at the lieutenant.

'Shrapnel pierced his right lung,' said Larrabee. 'Entered below the shoulder blade. Pulse of about forty.'

'Nurse,' called the doctor with a wave of his hand, summoning a slender VAD whose bib and apron were smeared bright red. Harrington was surprised to see that she was Kit. 'Get this man's wound cleaned and dressed,' commanded the doctor. 'He mustn't be moved.' The doctor quickly strode off, with the Ward Sister and orderly hurrying after him.

Kit studied the unconscious soldier for a moment and then glanced up at Frank. 'Oh, my,' she said. 'It's you.'

'Yes. We've just brought in these men...'

'C'mon, Frank. Let's go.' Larrabee's voice still had an angry edge.

'Wait,' said Kit, giving Frank an urgent look. He stared at her. 'I mean,' she said, 'can you wait a bit? I should be done here before too long.'

'Sure,' said Harrington, aware that Larrabee was listening. 'I'll, ah, be just outside.'

Once they stowed the stretcher and fastened the ambulance doors, Harrington turned to Larrabee and said, 'You can go on with the others. Don't wait on me.'

'That the gal you mentioned before?' asked Larrabee with a smile. Harrington nodded. 'She sure is cute,' said Larrabee as he tipped back his hat. 'See you later.'

Bone-tired, Harrington wandered over to a bench in the shade of a wooden hut and slumped down. Gazing at the blue–green water of the Channel between the rows of tents and the green fields filled with yellow wildflowers, he was struck by the incongruency of the beauty surrounding the encampment, the illusion of peace. He must have dozed, for he was momentarily confused when he heard his name. He looked up to see Kit. She'd discarded her cap and removed the bloodied bib and apron.

'Sorry,' he said, jumping up.

'You must be exhausted. Let's sit.'

Once she was seated beside him, he looked at her a bit awkwardly and said, 'It's been a long day.' She smiled encouragingly, and he added, 'We drove those poor fellows all the way from the aid station.'

'Where?' she asked.

'A place called Hooge Château,' he said. 'At the tip of the Salient.' At the name a shadow crossed her face and she briefly looked away. 'You know someone there?' he asked.

Kit nodded. 'Do you know the men's regiment?' she asked.

'The lieutenant they were making the fuss over is with, let's see, the King's Royal Rifles.'

'I see,' said Kit so softly he could barely hear her. 'You

55

mustn't think badly of the Sister,' she said in a stronger voice. 'We were having such a terrible time with the burn cases.'

'It was Bill who was out of line,' said Frank. 'He's planning to be a doctor, and he gets so worked up...'

'He was right. He may have saved that man's life. Oh, God, Frank. It's just so awful.'

Looking in her pale-blue eyes, he said, 'Yes. Yes it is.'

She tried to smile, but tears welled up and she fought back a sob. 'I'm sorry,' she managed to get out.

'Shh,' he said, putting his arm around her. She snuggled against him like a child, convulsed with sobs as he stroked her hair.

Regaining her composure, Kit sat up and brushed away her tears. 'Thank you,' she said quietly. 'I'm afraid I can't take much more.'

He thought back to the blackened men stacked like cordwood at the aid station. 'I'm not sure I can either,' he said. With a smile, he took her hand and stood up. 'I'm due for some time off,' he said. '*En repos*, as the Frogs would say. Maybe we could take a day down on the beach.'

'That would be lovely.' She rose and reluctantly let go of his hand. 'I should be going,' she said. 'Before we're seen.'

'We're just up the road at Dunkirk,' he said. 'Maybe on Saturday, if you're off...'

'Miss Stanley.'

They turned to see a senior RAMC nurse who evidently had been watching them. 'You're needed, Miss Stanley,' she said simply.

'Goodbye, Kit.'

She smiled and turned to follow the Sister down the path.

5

Whistling a cheerful tune, Frank Harrington turned off the sidewalk into a cluttered railway yard, clutching a sack with his morning's purchases. 'Morning, boys,' he called out as he strolled past the drab-green ambulances parked by the machine shop. A pair of muddy boots protruded from underneath one of the Fords, and two men were bent over the hood of another, their hands black with grime as they worked to adjust a temperamental carburettor. At the sound of hoof beats on cobblestones, Harrington turned as a sturdy Belgian mare rounded the corner, hitched to a dray piled with fruit and vegetables. He signalled to the driver, who brought the horse to a halt with a gentle tug on the reins. Harrington walked over to examine the produce while the mare stamped impatiently and swatted a fly with her tail.

'*Une poire, s'il vous plaît,*' he said, handing a coin to the driver, an old, bewhiskered Frenchman wearing a straw hat identical to the one perched on the horse's head.

Adding the pear to the contents of his sack, Harrington returned to the line of ambulances. He paused and squinted up at the cloudless sky, his ears attuned to a whining sound growing louder and higher in pitch. The artillery round exploded with a deafening *boom* in the next block, sending a plume of black smoke and ash spiralling over the rooftops and the horse-drawn cart clattering down the cobblestones.

Deac Caruth scrambled from underneath his car. 'Holy Jesus,' he said as he watched the smoke drifting away. 'That was a close one.'

Under intermittent shelling from long-range German guns, the French coastal city of Dunkirk was gradually being razed, with caved-in rooftops and demolished storefronts in virtually every block.

'Yeah,' said Harrington, 'and one of these days it's gonna be our turn.'

Hearing the familiar siren of a fire engine, he continued walking to the lean-to shed that served as their sleeping quarters while the others resumed their repairs. Inside the small, squalid structure, dubbed the 'monkey house' by its American inhabitants, he deposited his sack on the table in the corner and slumped on his cot, whose thin straw mattress was covered by a dark-brown blanket. Unbuttoning his jacket in the heat, he removed two envelopes from the pocket and examined the postmarks. The words 'Quincy, Massachusetts' stamped on the wrinkled envelope evoked a momentary pang of homesickness, but the postmark on the other envelope – San Antonio, Texas – aroused more curiosity. He slit open the envelope, unfolded several sheets of US Army stationery, and began reading his sister's letter:

Ft. Sam Houston, Texas
July 30, 1915

Dear Frank,

Sorry to have been such a pill about writing, but we've been so busy.

I fall into my bunk each night too exhausted to put pen to paper. But here's news – I've got my commission! 2nd Lieutenant E. L. Harrington, better known simply as 'Nurse'. Now I've got a black stripe on the sleeves of my 'Norfolk', the swell blue serge uniforms we wear.

It's so strange and wonderful here for a Yankee girl; hot, hot days with the bluest skies, a steady breeze blowing through our screened-in sleeping porch, and the marvellous chorus of the cicadas, great winged bugs in the pecan trees outside our barracks that rub their legs together in the evenings. The post is bristling with troops constantly on parade and cavalry on fine looking animals, lots of fellows for the nurses to see when we have time off from training. Everyone planning for war, certain that Uncle Sam is heading 'over there.'

I'm desperate for news, to know what it's really like. We're told that our boys are helping with the French Army, driving their wounded to the field hospitals. Have you been near the front? Have they given you a car? It must be *so* exciting.

Harrington put the letter aside and stared at the blank wall, trying to visualize Elsie in her dark-blue uniform and wide-brimmed hat. His kid sister, a commissioned officer, a trained army nurse. Like everybody back home, she seemed to think that the war was some grand adventure. Well, he supposed that was true enough ... an adventure and a nightmare. He picked up the letter and read her closing paragraph, imploring him to write and to take care of himself.

The letter from home was filled with the usual prosaic news, but beneath his mother's carefully chosen words was an ill-concealed anxiety for his safety and the fate of all of the American volunteers. Her descriptions of life at home, a cousin's engagement party, left him feeling strangely depressed. Tossing the letters aside with a sigh, he jumped up from the bed and walked over to inventory the contents of the sack: a bottle of *vin rouge*, round of cheese, baguette, a local sausage, and the plump, green pear. Patting the jackknife in his pocket, he considered that it should suffice for a seaside picnic ... if only he had some butter and jam. With a quick glance at the cracked mirror over the table, he slipped on his cap, scooped up the sack, and hurried outside.

'Anybody seen Borden?' he asked Bill Larrabee, who was hunched over the hood of his Ford.

'Over here, Frank.' Henry Borden was lounging in Harrington's Model T with his boots on the dash. 'Let's get a move on.'

'We'll see you fellows later,' said Harrington to the others. 'In Le Touquet.'

He walked around to the driver's side and secured the sack in the toolbox over the running boards. Moving to the front, he bent down and gave the crank a hard turn. With a grunt, he cranked it again, careful to let go just as the engine kicked in. Vaulting up on the seat next to Borden, he jammed down the clutch, gave the gear-lever a jerk, and drove out of the rail-yard with a cough of exhaust and cloud of dust.

Once they were out of town, driving south on the coastal highway toward Calais, he turned to Borden with a smile. 'We'll make a quick stop at the hospital,' he said. 'And then we'll be on our way.'

*   *   *

Even with the flaps wide open, Kit Stanley was uncomfortably warm in the bell-tent, propped up on her pillows on her cot, wearing only a camisole and cotton pantaloons. She picked up the envelope and examined the Belgian stamp with its image of King Albert, and Nigel's neat handwriting, so unlike the rough scrawl of the letters he'd penned from the trenches. In the days since she'd learned that his battalion – the 7th KRRC – had borne the brunt of the terrible German attack at Hooge Crater, she'd been consumed with worry. Although her fears abated with the arrival of his letter, another, deeper, unease had taken their place, and so she had put off opening it for hours. With a sigh of resignation, she tore open the envelope and began to read:

My beloved Kit,
I'm writing from the relative comforts of a rooming
house in Poperinge, complete with bed and bath, where
we've been sent to rest and refit. I say 'we' though
they're aren't many of us. Only a few dozen left in
my company, which was shot to pieces in the latest
fighting. The Huns employed a ghastly new weapon,
burning petrol, fired through hoses, raining down on
the brigade next to us...

Kit dropped the letter in her lap and closed her eyes,
her mind filled with images of the terribly burned men
they'd been struggling to keep alive. Patting perspiration
from her brow, she picked up the letter and continued:

Darling, after so many months in the line I've finally
obtained a three-day leave. We could meet in Paris
and for a few precious hours pretend that there's no
war, that things are as they were in that far ago time
of peace. Please, darling, you must find a way to come,
I'm desperate to see you, to hold you in my arms.
Just send a wire, tell me the day, and I'll be there to
meet you at the station.
                    Your beloved,
                        Nigel

Kit put the letter aside with an inward groan. She could
contrive some excuse about the Sisters' unwillingness to
spare her from her duties, but he would see right through
it. Besides, she pitied him, after the months of fighting in
such deplorable conditions. How could she possibly say
no? A few days and nights in Paris, sleeping in a decent
bed, with a decent bath, decent food at a pavement café...
But inevitably the question of their – she couldn't bear
the conscious thought – would be hanging over them like

a shadow more ominous than the war. They'd been through it all before, the arguments, the tearful remonstrations...

Swinging her legs over the side of the cot, she sat up and stretched. It was Saturday, a rare day off, and the sun well up in the summer sky. Determined not to let thoughts of Nigel spoil it, she slipped into her dress and began working on the buttons.

'I didn't think we'd find her,' said Harrington as he pulled out of the hospital's gravel drive onto the paved coastal highway. 'But I wanted to check, just in case.'

The unsmiling RAMC nurse at the Administration hut had begrudged him the information that 'Miss Stanley' had the day off and was presumably spending it with the other VADs at the nearby seaside resort of Le Touquet.

'Hmm,' said Borden as he glimpsed the jade water through breaks in the stands of tall pines, reminding him of Sullivan's Island, his home outside Charleston, South Carolina.

After driving a few more minutes along the twisting highway, eliciting curious glances from passers-by at the Indian-head insignia painted on the ambulance's side panel, they observed two young women walking along the roadside, one tall and slender, the other petite, both wearing the blue–grey uniform and white cap of a Red Cross nurse. Harrington depressed the clutch and let the vehicle coast by them, hoping for a decent look. He smiled as he recognized Kit in the rear-view mirror, holding a hand to her face to ward off the billowing dust.

'There she is,' said Harrington as the car came to a stop. With a pump of gas and grind of gears, he backed the Model T to the spot where the nurses were standing, arms crossed over their bibs, with an amused expression.

'You ladies look like you could use a ride,' drawled Borden.

'Hullo, Kit,' said Harrington.

'Do you think we might?' asked Kit's companion. 'It's against regulations, but perhaps...'

'We could lay you out on a stretcher and put you in the back,' suggested Borden with a grin as he opened the door and climbed out.

'Henry,' said Harrington, 'allow me to introduce Kit Stanley.'

'Hello,' said Kit, giving Borden a quick handshake. 'And this is Jane Tisdale.'

'Climb in, ladies,' said Frank. 'Don't worry about getting caught. It's just another mile to town.' Kit slid across the seat next to Frank, with Jane following and Borden squeezing in behind them. Harrington gunned the engine and accelerated down the highway, with the warm, salt-laden breeze blowing through the open cab, furling the women's hair.

'This is *much* better,' said Jane. 'My feet were killing me.'

'Are you working today, Frank?' asked Kit, conscious of the pleasurable sensation of being pressed so close to him. 'Or is this just an outing?'

'The latter,' he said. 'I've got the fixings for a picnic. And I thought I'd take a swim in the ocean.'

'Sounds lovely,' said Jane.

Kit merely smiled, stealing a quick look into Frank's dark-brown eyes.

Harrington slowed down as they entered the outskirts of the ocean-side resort, whose abandoned casino and golf courses were a stark reminder of the bridgeless gap that separated them from the innocent time before the war's outbreak almost exactly a year earlier. Pulling over on the shoulder, he said, 'Maybe you girls should walk the rest of the way. I'd hate for you to get written up by some martinet and sent back to the hospital.'

'We can wait for you at the estaminet,' suggested Borden.

'Of course,' said Kit as Borden opened the door and tumbled out.

'We'll have a cold beer waiting for you,' said Frank with a smile. 'It's the little place on the left in the block past the old hotel.'

It was dark and relatively cool inside the estaminet, a favourite of the off-duty RAMC personnel staffing the numerous field hospitals in the vicinity of Camiers and Étaples. Wearing their British khakis, Harrington and Borden hardly received a passing glance when they stepped inside and made their way to the bar.

'*Quatre bières, s'il vous plaît,*' said Harrington to the barmaid as he rested his arms on the scarred surface and hitched his boot on the foot-rail. A short, stocky lieutenant standing next to him studied Harrington's uniform with a sour expression.

'What's this?' he said, slapping the back of his hand on Harrington's shoulder. 'Where's your insignia, soldier?'

'He ain't a soldier,' answered Borden with a smile, as the plump barmaid returned with a tray bearing four half-pints of pale-yellow beer.

The British officer narrowed his eyes, weighing the strange reply and the even stranger accent. 'What, then, is he?' he asked, addressing the question to Borden.

'We're Americans,' said Harrington pleasantly. 'Volunteer drivers with the AFS.'

'The bloody what?' said the lieutenant. Several officers at a nearby table had now turned to watch.

'The American Field Service,' said Borden. 'We drive ambulances.'

A bright shaft of light flickered across the room as the door opened, admitting two women who stood gazing over the tables, their eyes adjusting to the dimness. Turning around, Harrington flashed a smile of recognition and motioned to Kit and Jane. The arrival of the two attractive VADs at the side of the Americans caused the inquisitive British lieutenant to pick up his glass and move to the end of the bar.

'Here you go,' said Borden, handing a glass to Jane. 'And for you, Kit.'

'Let's have a seat,' suggested Frank, pointing to a table in the corner.

When they were seated, Borden raised his glass, said 'Cheers' and took a long swallow. 'Mmm,' he said. 'Now *that's* beer. Not like that watered-down stuff they sell up in Flanders.'

'You're right about that,' said Harrington after taking a sip. 'And it's not just the beer, but the wine, the food. You'd think the Belgians were in this thing just to make money off the lousy soldiers.'

'Don't be too harsh,' said Kit. 'They were forced out of their homes, after all, their villages destroyed...'

'You should see Ypres,' said Borden.

'Have you actually been there?' asked Jane, fascinated with Borden's soft Carolina drawl.

'About a dozen times. We have to drive through on our way to the aid stations. All that's left standing of that Cloth Hall is one crumbling tower and part of a wall, and the rest of the town is just a pile of rubble.'

'How dreadful,' said Kit. 'We hear all the stories, but of course we never get any closer than the CCS at Bailleul.'

'Where we met,' said Frank with a smile. 'I've finally got my chance to buy you that drink I promised.' They briefly made eye contact.

'Now, ladies,' said Borden, 'what's it going to be? A stroll along the boardwalk, some shopping at the fancy boutiques?'

'Frank,' said Kit, unexpectedly placing a hand on his arm. 'You said something about a picnic...' He nodded.

Before Frank could answer, Borden turned to Jane and said, 'I was hoping to get a look around town. Maybe you'd like to come along…'

Jane smiled and said, 'Of course.'

Finishing his beer, Harrington rose and said, 'This round's on me, Henry. We'll see you later.'

Stepping out into the bright sunshine, Harrington straightened his tunic and began strolling with Kit at his side, hands clasped behind his back like a pensioner, absently inspecting the merchandise in the storefronts. The sidewalks were crowded with older men wearing straw boaters, reminding him of the scene at his Harvard graduation – a sea of straw against the emerald of the quadrangle. Was it only three months ago?

They stopped at the corner as two women passed by on fine black horses, riding side-saddle in their long dresses with wide bustles at the back. Crossing the street, Harrington stopped at a *pâtisserie* and stooped down to examine a wicker basket filled with fresh croissants behind the glass.

'Now that's what we need,' he said to Kit. 'A picnic basket. And I was hoping to find some butter and jam.'

Kit smiled encouragingly and followed him into the shop. When his turn came at the counter, Frank smiled at the young baker in her toque, whose hands were dusted with flour, and said, *'Je voudrais un pot de confiture de fraise, s'il vous plaît.'*

'Oui…'

'Et peut-être, un peu de beurre…'

'Et deux croissants,' interjected Kit.

'Yes,' said Frank, giving Kit a quick smile. *'Et le panier là-bas dans la fenêtre, si possible,'* he added, pointing to the window display.

When they were back on the sidewalk, the basket hooked on Frank's arm, Kit said, 'You speak French rather well.'

'I studied it in school. I'm afraid it's not doing me much good in Flanders.'

He led her back to the Ford outside the estaminet and removed the sack from the toolbox, adding its contents to the basket. Placing the basket on the seat, he helped Kit to climb in and then walked to the front to crank the engine. They drove past the shops on the main boulevard, turning at the sign for 'La Plage' and again on the corniche that ran parallel to the beach.

'This looks promising,' he said, glancing over at Kit, who'd removed her cap to let the wind toss her light-brown hair. He turned on a track between the dunes and parked on the wide beach a half-mile from the public bathing area whose colourful pennants were streaming in the steady onshore breeze. Though it was August, when the beaches would normally be teeming with the French on holiday, this stretch was virtually deserted, with only a few middle-aged couples strolling along and a group of children splashing in the shallows.

With the gentle roar of the surf and cry of the gulls in their ears, Frank helped Kit out and then removed one of the stretchers and a folded blanket from the back. Spreading the blanket on the sand, he took the picnic basket from the seat and arranged the stretcher so they could sit facing the sea. With Kit seated Indian-style beside him, he uncorked the wine and poured some into the tin mess cups he'd brought along.

'Lovely,' she said, taking a sip and tilting her face up to the sun.

'And now *le pain*,' he said, slicing the baguette with his jackknife. 'Butter?' he asked.

'Yes, thank you. And jam. Oh, and a croissant.'

'I'll sample the cheese and the pear.'

A quarter-hour passed with hardly a word spoken, sharing the bread and butter, nibbling morsels of sausage or fruit with cheese, pouring more wine. Kit shed her bib, apron and shoes, and Frank his jacket, and so they sat with the sun on their faces, sipping their wine, and watching the children at play in the surf.

'A penny for your thoughts,' Kit said at last.

'I've been trying', he said, 'to imagine that there's no war. That things are just, you know, like they were before, sitting here on the beach, watching the ocean...'

'Yes?'

'But it's only an illusion. My mind keeps filling up with other images...'

'I know.' Kit shaded her eyes and gazed at the horizon where the white sails of a sloop angled against the wind. 'I tried doing the same thing,' she said softly. 'But it doesn't matter.' She turned to him with a happy smile. 'We have today, and it's wonderful.' She impulsively leaned over and gave him a peck on the cheek.

He gazed in her eyes and said, 'Yes, we do.' Finishing what was left of his wine, he added, 'And now I'm dying to take a swim.'

'Do you have a suit?' she asked. He nodded and motioned to the car. 'I'm afraid,' she said, 'I didn't bring one.'

'I'll bet we can fix you up,' he said, standing up and dusting crumbs from his lap.

Harrington emerged from the red-striped dressing tent feeling somewhat self-conscious in his navy-blue swimming trunks and jersey. A middling crowd of bathers was enjoying the warm, sunny afternoon, though there were very few young men among them. He scanned the beach and rows of lounge chairs and, as he turned toward the women's dressing tents, saw Kit walking toward him in her brand-new bathing outfit, a bright-red, sleeveless top and matching skirt that revealed something of her shapely legs.

She smiled and said, 'Ready?'

'Last one in is a rotten egg.'

He dashed across the sand with Kit close behind, splashed into the shallows, and dove into the crest of a jade-green breaker.

'Oh,' said Kit, her head emerging from the foam, 'that's marvellous.'

They laughed and began swimming in a steady crawl out to a point beyond the line of scrolling waves. Harrington floated on his back on the mounded seas, delighting in the warmth of the sun on his face and the bracing cold water.

'You look like an otter,' said Kit, treading water beside him. He smiled, his eyes closed, and then started swimming toward shore. After a few minutes they were standing on the hot sand, shaking out their wet hair.

'I'll get some towels,' he suggested.

'And I'll look for two lounge chairs.'

At the end of the long summer afternoon, Frank and Kit, refreshed from a shower at the bathing pavilion yet pleasantly drowsy from too much sun, strolled side by side along the boardwalk, occasionally letting their hands brush together.

'Look,' said Frank, 'there goes Borden.'

A bicycle built for two, with Henry Borden in front and a Red Cross nurse on the seat behind, whizzed down the street and around the corner.

Frank smiled and glanced at his watch. 'I suppose we should be heading to the café,' he said. 'I told them we'd meet at that place with a view of the ocean.'

'Them?'

'The rest of our section,' Frank explained. 'You're in for a treat.'

By the time he found a place to park, the café was

packed with British officers, almost all of them RAMC. By unspoken stricture, a somewhat shabbier establishment further into town was the gathering place for the enlisted men. Kit hesitated at the entrance when Frank reached for the door.

'What is it?' he said.

'It's just that, wearing these' – she pointed to her uniform bib and dress – 'I'm bound to be noticed, and it's not allowed.'

'Hmm,' said Frank. 'Not allowed with the officers, that is.' He glanced at the empty tables under the red Dubonnet umbrellas on the terrace, with a view of the beach and ocean. 'Why don't you wait here,' he suggested, 'while I take a look inside.' After a few minutes he returned, holding two glasses of wine, followed by a waitress, who placed a simple menu before Kit. 'The others are on their way,' said Frank as he sat down beside her. 'As soon as they finish beating some of your countrymen in a game of darts.'

Glancing at the menu, Kit looked up at the waitress and in decent French ordered the mussels with *frites*. 'I'm famished,' she added to Frank.

'*La même chose*,' said Frank, handing his menu to the waitress. He lifted his glass to his lips and gazed at the red ball of the sun above the horizon.

There was a sudden commotion, and a tall young man tripped out the front door, followed by two others. Straightening his tunic, the tall man walked up, bowed slightly, and said, 'You must be Kit. I'm Herman Caruth.'

'Everybody calls him Deac,' said Borden. 'For Deacon. And this is Bill Larrabee.'

Larrabee, who was wearing his usual wide-brim western hat, smiled and said, 'Howdy.'

When they were all seated, Kit looked expectantly at Borden and said, 'What have you done with Jane?'

Blushing, Borden said, 'Gee, I had to leave her at that tearoom in town with the other VADs. She said they wouldn't let her near this place.'

'It's OK,' said Harrington, 'so long as Kit doesn't fraternize with the officers.'

'We won't let that happen,' said Larrabee with a grin.

After the dinner plates had been cleared away, and another bottle of inexpensive wine made its way around the table, Larrabee excused himself as the others watched the sun slip beneath the horizon, streaking the towering cumulus clouds with gold fading to pink. Inside, they could hear the tinny sound of a piano, and a rousing male chorus of 'Take Me Back to Dear Old Blighty.'

Larrabee emerged from the shadows with his guitar. Slipping into a chair, he hitched a boot up on the railing and strummed a chord.

'Play us a cowboy song,' said Borden. Turning to Kit, he explained, 'Bill's from Wyoming. Grew up on a ranch.'

After a series of introductory chords, Larrabee began singing in his pleasant baritone:

'I ride an old paint, I lead an old dan,
I'm bound for Montan' for to throw the hoolihan.
They feed in the gullies, they water in the draw,
their tails are all matted, their backs are all raw...'

Listening to the music, the sky suffused with the fading light and the air fresh with the sea breeze, Frank slipped his arm around Kit's shoulder. She nestled against him and closed her eyes with a contented smile, wondering for a moment what Nigel, or her parents, would think if somehow they knew she'd spent the evening in the arms of the tall, handsome American.

71

'Ride around, little ponies,' sang Larrabee in his lilting voice, and the others joined in: 'Ride around and slow. You're fiery and snuffy, and rarin' to go...'

6

Kit stood at the lieutenant's bedside and studied his features as he slept peacefully; his prominent forehead, the nose somewhat out of alignment, the cleft in his chin. An interesting face, she considered, not unattractive. Aware of his shallow breathing, she gently placed a finger on his inner wrist, just able to detect a faint pulse.

'You're the one they call Kit,' he said softly, speaking with his eyes closed.

'Why, yes, that's right,' she said. When she looked back at his face, he opened his eyes and gave her a weak smile.

'I'm Albert,' he said. 'Albert Barnes.' He looked at her expectantly.

'Well, Albert,' she said, returning the smile, 'I'm Kit Stanley. How are you feeling today?'

Ignoring the question, he said, 'I wonder how long I've been here? I haven't any notion of the time.'

Kit thought back to the dreadful morning when Frank and Bill Larrabee carried in the lieutenant, almost dead. He'd since undergone surgery and been moved to her usual marquee. A Dangerously Ill List tag was fastened to the foot-rail of his bed. She doubted he'd ever be taken off it. 'It's been over a week,' she replied. 'You were unconscious much of the time.'

'I see. It seems a blur.'

'You were brought in with the others who ... er ... had been burned...'

'The poor sods in the crater?' he said quietly. 'The Rifle Brigade. They were being relieved.' The lieutenant groaned

73

and then tried to cough, leaving a spittle of blood at the corner of his mouth.

'You should rest,' said Kit, gently placing a hand on his arm.

He shook his head slightly in protest. 'Are there any others here from my battalion?' he asked after a moment.

'Your battalion...'

'The 7th King's Royal Rifles.'

Oh, my, thought Kit, raising her hand to her lips. Nigel's regiment – his own battalion. 'No,' she said, 'not that I know of. But I understand they've been sent out of the line, to rest and refit.'

'Rest and refit,' murmured the lieutenant. He closed his eyes with a slight, inscrutable smile. 'You know someone in the battalion?' he asked after a moment.

'Yes. Ah, an old friend from before the war. He wrote to tell me his company's staying at Poperinge.'

Lieutenant Barnes slowly opened his eyes. 'His name?' he asked.

'Owen,' said Kit. 'Captain Nigel Owen. Do you know him?'

Barnes nodded. 'I should say so,' he said. 'He's my CO. So Owen made it...'

'Miss Stanley.'

Kit turned to see the Ward Sister approaching with the MO.

'Good morning, Lieutenant,' said the doctor, taking Kit's place at the bedside. 'Let's have a look.'

After removing the bandage and quickly checking the bright-pink incision, he lightly placed his stethoscope on Barnes' chest and carefully listened. 'I'm afraid we shall have to aspirate,' said the doctor with a frown as he removed the instrument's earpieces. Barnes gave him a questioning look. 'Your lung is continuing to haemorrhage,' explained the doctor. 'We'll draw off the blood and then, with proper rest, it should begin to heal.'

74

'I see,' said Barnes stoically.

An orderly rolled a cart up to the bed, with a tray of instruments, rubber tubing, and a glass bell jar. Pointing to the hypodermic on the tray, the MO turned to the Sister and said, 'Five ccs of the analgesic.'

'You'll have to sit up now,' he instructed Barnes.

Kit stepped forward and, taking the lieutenant by the arm and shoulder, helped him to a sitting position. For a moment it looked as if he might faint, but then his colour returned and he nodded to signal he was all right. As Kit steadied him, the Sister injected his back with a local anaesthetic.

The doctor wordlessly removed a large, stainless-steel instrument from the tray, connected by the tubing to the vacuum flask. Carefully inserting a long needle below the shoulder blade, he slowly withdrew the plunger, drawing off bright-red blood from the lieutenant's lung, which flowed into the bell jar with a hiss. Apart from an initial tremor, Barnes sat quietly, staring blankly at the far side of the marquee. After a few moments the doctor withdrew the needle. As the Sister affixed a gauze bandage to the lieutenant's back, the doctor held up the jar, half-filled with crimson blood, for Barnes to see.

'About six ounces,' said the MO. 'You should breathe far more easily now.' As Kit carefully helped Barnes to lie down, the MO instructed the Sister: 'See to it that he stays very still. Still, and plenty of rest. That should clear up the haemorrhage.'

'Yes, Doctor,' said the Sister with a slight bow.

Kit patted Barnes on the arm and moved on with the Sister to the next bed. When their rounds were finished, she returned to the lieutenant's bedside. He appeared to be sleeping, but then the suggestion of a smile curled his mouth, and he softly said, 'So you know Captain Owen?'

Though anxious for details about Nigel, she was reluctant

to disturb the lieutenant. 'Yes, I do,' she said. 'But you should be resting.'

He cocked one sleepy eye at her. 'You know him well?' he asked.

'Yes, very well. Now, hush. Go to sleep.'

'Owen's a bit of a cipher,' said Barnes. 'A good officer, but...'

Kit gave him a questioning look.

'But a bit stand-offish.'

She considered Nigel's cold, imperious demeanour. 'What happened?' she asked. 'To your company, I mean?'

Barnes stared at the top of the tent with a faraway look. 'The Germans launched an attack in force on the crater. The crater from the mine.' He glanced at her. 'You know about the mine?'

'Yes, I read the accounts.'

'They attacked at first light. Quite remarkable, pouring jets of fire on the poor devils in the crater just as they were being relieved. At all events, the Boche took the trenches to our left, got in our rear.' Kit nodded. 'I remember the captain standing there shouting commands, quite cool. And so over the top we went. I can't say that we threw them out – it's all a bit of a fog – but I rather think so.'

Kit patted his arm and said, 'You should go back to sleep.'

'I'm surprised Owen made it,' said Barnes weakly. 'I'm *glad* he made it.'

'Goodbye, Lieutenant,' said Kit. 'I'll be back later with some *consommé*.' As she turned to go she noted the time on the clock, determined to return in the afternoon with the promised cup of hot broth.

As she made her way through the maze of tents, her thoughts kept coming back to the lieutenant, how calmly he'd accepted the news that his lung was still haemorrhaging, how he'd scarcely flinched when the MO inserted the long needle ... It was amazing that he and Nigel were serving in the same company. What was it he'd called Nigel? Stand-offish? That was an understatement if she'd ever heard one. The lieutenant's chilling description of the German attack, pouring liquid fire on the men in the crater ... and Nigel was actually there, coolly giving orders. The thought was deeply disturbing. Despite his letters, she'd somehow never allowed herself to imagine Nigel actually in battle, with men dying all around him.

A wave of guilt passed over her as she reached her tent and glanced through the flap, relieved to see that Jane was elsewhere. Yes, Nigel had been there, she thought, as she kicked off her shoes and slumped on the cot, while she had been enjoying herself on the beach ... with Frank.

God, she couldn't go on like this any longer, ignoring Nigel's pleas to meet him in Paris. Of course she'd go, and the sooner the better, to face what would inevitably ensue. His insistence that she marry him. With a heavy sigh, she eased a cigarette from the pack and lit it, waving the match in the air as her thoughts turned to Frank. A wistful smile crossed her face, remembering the day at Le Touquet, the evening outside the café with his arm around her. Well, before sending a wire to Nigel she would write the note to Frank she'd been composing in her mind for days.

After depositing the envelope at the hospital post, she arranged a ride into Camiers to the telegraph office. She quickly filled out the form at the counter, suggesting that she take the afternoon train to Paris on Friday a week hence, and addressed it to Capt. Nigel Owen, 7th King's Royal Rifles, BEF, Poperinge. Handing it to the clerk, she hurried outside, the burden lifted at last from her conscience.

*   *   *

Leaning back against the wall, Frank Harrington stretched his legs on his cot and unbuttoned his shirt. He glanced at the cot next to him, where Henry Borden was lying on his side, reading a book. The door opened, filling the dim room with a shaft of bright sunlight.

'Mail call, gentlemen,' said Deac Caruth, whose tall form filled the doorway. 'The latest batch from Neuilly.'

Closing the door behind him, he sorted the bundle as he walked over to their cots. 'A letter from Mother,' he commented, tossing an envelope to Borden. 'Another from your gal, or maybe it's your sis, and the latest issue of *Outdoor Life*. And something from the parcel post. Your lucky day.' He dropped a package wrapped in brown paper on the end of the bed.

As Borden tore into the parcel, Frank sat up with an expectant look.

'OK, Harrington,' said Deac, 'what have we got here.' He shuffled through the stack and withdrew an envelope with a Quincy postmark, and then paused to examine a smaller, cream-coloured envelope. 'Curious,' he said, holding it up and then tossing it to Harrington. 'Not even stamped.' Harrington studied the neat handwriting on the envelope. 'Where's Larrabee?' asked Caruth. 'The rest of these are his.'

'Out in the yard,' said Borden. 'Working on his car. Gosh, look at this.' He unfolded a belted khaki coat with shoulder straps. 'A real Burberry trench coat,' he said with a grin. 'Mom ordered it out of the catalogue.'

Deac whistled and said, 'You'll look mighty slick, Henry.'

Harrington put the letter from home aside and slit open the cream-coloured envelope, which somehow had made its way into the AFS mail pouch without passing through the French postal system. He immediately saw that the note was from Kit. Smiling inwardly, he refolded it in the envelope and stood up. Seeing that Borden was immersed in his hunting and fishing magazine, he buttoned his shirt and walked outside, preferring to read the note away from the prying eyes of his comrades.

'Dear Frank,' it began. 'Last Saturday was one of the happiest days I've spent since leaving home.' He walked over to his Model T and sat on the running board. 'Our picnic on the beach, the swim in the ocean, and most of all, dinner at the café, watching the sunset and listening to the guitar, were perfect. It was almost as if we were back in the time before the war.' Harrington looked up from the letter and remembered the way Kit sat cross-legged on the beach, the breeze furling her light-brown hair. He smiled as he finished the short note, conscious of a strange lightness in his chest as he read her closing lines, telling him how she hoped to see him again soon.

Carefully folding the note in the envelope, he stood up and stretched. At that moment, a dark-green British staff car noisily turned into the rail-yard and came to a stop with a grind of gears. As the others filed out of the shed, a short, rotund RAMC officer, sporting a drooping moustache like Kitchener's, emerged from the backseat.

As the young Americans gathered around him, he said, 'The French have requested the return of your section to the 10th Corps at Arras.' The men nodded. 'But you men are needed here,' said the officer, tapping a leather crop on his palm. 'I intend to retain you as an auxiliary in the Salient at least through the push we're expecting in the autumn. And for now,' he concluded, opening the door to his vehicle, 'you shall return to billets outside Elverdinge. Be prepared to pull out at 1600 hours.' He slammed the door behind him, and the staff car sped out of the dusty yard.

After seeing to some last-minute adjustments to their Fords and topping off their gas tanks, they packed their clothes and few belongings and stripped their cots in preparation for weeks billeted in the Flemish countryside. Harrington sat on his mattress hunched over a wooden crate as he penned a hasty note to Kit. 'Thanks for your letter,' he began. 'The day we spent together in Le Touquet was the most fun I've had since...' He hesitated. Since when? Since as long as he could remember? '...since coming here,' he wrote. 'We've been ordered into Flanders for another spell, so it may be a while before we're *en repos* again in Dunkirk. But I'd love to see you just as soon as we're back.'

'C'mon, Frank,' said Bill Larrabee, standing in the doorway with a duffel bag on his shoulder. 'Let's go.'

Harrington quickly sealed the envelope and jotted her address. Slipping it in his pocket, he grabbed his bag and hurried out into the yard.

'I'll take the lead,' said Deac, at the open door of his Model T with one boot on the running board. 'Frank, you follow me, and then Borden and Larrabee. We'll take the road to Buerges and continue right on in to Poperinge.'

The men nodded in agreement and then glanced to their right at the sound of an incoming shell followed a split second later by a loud blast.

Watching the plume of black smoke drift over the rooftops, Borden said, 'Let's get the heck out of here before they drop one on the monkey house.'

After cranking the engine, Harrington climbed behind the wheel, shifted and followed Deac Caruth along the cobblestone streets to the paved highway heading south toward Belgium. With the afternoon sun in their rear-view mirrors, the convoy of drab ambulances passed into the lush green countryside, rolling expanses of farmland, ripe with grain, past neatly tended cottages with bright flowers in their window boxes, untouched by war.

Driving along the arrow-straight road with the pleasant late-summer breeze flowing over his face, Harrington was conscious of a certain excitement, a pleasurable anticipation. Kit's simple note, telling him she wanted to see him again, allowed him to admit how strongly he felt about her. If it wasn't infatuation, he considered, it was something close. Passing through the French village of Buerges, they soon crossed the border into Belgium and were abruptly surrounded by the vast British war effort, the long columns of supply vehicles and horse-drawn artillery caissons slowing their progress to a crawl.

As they approached Poperinge, the verdant fields and sturdy oaks gave way to the shell-pocked landscape, with splintered tree trunks jutting out of the muddy fields. The small convoy pulled over to let a column of British troops pass – new men, judging from their neat khaki uniforms and shining gear. Attached to the British battalion was a company of Belgian carabineers, wearing their distinctive leather hats, upturned on one side, complete with machine guns mounted on wheels drawn by teams of powerful, yellow dogs. Amazing, thought Harrington, as the last of the column passed, that the tiny Belgian Army had stood up to the German onslaught, a million men strong, when it would have been so easy to hand them the keys to the country.

'OK,' said Deac, tossing an apple core in the ditch. 'Let's go. A few more minutes and we should be there.'

'Great,' called Larrabee from the last ambulance in line. 'I could use a cold beer.'

The light was beginning to fade as they passed out of the congested streets and started down the narrow road toward the village of Elverdinghe, a few miles west of Ypres. Overtaking another horse-drawn limber, the road ahead was clear, and Harrington had to step on the gas to keep up with Deac, speeding up near the end of the journey like a horse headed for the barn. If only they had maintained their unhurried pace, Harrington reflected later, it might have saved them. Flinching at the unmistakable sound of an incoming high-explosive round, Harrington caught a glimpse of Deac's red tail lights in the same instant a deafening explosion plunged him into darkness. He blinked his eyes, trying to stop everything from spinning, dimly conscious that his car was in the ditch, miraculously in one piece. After a moment the spinning slowly stopped, and he could see that another Model T was lying upside down in front of him, engulfed in flames.

'Deac! Frank!'

Harrington, deafened by the blast, was unsure where the shouts were coming from. Henry Borden, wearing his new coat, dashed up to the door and peered inside. 'You all right?' he asked, looking at Harrington's bloody face. Harrington nodded, and Borden hurried on to the burning wreck.

Conscious that he was bleeding, Harrington lightly touched the gash over his eye. He tied a handkerchief around his forehead, tried the handle, and shoved open the door. His heart pounding, he hurried to the burning, overturned Model T, fearing that Deac was trapped inside. And then he saw Larrabee and Borden kneeling in the weeds in front of the wreck.

As he walked up, Larrabee looked up and said, 'Quick, Frank. Bring me some splints.' Borden was leaning over a body lying face down in the ditch.

'Is he...'

'He's alive,' said Larrabee. 'C'mon, Frank, hurry!'

As he searched the toolbox for a roll of tape and bundle of splints, some semblance of order returned to Harrington's mind. They'd been hit by a shell, he reasoned, and he was OK, but Deac had been thrown clear. The shell must have landed right in front of them. As Harrington trotted up, Larrabee and Borden were slowly turning Deac over on his back. His eyes were closed and his face was covered with blood. Larrabee took a knife from his pocket and quickly slit Deac's left pant leg, exposing an ugly compound fracture, the jagged point of the tibia piercing his shin. Deac let out a groan as Larrabee carefully straightened his shattered leg.

'OK,' said Larrabee, taking the tape and splints from Harrington. 'Go get a stretcher. I'll splint his leg and arm, and then we'll see to the head wound. We've got to get him to the CCS in a hurry. He's bound to be bleeding on the inside.'

Within minutes the three men carefully transferred their unconscious comrade to a stretcher, a bandage covering his face and splints tightly taped to his broken limbs. With the smoke from the burning car obscuring the lurid sunset, they loaded him in the back of Larrabee's undamaged ambulance. 'I'll ride with him,' said Larrabee. 'You drive,' he said to Borden. 'Can you find your way?'

'I think so.'

Larrabee turned to Frank. 'Are you all right?' he asked. Harrington nodded. 'Is your car OK?'

'Yeah, if I can get it out of the ditch.'

'Let's get moving,' said Larrabee, climbing in the back.

Harrington took a last look at the soles of Deac's boots and then shut the doors.

7

The platform below the vaulted ceiling of the Gare du Nord was crowded with older couples and young women awaiting the return of sons or lovers from the front. When the train came to a stop with a hiss of steam, the French officer across from Kit retrieved her bag from the overhead rack and politely gestured for her to go first. The trip from St-Omer had taken hours, with frequent stops in the congested areas to the rear of the front, more men crowding onto the train until the coaches were packed with *poilus* in their helmets and greatcoats and staff officers in dark-blue tunics and scarlet trousers. She'd whiled away the time in pleasant conversation with the two officers opposite her and an older chaplain with whom she was sharing a bench, the men blessing their good fortune to be seated with a pretty, well-dressed Englishwoman who possessed a good command of their language.

Standing at the top of the steps, Kit gazed out over the platform through the dim light filtering through the ceiling glass. After a moment she saw him standing beside a column with his hands in the pockets of his trench coat. Bidding her travelling companions adieu, she climbed down the steps and weaved through the crowd, certain that he hadn't seen her in the crush of soldiers exiting the train.

'Nigel,' she called out, and he turned, his eyes frantically searching the platform. 'Nigel,' she said with a wave and smile. 'Over here.'

He recognized her, stared for a moment, and then allowed himself the slightest smile as he began walking toward her.

At first she was unsure if he was going to embrace her, but after a moment of awkward hesitation he reached his arms around her and lightly kissed her cheek.

'Hullo, darling,' he said. 'I was beginning to think you weren't coming.'

'Yes, well, it took forever, with all the stops...'

'The French', he said irritably, taking her bag, 'can't even run their trains on time.'

As they passed under an ornate gaslight she could see that he was thinner than she remembered. How long had it been? The springtime ... that dreary weekend in April at Boulogne. It seemed a long time ago now. As they walked past the stairs to the Métro she gave him a questioning look. 'Aren't we taking the Underground?' she asked.

'No,' he said, making a face. 'It's filthy. We're taking a taxi.'

A gentle rain was falling on the early-September evening, the light from the streetlamps glistening on the pavement and reflecting on the black hoods of the taxis parked outside the station. 'No queue,' said Nigel distractedly. He walked up to the driver of the first car in line. '*Nous allons*,' said Nigel in his heavily accented French, '*à l'Hôtel Excelsior*.'

The driver gave him a blank look. 'The ... er ... Excelsior,' repeated Nigel, '*dans* the ... er ... rue Valette. Off the Boulevard St-Germain.'

'Valette ... *ah, oui*,' said the driver with a jerk of his head.

As Nigel held open the door, Kit slipped into the back, brushing raindrops from her hat. After the driver pulled away from the curb, Kit turned to Nigel and said, 'Where have you arranged for us...'

'The Excelsior,' he interrupted. 'Perfectly decent, clean, in the sixth arrondissement, I believe it is.' The driver gave them a quick look in the rear-view mirror.

'Well, I must say,' said Kit, 'you're certainly splurging. The taxi, a real hotel. I was expecting a young ladies' hostel.' This elicited a pained look. She quickly smiled and added, 'I think it's wonderful, after months sleeping in a bell-tent.'

He nodded and appeared to unbend.

Aware of his lugubrious mood, Kit said, 'I can scarcely believe we're in Paris. It's *wonderful* to be here.'

Glancing out the window, Nigel said, 'Yes, I suppose so...'

'And where are you taking us to dinner?' She was determined to try to buoy his spirits.

'Dinner? Oh, I've reserved a table at a little place off the place Vendôme. Is that all right?'

God, she thought, she'd never seen Nigel like this. 'Of course,' she said. 'I've been dreaming of a real restaurant, with tablecloths, fresh-cut flowers...'

She looked at him in the fading light, unable to penetrate his expressionless eyes. They spent the balance of the trip to the hotel in virtual silence, Nigel staring vacantly ahead and Kit merely remarking on the traffic and Notre Dame as they crossed the river. The small hotel was located on a quiet block in a fashionable neighbourhood in the Latin Quarter. As he paid the fare, she stood on the pavement, feeling a shiver of embarrassment at the thought of checking into a hotel with a man. Well, it *was* Paris, and perhaps that sort of thing went unnoticed. Inside the lobby, she was relieved when Nigel, gesturing toward the lift, said, 'I've taken the liberty of arranging for your room.' He reached into his pocket and produced a heavy brass key. They rode in silence to the third floor, where he accompanied her to her door.

'I'll wait for you downstairs,' he said as she worked the lock, 'while you freshen up.' Following her into the room, he placed her suitcase on the rack beside the dresser.

'I won't be a minute,' said Kit as he turned to go. Closing the door behind him, she tossed her hat on the bed, relieved to be alone, if only for a brief interval. The room was small but pleasant, with floral wallpaper, a soft bed, down pillows, and private bath, a rare luxury after so many months of spartan living. At home she would have indulged in a bath, taking her time to select a change of clothes, arrange her hair. But somehow it didn't matter. She washed her face, brushed her hair, applied a touch of rouge and, patting perfume on her wrists, was ready for the evening.

The *maître d'*, handsomely attired in a dinner jacket, seated Kit at the banquette in the corner of the small but elegant restaurant while Nigel checked his coat and hat. The dining room was suffused with pale-yellow light from sconces that gleamed on the dark panelling. She gave Nigel an encouraging smile as he sat down opposite her, looking handsome in uniform with his neatly trimmed moustache and carefully parted dark hair, creased just above his ears by his hatband.

'*Garçon*,' he said abruptly to a nearby waiter, who approached their table, bowed slightly, and said, '*Bonsoir, Madame, Monsieur.*'

'*Bonsoir*,' said Kit as Nigel simply nodded. In his odd combination of French and English he ordered a brandy and soda – '*Comprenez?* Selzer?' – while Kit requested champagne.

Once his drink was placed before him, Nigel reached into his breast pocket for a silver case and extracted a cigarette, tamping it on the face of his watch.

'May I?' said Kit as he snapped the case shut. He stared at her with slightly arched eyebrows. 'Don't tell me', she said, 'that you disapprove of ladies smoking...?'

'In public?' With a small shake of his head he removed another from the case and passed it to her. He struck a match, lit both cigarettes, and took a deep drag.

'*Merci*,' said Kit. She lifted her glass and said, '*à ta santé*.'

'Cheers.' Nigel took a long swallow.

He seemed to relax almost at once with the combination of brandy and tobacco, reverting to his old self, going on about their circle of friends in London – who was seeing whom – without a word about the war. His drink was gone in no time and he quickly ordered another. Kit paid little attention to the monologue, content to enjoy the champagne and the ambiance of faded elegance, just as she had imagined it, with fresh-cut flowers on crisp linen tablecloths and sparkling silver and crystal.

'At any rate,' said Nigel over the top of his menu, 'Mother wrote to say that Reggie and Delilah have announced a date in October. I gather he's managed a leave.'

Kit smiled, studying her menu.

'You know, darling, we should be thinking ourselves...'

'Nigel,' said Kit, 'what are you having?'

He glanced at his menu with a perplexed expression.

'You could have steak,' she suggested.

'Where do you see steak...'

The waiter appeared at their table. '*Madame?*' he said with a smile.

'*Le canard, s'il vous plaît*,' she said, '*et l'entrecôte pour le Monsieur.*'

'And a bottle of decent claret,' said Nigel, handing over his menu.

'*Très bien*,' said the waiter with a nod.

Once their dinner plates had been cleared away and the last of the wine poured, Kit looked at Nigel and said, 'You haven't asked me a question all evening.'

'A question?' His eyes seemed slightly unfocused.

'Yes, about my work, what life has been like.'

'Oh, well, I supposed it's a bit of a bore.' He took a large swallow of wine.

'Nor have you spoken a word about your own experience...'

'I prefer not to discuss it.'

'Well, it's *not* a bore. In fact, sometimes I feel I can't go on any longer, the sheer horror of it.' He avoided her intense gaze. 'And I know something about what you've been through.'

He gave her a curious look. 'What do you mean?'

'I've been nursing one of your men. A lieutenant named Barnes.' The mention of the name seemed briefly to sober him.

'I thought Barnes was dead,' he said softly.

'He should have been. He's a very determined man. At all events, he told me about the attack at Hooge Crater.'

'Barnes was reported dead. How odd.'

'He was brought in with the men who'd been burned. He'd have no doubt died at the Clearing Station, but they sent them direct to hospital. Nigel, I *know* how terrible it must have been...'

'Hooge,' he murmured. He downed the last of his wine. 'Bloody awful.'

'We should be going,' said Kit. 'It's growing late and it's been a long day.'

He rose from his chair and momentarily staggered. As she watched him, she felt a pang of pity, shocked by the change that had come over him at the mere mention of Barnes' name.

'We should get this soldier to bed,' she said, taking him by the arm to steady him. After helping him to settle the bill and draping his trench coat over his shoulders, she walked with him out on the rainy pavement.

*   *   *

Frank Harrington suppressed a yawn as he drove along the narrow roadway, waving away the dust that billowed from the wheels of the vehicle in front of him, a slow-moving army supply lorry. Though it was morning, he was unconcerned about enemy shellfire as he approached Bailleul from the north-west, a good six miles from Ypres. He'd left the others to collapse at their billet in a ruined barn after delivering a load of wounded to No. 4 CCS at Vlamertinge. It had been a relatively quiet night in the Salient – just desultory shelling from the batteries in the rear of the lines and the usual exchange of sniper fire. Harrington sensed the two sides were catching their breath, anticipating the next big push. Fighting a combination of drowsiness and the griping from his empty stomach, he slowed at the familiar high brick wall and turned into the monastery's gravel drive.

He had never seen the Clearing Station in daylight, and it struck him as oddly tranquil in the early morning. His was the only ambulance in the courtyard, and the orderlies, usually bustling about, were nowhere to be seen. Harrington stood by the Model T and studied the building, admiring its graceful arches and steeply pitched, red-tiled roof. He walked up to the heavy double doors and let himself in. The bright lights that lit the chapel at night had been doused, and in the dimness he could see that most of the cots, arranged in neat rows, were empty. As he gently closed the door behind him, a senior RAMC Sister approached him.

With a curious glance at his uniform, she said, 'You must be with the volunteers, the, er...'

Harrington slipped off his cap. 'That's right, ma'am,' he said. 'The AFS.'

'Well?' she said. 'Have you brought us more men? We weren't expecting another convoy.'

'No, ma'am. I just came by to look in on a friend.'

'I see.'

'Another driver, an American, who was wounded and brought here the other night. His name's Caruth...'

'You'll have to speak with the MO. Come along.'

As Harrington followed her to the back of the chapel, he said, 'Excuse me, Sister.' She stopped and looked at him. 'I don't suppose,' he asked, 'there's a VAD on duty named Stanley? Kit Stanley...'

'I don't believe so,' she said with a disapproving look. 'We have so many VADs coming and going it's hard to keep track.'

He followed her to a small, windowless office where a British captain sat behind a desk immersed in paperwork. He glanced up with a look of annoyance and said, 'Yes? What is it?'

'I was hoping to see a friend,' said Harrington. 'If he's still here. Caruth. Herman Caruth.'

The captain consulted a chart. 'Yes,' he said after a moment. 'Surgical case. Take him back to the ward, Sister. But just for a few minutes, young man.'

Harrington followed the Sister along a corridor to the monastery's smaller chapel, which had been converted to a ward for men whose wounds required immediate surgery before they could be evacuated to a general hospital on the Channel coast. Placing a finger to her lips, the Sister held open the door and gestured to him to go in. The pews had been removed to accommodate a row of beds on each side of the room, perhaps twenty in all. Harrington looked up at the vaulted plaster ceiling and then studied a large, painted crucifix on the far wall as his eyes adjusted to the light shining through the stained-glass windows. Raised a Protestant, he was troubled by the image of the bleeding and dying Christ in the midst of so much human suffering.

He walked slowly between the rows of beds, glancing

from side to side at the faces of the men, most of whom were sleeping. Deac was in the second-to-last bed on the right. Harrington recognized him by his unusual height, filling every inch of the bed, in contrast to the generally diminutive British soldiers. His left leg, in a plaster cast from the knee to the ankle, was suspended by a sling, another cast covered his right arm, and a bandage obscured half his face. As Harrington walked up to his bedside, Deac opened his eyes and managed a weak smile.

Gently placing a hand on Deac's uninjured arm, Harrington said, 'Hullo, pal. How are you feeling?'

In a barely audible voice, Deac said, 'Not too bad.' He then winced and added, 'It hurts.'

Harrington nodded. 'You were pretty badly smashed up.'

'What happened?'

'A 155 exploded right in front of us, and we went into the ditch. You were thrown clear. I just got a knock on the head.' Harrington touched the bandage over his right eye.

'What about the others?' asked Deac. He grimaced in pain.

'You shouldn't be talking...'

'It's OK.'

'The others are fine. They came by to see you yesterday, but the Sister wouldn't let them in.' He studied Deac's face below the thick bandage. There was no colour in his cheeks or lips. 'How long will they keep you here?' asked Harrington.

'They'll put me on a train in a day or so,' Deac whispered. 'They've got to keep this ward clear.' Harrington nodded, wondering how someone so badly injured could manage the long, bone-rattling journey to the coast.

'Say, Frank.' Deac looked up. 'Could you do something for me?'

'Sure,' said Harrington as softly as possible.

'My Bible should be there on the table.'

Harrington glanced at the small, worn book on the bedside table and picked it up.

'Could you read to me?' asked Deac. 'Something from the Psalms?'

Harrington nodded, embarrassed at his lack of familiarity with the contents of the slender volume. He noticed a stool against the wall and quietly placed it by the bed. He sat down and opened the Bible. Deac had neatly written 'Herman Caruth, St Louis, Missouri' on the flysheet. Unsure where to find the Psalms, he began leafing through the onionskin pages.

'Psalm 30,' said Deac. 'They're in the middle, before Proverbs.'

After a moment, Harrington found it and began reading in a quiet voice. 'I will extol thee, O Lord, for thou hast lifted me up ... O Lord my God, I cried unto thee, and thou hast healed me. O Lord, thou hast brought up my soul from the grave; thou hast kept me alive, that I should not go down to the pit...' He paused and looked at Deac, whose face had softened, the tension gone.

'Sing unto the Lord,' Frank continued reading, 'and give thanks at the remembrance of His holiness ... Weeping may endure for a night, but joy cometh in the morning...'

When the Sister came for him, Harrington was sitting on the stool, the Bible in his lap, watching Deac sleep, his breathing deep and regular. Outside in the corridor, Harrington turned to the Sister and said, 'Isn't there something you can give him for the pain?'

'We're short of morphia,' she replied. 'We have to wait until it's much worse.'

Harrington nodded, noticing a door that led outside. 'Can I get out that way?' he asked.

'Yes,' she said with a look that suggested the sooner he left the better.

Stepping into the sunshine, Harrington found himself in a small garden enclosed by a brick wall covered with climbing pink roses, alive with buzzing insects. Next to the building was a wooden bench. It was there, he was almost certain, that he'd first encountered Kit on that starlit night. The memory lifted his spirits from the deep sadness he'd felt sitting at Deac's bedside. He was determined to see her again just as soon as they completed this stretch. Slipping on his cap, he started down the path, the words from the Psalm playing in his mind: *'Joy cometh in the morning.'*

*   *   *

The evening rain was followed by a delightful morning, a cloudless sky with a hint of autumn in the air. Kit slept late, luxuriating in the soft bed under thick covers, the curtains drawn. When she finally rose, she treated herself to a room-service breakfast of tea, fresh orange juice and croissant, followed by an indolent soak in the tub. She knew Nigel was waiting impatiently for her somewhere, probably in the hotel dining room, but after the scene at the end of the evening she was content to let him wait. In all the years she'd known him she'd never seen Nigel in such a state, barely able to stand without her help, and then lunging for her, kissing her roughly, and trying to force his way into her room. Banishing the memory, she unlatched and threw open the windows, enjoying the breeze on her face as she gazed out over the mansard roofs.

She found Nigel in the lobby, dressed in uniform and seated on a sofa reading a London paper by a large potted fern. When she sat down in the chair next to him, he greeted her as if the scene at her door had never happened, no doubt lost in an alcohol-induced haze. After chastising her for sleeping late, he reverted to the silent, distracted state in which she'd found him at the station.

'As you don't seem to have a plan,' said Kit, 'I have a suggestion.' He folded his paper and stared at her. 'We can take a walk to the Seine and then ride out to the Bois du Boulogne. There's a wonderful restaurant where we can sit outside. It's such a lovely day.'

'Yes, very well, then.'

Despite taking her arm in his, and his monosyllabic replies to her occasional questions, Nigel had virtually nothing to say as they strolled along the pavements, a condition Kit found deeply disturbing but which he seemed completely at ease with. He waited on the pavement when she looked in at a fashionable boutique on the rue du Bac, choosing a pair of fine kid gloves to send to her mother and admiring the wide selection of ladies' hats, wide-brimmed with bright-coloured plumes and ribbons. Leaving the shop, Kit suggested a stop at the pavement café in the next block, where Nigel silently sipped his *café au lait* and watched the passers-by with a mildly bored expression.

Once they reached the river she persuaded him to take the Métro for the ride out to the Bois, arguing that his francs would be better spent on lunch than another taxi fare. He seemed ill at ease in the Métro carriage, choosing a seat near the back, away from the other, mostly middle-aged passengers. When a young French soldier boarded the car at an intermediate stop, Nigel visibly started, clutching the armrest with a frightened look, seeing something, thought Kit, that no one else could see. The moment passed, and he appeared to relax for the balance of the trip.

Arriving at Les Grandes Cascades, the fashionable Art Nouveau restaurant near the Longchamps racetrack, at the relatively early hour of one, they were seated at a sought-after table on the terrace with a view of couples strolling in the park amid horse-drawn carriages in the pleasant sunshine. Kit smiled encouragingly at Nigel as the waiter, clad in black with white shirtsleeves and apron, appeared at their table.

'I'll have a champagne cocktail,' she said.

'Monsieur?'

'*Pastis*,' said Nigel. Again, he waited until his drink was served before initiating a conversation, and he returned to his favourite theme.

'You know, darling,' he began after taking a large swallow of the powerful aperitif, 'we really should discuss a date.'

Kit looked away, trying not to show her resentment. 'A date for what?' she asked, though she knew perfectly well what he meant.

'Our nuptials.' He extracted a cigarette from his case and lit it, pointedly not offering one to her.

'Nigel,' said Kit. 'Doesn't it strike you as odd to be talking about a *date* to be married when we haven't even discussed marriage?'

'Haven't discussed? What do you mean? I mean, we've jolly well discussed it for years...'

'That may be, but you seem to forget that *you* haven't proposed, nor have *I* accepted.' She looked beyond Nigel and watched as two men in cycling club jerseys whizzed past.

Nigel finished his drink in a single swig, motioned to the waiter, and said, '*Encore un verre.*' Taking a deep drag on his cigarette, he stared across the table at Kit and said, 'I think Christmas would be an excellent time. I should be able to arrange leave, everyone who matters should be in the city, and...'

'Stop it, Nigel!'

He looked more surprised than hurt. They sat silently as the waiter returned with Nigel's drink and handed both of them menus. A fine black brougham drawn by a matched pair of greys halted on the street by the terrace. Two ladies alighted from the coach, wearing elaborate silk gowns and exceptionally large, feathered hats, followed by their husbands in tails and top hats.

'Off to the races,' commented Kit. 'Terribly posh.'

'Rather,' said Nigel, indifferent to the extravagant display of wealth in a time of such great suffering and sacrifice.

'Nigel,' said Kit, doing her best to suppress her anger and frustration. 'I don't know what's come over you. You're drinking far too much and you seem, well, not yourself. I know you've been under terrible stress, but, frankly...'

He narrowed his eyes and said, 'Yes, frankly what?'

'I resent the fact that you seem to take it for granted that I'll marry you...'

'But I'm right for you. We share the same friends, the same interests, why, we've been together for years...'

'Yes. Yes, we have.' She felt tears coming and fought them back. 'But as *friends*. Nigel, I don't know if I *love* you?'

'I see.' He stubbed out his cigarette and took another large swallow. 'Well, perhaps it's best not to discuss it. At the moment, that is.'

She stared into his eyes, feeling more pity than anger.

'But I'm not giving up, darling,' he concluded. 'Now – what shall we have for lunch?'

8

The rain poured off the tarpaulin stretched over the collapsed roof of the barn and splashed in muddy pools. The men huddled on straw bales, backs against the rough brick wall amid piles of broken tile, warming their feet at the glowing embers of a dying fire. 'So Deac was gone,' said Henry Borden, idly tossing shoots of straw out a window that framed the flat, grey Flemish landscape.

'Yep,' said Larrabee. He drew up his knees and clasped his arms around them. 'According to the nurse, they put him on a train yesterday afternoon.'

'I don't see how he could handle it,' said Harrington. 'In the shape he's in.'

'Something like four hours just to get to Calais,' said Borden.

'If anybody's tough enough,' said Larrabee, 'it's Deac.' The others nodded. The steady drumbeat of rain muffled the distant thunder of cannons.

'I reckon they'll be sending someone to take his place', said Borden, 'when we get back to Dunkirk.'

'I wonder how much longer that'll be?' said Larrabee. 'I've about had it with this lousy billet.' The rain poured down even harder, silencing the guns.

'Well, at least we've got a place to keep dry,' said Harrington. 'Think about the poor s.o.b.'s in the trenches.'

'I don't get it,' said Larrabee. He leaned over and stirred the fire with a stick. The others looked at him, waiting for an explanation. 'They send out their patrols at night,' he said. 'Toss a few bombs into the other side's trench, if they're lucky. Keep up the sniper fire, the shelling. We haul off the casualties night after night.'

Harrington sat up straight. 'What's your point, Bill?' he asked.

'How are they ever gonna end this thing?' said Larrabee. 'It's a stalemate. And every time the British try to punch through the German lines, it's a slaughter.'

Harrington nodded. 'You don't send men across open country like this,' he said, 'to attack an entrenched position. We learned that in the Civil War.'

'Like Burnside at Fredericksburg,' said Larrabee.

'Or Pickett's charge,' agreed Borden. 'And the Yanks didn't have machine guns.'

'And why in heck did the British pick this ground to defend,' asked Harrington, 'when they could've placed their trenches up there on Mount Kemmel?' He motioned toward the solitary steep hill that overlooked Ypres and the surrounding countryside.

'And on the west bank of the canal,' said Larrabee. 'Instead of out there on that flat, exposed ground.'

'You forget', said Borden, 'that the Brits were on the offensive.' He shook his head.

'Well, there's no way they're backing down now,' said Larrabee. 'Not when the Germans keep upping the ante.'

'I think the Brits are counting on the French', said Harrington, 'to break through the German centre. Meanwhile, they'll just keep up the pressure around Ypres.'

'From everything I've heard,' said Larrabee, 'I wouldn't be surprised if the British try another offensive.'

'"Into the valley of Death", said Borden, 'rode the six hundred."'

The three men lapsed into silence, listening to the rain on the canvas, the hissing fire.

'And what about this Gallipoli campaign?' asked Larrabee after a while.

'Another bloody balls-up,' said Borden, 'as the Tommies would say.'

'Listen, fellas,' said Harrington, standing up and stretching his arms. 'The only way this war's gonna be won' – he paused to look at them – 'is if *we* come in.'

'Wilson will never let that happen,' said Borden flatly.

'He may not have any choice,' countered Harrington, 'if Fritz keeps torpedoing our ships.'

'Well, one thing's for sure,' said Larrabee. 'They're gonna need more ambulance drivers.'

*   *   *

After weeks of rest in Poperinge, during which the decimated ranks of the 7th Battalion were filled with new recruits and the officers were afforded five days' leave, the men of the King's Royal Rifle Corps moved out, under orders to march south-southeast to the French city of Béthune, and thence to billets in nearby villages.

The battalion officers were billeted in a manor house outside the village of Givenchy. A rigid protocol was observed at their mess in the large dining hall; the subalterns speaking only when responding to their superiors, and the dinner-table conversation dominated by the colonel and his company commanders. Nigel Owen, more at ease with the hierarchy of class and rank than the more casual conditions of life in the trenches, was pleased by the change from Flanders. The mess-boys kept carafes of decent French claret on the table to accompany servings of roast beef, lamb and rabbit prepared by a local French cook, a welcome change from tins of bully beef. Most afternoons were spent at the riding ring – decent horsemanship was expected of all infantry officers – or overseeing the parade and battalion guard-changing.

Besides Barnes, C Company had lost another lieutenant, killed by machine-gun fire in the attack at Hooge. Seven of the battalion's eleven officers had been killed or wounded, leaving Owen the only company CO who remained from the regiment's deployment in the autumn of 1914. With all the fresh faces, most of them new men, just arrived in France direct out of school, it was not a particularly congenial billet. Owen generally avoided the new subalterns, observing with perverse satisfaction their humiliations at the hands of the colonel for mistakes in the riding ring or in the handling of the men on the parade ground. He messed with Captain Henderson, the CO of A Company, whom he'd known slightly in their public school days, and Lieutenant Parker, the only other officer in C Company who'd come through the summer in the Salient unscathed and who treated Nigel with grudging respect if not friendship. The veteran officers seldom, if ever, spoke to the new men about their experiences in the trenches, not so much to spare them as to avoid conscious thought of the images that haunted their sleep.

The British lines ran due south from the Belgian border, passing just to the east of Béthune, joining up with the French 10th Army at Arras. The sector had been relatively quiet, in contrast to the fierce fighting to the north in Flanders throughout the spring and summer. But now the roads were clogged with supply lorries and troops on the move. At Givenchy's only estaminet, Owen and Lieutenant Parker had a table to themselves on the terrace, affording them a view of the busy crossroads on the highway to the east toward La Bassée.

'*Pardon*,' said Parker, waving down the young waitress as soon as she appeared on the terrace. '*Une bière, s'il vous plaît*. Captain?' he said, turning to Owen.

'*Pastis*. I've grown rather fond of the beastly stuff.' The waitress nodded and went inside.

'It's a damned sight better than that rotgut they call cognac in Poperinge,' said Parker.

'Drink's not the only thing that's improved since we left Belgium,' said Owen. 'I've noticed the queue's twice as long at the local brothel.'

'Yes, so I gather from the men. I've warned them about disease, though to no avail.'

'There's no stopping the Welshmen,' said Owen with a faint smile. 'The randiest chaps I've ever known.' The waitress reappeared with a tray and lowered their drinks to the table. Owen took a sip of the aperitif and lit a cigarette.

'There goes more artillery,' said Parker, pointing to the crossroads. 'More of the heavies, the 155s.'

Owen turned in his chair to look at the column of horse-drawn limbers, sending up a cloud of pale-brown dust. 'Earlier this morning,' he said, 'an entire brigade of cavalry passed through town.'

'I saw them,' said Parker. 'A splendid sight, with their spurs and sabres jangling. Now why do you suppose they're sending up cavalry?'

Owen took a deep drag and expelled the smoke from his nostrils. 'Almost all the general staff are cavalrymen,' he said. 'French, Haig, the lot of them. I suppose they're still dreaming of a fine cavalry charge to sunder the German line once the infantry's broken through.'

'From the look of things, Sir John's planning a big show.'

Owen knocked back his drink and raised his glass to signal the waitress for another. 'I should say so,' he agreed. 'Besides our regiment, they've sent down the Royal Welch, the Middlesex, and the Argyll and Sutherland. It must be obvious to the lowliest peasant that a big push is in the offing. *Merci,*' he added to the waitress as she placed another glass before him.

'With all due respect, Captain,' said Parker, 'I hate to see the army smashed to pieces in another fruitless attack. It will be Neuve Chapelle all over again.'

'Oh, but this time the Huns are in for a nasty little surprise.'

Parker gave Owen a questioning look, observing the slightest tremor as he raised his glass.

'Haven't you heard?' said Owen. He reached into his pocket and produced a folded slip of paper. 'This is a special notice from GHQ: "Under no circumstances...",' he read from the note, '"... shall any reference be made to gas cylinders."'

'Gas?' said Parker.

'"They shall be referred to only as 'the accessory'..."' Owen continued reading. He refolded the note and tucked it in his pocket. 'That's right, Parker,' he said. 'The accessory.'

'So we're planning to use gas on the Boche.'

'Anything wrong with that?'

'It's fighting dirty, Captain, if I may be permitted to say so. And once we've gone down that path, there's no turning back.'

'I only pray that it works,' said Owen. He finished his drink in a swig and reached for another cigarette. 'I'm afraid our chaps will botch it.'

All through the third week of September the British heavy guns pounded the German lines along a five-mile front opposite the town of Loos. The incessant shelling, rattling the glasses on the shelves in the bars, causing the ceilings to tremble, almost convinced the anxious Tommies that no living thing could be left in the blasted German trenches. The men in the forward areas suffered casualties from rounds falling short, owing to the narrow gap, only a few hundred yards, that separated the British and German lines and the often defective artillery shells. Meanwhile, teams of Royal Engineers dug pits at intervals along the British front for the 'accessory' cylinders that were brought forward in due course. Sir John French and his staff were convinced that the combination of high-explosive artillery and a cloud of chlorine would render the Germans incapable of resistance when the whistles blew for the infantry to go over the top and dash across No Man's Land.

Owen returned from the briefing at battalion HQ and assembled his officers, Parker and the two new lieutenants. 'Here is a map for each of you men,' he began. 'Take notes on the back, as you'll have to explain our orders to your platoons this afternoon. Tomorrow we return to Béthune, where we shall dump our kit. The following morning we attack.' The new lieutenants gave each other a nervous glance as Owen reached into his pocket for his cigarettes.

'Our first objective', said Owen, 'is a large house that's plainly visible beyond the first line of trenches. Beyond the house we cross a railway line. Our second objective is the town of Auchy, four hundred yards past the railway, as you can see on your maps.' The lieutenants scribbled to keep pace with Owen's rapid-fire presentation. 'And our final objective is the village of Haisnes, whose church spire can be easily seen.' Owen paused and then said, 'Questions?'

'Hohenzollern Redoubt, sir,' said Parker, studying his map, 'is roughly opposite our position. Are we expected to bypass it?'

'Hohenzollern Redoubt', said Owen, 'shall have been destroyed by our artillery. Now, the attack all along the front will be preceded by the discharge of the accessory for a period of forty minutes.' He paused to look into the eyes of the three young men, who blinked back at him. 'Attacking on our right are the Middlesex, and following behind us will be additional infantry and the Cavalry Corps.' Owen proceeded to enumerate the ammunition, wire-cutters, dressings, and other equipment the men were to carry, leaving their entrenching tools, blankets and greatcoats behind.

'Pardon me, sir,' said one of the new officers. 'Are the men to be warned about the use of the ... er ... accessory?'

Owen stubbed out his cigarette and said, 'They should be cautioned not to linger in the enemy's trenches where the accessory is likely to gather. Gas-helmets, naturally, are to be worn. Well?' he said, glancing at the men. 'That's about it. Brief your platoons. Each man is expected to do his duty.'

* * *

Daylight was fading as the three AFS ambulances entered the cobblestone streets of Dunkirk. Harrington glanced at his wristwatch, noting that the sun was now setting much earlier after the long days of summer. They drove past wrecked houses and storefronts, the rubble heaped on the sidewalk or spilling into the streets, and were forced to make a detour around the bloated corpse of a horse that blocked their path, still yoked to an overturned cart whose fruit and vegetables littered the cobblestones. What was the point, he wondered, of shelling the city, needlessly causing such suffering to the civilian population? The Germans were brutes, a menace to civilized society, and had to be beaten. It was as simple as that.

It was almost dark as the convoy approached the rail-yard. Even in the twilight Harrington could sense something was wrong. He followed Borden into the yard, killed the engine, and jumped out.

'Holy cow,' said Borden, standing by his car with his hands on his hips.

The shed had been flattened. Only a pile of bricks and blackened rafters remained on the spot where the 'monkey house' had stood. Harrington grabbed a flashlight from his toolbox and walked over to the rubble, where Larrabee and Borden were standing with their hands in their pockets. He switched on the light and shone the yellow beam across the wrecked and burned-out building, pausing to examine the occasional artefact lodged amid the bricks: a shoe, a broken bedstead, the twisted springs of a mattress.

'Direct hit,' said Borden. He chose not to complete the thought, the obvious fact that but for their purely fortuitous absence they might all be dead, blown to smithereens by a random shell from somewhere over the horizon. For a moment Harrington was conscious of a novel sensation, intense fear and relief at the same time.

'We might as well get something to eat...' said Borden.

'And drink,' added Larrabee, turning away from the rubble.

'...And then we can decide where we're gonna sleep.'

Harrington awoke with a pounding head and stabbing pain behind his eye-sockets, the result of too much cheap wine and sleeping on the hard ground with his rolled-up coat as a pillow. Sitting up, he gently massaged his eyes. A shave and a bath, he considered, would do wonders. But where? He noticed Bill Larrabee picking through the remains of the shed and walked over to confer.

'Find anything?' asked Frank.

'This,' said Bill, squinting in the strong sunshine. He held up a small notebook. 'And somebody's boots.'

'Listen, Bill. I could sure use a shave and a change of clothes. Where do you suppose we...'

'There's a little hotel a couple of blocks over. I figure we can get rooms till they find us another place to stay.'

'Or send us off. Sounds good to me. After breakfast let's drive down to Boulogne and see if we can find Deac.'

There was a claw-foot tub and washbasin down the hall from the third-storey rooms the Americans had secured for a modest outlay. With the war and the constant bombardment, there were few visitors to Dunkirk, and the proprietor of the simple establishment had been more than happy to accommodate them. Frank, having politely offered the others the first turns at the bath, promptly fell asleep, savouring the sensation of a pillow and mattress for the first time in weeks. He awoke to the sound of whistling in the hallway, opening his eyes as a thin young man, with skin as white as the towel wrapped around his waist, appeared in the doorway.

'Your turn, Frank,' said Henry Borden. 'If there's any hot water left.'

'Umm,' said Harrington, rolling over on his side. 'I could sleep all morning.' Reaching for his shaving kit, he stood up and slipped his suspenders over his shoulders.

Twenty minutes later, clean-shaven, refreshed by a hot soak, and wearing his one remaining clean uniform, he stood before the mirror combing his dark-brown hair. He wanted to look sharp, he realized, on the off chance that he might see Kit. If only he had something for her ... Flowers? A box of candy? The thought made him feel foolish, like a schoolboy on Valentine's Day. Besides, what were the chances of running into her? He slipped the comb in his pocket and hurried out the door.

Seated at a sidewalk café next door to their hotel, the three men were finishing their coffee, the sludgy French variety with hot milk. They looked up from the plate of fresh croissants and brioches to the sound of an incoming artillery shell and winced at the explosion on the other side of town.

'You'd think you'd get used to it,' said Larrabee, pouring his spilled coffee from the saucer back into the cup.

'Let's get out of here,' said Borden, scoffing down his

pastry. Harrington stood up and pulled several bills from his pocket.

Returning to the rail-yard, they piled into Borden's ambulance and were off, bumping along the cobblestones until they reached the coastal highway. A low cloudbank drifted over the dunes from the Channel, blotting out the sun and filling the open-air cab with a fine, cold mist. At thirty miles an hour, the sound of the tyres on the pavement and rushing air made conversation difficult, and the 45-minute drive to Boulogne passed in silence.

'There's so many hospitals around here,' said Borden, after they passed through the city and turned back on the highway, 'how are we going to figure where they've taken him?'

Harrington was tempted to suggest driving on to No. 4, but instead he said, 'Just pull in at the first one we come to. We can ask.'

By the time they reached No. 18 Red Cross Hospital, the mist had turned to light rain, dripping down the canvas sheets tied over the doors and blowing over the Model T's windscreen.

'Leave the engine running, Henry,' said Larrabee as he climbed out, 'while I check inside.'

Five minutes later he returned with the information, pried out of the Sister at the front desk, that Herman Caruth was listed at No. 11 General Hospital, near Étaples.

The morning was almost gone when they finally reached their destination, damp and chilled to the bone. Apart from next of kin, visitors were rare at the temporary military hospitals, but as they were in uniform, and ambulance drivers, the commanding officer agreed to allow them a brief visit.

'Besides,' he said gruffly, 'I expect he shan't be here much longer. Your friend's in marquee 7.'

After wandering among the maze of tents in the light

rain, passing by a vegetable garden whose vines had withered, they found the entrance to marquee 7 and let themselves in. The long A-line tent was identical to the wards of all the other RAMC hospitals they'd seen in the course of transporting the British wounded. The young soldiers in the cots by the door stared at them with curiosity.

'Looks like Sister's in the back,' said Larrabee in a low voice, 'talking with the MO.' A doctor and nurse were engaged in a hushed conversation at the far end of the marquee.

'Why don't you let them know we're here?' suggested Borden.

Larrabee slipped off his cap and started down the marquee as Borden and Harrington held back by the entrance.

'He simply must be moved,' said the MO as Larrabee walked up. 'There's a civilian hospital in town.'

'But, doctor...' The Ward Sister paused to look at Larrabee.

'Yes, what is it?' the MO asked with asperity.

Larrabee could see Deac in the bed beyond the MO and the Sister, his left leg in a cast from the thigh to the ankle. Larrabee gave him a wink. 'We're here to look in on our friend,' replied Larrabee. 'Mr Caruth.'

Both the MO and the Sister glanced at the end of the marquee where the others were waiting.

'This man is your friend?' asked the MO.

Larrabee nodded, feeling anger rising on the back of his neck at the doctor's tone.

The MO turned to the Sister and said, 'He'll have to be moved immediately. I'm afraid the regulations are quite clear.'

'Moved?' said Larrabee.

The doctor gave him a look of annoyance and said to the Sister, 'This hospital is for British army personnel only. The man's an American, and what's more, a civilian...'

'Now hold on just a minute,' said Larrabee.

Hearing raised voices, Harrington and Borden sensed trouble and began walking down the marquee.

Taking a closer look at Larrabee's uniform, the MO said, 'Who are you?'

'Listen, Major,' said Larrabee hotly, 'We're with the AFS. And so's our friend lying there with a compound fracture. Which, by the way, he got from a German 155 driving an ambulance to pick up *your army's* wounded in the Salient. Under direct orders of the RAMC Ambulance Corps.'

Harrington and Borden arrived in time to hear the last of Larrabee's words.

'That may be, young man, but the fact remains...'

'Hold on a second, Doctor,' said Harrington. 'Maybe we can straighten this out.' His calm tone seemed to defuse the escalating confrontation. 'Why don't you and I discuss this, say, outside ... away from the patient,' he added quietly. 'While my buddies have a chance to visit with their friend?'

The MO frowned and nodded. 'All right, then,' he said.

Five minutes later Harrington and the MO returned to the nursing station, where Larrabee and Borden were discussing Deac's condition with the Ward Sister. 'I'm satisfied,' said the MO to the Sister, 'for the time being, that the young man was wounded in the line of duty under orders of the RAMC. Of course, I shall have to confirm this ... er ... rather unusual arrangement with my superiors.'

'Thank you, Doctor,' said the Sister. 'It would have been very dangerous to move him.'

The MO briefly studied the three young men and then said, 'I'm afraid the fracture to the tibia has gone septic.'

Larrabee grimaced. 'I suppose that means', he said, 'you'll have to take it off?'

'Yes, it does.' In response to their questioning expressions, he added, 'We'll schedule him for surgery this evening.'

Once the MO had gone, Harrington stood with Larrabee and Borden at Deac's bedside and quietly said, 'We're awful sorry, Deac. But they've got to do it.'

With the large bandage removed from his face, leaving only a patch of gauze taped over the wound at his hairline, Deac smiled faintly and slowly exhaled. 'I'll be OK,' he said in a strong voice. 'Don't worry about me.'

Harrington glanced at the Bible on the corner of the bedside table. 'Anything we can do?' he asked.

'Write my mom and dad,' he said. 'Let them know what's happened. You've got the address?'

The men nodded. Placing a hand on Deac's uninjured arm, Borden said, 'We've got to go now, buddy. They won't let us stay.'

Deac nodded.

'But we'll be back in the morning,' said Larrabee.

'Good luck,' said Harrington. 'We'll be praying for you.'

The short drive from Étaples to Camiers was spent in silence, the men left to their ruminations. The rain had ceased, leaving a cold breeze blowing through the open cab. When they approached the entrance to No. 4 General Hospital, Frank turned to Borden and said, 'Say, Henry, would you mind stopping here?'

'Want to look in on your girl?' asked Larrabee.

Harrington nodded and said, 'If she's around.' Borden pulled into the drive and stopped outside the administration hut. 'I won't be long,' said Harrington as he climbed out. He returned in a few minutes. 'You can leave me here,' he said with a weak smile. 'I'll hitch a ride back to Dunkirk.'

9

'I'm sorry,' said the matronly Sister at the front desk, 'but the young ladies are not allowed visitors. Now tell me again the name of your organization?'

Harrington straightened his tunic and said, 'The American Field Service. We work mainly with the French Army.'

'I see.' She briefly studied his uniform. 'Volunteer ambulance drivers?'

'Yes, ma'am.'

'Very commendable. Well, good afternoon.'

As he turned to go, he heard the crunch of tyres on gravel and a throaty exhaust, deeper than the distinctive Model Ts. An RAMC convoy, he concluded as he let himself out. Four drab-green ambulances, with a bright-red cross on a white field painted on their sides, were lined up in the drive, engines idling, the wipers slapping the windshields in the lightly falling rain. Windshields would be nice, thought Harrington as he started down the steps, though he wouldn't trade his manoeuvrable Model T, with its short wheelbase, for one of the bulky RAMC vehicles. Standing under the awning, he slipped on his cap and watched the British orderlies unload the stretchers. Maybe he could talk one of the drivers into giving him a ride. He approached the lead ambulance.

'Sorry, mate,' the driver replied to Frank's enquiry. 'But we're going the other way, to Étaples.'

Harrington smiled inwardly at his mangling of the name. Étaples usually came out as 'eat-apples', and Ypres was rendered 'wipers'. 'Thanks, anyway,' he said.

112

He decided to stroll the duckboards between the neat rows of tents and huts. As he paused to inspect a single rose bush, a petite VAD hurried past, sheltering under an umbrella. She stopped and turned around to look at him. With a white scarf tied about her head, her red cross bib and ankle-length dress, she could have been any of the dozens of volunteer nurses in the compound.

'Frank?' she said.

He paused in the act of picking a rose. 'Jane,' he said with a smile. 'Sorry, I didn't recognize you.'

'These scarves make us look like nuns. What are you doing here? You're dripping wet.'

Brushing the raindrops from his face, he said, 'Well, I dropped by to see Kit. But I've been advised that's out of the question. So I'm wandering the grounds.'

'Kit's just coming off duty,' said Jane, holding her umbrella over both of them. 'I'll let her know you're here. You can wait for her in the canteen. It's down the next row.'

Frank snapped off a stem with a pale-yellow rose and started down the path. Rounding the corner, it seemed the entire hospital was converging on the canteen, which struck him as odd until he glanced at his watch and saw the time – nearly four. You could set a clock, he considered, by the British taking tea. Two lines were forming in the long, wooden structure, dimly lit by hurricane lamps, where Red Cross volunteers were serving out tea with scones and finger sandwiches. By unwritten stricture, the doctors, all officers, gathered at one end of the building, segregated from the nurses at the other end.

Harrington chose a table more or less in the middle, against the wall. Sitting alone in his rain damp uniform with the rosebud in his lap, he endured the curious stares and giggles of the young nurses walking past him with steaming mugs of tea and plates of cakes and sandwiches. After a few minutes he saw her, standing just inside the

113

door in the midst of a group of VADs, taller than the others and, unlike Jane, with a small, white cap pinned atop her thick brown hair. He watched as Kit scanned the crowded room, and after a moment his eyes met hers, eliciting the slightest smile and wave. She soon appeared at his table, holding two mugs.

'May I join you?' she said with a smile. 'You look awfully alone.'

Frank rose from his chair. 'Hullo, Kit,' he said, accepting his mug of tea. 'We have a way of running into each other.'

Once she was seated, modestly leaving a vacant chair between them, he said, 'Oh, and I've got something for you.' He handed her the rose.

Lifting the blossom to her nose, she inhaled the bouquet. 'Lovely,' she said. 'Frank, I'm so happy to see you.'

'We were in the area, so I thought, why not drop by? But the Sister at the front desk said no dice.'

Kit gave him puzzled look. 'The young ladies are forbidden to receive visitors,' he explained, mimicking her accent. 'I felt like I was calling on my sister at boarding school.'

'Well, here we are,' said Kit, 'and' – she lowered her voice – 'the Sister be damned!'

Frank smiled and took a sip of tea. 'You got my note?' he asked.

'Yes. How was your latest stint?'

'Pretty uneventful, except for the day we left Dunkirk.'

'What happened?'

'We were just outside Poperinge when a heavy landed right in front of us. I was following Deac, and we both went into the ditch...'

'Oh, my God, Frank. Are you all right?'

'Yes, I'm fine, except for this.' He pointed to a small, pink scar above his right eye. 'But Deac wasn't so lucky.' He gave Kit a rueful smile. 'You remember Deac?'

'Yes, of course. The tall one.'

114

'He was hurt pretty badly. Broken leg and arm, internal injuries. We got him to the CCS at Bailleul and now they've transferred him to one of the hospitals outside Étaples. I've just come from there.'

'And how is he doing?'

'Not very well, I'm afraid. The doc said his leg – he had a compound fracture – has gone septic. What exactly does that mean?'

Kit frowned. 'It means', she said, 'there's an infection. Gas gangrene, in all likelihood. I expect they'll want to amputate.'

Frank nodded. 'It's scheduled for tonight.'

'I'm so sorry. But the surgeons are very good. He should be well taken care of.'

'Anyway,' said Frank, holding his mug of tea in front of him, 'when we got back to Dunkirk, we found our quarters had been blown to bits, a direct hit.'

'How terrible.' She gazed into his eyes and said, 'It doesn't seem right.' He gave her an expectant look. 'After all,' she continued, 'we're here because it's our country, our boys, in the war. But you and your friends are just here to help. And now one of you has been terribly injured.'

'Well, we knew it wouldn't be a Boy Scout outing when we signed up. But it makes you stop and think when it's one of your own men.' He looked in her eyes and smiled. 'It's wonderful to see you, Kit. How have you been?'

'I'm fine. Things have been relatively quiet here, quite a change from the summer.'

'Rumour has it', he said, 'that General French is planning another offensive.'

'Another "push",' said Kit with a nod. 'So we hear. They've been emptying the beds in all the wards, a sure sign something big is up.'

'Well,' he said, 'with the pleasant weather, what have you VADs been doing in your spare time?'

'I've been to Paris.'

'Really? I'm dying to go. Did a group of you…'

'No. I went to see a friend for the weekend.'

'That must have been grand, after all the months cooped up here.'

'Paris is delightful.' An image of Nigel on the Métro came to mind. 'But frankly, it was rather depressing. Not Paris,' she explained, 'but being with my friend. So unlike the times before the war.'

'I see,' said Frank, politely pretending to understand. 'Anyway, Kit, I was hoping I could see you again. Now that I'm *en repos* for a week or two. Do you have any time off?'

'On weekends. Saturday afternoon till Sunday noon.'

'I could pick you up on Saturday and we could drive over to Montreuil, have dinner.'

'I'd love to,' she said with a smile. 'I'm told there's an excellent restaurant.' She glanced around the crowded room. 'Rather than come here,' she said quietly, 'could you pick me up on the road outside the compound?'

'Picking up nurses is our specialty. What time?'

'How would two be? We could wander the town.'

'Two it is. I'll look for you just outside the gate.'

'Perfect.' Kit glanced over at two VADs at a nearby table, who were pretending not to listen to their conversation. 'Well, Frank,' she said, pushing back from the table. 'I should tell you goodbye, before we attract too much notice.'

'Bye, Kit,' said Frank, standing up. 'I'll see you Saturday.'

As soon as he had gone, with a second mug of tea, Kit took her place next to Jane at one of the tables crowded with VADs.

'Well, Kit,' said Emily Goodall, a tall, slender girl with blonde hair tucked under her scarf. 'Are you going to see him again?'

'He's awfully good-looking,' ventured Catherine Hewitt with an envious smile.

116

'Yes,' said Kit. 'He's picking me up on Saturday. We'll have dinner.'

'Some girls have all the luck,' said Polly McBride. Unlike the others, who were educated young women from well-to-do families, Polly was a working-class Scot from a mill town south of Edinburgh. 'Seein' as he's an American,' she explained, 'drivin' an ambulance, he's not liable to get shot.' Virtually every VAD had a brother or beau, or both, serving in the BEF, a number of whom had been wounded, and several killed.

'Well, the drivers *are* in danger,' rejoined Kit.

'And don't forget, Polly,' said Jane, giving Kit a look of mild disapprobation, 'that Kit's also seeing a captain with the KRRC who was in the thick of the fighting at Hooge.'

'Just as I was sayin',' said Polly in her brogue. 'Some girls have all the luck.'

*   *   *

Seated between the colonel and a fellow captain, Nigel Owen took a swallow of wine and a carved a hearty bite of roast beef. The roast was too well done, but how could you expect the French to understand the Englishman's penchant for rare beef? The officers of 7th Battalion, King's Royal Rifles, were enjoying a final, elaborate repast in the château's dining salon. When they arrived at their former billet outside Béthune, hot and thirsty after a ten-mile march, they were dismayed to discover that the headquarters staff of the 21st Division, part of Kitchener's 'New Army', was insisting on occupying the château. The ensuing argument resulted in a compromise: the officers of the 7th KRRC would dine at the same table with the staff of the 21st. Kitchener men, thought Owen disdainfully as he surveyed the officers seated on the other side of the long table. He buttered a roll and carved another bite of beef.

'You see that pompous ass at the head of the table?' the

117

colonel, the battalion CO, quietly asked his adjutant. Both men were career officers who'd served together in India years earlier. Owen looked down the table at the portly, silver-haired officer with the red tabs of a general on his lapels.

'The commanding general...' said the colonel with a trace of sarcasm, taking a sip of whisky. His adjutant nodded. '... Hasn't any experience commanding troops, no experience in the trenches, none whatsoever.'

'Yes, and he's marched his poor lads to the point that they've blistered their feet and thrown away their gear,' said the adjutant.

Owen downed the last of his wine and gestured to the mess-boy for more. The young subalterns seated to his right, new men who'd taken the places of the lieutenants killed or wounded at Hooge, were laughing raucously, unaccustomed to whisky with their mess and keyed up at the prospect of the coming fight.

'Well,' concluded the colonel, 'tomorrow morning this *general* is sending his men over the top to assault the German line.'

'Another bloody disaster, no doubt,' grumbled the adjutant. Owen shuddered involuntarily.

'And then, I suppose,' said the colonel after taking another sip of his drink, 'he'll be on his merry way back to London with a bright new ribbon on his chest.'

After dumping their extraneous kit – greatcoats, packs, tools – the battalion moved out to Vermelles, the jumping-off point for the attack; a long column moving along the road in darkness. The men sang as they marched, familiar hymns for the most part, but gloomy songs as well about death and home. With frequent stops to allow ammunition lorries, horse-drawn artillery and cavalry to pass, the ten-mile march dragged on past midnight. The heavy British guns thundered almost continuously, and brilliant flashes on the horizon momentarily illuminated the men, horses, and vehicles clogging the road. When at last they reached Vermelles, the sergeants passed the word to move into the long, shallow communication trench that led to the front lines. The 7th Battalion was assigned the second place in line, and in the darkness the men soon crowded the narrow trench, scarcely wide enough for two abreast. Owen pushed his way forward, searching for the sergeant-major.

'Pearson,' he said at last. The column had halted, waiting for a squad of engineers to pass through a bottleneck.

'Sir.'

'Do you suppose these lieutenants understand their orders?' asked Owen. 'Not Parker, but the new men?'

'I wouldn't rely on it, sir,' replied the sergeant. 'I've gone over it all again with the other sergeants. They'll look after the lieutenants.'

'I only wish we had Barnes,' said Owen. 'A man with nerves.'

'Aye,' said Pearson, 'Barnes was a steady one.'

Owen reached into his pocket for a cigarette and match. Lighting it, he exhaled and looked up at the dark sky, where the faint sliver of the moon momentarily appeared through a break in the clouds. 'Despite what HQ told us,' he said, 'there won't be an infantry division or cavalry brigade supporting our attack.'

'No, sir,' said Pearson. 'I didn't think so.'

'We'll be on our own,' said Owen. 'Ours is a "subsidiary" attack. The main force is to our right, the Middlesex and the Argyll and Sutherland.'

'Right, sir.' The sergeant was barely visible in the darkness.

'Calm night,' said Owen. 'No breeze.'

'No, sir.'

'I don't like it,' said Owen. His hand trembled slightly

119

when he raised his cigarette. He thought he detected a questioning look on the sergeant's face. 'The gas, Pearson,' said Owen. 'The idea is for the wind to blow the stuff across No Man's Land into the Huns' trenches.'

'No bloody good, sir,' said Pearson, 'if there's no breeze.'

'I wonder if Sir Johnny French thought about *that*,' said Owen, taking a final drag on his cigarette and tossing it into the dirt. The men crowding the narrow trench began moving forward again. 'Well,' he said, squaring his shoulders, 'we shall have to see.'

* * *

Leaning back on the soft turf of the embankment, Frank Harrington watched a sailboat gliding along the river, a blond-haired boy at the tiller, a girl in a sun-bonnet reclining in the cockpit. The late-afternoon sun glittered on the water. He studied the shadows on the water from the supports of the bridge, a graceful stone arch over the wide, placid river, whose banks were lined with tall oaks stirring in the gentle breeze. 'If I were a painter,' said Frank, 'I'd paint this place. The cottony clouds in that perfect blue sky; the way the light sparkles on the water.'

'Mmm,' said Kit. 'It is lovely. Reminds me of home, punting on the Avon.'

Frank looked over at her and smiled.

'We used to go to Bath,' she explained. 'We'd take picnics on the Avon. Not as grand a river as this, but beautiful all the same.'

He gazed into her pale-blue eyes and then leaned over and kissed her lightly on the lips. For a moment she looked at him and then closed her eyes, inviting him. Draping an arm around her, he kissed her again, savouring the sensations, her fragrance, the warmth, the softness, of her body moulded against his. After a while he rolled over on his back, clasping his hands behind his head on the soft grass, staring up at the sky. She drew closer to him, lying with her head on his chest.

Lightly stroking her hair, he said, 'I'd never seen you without your uniform on, other than that time we went for a swim.'

'I'm sick of that dreadful uniform...'

'It's not so bad.'

'It makes me feel so ... so matronly, all covered up from head to toe.' She dangled a bare foot, exposing a slender calf below the folds of her dress.

'Seeing you without the uniform', said Frank, 'helps me to imagine what it would be like to be together, if there weren't any war.'

'Yes, it does. Lying here like this, watching the boats and the children, I could almost forget about the war.' She thought back to Paris. 'The funny thing,' she said, propping herself up on an elbow, 'that weekend I spent in Paris with my friend, it seemed the war was always there. You couldn't get away from it. Do you understand?'

He looked in her eyes. 'Yes,' he said, 'I think so. Some horrible image always in the back of your mind?'

'I don't know why, but today it's just different.' She smiled happily.

'Maybe the difference was your friend,' he suggested. 'Maybe she couldn't stop talking about it. Is she another nurse?'

Of course that was the difference, Kit realized. 'No,' she said after a moment. 'Just an old friend ... from school.'

He sat up and ran a hand through his hair. 'Well, if I ever make it to Paris – maybe you'll come with me – I intend to enjoy it.' He stood up and brushed the grass from his corduroys and then took her by the hands and pulled her to her feet. 'Why don't we stroll along the towpath,' he suggested, 'the rest of the way into town?

And then we can take a look at that restaurant you were talking about.'

Kit studied his features in the flickering light of the chandelier at the centre of the small room. His thick brown hair, parted on the left, a wide, intelligent forehead and dark-brown eyes, a strong chin ... handsome in what she considered a typically American way, though she hardly knew any Americans besides Frank and his friends, but so unlike the boys at home.

'What are you thinking?' he asked, folding his napkin beside his dinner plate.

'About you. How you look.'

'Oh, c'mon now.' He smiled, looked in her eyes, and then self-consciously looked away.

'What's wrong with that?' said Kit. 'I like the way you look.'

'Well, I like the way you look, and just about everything else about you, Miss Stanley.'

A waiter appeared at their table. '*Un dessert, peut-être?*' he said. '*M'am'selle? Nous avons des profiteroles délicieuses.*'

'Profiteroles,' said Frank. 'How about it?'

'*Pour deux,*' said Kit. '*Avec deux cafés, s'il vous plaît.*'

'You know,' said Frank as the waiter turned to go, 'I like the way you speak French, with that high-class British accent.'

'High-class?'

'Yep. And I'm just an ordinary Yank from Quincy, Mass.'

'Tell me about Quincy, Mass. What does your family do there?'

'It's just outside Boston. My father's people have been there for ... well, since before we threw the British out. My dad's a lawyer.'

'Is that what you're planning to be?'

'I don't know. It's what he'd like me to be. To go back to Harvard law school when I'm finished here.'

'I see,' she said quietly. She was struck by the transience of everything. What little time they had together would, in all likelihood, be over no sooner than it had begun. 'And when will that be?' she asked.

Before he could answer the waiter reappeared with a tray and served their dessert and coffee with an elaborate Gallic display. 'Mmm,' said Frank, 'that's some combination. Ice cream, chocolate and these little pastries. What were you saying? Oh, when am I going home. I suppose I signed up for a year, more or less. But I'm hoping we'll get into the war and I'll join the Army Ambulance Corps.'

'Really?' It hadn't occurred to Kit that the US might enter the war. 'Why would America want to fight?' she asked.

'To help beat the Germans, of course.' He gave her a questioning look.

'I can't even remember what we're fighting about,' said Kit with a sigh. 'It's just a bloody slaughter all the way round, as far as I can tell.'

'Well,' he said gently, 'there *was* the invasion of Belgium.'

'Yes, I know, but now it seems there's no way out of it. I'd hate to see America dragged into the war. So many of your boys would be killed or, like your friend Deac, . . .'

Frank nodded and had another bite of dessert. 'When we were talking earlier,' he said after a moment, 'lying by the river, we thought we could forget about the war. Looks like we were wrong.'

'Yes. I'm sorry, I'm afraid it's my fault.'

'Don't be silly.'

'Frank . . .' She impulsively reached across the table and placed her hand on his arm. 'I don't want to think about your going back, or going into the army. I just want to have this time.'

He placed his hand on hers and gazed into her eyes. 'OK,' he said. 'We won't talk about it. I want to see you, Kit, whenever we get the chance.' She nodded. 'Maybe,' he said with a smile, 'we could even get away to Paris.'

She looked down at her plate, noticing that the ice cream was melting. 'There's something I should tell you,' she said quietly. 'Promise me you won't be angry.'

'Angry? What could I possibly be...'

'I lied to you. Well, not exactly lied. I misled you...' She hesitated. 'The friend I went to see in Paris ... It wasn't an old girlfriend from school. It was an old boyfriend from home.'

'I see.'

'Frank, I'm sorry. I should have just been honest.'

'And is there something between you and this ... er ... old boyfriend?'

'No. I mean, not now. We were seeing one another before the war. In fact, I suppose he fancied marrying me. But I ...'

'Were you in love with him?'

'No.' She shook her head. 'That summer before the war, looking back, everything seems so, well, so frivolous. There were parties, weekends in the country ... Nigel was always with me, perhaps it was assumed that we...'

'Nigel?'

'Yes, Nigel Owen. He's a captain in the army. The King's Royal Rifle Corps.'

'I've heard of them.'

'Our families are old friends. We've more or less grown up together.'

Frank nodded. 'Well,' he said with a sigh, 'like I said, I'm just an ordinary Yank. I'm not sure I can compete.'

'Frank.' She squeezed his hand and stared into his eyes. 'Will you forgive me? The trip to Paris was nothing. Let's not let it ruin our time together.'

'Forget it,' he said. 'You're forgiven,' he added with a smile. 'Now, I'd better be getting you back or it's going to be past the curfew.'

10

Amid the roar and flash of the guns, the black night was split by an arc of lightning and deep, reverberating thunder. With a sharp gust of wind, the clouds opened, pouring down on the men sheltering in the trenches. Looking up as another bolt flashed, Nigel Owen smiled, feeling the cold rain on his face and streaming from his coat into the top of his boots. The wind kicked up with the sudden storm, blowing hard out of the west-southwest toward the German lines. The men huddled in the narrow trench, oblivious to the rain, too afraid to sleep.

After a while the storm receded, turning to soft rain, the sharp wind gusts lapsing into a gentle breeze. Leaning back against the trench wall with eyes closed, Owen prayed it would hold. But as the rain drifted away and first light glowed on the horizon, the breeze slowly died, a stillness in the midst of the thundering cannonade. A few objects beyond the German lines gradually came into view: slag heaps, a rooftop, a distant church spire. Owen glanced at his watch. Five forty-five. Surely in the dead calm they'd scotch the plan to use gas. He shoved his way past the men, desperate to find the sergeant-major.

'Pearson,' he said, grabbing the sergeant by the shoulder. 'Sir.'

'Locate the accessory company,' said Owen, 'and ask them about their orders.' Pearson nodded and scrambled down the trench. He returned after a few minutes during which the British bombardment slackened.

'They telephoned battalion HQ', reported Pearson, 'to request suspension of the discharge.'

'Yes?' said Owen.

'They were advised, Captain, to discharge the accessory, regardless of wind conditions.'

'Good God. Order the men to put on their gas-helmets and fix bayonets.'

'But, sir! What about the rum ration?'

'Find the bloody storemen and tell them to get on with it.'

Owen estimated they were several hundred yards from the front-line trench. Alpha Company would go first, to clear the way for C Company. The order to go over the top would be given forty minutes following discharge of the 'accessory', on the theory that the Germans' gas masks only afforded them thirty minutes' protection. He looked at the men huddling in the shallow trench, cold, soaked to the skin, and exhausted from the previous day's march and lack of sleep. In no condition to go into battle, he considered. Well, perhaps a double tot of rum would buck them up. A burly sergeant appeared with a three-gallon demijohn on his hip.

'All right, lads,' he grumbled as he unstoppered the bottle. A diminutive corporal stood beside him with a battered tin cup. The sergeant splashed rum into the cup. 'Here you are, sonny-boy,' he said to the nearest soldier, a young Welshman with fear etched on his pale face. He gulped down the drink with a splutter.

As the storemen made their way down the line, Owen followed behind, reminding the men to wear their gas-helmets snugly, commanding them to snap bayonets on their Enfields and stand to. By now the light was strong enough to illuminate the thick coils of wire beyond the British line. Owen took another glance at his watch. Almost six. Where in God's name was the gas? As he stood watching for some sign of activity, he suddenly became conscious of a hissing sound. The gas teams had turned the cocks, releasing plumes of chlorine from cylinders located at intervals along the trenches, piped through long tubes into No Man's Land. As Owen watched, the gas billowed into a dense cloud, heavier than air, and slowly began to drift, like a cat on tiptoes, away from the British lines.

Go on, thought Owen desperately. He pictured some wind god in the heavens, blowing the cloud toward the Germans. The tubes continued to hiss, spewing more of the deadly toxin. The cloud hovered over No Man's Land, no more than forty yards beyond the British trenches, and then, in the light and variable breeze, it wandered back, obscuring the double line of wire. The sound of escaping gas was suddenly joined by men shouting, the crackle of rifle fire, and the crash of shells – incoming shells. Somewhere to the right Owen could hear the skirl of bagpipes as the men of the Argyll and Sutherland and the Middlesex stormed out of their trenches toward the German line. In his immediate front, there was chaos as the gas cloud settled back on the British troops. After a few minutes the victims began streaming down the trench, men choking, retching, clutching their eyes, their brass buttons tarnished green.

'Effing balls-up,' muttered Sergeant Pearson, standing beside Owen as the gas cases blindly stumbled past. Next came the wounded on litters, squeezing their way through the tight bends in the trench.

'All right, Sergeant,' said Owen, 'get the men moving. We've got to get up into position. There won't be any forty-minute delay.'

The sound of battle to their right intensified, the rifle fire mixed with machine guns and exploding shrapnel. The men slowly crept forward, impeded by sections of the trench that had been blown in by shellfire, forcing them to climb awkwardly up and around. More stretcher cases emerged, struggling to get through to the dressing station. Wearing their gas-helmets and battle kit, the men were exhausted by the time the column was forced to halt some fifty yards from the jumping-off trench. Owen pushed his way to the front.

'What is it?' he asked a young lieutenant, one of the new men with terror in his eyes behind the glass of his helmet. Aware that he couldn't be heard, Owen stripped off his helmet and repeated the question.

'Alpha Company is waiting for orders,' replied the lieutenant, ducking as a whiz-bang exploded to their left. 'The attack hasn't gone forward. The telephone wire's been severed by shellfire.'

Owen's nose twitched at the lingering stench of chlorine. 'Send a runner to battalion HQ,' he said calmly. 'Advise them of our position and request clarification.'

Slipping on his gas-helmet, he pressed ahead to the front of the column. It was apparent that A Company had suffered terribly from the botched attack, which, of course, had done no harm to the enemy, and that its commander had wisely delayed the attack pending further orders. Five hundred yards to their right, the cloud of gas had inexplicably drifted across No Man's Land and settled in the German trenches, allowing the Argyll and Sutherland and the Middlesex to charge across in good order. To the left the line was manned by the green troops of the 21st Division, with whose staff the battalion officers had messed the day before.

Hearing the shrill blast of a whistle, Owen climbed up on the rim and watched as a battalion of the 21st, almost a thousand men strong, scaled trench ladders and plunged ahead into No Man's Land. Pulling off his helmet to see clearly, he was astonished at the spectacle. Within moments the British troops were caught in their own wire and swept by withering machine-gun fire and shrapnel, literally mown down, thought Owen. A small body of men managed to get through, moving forward in a crouching trot.

Dropping down, Owen squeezed past his terrified men, looking for the lieutenant. Wearing gas-helmets, the men all looked alike. He found him at last, on one knee in an attitude of prayer.

'Well?' said Owen.

'Oh, Captain,' said the lieutenant, standing partially upright. 'The word from battalion HQ is to hold in position.'

'Very well.'

Owen turned and started for the head of the column. Moments later a tremendous concussion flung him face-first into the mud. Dazed, he struggled to his knees and turned to look back. Twenty yards behind him was a smoking crater filled with body parts, all that was left of the lieutenant and the two men standing beside him.

'My God,' muttered Owen, picking dirt from his eyes. He stood up and pushed his way past the boys gaping at the crater.

When he reached the front-line trench, he found it littered with abandoned equipment and almost empty, except for a sergeant and a few others crouching among their fallen comrades.

'Where's your lieutenant?' demanded Owen.

The sergeant gave him a vacant look. 'Dead,' he said after a moment.

Owen could hear the cries of the wounded. It was obvious that A Company had lost all its officers. Sergeant-Major Pearson appeared beside him.

'Organize a patrol,' said Owen. 'We're going to bring those wounded in.'

He mounted the fire-step and peered over the parapet.

The gas cloud had dispersed, settling in pockets in shell craters, and the morning sun was up.

'Water!' cried the wounded, lying in clumps some thirty yards beyond the coils of barbed wire. Stumbling through the gas, they'd been raked with machine-gun fire. Owen glanced at Pearson, who was standing with two teams of stretcher-bearers.

'All right, then,' said Owen. 'We're going out. Let's make quick work of it.' He jumped down from the fire-step and led the way to the ladders resting against the parapet.

With a grimace, Owen climbed up and over, dashing through a gap in the wire. He dove to the earth at the sound of a machine gun. Looking back, he saw the sergeant-major sprawled beside the other men.

'C'mon!' shouted Owen with a wave. 'You don't think I can go it alone?'

'It's no use, sir,' groaned Pearson. 'They're all dead.'

* * *

Leaning back against the iron frame of his bed, Frank Harrington stared at the double-ruled page of the writing tablet balanced on his knees and considered how to begin. With a frown, he wrote 'Dear Kit,' and then:

Despite the fact that you're just down the road, you seem so far away. If only I could drop by and share another cup of tea with you. The problem is, they're liable to send for us any time now, with all the talk about the big push. We've got new sleeping quarters in an abandoned boys' school, and we've been told to sit tight and wait...

He looked up as Bill Larrabee pushed open the door and tossed his hat on one of the empty beds. Turning back to the tablet, Harrington wrote:

131

I got a letter the other day from my sister Elsie, who's training as an army nurse in Texas. She volunteered for a medical team the army's sending to France and they picked her! I would have told her to stay home, but now it's too late. My mom and dad will be worried sick. It seems there's a group of American doctors from Harvard attached to an RAMC hospital outside Étaples, which is where Elsie's headed. You'll have to look after her for me, as I doubt we'll be here much longer. If only there were a way I could see you before we're sent out. I think about you all the time.

He chewed on the end of his pen and knitted his brow. How should he close? 'Love, Frank'? He couldn't say 'I love you,' though he wished he could. Conscious that Larrabee was watching him, he hurriedly wrote:

Are you thinking about me?
Love, Frank

He still found it hard to believe that Elsie would do something so rash without asking his opinion. Didn't the folks back home understand that there was danger even for the medical personnel in the rear areas? Hadn't they read about the air raids? Well, he considered after a moment, she *was* in the regular army, a commissioned officer. He just couldn't help thinking of her as his kid sister.

Bill Larrabee walked over and dropped down next to Frank.

'Well,' he said, 'things are gonna be a little different around here.'

'How do you mean?' asked Harrington.

'With this new fellow they've sent us.'

'I didn't know.'

'Just arrived. Borden's showing him around.' Frank

132

responded with a curious expression. 'He's a quiet little fella,' explained Larrabee. 'I'd swear he's not old enough to shave.'

'Hmm,' said Frank with a frown. 'Have you heard any news about Deac?'

'Word is he's almost well enough to ship out. They'll put him on a boat to Blighty and eventually send him home.'

The door swung open, admitting Henry Borden and a diminutive young man wearing wire-rimmed spectacles and a brand-new uniform. The collar was a size too large, so that his thin neck stuck out like a turtle's.

'Frank,' said Borden. 'Allow me to introduce Talbot Pierce.'

Harrington jumped up and gave the new man a quick handshake, surprised by his flaccid grip. 'I'm Frank Harrington,' he said. 'Where are you from, Talbot?'

'Outside Philadelphia. A place called Norristown.'

Larrabee sat up on the side of the bed, reached for his guitar and strummed a chord. Pierce stared at it with a look of mild surprise.

'You play?' asked Larrabee.

'The guitar?' said Pierce. 'Why, no. I ... er ... play the clarinet, though I didn't think to bring it along.'

This elicited an amused look from the others, though they refrained from laughing. 'This must be our barracks,' said Pierce, glancing around the long room.

'No, it's the boys' dorm,' said Larrabee after playing another chord. 'But the boys are all gone ... the schoolboys, that is. The Lycée St-Jean, for Dunkirk's finest.'

'I see,' said Pierce with a perplexed expression.

'Besides, we don't have barracks,' said Borden. 'We have *billets*.'

'Well, ah, Henry,' said Pierce, 'when will we be going into action?'

'Action?' repeated Larrabee, putting the guitar aside. 'We try to stay out of action.'

133

JOHN C. KERR

'But I thought...'

Borden cut him off. 'Listen, Talbot, a buddy of ours, the man you were sent to replace, just lost his leg to a German howitzer. You'll see more *action* than you'd care to.' A thud sounded in the distance, rattling the window-panes. 'See what I mean?' said Borden. 'The Boche are constantly shelling this place.'

A car horn sounded in the courtyard below the dormitory windows. Harrington walked over and looked down. 'We've got company,' he said, turning to the others. 'An RAMC officer.'

The four young men walked out into the bright sunshine where a British officer was standing beside a staff car, its engine running.

'What can we do for you, Captain?' asked Larrabee.

'All available ambulances are needed immediately in the Béthune–Loos sector,' he replied. 'There's a major offensive underway, and the casualties are quite heavy.' He handed Larrabee a map. 'You'll be assigned a billet in the area. Is that clear?'

'Yes, sir,' said Larrabee as he examined the map. 'We'll saddle up and get on the road.'

The captain opened the car door and then hesitated. 'There's one more thing,' he said. 'I'm told we made a gas attack on the Germans.' The Americans looked at one another. 'But it went badly,' said the captain. 'It seems we gassed our own men. So you'll know what to expect.' He climbed in and slammed the door. They watched as the car sped out of the courtyard.

'OK, boys,' said Borden. 'You heard what the man said. Let's grab our gear and get underway.' He looked at Pierce. 'Talbot, you ride shotgun with Frank.'

* * *

Lieutenant Barnes sat on the side of his bed wearing a

134

regulation dark-blue robe over his pale blue pyjamas. He took a deep breath and placed his hands on the mattress.

'Here,' said Kit, reaching out to him.

'No,' he said with a shake of his head. 'I can do it myself.' He slowly but steadily rose to his feet. 'There, you see?' he said with a smile.

Kit glanced at the foot-rail, where the Dangerously Ill List tag had been replaced by a red card with the block letters 'BL', evacuation to England by hospital ship. In the early weeks she had doubted that Barnes would ever make it out of the hospital. He took a few hesitant steps, paused for a breath, and continued walking slowly to the end of the marquee. Kit followed behind him.

'Do you realize,' he said, standing at the screen door, 'how long it's been since I've been out of doors?'

She thought back to the early-August morning when he'd been brought in with the burn cases, all of whom had long since either died or been evacuated. 'Well,' she said, 'you'll soon be in a real hospital with ample time to stroll the grounds.'

'The MO informs me I'm bound for the lung hospital in Kent.' He looked down the length of the marquee, most of whose beds were empty. 'Believe it or not, I'm actually going to miss this place.'

'Once you've recuperated, what will you do? Will the army discharge you?'

'Assuming they pronounce me fit for duty, I intend to rejoin my regiment.'

'What? Return to France?'

Barnes nodded and began walking toward his bed. She sensed he was too weakened by the exertion to continue talking and so let the matter drop. When he reached his bedside he willingly allowed her to take him by the arm and help him down. At the corner of the bedside table was the leather case containing his Victoria Cross. The entire staff of doctors, nurses, and VADs had crowded into the marquee when the colonel of Barnes' battalion had arrived to pin the medal on the lapel of his robe, reading aloud the citation 'for conspicuous gallantry in leading his men to dislodge the enemy from the mine crater at Hooge Château.'

Once he was settled comfortably, Kit smiled at him and said, 'We're going to miss you, Albert. You're the only patient who's passed through this ward with scarcely a complaint.'

As she turned to leave, he said, 'Kit ... what have you heard from Captain Owen?'

'From Nigel?' She was surprised, as there had been no mention of him apart from the one conversation shortly after Barnes' arrival. 'He wrote to say,' she said, 'that the regiment has moved out of Flanders, somewhere to the south, in France. He wasn't at liberty to say where.'

Barnes nodded. 'To the south,' he said quietly. 'I shouldn't be surprised if they sent the KRRC to take part in this latest push.'

'We're told', she said, 'the casualties are very heavy.'

'That's why the MO was so anxious to empty the ward,' said Barnes, pulling the blanket up to his neck. 'Issuing tickets to Blighty to chaps like me.' He looked up at the sound of voices at the entrance, the senior Sister arriving with a VAD and orderly. 'For your sake, Kit,' he said, 'I pray that Captain Owen's safe.'

She lightly touched his arm and said, 'Thanks. I see my relief's arrived. But I'll be back before they come for you.'

Suddenly exhausted as she walked along the duckboards, she decided to skip tea and head straight for her tent for a nap. The sky was darkening when she opened the flap and ducked inside. Jane, who was working the evening shift, had placed two letters on Kit's cot. Kicking off her shoes and removing her bib and apron, she slumped on the thin mattress and examined the envelopes. She recognized a letter from home by the postmark. And the other – she could tell immediately from the neat, masculine cursive – was from Frank. She decided to save it for last. She struck a match and lit the candle on the folding campaign table.

After lighting a cigarette, she opened the letter from home. Her mother began with the usual news, an account of a weekend at an aunt's country house and a description of her sisters' social life, but soon turned to the war, her fears for the boys in the trenches and worries about Kit's safety, closing with an urgent appeal that she return home as soon as she was able. She tossed the letter aside with a sigh and picked up the letter from Frank. She tried imagining him writing it, but realized she had no idea where he was living since his quarters had been destroyed. She tore open the envelope and quickly read the brief note.

She smiled at his closing question. Was she thinking about him? She took a drag and expelled a cloud of smoke, watching the flickering shadows on the swaying canvas. She thought about him all the time, when she first awoke in the morning, and at odd moments throughout the day. She compared the note to Nigel's letters, so full of dramatic professions of love and devotion, always addressing her as 'darling'. Somehow in Frank's few, simple words, genuine sentiment came through. Was she falling in love with him? She'd never loved anyone before, so she couldn't be sure. If only she could see him again ... But it was apparent his section was being sent away, to help with the wounded from this latest offensive. And Lieutenant Barnes seemed to think that Nigel's regiment was there too. Oh God, it was just too awful. She couldn't bear the thought of something happening to either of them. She leaned over to stub out her cigarette, blew out the candle, and slumped back on the pillow. Listening to the wind and the rain, she closed her eyes and soon fell asleep.

When she awoke, it was dark and utterly still, the wind having died after the storm. Groggy and disoriented, Kit was unsure whether it was evening or the middle of the night. She groped for the matches, struck one, and lit the candle. With a yawn, she looked at her wristwatch, surprised to see that it was only a quarter past seven. She debated rushing over to the mess tent to join the other girls for dinner, but decided she would go later to the canteen, which served soup and sandwiches until late in the evening for the doctors and nurses coming off shift. She would take advantage of the quiet moment. Reaching under the cot for her writing case, she removed several sheets of cream-coloured stationery and her fountain pen. Sitting cross-legged with the case on her lap, she wrote:

Camiers
27 September 1915

Dear Frank,
I returned to my tent late this afternoon just before a storm struck and found your letter on my cot. Just seeing your handwriting lifted my spirits. You asked if I'm thinking of you, and the answer is – night and day. I find myself daydreaming of the day we spent at the beach, the afternoon on the riverbank, sitting across from you in the restaurant. Oh, Frank, I miss you so much! And now you're going away again.

Kit's hand trembled and tears welled in her eyes. Brushing them away, she continued:

How brave you are, driving at night under shellfire to the front lines to pick up the poor wounded boys. It makes me very proud. But I worry so much that something could happen to you. Please promise me you'll be careful. Please come back to me safe and sound. We can have that time in Paris together we've been dreaming of.

I was surprised to read of your sister's plans to come to France. But I've heard the MOs talking about the doctors from Harvard at No. 22, a very fine lot. Of course I'll look after her while you're away, but as she's a real nurse, I fancy there's a great deal I could learn from her.

With the terrible fighting in this latest push, I'm almost certain you will have been called back to duty, and so I don't know when or where this letter will find you. I can only pray that you're safe, that you're thinking of me, and count the days till I see you again.

Love,

Kit

She gently blew across the sheet to dry the ink. Carefully folding the pages, she put aside her writing case and stood up. Somewhere, she considered, on this dark night Frank was driving his ambulance into the battle, and somewhere, no doubt sheltering in a trench, possibly wounded, or worse, was Nigel. Dear God, she prayed, her eyes squeezed shut, keep them safe.

11

Frank Harrington brought the Model T to a halt. In the light filtering through tall trees, he could make out a column of horse-drawn artillery crossing the road, the limbers and cannons painted a dull grey in contrast to the dun-coloured guns of the British Army. French 75s, thought Harrington. In the chaos of the rear areas, elements of the French 10th Army were intermingling with the British forces reinforcing Loos. He glanced over at Talbot Pierce, trying to sleep with his head resting on the metal frame of the cab. With his glasses folded in his pocket, he looked even more boyish. As the last of the limbers disappeared across the road, Harrington eased off the clutch and started forward, checking his mirror to make sure Borden and Larrabee were still following him.

Pierce stirred. 'Where are we?' he asked with a yawn, rubbing his eyes. A shaft of sunlight glinted on the hood.

'Somewhere on the road between Lillers and Béthune.'

'It's morning,' said Pierce dully.

'That it is,' said Harrington. 'We've driven all night. I could sure use a cup of coffee.'

'Is it always this slow?' The American ambulances had driven south from Dunkirk at a snail's pace, pulling over to let supply vehicles and artillery pass, with frequent stops at crossroads for columns of troops and cavalry.

'No.' Harrington resented the fact that the new man had slept most of the long night while he had struggled to keep the Ford from running off the road. He didn't particularly care to converse with him. In the patches of ground fog swirling among the hedgerows he could faintly see a solitary French officer standing at the roadside, a dash of scarlet and blue in the mist. Harrington slowed to a stop and peered over the passenger door.

'*Bonjour,*' said Harrington. '*Avez-vous besoin de secours?*'

'*Oui, merci,*' replied the officer, touching a hand to the bill of his kepi. 'I'm afraid I'm lost.' He glanced at the insignia and block letters stencilled on the side of the ambulance. '*Vous êtes américains?*' he said with a smile.

'*Mais oui,*' replied Harrington with a nod. 'We're on our way to Béthune,' he added in passable French. 'We'd be happy to give you a ride.' He motioned to Pierce to open the door and let the officer in.

'You speak French, Talbot?' asked Harrington as he eased off the clutch.

'No, other than a few guidebook phrases.' He looked at the officer's colourful uniform with curiosity. After driving in silence for several miles along the narrow road, flanked by tall trees and shrouded in morning fog, Harrington came to a stop at a stone signpost by a fork in the road. He studied the weathered inscription beneath the cross, just able to make out the words 'Béthune' and 'La Bassée'.

'*À gauche?*' Harrington asked the officer, pointing to the road to the left. '*À Béthune?*'

The officer scratched his chin. '*Tout droit,*' he commented after a moment. Harrington started forward. '*Non,*' said the officer, changing his mind. '*À gauche.*' Harrington put the Model T in a tight turn down the road to the left. As they started up a long, gentle hill, the bark of heavy guns grew louder.

'*Arrivés?*' said Harrington. '*Ou départs?*' Turning to Pierce, he translated, 'Incoming or outgoing.'

The officer narrowed his eyes and listened. '*Départs,*' he said as the cannons thundered. As they breasted the hill, the fog lifted with the morning sun, exposing a ridgeline a half-mile to the east. A battery of German howitzers was clearly visible on the hillside, a stack of bronze shells glinting in the sunshine beside the gunners in field grey.

'*Vite!*' shouted the officer, pointing toward the battery. '*Pour l'amour de Dieu, vite – ils nous ont vus!*'

A shell exploded thirty yards to their left, throwing up a plume of smoke and earth that showered the speeding ambulances. Harrington hit the accelerator and shifted gears, racing toward a curve where the road disappeared into a tree line. He glanced in the mirror, just able to make out Borden's panicked face, and rounding the curve too fast, bounced the Ford into a shallow ditch, just missing a sturdy tree. As the ambulance ground to a halt he was conscious of a loud *bam*. Harrington leaned out and looked back. The fender of Borden's Ford was wrapped around a young poplar, flattening the front right tyre. After checking to make sure they were out of sight of the guns, Harrington scrambled out and hurried over to the wreck.

'Damn!' said Borden, banging his fists on the steering wheel.

'You all right?' asked Harrington.

'Yeah, I'm OK.' Borden opened the door and jumped down.

Bill Larrabee, who'd managed to keep his ambulance on the road, walked over and knelt down to examine the fender. 'We ought to be able to straighten that out,' he said, rubbing his hands together.

Harrington reached his hand through a hole in the hardboard siding, gouged out by a piece of shrapnel. 'Guess we took a wrong turn back there,' he said with a shrug.

The French officer had meanwhile wandered over to the edge of the woods, kneeling down to observe the German battery, which was now directing its fire over the horizon. Borden crawled underneath the front end to check the axle.

'Frank,' said Larrabee, reaching into the toolbox for a

crowbar. 'Why don't you give me a hand while Borden gets to work on the spare.'

'Sure.'

'Where's Peach?' asked Borden, lying on his back under the chassis. Soon after his arrival, Talbot Pierce had been dubbed 'Peach-fuzz' by Larrabee, owing to the sparseness of his beard, which had quickly been sawn down to simply 'Peach'.

Harrington looked over at his ambulance, unable to see Pierce, wondering whether he might have followed the officer to observe the Germans. Walking back to the car, he found him cowering on the front seat, keeping his head down. 'What are you doing?' asked Harrington.

'They're still firing,' said Pierce. 'I can hear them.'

'Sure they are. But not at us. C'mon, Talbot. Give us a hand.'

'They were aiming at us, Frank,' said Pierce, not budging. 'Why would they aim at an ambulance?'

'I don't know. Maybe for sport. Now get out of there.'

'What are we going to do? We can't go back.'

'Look, Talbot, leave that to us to figure out. First we've got to get Henry's car running again.'

Harrington opened the passenger door, grabbed the diminutive Pierce by the arm and pulled him out.

By the time they'd changed the front tyre and straightened the fender sufficiently to fit the starter crank through the slot in the grill, the men's hands were black with grime and their faces streaming with sweat.

'OK, Frank,' said Larrabee, 'you got us into this jam. How do you aim to get us out of it?'

The French officer, having lost interest in the German battery, was sitting on the grass, resting his back against a tree.

'If we keep on this road,' said Harrington, 'it'll take us right into the German lines. We've got to go back the way we came.'

'Go back?' said Pierce, his face pale. 'That's ... I mean, they'll just shoot at us again.'

'We'll have to take that chance,' said Harrington, wiping his hands on his trousers. 'Make a dash for it.'

'Run the gauntlet,' said Borden. 'Assuming we can get ol' Betsy cranked up again.'

'You go on,' said Pierce softly. 'I'll stay here.'

'The hell you will,' said Larrabee, taking a step toward him.

'Easy, Bill,' said Harrington, raising his hands. He walked over to Pierce and placed a hand on his shoulder. 'I don't blame you for being scared,' he said in a low voice. 'We're all scared. Just trust me. I'll get us out of here.'

With a terrified Talbot Pierce squeezed in next to the Frenchman, Harrington drove a short distance down the winding road, turned around, and revved the engine. 'Here we go,' he said under his breath. 'Hang on.' He jammed the pedal to the floorboard, rounding the curve into the open at full tilt. The dash across the open ground was no more than 400 yards, a thirty-second run that felt more like minutes. The German gunners had just enough time to get off a single shot – a whiz-bang, or shrapnel, round – aimed at the lead vehicle. The shell exploded just to their right and rear, harmlessly, thought Harrington with a rush of adrenalin as they approached the protective brow of the hill.

With a groan, the officer slumped on Pierce's lap.

'Dammit!' cried Harrington as he made it to safety, checking his mirrors to confirm that the others were still with him. He quickly pulled over and jerked on the handbrake.

The officer was moaning and clutching his neck, and

his blue tunic was covered with bright-red blood that spilled onto Pierce's lap.

'Let's get him out,' said Harrington, throwing open the door. 'The Frenchman's hit,' he shouted to Larrabee, who'd pulled up next to him. Harrington hurried around to the passenger door while Borden and Larrabee pulled a stretcher from the back.

'C'mon, Talbot,' said Harrington. 'Give me a hand.'

Pierce, his face ghostly white, stared silently back. Harrington reached inside and hauled out the injured man, gently lowering him onto a stretcher. They examined the wound, a gash below his right ear.

'Missed the carotid,' said Larrabee. '*Vous avez de la chance*,' he added to the officer, who was lying stoically still with his eyes closed. They quickly staunched the bleeding and bandaged the wound.

'That should hold him till we can get to the CCS,' said Harrington. They hoisted the stretcher and loaded it in the back. Harrington climbed behind the wheel and looked over at Pierce, who was slumped dejectedly on the seat, staring at his bloodstained khakis.

'Is ... is he all right?' Pierce asked quietly.

Harrington nodded. 'He should be fine. You'll see a lot worse before the day's out. Now let's get the heck out of here.'

* * *

Kit stood at the foot-rail, her hands folded at her apron, staring at the canvas beyond the iron bed. The marquee was filled with victims of the botched gas attack at Loos, recently evacuated by hospital train from the Casualty Clearing Stations. Kit closed her eyes and listened as the young soldier fought for breath. After a moment she forced herself to look at him, noting the bluish pallor of his puffy cheeks and his hands, mottled and grey like an old man's.

With his eyes closed, he gasped, coughed weakly, and then relapsed to the steady rale from deep in his chest, caused, she knew, by oedema. Was he dreaming, she wondered? Dreaming of home as his lungs filled slowly with fluid?

She turned at the sound of footfalls on the scrubbed floorboards. A distinguished-looking older man strode into the marquee, followed by an entourage of RAMC physicians and the senior Ward Sister. Kit had heard something about the specialist from London who'd been sent to evaluate the gas cases. As she stood at the foot-rail, he walked up and gazed down at the young soldier. Unlike the MOs in their khakis, the specialist was wearing a heavy wool suit, and his thick hair and full beard were flecked with grey.

'Blue asphyxia, with intense venous congestion,' he commented as he studied the patient. 'The hallmarks of chlorine poisoning.' The others merely nodded. 'The lividity', continued the specialist, 'is not the result of abnormal pigmentation, but rather is due to cyanosis. Imperfectly oxygenated blood.'

He stooped down and placed the silver disc of his stethoscope on the patient's chest. The young soldier opened his eyes, wide with fear. 'Acute bronchitis,' observed the specialist. Drawing back the covers at the end of the bed, he exposed the patient's left foot, severely swollen and turning greyish-blue. 'Gangrene,' said the specialist with a frown. 'Caused by vascular thrombosis.' He draped the covers over the boy's foot.

'Doctor,' said the Sister, taking the specialist aside. She resembled a nun with her steel-rimmed spectacles and long, white scarf tied tightly about her greying hair. 'Is there nothing we can do?'

'I'm afraid not,' replied the specialist. 'Some will recover with rest,' he said as he moved away from the bed. 'Others,' he added in a voice just above a whisper, 'will not.'

As Kit studied the young soldier's swollen and discoloured

face, the marquee suddenly swam before her eyes and her knees buckled. 'Ohh,' she groaned as she crumpled to the floor. The Sister knelt beside her and gently patted her clammy forehead with a handkerchief. Blinking, Kit stared up at the out-of-focus face hovering over her.

'There, now,' said the Sister. 'Can you sit up?'

Kit took a deep breath, fighting back a wave of nausea. 'I'm sorry,' she murmured as she righted herself. 'I don't know what happened...' A kindly, older orderly helped her to her feet.

'You've had a long day, Miss Stanley,' said the Sister as the retinue of physicians moved on to the next bed. 'Let Mr Hodges show you to your tent.'

Kit awoke with a shaft of bright sunlight streaming through the tent flap. Raising herself up on an elbow, she rubbed her eyes.

'Sorry,' said Jane Tisdale, standing in the opening. 'I didn't expect to find you sleeping...'

'Yes, well, I was feeling ill, and Sister let me go.' Kit sat up and swung her legs to the side of the cot. 'The truth is, I fainted dead away in the ward.'

'Oh, my,' said Jane, ducking into the bell-tent and sitting on her cot. 'Are you all right?'

Kit nodded, aware that the churning in her stomach was not due to nausea but rather lack of food. 'I don't know what caused it,' she said wearily. 'Something about those poor gassed men.' Jane nodded. 'I say,' said Kit in a stronger voice, 'you don't suppose they're still serving? I'm famished.'

Holding a steaming mug and a plate of cakes and biscuits, Kit made her way to a table at the back of the canteen where several other VADs were having tea.

'A lucky thing we made it,' said Jane as she sat down next to Kit. 'As they promptly stop serving at five.'

Kit brushed back a stray wisp of hair and munched an oatmeal biscuit. She took a sip of tea and said, 'Mm, that's much better. I hadn't eaten a morsel since breakfast.'

'With every ward full to overflowing,' said Emily Goodall, 'there's scarcely time.'

Kit nodded glumly. 'I would never have thought', she said between bites, 'that things could be worse than last summer, with the fighting in the Salient. But these gas cases are so dreadful. There's simply nothing to be done.' Kit noticed Polly McBride sitting at a table in the corner with one of the few other girls who shared Polly's small-town, working-class background.

'It's not just the gas cases,' said Emily. The others gave her a questioning look. 'There's a man in my ward,' said Emily, 'which is filled with surgical cases – amputees and chest wounds – who professes to be unable to walk.'

'Professes?' said Jane.

'The odd thing is, there's not a scratch on him,' explained Emily. 'And at night, my God, you should hear the screams. Terrible nightmares. It's driving the other poor men mad.'

'What's wrong with him?' asked Kit.

'The MO calls it shell shock, though Sister says not to use the expression.'

'Shell shock?' said Jane.

'Neurasthenia is the proper term,' said Emily. 'He's not right in his mind. They're sending him home as soon as possible.'

'That doesn't seem fair,' said Kit. 'A ticket to Blighty with not a scratch on him? When so many of the wounded are sent back to the front?'

'He's not shirking!' said Emily. 'It's the horrors of the trenches ... At any rate, have you heard anything from your captain? Was his regiment in this latest push?'

Kit nodded. 'The KRRC were in the thick of it. A good many of them are here. But I haven't heard a word from Nigel.'

'Well,' said Jane with an encouraging smile, 'I'm sure you'll hear from him soon.'

'And what of your American friend?' asked one of the other girls.

'He wrote to say they were being sent away,' said Kit, 'and that's the last I've heard. Well,' she said after finishing her tea, 'I'm going to bathe and change. But first I think I'll look in at the post office.'

When her turn came at the counter, the clerk riffled through a thick stack of envelopes and extracted a slender one with the distinctive markings of the French telegraph company. Her heart pounding, Kit leapt to the conclusion that the cable was from the army, notifying her of Nigel's death. No! she thought desperately as she examined the envelope ... why would they notify her? 'Nothing else?' she asked as she tucked it in her pocket.

'Sorry, miss.'

Kit waited to read the telegram until she was back in her tent. She kicked off her shoes, lit the candle and slumped back on her cot. Tearing open the envelope, she quickly scanned the single sheet:

DARLING STOP AM OUT OF THE LINE IN VERMELLES STOP
DESPERATE TO SEE YOU STOP ARRANGED 12 HOUR PASS SATURDAY NEXT STOP
MEET ME BOULOGNE STATION STOP NIGEL STOP

Kit tossed the yellow paper on the blanket with a sigh. Thank God he was alive and unhurt. But there was something about the peremptory summons to meet him, with so little notice, that she resented. Why did Nigel always take for granted that she wanted to be with him? She reached for the cigarettes on the campaign table, ashamed that her fears for Nigel's safety had fled so quickly. Why couldn't he have cabled to *ask* if she would see him? Now she'd have to plead with the Sister for time off, with the hospital so terribly busy. She took a deep drag and stared up at the peaked canvas. She'd meet him, of course, in a mere three days. But what would she have to say?

*　　*　　*

The American drivers had been appalled by the scene at the CCS near Béthune when they arrived with the wounded French officer: dozens of gas victims, their faces livid, gasping on litters in the courtyard, convoys arriving almost hourly from the still raging Battle of Loos with fresh loads of badly wounded men, the operating theatres unable to keep up.

Now, after almost two weeks, the pace had slackened but the routine seldom varied: driving to the aid stations at the front in the middle of the night, delivering the wounded, and returning by dawn to the abandoned farmhouse where they slept, scrounged for food and whiled away the empty time in card games, reading and endless discussions of the war. With his slight stature and diffidence, Talbot Pierce was a natural target for the others' gibes. But once he overcame his revulsion at the sight of blood, he cared for the wounded soldiers with a tenderness and calmness under fire that impressed his more experienced and hardened comrades.

If only, thought Harrington, as he sat before the fire in the squalid living room, they could trust Talbot to take out his own car. That would add room for another five wounded. But Talbot just couldn't get over his fear of driving at night without headlamps. He rode with Frank or Borden, who'd patiently explain techniques for negotiating the narrow roads in the darkness, reading the crude maps and avoiding shellfire, but when the time came to solo he lacked the confidence.

Harrington reached for a poker and stirred the embers in the blackened hearth. Out of the corner of his eye he spotted a rat at the baseboard, eying a crusty piece of bread. He angrily flung the poker; just missing the animal, it clattered loudly on the stone floor.

'What the hell...?' drawled Bill Larrabee, standing in the doorway with an armload of firewood.

'Another lousy rat,' said Harrington sourly. 'This place is crawling with them.'

'I hear it's even worse in the trenches,' said Larrabee as he dropped his load on the floor. 'Rats everywhere, eating the corpses; everyone covered with lice...'

'*Bonjour, mes amis,*' sang out Henry Borden. 'Look what I've got.'

He walked into the room and placed a burlap sack on the rickety table. 'Fresh-laid eggs, a side of bacon, and a loaf of bread. Courtesy of the farmer's wife down the road.'

Talbot Pierce entered the room from the darkened hallway and stood with his head cocked to the side, listening to the sound of aircraft engines in the distance. The others listened for a moment, and then Harrington stood up and said, 'Let's go outside and have a look.'

Staring up at the pale-blue sky, the four men watched as a line of red triplanes dropped down out of the thick cumulus clouds, banking away from the sun in a steep descent.

'How many?' said Borden, shading his eyes.

'Four,' said Larrabee, pointing at the sky. 'No – five.'

'Look!' said Harrington excitedly.

Three tan British biplanes swooped down from the clouds,

scattering the German Fokkers like a covey of quail. Desperate to elude the attackers, the manoeuvrable triplanes rolled and weaved, trailing wisps of smoke in their slipstreams. Staccato bursts of machine-gun fire could be heard over the droning of the engines.

'It's a regular dogfight!' yelled Larrabee, pointing to the British Sopwiths close on the tail of two of the Fokkers.

'Dogfight?' said Talbot.

'That's what they call it,' said Harrington. 'Damn!'

Dense black smoke poured from the nose of one of the Fokkers, spiralling toward the earth as the Sopwiths banked away. The men listened as the engine noise grew louder and watched in fascination as the plane disappeared over the horizon with a loud explosion and a plume of smoke and fire.

'Poor sonofabitch,' said Larrabee.

'That Sopwith better watch out!' called Harrington.

Shielding their eyes from the sun, they watched as the tan biplanes climbed for the cloud deck, disappearing before the pursuing Fokkers could execute an attack. Within moments the battle was over, the red German planes with the black crosses on the fuselage banking to the east for the safety of their own lines.

'An honest-to-goodness dogfight,' said Harrington as he turned to go back inside. 'I can't wait to write my old man.'

Seated in a semicircle around the hearth, the four men stared into the dying fire as they listened to the gently falling rain. Bill Larrabee lifted the spatter-wear coffee pot from the embers and reached over to pour Frank another cup. 'I'm not sure how much longer I'm good for this duty,' he said as he offered the pot to the others.

'Oh, really?' said Frank.

'I've been out here longer than the rest of you,' said Larrabee, clasping his arms around his knees. 'And my dad's been after to me to come home and help with the ranch.'

'Will you do it?' asked Borden.

Larrabee shook his head. 'No. Not to Wyoming. After everything I've seen over here, I'm ready to go back to school.'

'He's planning to be a doctor,' Harrington explained to Talbot.

'What about you, Frank?' asked Larrabee.

'I keep thinking, the US is bound to get into the war, and then I can switch over to the Ambulance Corps. For now, I'm just hoping to have some time off with Kit.'

'Some guys have all the luck,' said Borden. 'I came over here thinkin' I was gonna meet some cute French girls. Hah.'

'Well, Frank,' said Larrabee, 'I hope you're wrong. Why should we get involved?'

'It's the only way the stalemate will ever be broken.'

'Not according to these officers I was carrying the other day,' said Borden. 'They were braggin' about the fine "New Army" Kitchener is building up – a million men – for a big push next year to break through the German lines and finish the war.'

'That's ridiculous, Henry,' said Larrabee with a shake of his head. 'You'd think the British would learn *something* from their mistakes. Just look at this last offensive. What a waste. And for what? A couple of lousy miles?'

'Well,' said Harrington, 'I think folks back home are fed up with this so-called neutrality after this latest German atrocity...'

'Edith Cavell, you mean,' said Borden.

'You're damn right,' said Harrington. 'They drag a Red Cross nurse, a *woman* for God's sake, before a firing squad?'

'Story going around', said Borden, 'was that she fainted on her way in, and this German officer just pulled a gun and shot her lyin' there on the ground.'

'Well,' said Larrabee, 'apparently she was helping British prisoners escape into Holland...'

'C'mon, Bill,' said Harrington. 'So what? They didn't have to shoot her!'

'Look,' said Larrabee angrily. 'I don't have to like the goddam Germans. It's just that it's not our fight!'

Borden turned to Pierce and said, 'What do you think, Peach?' Pierce almost never spoke up during their frequent arguments about the war.

'Me?' Talbot steepled his fingers at his lips and stared at the glowing embers. 'I don't know. I mean, I sure hope we're not dragged into it.' He glanced from Borden to the others. 'We – my family, that is,' he continued, 'don't believe in war.'

'In any war?' asked Borden.

Talbot nodded. 'We're Society of Friends. Quakers.'

'I'll be damned,' said Larrabee.

'Besides,' said Talbot, 'no one in this war seems to know what they're fighting for.'

12

Kit strolled through the quiet railway station, pausing to study the departure and arrival times posted above the ticket counter. The next train from Paris wasn't due for hours, which explained why so few men and women were waiting on the wooden benches. A young girl was selling flowers from a basket hooked over her arm, an incongruous dash of bright colours against the drab station wall.

Kit wandered over to a newsstand and examined the bold headlines of the Paris papers, reporting the heavy Zeppelin air raids on London, killing 71 civilians asleep in their beds. My God, she never thought she'd have to worry about the safety of her family back home. Her eyes were drawn to the illustration on the cover of *Le Petit Journal*, a Red Cross nurse prostrate on the ground, her arms outstretched, with a German officer standing over her, revolver in his hand. Edith Cavell. How terrible.

Kit studied her reflection in the mirror. Wearing a wide-brimmed hat with a black satin ribbon and a long, yellow dress that showed her trim figure to full advantage, she felt pretty for a change and wondered whether she'd dressed to please Nigel or merely to satisfy her vanity. As she adjusted her hat, she heard a long, piercing whistle and the rumble of an approaching train. With a quick glance at the tall, gilded clock at the centre of the station, she knew it was his.

Standing midway down the platform, Kit watched as the train came slowly to a stop. She peered at the faces in the windows of the celadon-green carriages, and then began strolling toward the back of the train. After a moment she saw him alight from the steps to the platform, wearing his khaki uniform with Sam Browne belt and polished cavalry boots, a coat over his arm. Kit waved and began walking toward him, meeting him halfway with an awkward embrace and a light kiss on the cheek.

'Nigel,' she said with a smile. 'Right on time. It's wonderful to see you.'

Casting a nervous glance up and down the platform, he said, 'Yes, well, not much of a crowd, is it?'

Kit continued to smile, unable to think of a response. 'Do you have any luggage?' she asked after a moment.

'Luggage? I should say not. I'm on the five o'clock return to Béthune.'

'Of course,' said Kit, taking him by the arm and starting for the terminal. 'How stupid of me.'

Two French military policemen slowly walked toward them, one tapping a baton on his gloved palm. He paused to give Kit an approving look.

'Well, darling,' said Nigel, oblivious to the MPs, 'where ... shall we go?'

Kit glanced up at him, staring straight ahead as he walked. 'Perhaps,' she suggested, 'we could talk over a cup of tea. The cafés should be open by ten.'

Nigel silently led Kit through the dimly lit terminal and out onto the pavement in the pleasant, mid-October sunshine.

'Rather a gloomy town, isn't it?' he said as he surveyed the square. 'All pretty much alike, these French cities in the north.'

'Well, compared to South Kensington, I suppose. But I did find a decent café in the next block.'

At the early hour, they had the establishment to themselves, seated at a booth by the half-curtained window.

'You're looking well,' said Kit after taking a sip of tea. 'Though a bit too thin.' With his neatly trimmed hair and moustache and sharply creased uniform, he fitted her image of a dashing young officer, though she noticed the slightest tremor in his hand as he buttered a piece of brioche. 'I imagine you're not fed very well...'

'The officers' mess has been quite satisfactory, actually, since we moved down from Flanders.' Taking a bite, he stared beyond Kit out the window, a vacant look in his eyes.

'Nigel,' said Kit. She hesitated, pressing her lips together. 'I know that your regiment was involved in this latest push...' His gaze travelled from the window to her face, seeming not to register recognition. She bit her lower lip. 'The attack at Loos,' she added after a moment.

'At Loos,' he said absently, as though trying to place the name. He reached for his cup, spilling tea into the saucer. He nodded and lifted the trembling cup to his lips. 'Ours was a subsidiary attack,' he said quietly.

'Oh, Nigel, it must have been dreadful. I've been worried sick about you.'

'I'd prefer not to discuss it.'

'I'm sorry, but I've been nursing these poor men who were gassed, and knowing your regiment was there, I...'

'Gassed?'

'Yes, evidently by our own side, a mistake of some kind...'

'You're not to use the term *gassed*,' said Nigel with surprising vehemence. 'It's termed the *accessory*.'

'Accessory?' said Kit. 'I'm afraid I don't understand...'

Attempting to return his cup to the saucer, Nigel started violently, overturning it on the table. 'Damn!' he exclaimed. 'Look what you've made me do!'

She responded with a pained expression as a waiter wearing a stained apron quickly walked over and wiped up the spilled liquid with a dishcloth. '*Encore une tasse de thé, Monsieur?*' he asked.

'What?' said Nigel as he dabbed at his lap with a napkin. 'Oh. Not tea. *Un pastis.*'

With a slight arch of his eyebrows, the waiter turned and walked away.

'I'm sorry, Nigel,' said Kit. 'I shouldn't have brought it up.'

'Don't.' He turned back to the window.

'All right,' she said quietly. 'I won't.'

They sat in wounded silence until the waiter returned, placed a glass on the table and poured from a bottle. Nigel took a sip, licked his lips and slowly exhaled. He looked at Kit and said, 'I think you should go home.'

'Go home?'

'Yes. This volunteer nursing is obviously not right for you. It's bad for your nerves.'

She considered saying, my nerves are fine, but thought better of it. 'Nigel,' she said, 'even if I wanted to, I'm needed too badly here. Perhaps you don't realize it, but our hospitals are overflowing. The RAMC want more VADs, not fewer.'

He knocked back the rest of his drink and gestured to the waiter for another. 'Nonsense,' he said. 'You should be b-b-back in London, enjoying your ... self, with your friends.' He gratefully watched the waiter fill his glass and then reached for his pack of Gauloises and shook one out. 'Wretched French cigarettes,' he muttered as he fumbled for a match.

'Nigel,' said Kit calmly, placing her palms flat on the table. 'I wouldn't know what to do in London. I'm *needed* here,' she said earnestly. 'At first I wasn't sure if I could take it, but now I feel almost as if I were a regular nurse...' She paused and watched as he downed his drink in a single swig and took a deep drag on his cigarette.

'Nigel,' she said, leaning forward. 'I'm worried about you. You're drinking too much. You're not yourself.'

As he met her steady gaze, he seemed to unbend from the effect of the powerful aperitif.

'You should take some leave,' Kit insisted. 'Go home and rest.'

'Leave?' he said. 'What, abandon my men?'

'You must be overdue for a furlough.'

He stared into his empty glass and took a deep breath. Raising his eyes to hers, he said, 'Darling ... I've come to ask for your hand.'

'Oh,' said Kit, raising her fingertips to her lips.

'I've been saving my leave for our wedding, you see. And our honeymoon. Nothing very elaborate, I'll grant you. But there's the lovely old hotel in Brighton. We could have a few days.'

'Oh, Nigel,' she finally managed to say. 'I'm afraid I wasn't expecting this...'

'Will you?' he asked. 'Will you marry me, darling?'

'I'm not quite sure what to say. This is so sudden.'

'We could wait, of course,' he said, adopting a conversational tone. 'But, with the war, I mean, what's the point of waiting?'

Kit nodded, avoiding his eyes. She sighed and said, 'I'm sorry, Nigel, but I can't say yes.'

'But why?' he said a bit too loudly.

'It's just that I'm not ... That we're not...'

'Don't be absurd. We've been together for years, why, with our families and friends, we're perfectly matched.'

'That may be,' said Kit. 'But I'm not sure we're in love...'

'Love? Why, what do you mean?' He glanced at the waiter standing by the bar and snapped his fingers.

'There's something I've been meaning to tell you,' said Kit. 'I intended to write to you, but now, as you're here, and as you've, well, proposed...'

He gave her a curious look and quietly said, 'Yes, go on.'

She bit her lower lip. 'There's someone else whom ... Well, whom I've been seeing.'

'Someone else?' When the waiter appeared, Nigel gestured to his glass.

'Yes. We met at the hospital. Not the hospital, actually, but at Bailleul, the CCS...'

'Do you mean to say, a *man?*'

Staring across the table at Nigel, with the ludicrous look of disbelief in his eyes, Kit was overwhelmed with embarrassment and pity. She paused and massaged her forehead. 'Yes,' she said quietly after a moment. 'A man.'

Nigel took a last drag on his cigarette and crushed it in a porcelain ashtray. Expelling a cloud of smoke through his nostrils, he said, 'I've come here to ask for your hand, and you tell me you're seeing another man.'

'Nigel, I didn't *intend* to. I thought we could have a pleasant day together, but when...'

'Who is this man?' he demanded in an indignant tone. He reached for another cigarette and quickly lit it.

'Oh, Nigel, must we?' He glared at her. 'He's an ambulance driver,' she said softly. 'A volunteer ambulance driver.' At this Nigel's eyes narrowed. 'An American,' Kit explained.

'An American? Dear God, not one of those, ah ... what's the name...'

'The American Field Service,' said Kit in a stronger voice. She realized that the embarrassment she'd felt a moment ago had turned to the more familiar feeling of resentment. 'And the truth is, I care about him. I hadn't intended to bring it up, but you really left me no choice.'

'An American.' Nigel shook his head and then finished his drink. 'Well,' he muttered, looking away from her, 'I should have known. Working here as a VAD, no supervision, good heavens. If your father knew...' He paused and stroked his moustache. 'As I said earlier, Kit ... You should go home.'

* * *

Standing on the Calais pier, Frank Harrington watched as

the steamer shuddered against the moorings with a sharp blast of its horn. Inhaling the salt-laden air, he impatiently studied the faces at the railing as the crew lowered the gangway. A military band was standing in the midst of the small crowd on the dock, a brass ensemble with scarlet uniforms trimmed in gold and instruments gleaming in the bright midday sunshine.

The first passengers slowly descended the gangway, middle-aged couples, as this was no troopship, followed by a group of older men in topcoats and silk hats; a contingent of French officials, surmised Harrington, returning from business in England. And then, after a pause, a group of young women, wearing identical wide-brimmed hats and dark-blue dresses, appeared at the top of the gangway. As they started down, three abreast, the band struck up a spirited rendition of 'The Star-Spangled Banner'. With a flutter in his chest and a wide smile on his face, Frank watched as his sister Elsie, proudly wearing her Norfolk blues, crossed over the gangway to France.

As the horns blared the closing refrain, with Frank softly singing 'and the home of the brave', the American nurses marched smartly onto the pier, halting before the smiling bandleader. Elsie stood erect on the end of her row, hands at her sides, chin out, and looking straight ahead, though Frank would have sworn she stole a glance at him out of the corner of her eye. He noticed the single black stripe on her sleeve and the silver 'US' badge on her collar. A severe, older nurse with three stripes, wearing gunmetal wire-rimmed glasses, strode to the front and gave the command, 'At ease.' As the young nurses relaxed, Frank walked quickly up to Elsie and reached over to give her an embrace. At the last second he hesitated, and, with a peck on her cheek, took her by the hand.

'My God, Elsie,' he said. 'Just look at you.'

'Oh, Frank,' she said with a happy smile. 'I'm so glad to

161

see you.' Conscious that the senior nurse was standing nearby, she let his hand go and turned around. 'Major Hollimon,' said Elsie, 'I'd like you to meet my brother Frank.'

The major walked over and gave him an appraising look.

'Hullo,' said Frank, extending his hand. 'Welcome to France.'

With a quick, businesslike handshake, she said, 'Thank you, Mr Harrington. I see by your uniform that you're...'

'With the AFS,' he said.

'The American Field Service,' added Elsie. 'Volunteer ambulance drivers.'

'I see,' said the major with a thin smile. 'It was the British uniform that threw me.'

'Our section's attached to the RAMC,' explained Frank.

'As *we* shall be,' said the major. Turning on her heel, she said, 'All right, ladies. Just as soon as our trunks are unloaded, we'll be boarding a bus for the hospital.' As the nurses dispersed to look for their luggage, Elsie leaned over to Frank and whispered, 'Tough old boot.'

Waiting for their transportation, Elsie, sitting on the end of her steamer trunk, looked up at her older brother with a smile. 'Can you imagine what Mom and Dad would think if they could see us now?' she asked.

Hitching a boot up, he said, 'I suspect they'd wring your neck, Els, for volunteering to come over here.'

She slipped off her soft, velour hat. 'I don't see how it's any different from what you did,' she said with a toss of her light-brown hair. 'And, besides, I'm more independent now than you think.'

'So what did they teach you down in Texas?' he asked, squinting into the sunshine.

'How to drink beer. *Cold* beer. And to eat chilli.'

'Chilli?'

'Spicy beef stew. The Mexican ladies sell it all night on Military Plaza.'

Frank shook his head. 'My kid sister. So where are they sending you?'

'The No. 22 General Hospital, I think it is. With the Harvard Unit.'

'You'd better get used to working and sleeping in tents. No. 22. That's outside Étaples, down the road from a friend of mine.' She cocked her head with a mildly curious look. 'She's a VAD,' said Frank.

'A what?'

'A volunteer British nurse. And she's mighty cute.'

'Francis Harrington...'

They both turned at the sound of an approaching vehicle, a drab-green bus with a red cross on the door that came to a stop by the pier with a noisy squeal of brakes.

'Here's our ride,' said Elsie, standing up and putting on her hat. He lifted the trunk and followed her to the group of nurses clustered at the curb.

'I'll be by to look in on you, sis,' he said as the bus doors swung open. 'And I want you to meet Kit.'

'Kit?'

'My gal.'

'Thanks for coming,' said Elsie a bit wistfully. She turned to go and then stopped and threw her arms around him.

'Oh, Frank,' she whispered. 'I'm so nervous.'

He gave her a gentle hug and said, 'Don't worry, Els, you'll be fine. And besides, I'm just up the road.'

She nodded and fell into line with the others boarding the bus. After stowing her trunk in the rack, he waved to Elsie at the window and watched as the doors swung shut and the bus pulled out on the roadway.

Returning to the dormitory at the boys' academy, Harrington

found Bill Larrabee reclining in braces and shirtsleeves, strumming his guitar. Borden was face down on the bed next to him, absorbed in his outdoors magazine, while Talbot Pierce sat in the corner, reading.

'As I was out walkin' this mornin' for pleasure,' sang Larrabee in a pleasant baritone, 'I spied a cowpuncher a-ridin' along...'

Harrington sat down on his bed to listen.

'...His hat was throwed back, and his spurs were a-janglin', and as he rode toward me he was singin' this song...'

'Whoopee ti-yi-yo, git along little dogies,' harmonized Borden, propped up on an elbow. 'It's your misfortune, and none of my own...'

They'd worked out the routine to impress the barmaids in the estaminets.

Harrington grinned as they finished the duet with a flourish on the guitar. 'Not bad,' he commented. He noticed that Talbot had scarcely looked up from his book.

Larrabee put aside his guitar and said, 'What's up, Frank?'

'I've been to Calais. To the docks.'

'Oh, really?' said Borden, swinging his legs over the side of his bed. 'Did her ship make it in?' Elsie had wired from England the expected date of their Channel crossing, an event Henry Borden, luckless thus far in his flirtations with the British nurses, was eagerly anticipating.

'Sure did,' said Frank. 'Right on time.'

'Dang it, Frank,' said Borden. 'You promised to take me along...'

'Relax, Henry. I didn't want to scare my poor sister on her first day in France.'

This diverted Talbot's attention from his book. 'Your sister?' he said with a glance over the top of his glasses.

'Yep. Just arrived from New York via Southampton.'

'What's she doing over here?' asked Talbot.

164

'She's a US Army nurse, Peach,' said Borden.

'They've sent over a team to work in one of the RAMC hospitals,' explained Harrington.

'Any cute ones?' asked Larrabee.

'I'd say so,' said Harrington. 'And they've got these swell-looking uniforms, dark blue with matching hats.'

'Maybe', said Borden, 'we can drive over tomorrow and say hullo.'

'You better be quick about it, Henry,' said Larrabee. 'Word is they're pulling us out any day now.'

When the others returned to their reading, Harrington stretched out on the bed with his writing tablet and pen. After thinking for a few moments, he wrote:

October 20, '15
Dunkirk

Dear Kit,

We're back from our latest stint at the front, but not for long. After six months attached to the RAMC, our section is being reassigned to the French Army with the rest of the AFS. I expect they'll send us first to the American hospital at Neuilly, outside Paris, for a week or so to relax and work on the cars. Is there any way you could meet me there? It may be our only chance to see each other for a while. Nothing could make me happier.

I mentioned that my sister is with the team of army nurses coming over to work with the Harvard doctors at No. 22. Well, I met her ship this morning at Calais! Promise me you'll look her up and keep an eye on her while I'm away.

These past few weeks, which were pretty miserable with all the fighting, I found myself thinking about you all the time. I'd give anything to stay right here where we could be together, but goodness knows where

I'm going and how long it will last. As we're pulling out any day now, please write me in care of AFS headquarters at Neuilly. I hope and pray to see you in Paris.

Love,

Frank

Quickly folding the pages in an envelope, he hurried out of the building to the nearest postal box.

*　　*　　*

The dolorous strains of a bugle, borne on the steady onshore breeze, drifted across the dunes to the hotchpotch of tents and huts of No. 4 General Hospital. Sitting on the wooden bench outside her marquee, Kit wiped away a tear as she listened to the final notes of the Last Post. She closed her eyes and waited for the rifle salute – three sharp reports in quick succession. She couldn't rid her mind of the image of the poor mother and father standing at their son's bedside, watching him gasp for breath as he slowly died from asphyxia. And now they were at the windswept cemetery just outside the camp, the third burial in less than a week from Kit's ward. The parents were notified at the very end, afforded the opportunity to pay a final visit. For many it was too late, crossing the Channel only in time for the funeral behind the dunes. Craving a smoke, Kit stood up and started for her tent.

Wandering the maze of duckboards, she happened on a solitary rosebush whose few blossoms were shrivelled and brown, shedding petals on the path. She immediately thought of Frank, sitting in the canteen with the yellow rose in his hand, which evoked a pang of longing as sharp as the sadness that swept over her listening to the bugle's wail. The memory brought Nigel to mind, the look of amazement on his face when she confessed she was seeing

166

someone else. Nigel had relapsed into his usual brooding silence, more pronounced on this visit than before in Paris, a vacancy of expression and emotion that she imagined masked some horror from the fighting. They'd spent the rest of the day wordlessly strolling the pavements and making futile attempts at small talk over a late bistro lunch. The farewell scene at the station was more pitiful than poignant, with Nigel adopting an almost avuncular tone, counselling her to go home to her family and assuring her that he would be fine, out of harm's way. But a week had passed without a word, leaving her guilty and depressed.

She stooped to pick a drooping rose blossom, banishing thoughts of Nigel. As she rounded the corner, she almost collided with the camp postman, carrying a bulging leather pouch on his shoulder. She recognized him as one of her orderly's card-playing acquaintances.

'Sorry, miss,' he said with a kindly smile. 'Didn't see you.'

'The fault was mine,' said Kit. 'I wasn't looking where I was going.' As he adjusted the strap of his pouch, she asked, 'I don't suppose you've got anything for me?'

'Let's have a look,' he replied, lowering the pouch and stooping down.

'It's Stanley,' she said. 'Kit Stanley.'

After a few moments searching the bundles he produced a single army-issue envelope. 'There you are,' he said, handing it to her.

'Thanks so much.'

Tucking it in her pocket, she hurried to her tent, relieved to find it unoccupied. Slipping her bib over her head, she kicked off her shoes and settled on her cot to examine the envelope. The masculine handwriting was Frank's and the postmark Dunkirk. She quickly slit it open and read his brief note.

So they were leaving, she thought with a sigh. Frank and

Borden, and Larrabee with his guitar and cowboy songs. Oh, God, with Frank gone she wasn't sure how much longer she could take it, and winter, dark, cold and wet, would soon be coming. She put the letter aside and considered what it would be like to meet Frank in Paris. That sunny afternoon on the riverbank outside Montreuil, watching the sailboats, he'd sworn if he ever had the chance to go, he meant to enjoy it. She smiled at the thought of stopping at a pavement café or wandering through the Tuileries … With no end in sight to the war, and the prospect of another long winter at the windswept hospital, filled with suffering and death, at least she could be with him in Paris.

13

Frank Harrington gazed out at the blue–green sea beyond the hillside, feeling comfortable in his greatcoat, wool cap and gloves despite the cold. He'd invited Talbot Pierce to drive and observed with satisfaction the confident way he handled the Model T, down-shifting and braking smoothly as a truck pulled out on the highway in front of them. The order to abandon their quarters in Dunkirk had come without warning the evening before, delivered by a senior AFS official, the first they'd seen in months. Rather than make the long trip in convoy, the Americans set out separately, their few possessions stowed in their ambulances, with Harrington taking a detour to look in on Elsie at No. 22 General Hospital.

Leaving Boulogne behind, Pierce drove steadily south, passing the entrance to No. 4 outside Camiers without slowing down. Harrington allowed himself a last look at the seaside tents and huts, suppressing a sharp pang of longing. He'd considered asking Talbot to stop on the chance of seeing Kit, but, with the urgency of their summons to Neuilly, he had decided against it. How long would it be before he saw her again? What were the chances she would meet him in Paris? In another ten minutes they approached an intersection with a sign for Étaples to the left – eight kilometres. Pierce coasted to a stop and gave Frank a questioning look.

'Turn left,' instructed Harrington. 'We should reach the hospital in a mile or so.'

After a few minutes Pierce steered the Model T onto

the hospital's gravel drive and parked next to an RAMC ambulance in front of the administration hut.

'Good job, Talbot,' said Harrington as the engine coughed and died. 'You can handle this thing as well as the next fellow.'

'Thanks,' said Pierce with a small smile. 'You know, I could hardly drive before coming over here.'

Harrington opened the door and climbed out. 'One of these days,' he said, 'you'll be going out at night on your own.'

As they walked up to the entrance, Pierce stopped to examine an arrangement of flagstones and gravel on the drive. 'What's that?' he asked with his hands on his knees.

'I'll be darned,' said Harrington. 'It's the Harvard shield.' They walked up the steps past a Union Jack snapping in the cold breeze, entered the hut and slipped off their hats. 'Morning,' said Harrington to the middle-aged nurse seated behind the desk. 'I'm here to see my sister.'

'One of the Americans,' she said, 'no doubt.'

'That's right. *Lieutenant* Harrington.' Frank shot Talbot a quick smile.

'Very well,' said the Sister. 'You may wait here while I send for her.'

After a few minutes the Sister returned with Elsie, wearing her navy-blue uniform and accompanied by a man in civilian clothes with a stethoscope around his neck.

'Hey, sis,' said Frank, stepping forward to give Elsie a brief embrace.

'Frank,' said Elsie with a smile, 'this is Dr Bruce Carey, with the Harvard Unit.'

'Hullo, Frank,' said the doctor with a quick handshake. With sandy hair and a ruddy complexion, he appeared to be in his late twenties.

'And this is Talbot Pierce,' said Harrington. 'He's with our section.'

'Pleased to meet you,' said Talbot. He started to give Elsie a handshake and then awkwardly shifted to Dr Carey. 'I see you're serving with the RAMC,' said the doctor, 'judging by your uniforms.'

'Well, we have been,' said Harrington. 'Working in the Flanders sector since summer. But we're about to trade in our khakis for horizon blues.' He turned from Dr Carey to Elsie, who gave him a searching look.

'That's right,' interjected Talbot with a bit too much enthusiasm. 'We're on our way to join the French Army.'

'But Frank...' said Elsie.

'I wonder', said Harrington, 'if Elsie and I might have a few minutes to visit?'

'Why don't you go outside,' suggested Dr Carey, 'in what we like to call the garden, and Talbot here can fill me in on the AFS.'

They sat together on a wooden bench, sheltered by canvas from the cold breeze blowing off the Channel, facing a few rows of flowering shrubs bordered by a gravel path. Wearing her long blue cape buttoned at the neck, Elsie shivered under the pewter November sky. 'It's not at all what I expected, Frank,' she said. 'It's much worse.'

'I might have warned you,' he said with an affectionate smile. 'If I'd had a chance.'

'They bring in more cases day and night. And fill up the wards just as soon as the British MOs can clear them out.' Frank nodded. Looking him in the eye, she said, 'Most of them have lost so much blood by the time they get here, they're too weak to make it through surgery. And the rates of infection are far higher than anything we'd anticipated.'

'Gas bacillus,' said Frank. 'It's got something to do with the manure in the soil. Or so I'm told. I wonder', he said,

171

looking away, 'whether conditions will be any better in the French hospitals.' Hearing Elsie sigh, he turned to her and said, 'I'm sorry about leaving so soon after you got here. But I don't have any choice.' Elsie nodded. He put his arm around her shoulder and gave her a squeeze. 'You'll be all right, Els,' he said. 'And these Harvard doctors seem fine enough fellows.'

'Thanks,' she said with a weak smile. 'I'll be fine.'

'I want you to meet Kit.'

'The British nurse? What did you call her?'

'A VAD.'

'I'm sure she'll have some helpful advice.'

'It's not just that.'

Elsie gave Frank a questioning look. 'What is it then?' she asked.

'I want you to meet her because...' He hesitated.

'Oh, come on,' said Elsie with a playful shove on his shoulder.

''Cause I think I'm in love with her.'

Elsie stared at him, her mouth open. 'In love?' she said after a moment.

'It does happen, you know.' It was his turn to give her a gentle shove.

'Is she pretty?'

'Of course she's pretty.'

'So you want *me* to keep an eye on *her*, with all the other fellows around.'

'I'm not worried about that. I just want Kit to get to know you. She's a wonderful girl.'

Elsie abruptly stood up. 'It's cold out here,' she said, giving her arms a rub under her cape. 'When do you have to go?'

He stood up and looked at her. 'Right away, I'm afraid.'

'Is it safe, Frank?' she asked. 'Do they keep you away from the fighting?'

172

'We pick up the wounded at the aid stations, right at the front lines. We drive at night, so their gunners can't see us. But sometimes...'

'What, Frank?'

'Our convoy was hit by a German shell a while back. One of our men was hurt pretty bad. He wound up losing his leg.'

'Oh, my,' said Elsie.

'And you'll need to be careful, too, Els.'

'Careful? Here?'

Frank nodded. 'You never know. The Boche send aeroplanes on raids. And they fire long-range artillery.'

'You're not saying they'd attack a hospital?'

'You never know with the Boche. You should see what they've done to Dunkirk. Be alert, especially for planes.' With a shiver, she put her arm around his waist and began walking toward the warmth of the administration hut.

Five minutes later, with Talbot in the car warming up the engine, Frank stood on the front steps holding Elsie's hands. 'Goodbye, sis,' he said before kissing her lightly on the cheek. 'Remember to be careful.'

'You too.'

'I'm sure Kit will be by to look in on you. And remember to write.'

She squeezed his hands and murmured, 'Goodbye,' and then watched as he climbed in the Model T and disappeared down the drive.

* * *

Uncomfortably warm inside the Métro station, Harrington slung his coat over his arm and unbuttoned his jacket. The benches were packed – mothers with infants in their arms, or suckling at their open blouses; old men in tattered suits and scuffed boots. The air reeked of tobacco smoke and unwashed bodies.

Unsure of the distance from the American Hospital at
Neuilly in the suburbs, Harrington had arrived at the stop
for the Gare du Nord an hour early. Desperate for fresh
air, he pushed his way through the crowd up the stairs to
the exit, pausing at the door to examine the large war
bond poster on the wall, depicting a *poilu* in helmet and
greatcoat, clutching his rifle and shouting to his unseen
comrades, '*On les aura!*' – We'll get them! The artist had
captured, perhaps unconsciously, the merest suggestion of
terror in the soldier's eyes.

Harrington walked out onto the sidewalk, shrugged on
his coat and took a deep breath. Even in the open air he
couldn't escape the mingling smells of exhaust fumes, cheap
perfume, and urine from the *pissoir* at the corner. Though
enchanted by the graceful architecture of the churches,
monuments and bridges, like many an American before
him he was repelled by the city's filth and shabbiness, an
old lady down at heel.

Despite the odours, the cold air felt good on his face.
Halfway down the block an uneven row of tables and chairs
spilled out on the sidewalk from a crowded café, the faces
of the patrons obscured by the pages of *Le Figaro*. He sat
down at one of the few unoccupied tables and promptly
ordered a *vin chaud* from a passing waiter. With the glass
of mulled wine warming his hand, he reached into his
pocket for Kit's letter and quickly reread it. She cautioned
that the 4:40 from St-Omer might be running late and
suggested that she stay at a young ladies' hostel in St-
Germain-des-Près. Harrington took a sip of wine and smiled
as he read her closing line: 'I'm desperate to see you ...
Love, Kit.'

Looking up, he noticed that a middle-aged couple at
a nearby table was staring at him with obvious disapprobation. In his civilian clothes, they undoubtedly
assumed he was dodging conscription. Well, he considered,

as he reached into his pocket for a few francs, perhaps they'd lost a son.

Harrington studied the time, a few minutes before five, on the large clock beneath the vaulted glass ceiling of the cavernous railway station. He walked over to the ticket counter and quickly ascertained that her train was arriving on platform six. He found himself in a gathering crowd, impatient to secure a place on the platform among the porters and baggage carts. Almost all of them were young women, staring nervously down the empty tracks. Harrington, feeling slightly ridiculous out of uniform in the midst of so many women, considered that the Gare du Nord was the terminus for all the trains arriving from the Somme sector. 'Pardon,' he muttered with mild annoyance as an older couple jostled past him, pushing to the front.

The roar of an approaching train and a shrill blast of its whistle echoed through the station. Standing a head taller than the women, Harrington peered over their fancy hats as the locomotive chugged by, pulling a long line of drab-green carriages. The young soldiers pressed against the windows, searching the faces on the platform. After a moment, they began to alight, wearing pale-blue greatcoats and steel helmets. With so many soldiers pouring onto the platform, there were anxious moments as the women, calling and waving, fought through the throng to embrace their husbands or lovers. With growing concern, Frank stood up to his full height and searched the platform as the crowd began to disperse.

At last he saw her, standing alone at the top of the steps, tall and trim in a blue coat and matching hat. Their eyes met, and she raised a gloved hand and smiled. Threading his way, Frank hurried to her coach and held her hand as she took the final step down to the platform. Neither spoke, but stared for a moment into each other's eyes until he folded her in a warm embrace.

'Oh, Frank,' she murmured, pressing her face against him.

Aware of his pounding heart, he held her tighter and said, 'For a minute I was afraid you weren't on the train.'

'There were so many soldiers,' she said, separating and happily looking up at him, 'it took forever to get off.'

'Home on leave,' he said. 'Anxious to see their girls. Let me get that,' he added, reaching down to pick up her bag where she'd let it drop.

He took her by the hand, and they began walking toward the terminal. 'I can't believe we're really here,' he said, stealing a look at her. 'Really here in Paris.' She responded with an encouraging smile. 'I thought we'd take the subway,' he said, pointing to the stairs in the corner of the station. 'The Métro.'

She gave his hand a gentle squeeze and said, 'Lead the way.'

The subway was every bit as crowded as the station, with Frank hanging on to a strap in the swaying car, looking down at Kit, squeezed into a seat beside an older woman in a heavy wool coat. After consulting a pocket Métro map, he'd suggested they take the blue line to a stop in the sixth arrondissement, though it was his first trip into the heart of the city. Unable to converse over the noise, he smiled at her and helped her to stand when the conductor announced the stop for St-Germain-des-Prés. Darkness had fallen when they emerged, the night air free of noxious fumes and smells. Waiting to cross the wide boulevard, filled with taxis and clattering horse-drawn carriages, they watched as a lamplighter held up his long pole to light the gaslight at the corner. Frank turned to Kit and asked, 'Where to?'

The air grew colder as they walked along the busy sidewalks, and a fine mist began to fall, visible in the streetlamps. With her arm through his, Kit leaned against Frank's shoulder. Halting at the intersection opposite the Romanesque cathedral, she said, 'I'm quite sure if we go left here, it's down the side street in the next block.'

'It's beautiful,' said Frank, pointing to the church. 'Just the way I pictured it.'

After a few more minutes, they entered through an inconspicuous doorway into the small lobby of the hostel, where a matronly woman in black silk stood behind the counter.

'*Bonsoir*,' she said, casting a disapproving eye at Frank, who smiled back at her before wandering over to inspect an arrangement of prints above the sofa.

'*Bonsoir*,' said Kit. '*Je suis M'amselle Stanley*. I wired ahead for a room for one night,' she added in decent French.

Consulting a worn notebook, the matron said, '*Eh, la voilà*. And Miss Stanley...' She paused and gave Kit a stern look. 'Visitors are absolutely prohibited.'

'*Je comprends, Madame*,' said Kit with a smile. 'Frank – would you bring me my bag?'

Frank walked over, and placing Kit's suitcase by the counter, turned to the matron and said, '*Pourriez-vous me dire, Madame, s'il y a un hôtel tout près? Pas cher.*'

Surprised, the woman said, '*Mais oui, Monsieur. La Mirabelle, dans la rue Lobineau.*' She gestured vaguely.

'One street over,' said Kit. 'I'll meet you in the lobby of your hotel.'

Frank consulted his watch. 'Shall we say in an hour?'

Not quite an hour had passed when Frank emerged from

the lift with his coat over his arm. Kit was at the entrance to the dining room, wearing a fur hat and dark-grey coat trimmed in red. 'I didn't expect you so soon,' he said as he gave her an admiring look.

'Actually, I've been waiting for a quarter-hour. I was dying to get out.' She leaned over and kissed him on the cheek.

'Ready?' he asked, slipping on his coat. He took her by the arm and led her out to the sidewalk. 'We could walk,' he said, 'but it's a bit cold.' He glanced up at the sound of hooves on the pavement and bells jingling. 'Look,' he said, 'a hansom cab.'

'Let's take it.'

Frank motioned to the driver, who reined in his horse, climbed down from his step and pulled open the door. '*À l'Île St-Louis, s'il vous plaît*,' said Frank as the driver gave Kit his hand and helped her up to the seat.

'*Mais oui*,' said the driver.

'*C'est un restaurant qui s'appelle Le Tastevin.*'

'*Eh bien, Monsieur. Je le connais.*'

Frank grasped the handle and swung up beside Kit as the horse started with a snort and shake of its harness bells. Looking at Kit in the flickering light of the coach lamps, Frank said, 'Swell, isn't it?'

She nodded and adjusted the thick blanket across their laps. 'You never see the hansoms in London any more. They're dying out.' As if to emphasize the point, an automobile rumbled past and sounded its horn.

Holding Kit's hand under the blanket, Frank took a deep breath of cold air and gazed out at the gas-lit cafés and storefronts as they rolled by at a leisurely pace. 'It's beautiful,' he said with a squeeze of Kit's hand.

'Yes,' she agreed, looking at him in the dim light. 'So romantic.'

The two-wheeled carriage rumbled over the bridge to

the Île St-Louis. Too narrow for automobiles, the ancient cobblestone streets lent even more of an Old World aspect to the place. Turning on the rue St-Louis, the driver continued down the block and then reined in his horse with a sharp '*Arrêtez, mon cher!*'

Frank climbed out and then took Kit's hand for the long step to the sidewalk, holding her close for a moment, her hair brushing his face. Savouring the fragrance of her perfume, he let go of her hand and reached into his pocket for several bills. '*Merci,*' he said to the driver, who accepted the fare and generous tip with a slight bow. Placing his arm around Kit's waist, Frank began walking along the sidewalk.

'You act as if you know where you're going,' observed Kit.

'Here we are,' said Frank, pointing to the sign over a dark-red door. He held it open for Kit and then helped her out of her coat as she inspected the tiny restaurant, whose exposed beams and varnished panelling were dimly illuminated by sconces and candles flickering on the linen-covered tables.

Once the trim *maître d'* had showed them to their table, Kit looked happily at Frank and said, 'How did you ever find this place? I feel like we've gone back in time.'

'One of the doctors at Neuilly recommended it. He's sampled all the best restaurants in town and said this was the place to take your special girl.'

'Is that what I am?'

Slightly embarrassed, Frank smiled and said, 'Yes. That's what you are.'

A waiter appeared at the table. 'What would you like?' asked Frank. 'We could have wine.'

'That would be lovely.'

Frank briefly consulted the wine list and ordered a Burgundy. After the sommelier returned, decanted the

179

bottle, and poured each of them a glass, Frank proposed a toast. '*Votre santé*,' he said, '*et notre bonheur.*'

Kit smiled and took a sip. 'And to victory,' she added. 'Yes,' said Frank. 'Of course.'

At the end of a three-course dinner, enlivened by stories of Frank's experiences on the Loos front, Elsie's arrival, and his section's impending move to the Champagne–Ardennes sector, they contentedly settled back to finish the last of the wine.

'You know,' said Kit, 'the horse-drawn hansom, and this lovely old place, without electricity, make me think what life must have been like when our grandparents were young.'

Frank nodded, noticing the candlelight reflecting in her eyes. 'Those were simpler times. No automobiles, no aeroplanes...'

'And no war.'

'I suspect that generation had forgotten what war was all about,' said Frank. 'Otherwise, they wouldn't have gotten us into this one.'

'Do you really think so?'

'That generation of Europeans, I do.' Kit gave him a questioning look. 'We Americans had the Civil War,' he explained. 'My grandfather fought all through it, and to this day he won't talk about it. It's why so many Americans are dead set against our getting involved.'

'Frank,' said Kit, putting her glass aside. 'Let's bundle up and take a walk along the river.'

The temperature had dropped, but the night was still and free of mist. They held each other close, silently watching the lights of the boats reflecting on the dark water, pausing to admire the arches and buttresses of Notre Dame bathed in floodlights. As they continued along the path they were

aware of dim forms embracing in the shadows. Passing out
of a pool of lamplight, Frank stopped and turned to Kit,
briefly looking in her eyes before pulling her to him. They
kissed for what seemed a long time, holding each other
tight, oblivious to the couples strolling along the quay.

'I should take you back,' said Frank at last. 'Or you'll
be late for your curfew.'

'Oh, Frank,' she whispered. 'Do we have to go?'

He kissed her again, gently, and then said, 'I'm afraid
so. But we have tomorrow.'

'Frank,' she said, searching his eyes in the darkness.
'Frank ... I love you.'

He kissed her again and murmured, 'And I love you
too.'

Kit awoke with bright sunlight streaming through a crack
in the cheap curtains. She'd been dreaming of the hospital
and was relieved to discover that in fact she was in a room
at the hostel. Rolling over, she considered going back to
sleep and then suddenly the scene at the end of the evening
came to mind and she stared up at the whitewashed ceiling
with a feeling of intense happiness, remembering his kiss,
the sensation of his arms around her ... She threw back
the covers and stood up, shivering in her light flannel
gown, anxious to dress and seize every moment of their
brief time together.

Following a breakfast of coffee and pastries at Frank's
hotel, they ventured out into the quiet neighbourhood,
bundled up in coats, hats and gloves. There were almost
no soldiers on the sidewalks but rather the typical bourgeois
Parisians out for their Saturday-morning shopping. Frank
was content to play the part of an American abroad, taking
in the usual sights, with Kit, who'd travelled often to Paris
before the war, as his tour guide. Midway down the block,

a pale, young soldier, bundled up in his greatcoat, sat on the sidewalk with a crude sign suspended from his neck that read: 'Alms for a Patriot'. Staring ahead through sightless eyes, with both legs amputated above the knee, the veteran rattled the change in his battered tin cup. Frank reached down to drop a few coins in the cup, shook his head, and continued walking with Kit's arm through his.

Stopping at a newsstand by the entrance to the Métro, Frank's eyes were drawn to the colourful lithograph on the cover of *Le Petit Journal*. Taking the paper from the rack, he read aloud the caption: '*Ils bombardent les hôpitaux et assassinent les blessés.*'

Peering over his shoulder, Kit said, 'Oh, my God,' as she studied the illustration of the bombing raid on an Allied hospital, with nurses and orderlies helping the wounded to escape the flames. 'Where did this happen?' she asked.

'Let's see,' said Frank. He removed the paper from the rack and handed a coin to the young boy behind the counter, who was wearing a soft wool cap low over his forehead. Frank quickly scanned the text. 'The No. 7 Canadian Hospital,' he said with a frown. 'Outside Boulogne. It says the German planes dropped their bombs at night, killing two nurses and four of the wounded men in their beds.'

'How ghastly,' said Kit, placing her arm around his waist and clinging to him.

Frank folded the paper under his arm as they resumed their stroll.

At the end of the morning, their cheeks rouged by the cold and feet growing weary, they stopped for lunch at an Art Nouveau café on the Champs-Elysées, seated at a table for two in the crowded dining room. Stripping off their gloves and coats, they motioned to a waiter and ordered two glasses of wine.

'Mm, that's much better,' said Kit after taking a sip.

Frank raised his glass and nodded. A group of French officers at a nearby table, smoking and passing a bottle of *pastis*, gave him a curious look. 'They probably think I'm a shirker,' said Frank.

'Why would they think that about an American?' Kit glanced at the officers. At the sight of the *pastis* she thought of Nigel, his hand trembling and a faraway look in his eyes.

'At any rate,' said Frank, 'in a few days I'll be trading in this suit for a French uniform.' All morning he'd avoided mention of his impending transfer to the French Army.

A dark look clouded Kit's face. 'Oh, God, Frank,' she said. 'If only the war would end. But it's not going to, not any time soon. Especially after this latest disaster in the Dardanelles.'

'I read that Kitchener is considering evacuating the troops from Gallipoli.'

'Yes, and the press are heaping all the blame on poor Winston.' In response to Frank's surprised expression, she explained, 'Our families are friends. Mother and Clementine Churchill are very close.'

They lapsed into an uncomfortable silence, interrupted by the arrival of a waiter. Fighting a feeling of inferiority at the further evidence of Kit's elevated social status, Frank studied the complex menu and said, 'Gosh, lots to choose from.'

'Frank,' said Kit. He put the menu aside and looked in her eyes. 'What you said last night?' she continued in a soft voice.

'Yes?'

'Did you mean it?'

'Of course I meant it, Kit. I've never felt this way before.'

'Nor have I. There's something I should tell you.' He lifted his glass and took a sip, waiting for her to explain.

'Nigel recently came to see me,' she said. 'He came because, well ... to ask me to marry him.'

Frank looked away and said, 'I thought you told me it was over between you...'

'It *is* over, Frank. That's what I want you to understand. I told Nigel no. And I don't intend to see him again.'

'Are you sure *he* understands?'

'Frank, please. I love you,' she said in a voice just above a whisper. 'It doesn't matter what Nigel thinks. I just want to be with you.'

He reached across the table and took her hand. 'That's all I care about. I only wish we could be together.'

'I'm going home for Christmas. I've been away for over a year and I'm due for a leave. Perhaps you could come ... You could meet Mother and Father.'

With a rueful smile, he said, 'I'd love nothing better. But I doubt the AFS will let me.' He leaned over, placed an arm around her shoulder, and kissed her softly on the lips. 'Just promise me,' he said, 'you'll wait for me.'

14

Lieutenant Parker slowly picked his way down the trench, his breath frosting before his face and his feet pinched and numb in mud-caked boots. Indifferent to the shelling in the distance and the occasional crack of a sniper's rifle, his mind was fastened on a single thought: a warm room and a hot meal. He glanced down at his boots, paused, and stepped gingerly over a finger bone protruding from the mud. Stumbling down the final steps to the dugout, he pushed the blanket aside and stiffly came to attention.

Captain Nigel Owen was seated on an ammunition case, reading a book by the light of a candle on a sagging table. He looked up at the lieutenant with a puzzled expression. 'Oh, Parker,' he said after a moment. 'What is it?'

'Colonel's compliments, sir,' said Parker. 'He sent a runner with orders to retire the company at 1600 hours. We're being relieved.'

Owen seemed lost in concentration, unable to assimilate the information. 'Sixteen hundred hours,' he finally repeated and then pulled back his sleeve to look at his watch. 'Two hours hence.'

'And not a minute too soon,' said Parker, shivering under his greatcoat.

'Very well,' said Owen, resuming his reading.

Parker touched the bill of his hat and disappeared through the blanket. Owen fished in his pocket for a cigarette and lit it with the candle. Taking a deep drag, he reached down for a half-empty bottle of whisky wrapped in a blanket and poured an inch into the tin cup on the table. Closing his book, he sat smoking and sipping whisky with a vacant expression, as though he were at his club in Mayfair. After a while he stubbed out the cigarette in the miniature frying pan ashtray, stood up and twisted the belt of his coat into a tight knot.

Ascending the steps to the trench, he casually looked to his left and right, noting that the men were resting in their dugouts apart from the sentries standing with their backs against the trench wall. He walked a few paces and stopped where a periscope was mounted on the sandbags at the top of the trench. Climbing up on the fire-step, he hunched over the eyepiece and looked out on the small square of No Man's Land reflected in its mirror. The earth beyond the rolls of wire was utterly wasted – pocked with rainwater-filled craters, the tree trunks blasted to splinters a few feet above the muddy ground.

Squinting, he gazed across toward the German line. Startled, he sucked in a deep breath and tried to focus. A dim shape was slowly coming toward them from the German side. What the devil was it? As it grew closer he could see that it was a group of men, not German infantrymen in their helmets, but men in dark suits, like undertakers, he wildly reasoned. Why weren't his men firing? Wait … it was Barnes, Lieutenant Barnes, he was sure of it, leading the strange body of men! Owen jumped down and staggered to the nearest sentry.

'Get up!' he shouted. 'Up on the fire-step and look!'

'What, sir?' said the startled private. 'On the fire-step?'

'Look!' cried Owen. 'They're coming!'

Climbing up on the step, the sentry warily raised his head over the rim of the parapet. 'What is it, sir?' he asked, gazing across No Man's Land. 'I don't see a thing…'

With a single report that echoed in the still air, the sentry silently collapsed, tumbling backwards into the trench, a bullet hole in his forehead. Owen gaped at him, at the dark blood streaming down his face and the puzzled expression frozen in his lifeless eyes. Other men appeared in the trench but Owen, oblivious to them, watched in horror as the dead man smiled at him and then his form seemed to rise up out of his body, slowly coming toward him. Owen tried to scream, but could make no sound. He turned, slipped down, and then began to run, wildly stumbling past his astonished men until Parker finally caught up with him, cowering on the ground at a bend in the trench, one arm protecting his face, tears streaming down his cheeks ...

*   *   *

Sandwiched between the driver and a burly sergeant whose hand kept roaming to her knee, Kit was greatly relieved when the ambulance finally came to a stop.

'Cheerio, Sister,' said the sergeant with a lecherous look as Kit climbed out.

'Thanks for the lift, I suppose I should say,' she replied. 'Though I'll remember next time to be more careful with whom I ride.'

She turned and began walking toward the administration hut, ignoring the sergeant's derisive laugh. She went inside and stood at attention before the matronly nurse at the front desk.

'Good morning, Sister,' said Kit.

'Good morning, miss, ah...'

'Stanley. From No. 4.'

'I see,' said the senior RAMC nurse. 'And what may we do for you, Miss Stanley.'

'I'm off duty till later this afternoon and I came by in the hope of seeing a friend.' In response to the Sister's slightly raised eyebrows, she added, 'One of the American nurses. Miss Elsie Harrington.'

'I would be happy to enquire of her superior officer,'

said the Sister, sliding off her stool, 'if the young lady is available.'

The Sister returned after a few minutes and said, 'You may visit with Nurse Harrington in the canteen. I trust you can find your way?'

Walking along the duckboards among the maze of tents, Kit felt a flutter of apprehension. How would she measure up to Frank's sister, a trained army nurse? Don't be ridiculous, she chided herself, there was a thing or two she could teach the Americans after the year she'd spent in France. She almost collided with an attractive man in civilian clothes, presumably a doctor by the stethoscope around his neck, who smiled pleasantly at her in a distinctive American way.

'Lost?' he said.

'I'm looking for the canteen...'

'Over yonder,' said the doctor, pointing to the next row of marquees.

'Thanks,' said Kit as she continued walking.

At the mid-morning hour the wooden structure was almost empty, save for the Red Cross volunteers dispensing coffee and tea from large urns on one side of the room. Kit immediately recognized Elsie, seated by herself at a table against the wall, with the same dark-brown hair as Frank's and a striking family resemblance. She was wearing a plain white nurse's uniform, with insignias on the collars, and a nurse's cap with 'US' embroidered in blue on the front. Rising from her seat as Kit walked up, she held out her hand and smiled.

'You must be Elsie,' said Kit, giving her hand a quick shake.

'And you're Kit. I recognized you the moment you walked in.'

'These, you mean?' said Kit, touching her white bib with its faded red cross.

'No,' said Elsie. 'Frank described you to a tec. Why don't we get a cup and sit down?'

Seated across from Elsie with a steaming mug of tea, Kit smiled politely and said, 'I've been so looking forward to meeting you.'

'I've been dying of curiosity,' said Elsie. This elicited a look of surprise. 'I mean,' said Elsie, 'I've never heard Frank go on like that about a girl.'

'Oh,' said Kit, feeling a slight blush on her cheeks.

'He's crazy about you. So I've been curious to get a look for myself.'

Slightly unnerved by Elsie's directness, Kit decided to take another tack. 'I understand,' she said, 'that you've been training in Texas?'

Elsie nodded and took a sip of tea. 'Good old Fort Sam Houston,' she said. 'All the way from San Antonio to Ehtopple. Now there's a change of scenery!'

'And what', asked Kit, 'are your impressions of conditions here?'

'To be honest, I was shocked at first. We all were.'

'Yes,' said Kit. 'It's rather appalling. And things seem to keep getting worse, rather than better.'

'In what way?'

'At first the problem was infection, gas gangrene, mainly the shrapnel cases.' Elsie nodded. 'We've been able to reduce the rate of amputations with the Carrel and Dakin solution.'

'Hypochlorous acid?'

'That's right. But then came the burn cases. The Boche turned liquid fire on our boys at Hooge Crater,' explained Kit. 'Last July. And lastly the gas cases, of course. Chlorine and phosgene. In this last push, it was dreadful, there were so many gassed.'

'You've been through quite a lot.'

'Well,' said Kit with a smile, 'we VADs are simply here to help out.'

'In the wards?'

'Yes, in the wards, mostly changing dressings. But assisting in the operating theatres as well, and with triage at the Casualty Clearing Stations, where the wounded are brought in from the aid stations.'

'That's what Frank does, isn't it?' asked Elsie.

'Yes,' said Kit. 'They pick up the men at night, near the front lines. They're very brave men, the ambulance drivers.'

Elsie nodded with a proud expression. 'All the experience you've had', she said, 'is worth years of nursing school.'

'Thanks for saying so,' said Kit. 'We don't get many compliments from the Sisters and MOs.'

'There's something the Harvard doctors have been working on,' said Elsie, feeling a growing bond between them, 'that you might find interesting.' Kit looked expectantly over her mug of tea. 'A technique for transfusing blood,' said Elsie.

'I've heard of it being attempted,' said Kit. 'Though without success.'

'By the time they reach the hospital, so many of these men are suffering from shock from loss of blood.'

'At No. 4,' said Kit, 'they're placed in what's termed the "moribund" ward.'

'At any rate,' said Elsie, 'the doctors here have devised a way to prevent the blood from clotting during the transfusion. First they have to match the blood to a donor with the same blood type, of course.' Kit nodded. 'The donor's blood goes into a flask, where it's mixed with sodium citrate, and then from the flask into the patient.'

'You're doing that here?'

'Routinely. And it's amazing how the men respond. After being in shock, they're alert and strong enough for surgery. It's saving lives by the dozens.'

Kit put down her mug and said, 'That's remarkable. I'll pass it along to my superiors. I'm sure the RAMC will want to send a team over to learn the technique.' Feeling completely at ease now, Kit asked, 'What have you heard from Frank?'

'He wrote the other day to say that his section's been sent to a town in Champagne, somewhere east of Paris.'

'Yes, he wrote to me as well. A village called Châlons-sur-Marne, I believe it is.'

'He said they were bored stiff,' said Elsie. 'Not much fighting in that sector.'

'It's the far right of the French line,' said Kit. 'I expect it will stay rather quiet, with winter coming on.'

'Frank wrote that he was hoping to arrange a leave, to see you in London over Christmas.'

'Yes,' said Kit. 'I'm hoping he'll come.'

'He *is* crazy about you, you know.'

'Yes, and I'm mad about him.' Kit abruptly stood up. 'I should be going,' she said.

'I've so enjoyed this visit. You shall have to come to Camiers on your day off and we'll have lunch.'

'I'd like that.' They began walking toward the exit. Standing at the door, Elsie said, 'I'll write Frank that I've finally met his girl.'

'I'm so glad to get to know you,' said Kit with a smile. 'Goodbye.'

* * *

'You say he snapped?' The colonel rested his elbows on the cluttered table in the farmhouse that served as headquarters for 7th Battalion, King's Royal Rifle Corps.

'Yes, sir,' said Lieutenant Parker, standing rigidly at attention. 'Snapped.'

'Sit down, Lieutenant,' said the colonel. 'At ease.' He dug into his pocket for a tobacco pouch and began filling his pipe. 'Owen was one of my best officers,' he said thoughtfully. 'And he snapped? Just like that?'

Parker sat down in one of the straight-back chairs and said, 'He bolted down the trench like a rabbit, after one of the men was shot by a sniper. Bloody fool was gazing out over No Man's Land in broad daylight. By the time I caught up with him, the captain was curled up on the ground, blubberin' like a child.'

'Good God, man, what did he have to say?'

'Didn't make any sense, sir. Something about "they were coming" and "Barnes was with them". Had this queer look in his eyes. Barnes was a lieutenant in the company. Wounded last summer.'

'Yes, I remember Barnes. The Victoria Cross.' He struck a match and cupped it over the bowl of his pipe. Expelling a cloud of aromatic smoke, the colonel said, 'What have they done with Owen?'

'We laid him on a stretcher and carried him out to an aid station. I went along to explain. The ambulance man took one look at him – he was still blubberin' – and said "shell shock". They've taken him to the Clearing Station.'

'Shell shock,' repeated the colonel with an expression of revulsion. 'Owen ... Well, perhaps he'll pull out of it. Meanwhile, Parker, you're acting CO. Keep me informed if there's anything new on Owen.'

*　　*　　*

The Ward Sister leaned over to the MO and quietly said, 'He's in the last cot on the right. Captain Owen.'

'And you say he won't respond?' asked the MO with a frown.

'Well, he won't answer *my* questions. But at night, oh my, you should hear the commotion. None of the others can get any sleep.'

'Very well,' said the MO as he started walking down the

marquee. When he reached the bed he glanced at the note on the foot-rail and then looked at Owen, in peaceful repose, appearing to be sleeping until his eyes opened a crack.

'Good morning, Captain,' said the MO, a major in his mid-thirties with a surgical practice in Birmingham before the war. When Owen failed to respond, other than by closing his eyes, the doctor said, 'I see you're sloughing.' Owen opened his eyes just wide enough to give the MO a brief, hateful look.

'Can't have that here,' said the doctor, walking to the head of the bed. 'Bad for morale.'

Owen re-opened his eyes and tried to speak. 'S-s-send m-me b-b-back, w-w-why d-don't you...'

The doctor looked down with a grim smile. 'What happened to you out there, Owen?'

Nigel looked up at the doctor, avoiding eye contact. For a moment he thought his face was starting to change, the same way the other face had changed, with the neat bullet hole in the centre of its forehead, a perfect shot ... Nigel swallowed hard and closed his eyes, blotting out the image, but another image, a small, dark cloud slowly coming toward him, took its place.

'What is it, Captain?' said the doctor. 'Spit it out.'

Nigel opened his eyes. He tried to spit at the doctor, but it just came out as a dribbling splutter.

'Good God, man,' muttered the MO. 'Get control of yourself.'

Nigel wiped his mouth with the sleeve of his pyjama. 'I ... I s-see things,' he said after a moment in a barely audible voice.

'You what?' said the doctor. 'See things?' Nigel nodded. 'What sort of things?'

'Shapes,' whispered Nigel. 'F-f-faces. I ... I can't g-get rid of them.'

'Well,' said the doctor with a frown. He stroked his chin. 'We can't have you disturbing this ward with your bellowing all night. I'm writing you up as unfit for duty. You'll be marked BS on the next available ship. Perhaps the doctors in London will know what to do with you.'

Nigel watched as the MO walked briskly to the end of the marquee and out the door. Closing his eyes, he let the warm tears trickle down his cheeks.

* * *

'I don't understand it,' said Kit with a heavy sigh. 'I can't get over the feeling that something's happened to him.'

'How long has it been?' asked Jane. Both women were stretched out on their cots in stocking feet.

'Let me think,' said Kit. 'What day is it? December second?'

'Third,' said Jane with a yawn. 'Wednesday's the fifth, my eleven-month anniversary.' Though just past four in the afternoon, the light outside the bell-tent was fading. Propped on an elbow, Jane struck a match and lit the candle on the table between their cots.

'It's been almost a month since Nigel's last letter,' said Kit pensively. 'He was so hurt after I turned down his proposal. His letter made me feel guilty, and so I wrote him back and asked him to forgive me...'

'Forgive you?'

'Well, not forgive, but asking him to remain friends, not to be angry with me.'

'And he hasn't responded?'

'No.' Kit stood up and stretched. 'I'm going to call on Major Evans. I put in for that leave and she still hasn't given me an answer.'

'You've served your twelve months,' said Jane. 'And it's relatively quiet around here.'

'Yes, I know,' said Kit, slipping on her shoes. 'I'm sure

194

she'll let me have it.' She draped her cloak over her shoulders and pushed through the tent flaps. Light rain was falling, with a cold breeze off the Channel. Shivering, Kit hurried along the path to the administration hut.

'Is Major Evans available?' she asked.

The nurse on duty at the front desk looked up from her novel. 'I suppose you'll find her in her office, Miss Stanley.'

Kit walked down the hall and knocked on the door next to the Chief Medical Officer's office. Hearing a muffled 'come in', she turned the handle and stepped inside. The senior RAMC nurse, a tall, severe woman in her fifties, looked up from her paperwork.

'What is it, Miss Stanley? I'm rather busy at the moment.'

'It's about my leave.' Regretting her impertinent tone, she quickly added, 'Ma'am.'

The older woman eyed her coldly. 'You're not the only VAD', she said, 'who's hoping to spend Christmas at home with her family.'

'I suppose not, but I have served more than my twelve months without a furlough.'

'Are you certain of that?'

'Yes, quite. You can check the records...'

'That won't be necessary.' She consulted a calendar on her desk. 'I'll grant you one week, beginning, let's see ... on Saturday the 22nd, returning no later than 5:00 p.m. on the 29th.'

'Thank you, ma'am.'

'You're welcome. I'll sign the papers tomorrow.'

Anxious to leave before the major changed her mind, Kit let herself out. She hadn't allowed herself to believe she was really going home, but now the certainty of her leave filled her with happiness. What a joy to be in London again, away from the miserable bell-tents, the men in agony, working late into the cold nights or rising before day. Back

195

in her family's townhouse in South Kensington, reunited with her mother, father and sisters ... and at Christmas! If only Frank could come. The thought of Frank reminded her of Nigel, triggering a wave of guilt and worry that abruptly cancelled her happy expectation. There must be some way to learn if he was all right. What if he was lying in a hospital somewhere, or worse? She had a friend who worked in patient records – why not ask her to check with the other RAMC hospitals in the area? She quickly found her way to the medical records hut, feeling like a fool for not having thought of it sooner.

Though it was past five, the clerks were still at their desks, typewriters chattering as they recorded the nationality, date of birth, height, weight, diagnosis and other pertinent information for each patient admitted to the hospital. Kit walked up to her friend's desk.

'Sorry to interrupt, Violet,' she said, 'but I have a question for you.'

'Quite all right.' Violet looked up over her tortoiseshell glasses, fingers poised over the keys of her Royal.

'I'm concerned about a friend of mine,' said Kit. 'A captain with the King's Royal Rifles.'

'Has he been wounded?' asked Violet.

'I'm not sure. Is there a way to run a check with the other hospitals to see whether he's been admitted?'

'Well,' said Violet in a quiet voice, 'if you were to ask, they'd refuse to give it out. But I'm sure they'll share it with me. What's his name?'

'Owen. Captain Nigel Owen, the 7th KRRC.'

Violet took a pencil from her thick red hair and made a note. 'I'll telephone first thing in the morning. I should know something by noon.'

'Thanks, Violet. I knew I could depend on you.'

She hurried back to her tent, the worry lifted. She found the lantern lit but Jane's cot empty, not surprising as the first serving of supper was about to be begin. Retrieving her writing case from under the cot, she sat cross-legged with a clean sheet of stationery and her fountain pen. After thinking for a moment, she wrote:

3 December 1915
No. 4 Gen. Hosp.
Camiers

Dear Frank,

I've just come from Major Evans' office – she's in charge of the VADs – and I've got my leave! One whole week, starting Saturday Dec. 22. Is there any way you could come? There's plenty of room to put you up. London is so beautiful at Christmas, and I so want my family to meet you. I hope and pray you can talk your superiors into granting you a few days' leave. As you're only a volunteer, surely there's a way.

I hitched a ride the other day to No. 22 and had a lovely visit with Elsie. I confess to having been a bit nervous, wanting to make a good impression I suppose, but we 'hit it off' right away, as you would say. Elsie is so attractive Frank, and obviously a well-trained army nurse, but without the condescension our Sisters are always obliged to display toward the lowly VADs. She described a method for transfusing blood the Harvard doctors at No. 22 have worked out, which I've passed along to our MOs.

Kit put aside her pen for a moment and thought back to her conversation with the British doctor about the Harvard technique for transfusions, how his scepticism had turned to keen professional interest when she mentioned the use of sodium citrate to prevent the clotting.

Taking another sheet, she wrote:

197

Please write to me about your new posting with the French. How do their hospitals compare to ours? I've found the village you mentioned on the map – it appears to be tiny. If there are any pretty French girls in the vicinity, you must strictly avoid them. It seems you're in a quiet sector, and I trust it will stay that way with winter coming on.

Oh, Frank, I miss you so much. The time we had in Paris was the most wonderful of my life. I'll never forget that night walking in the cold along the river. Please promise me you'll take care of yourself. I can't wait to hold you in my arms again, and pray it will be soon, in London. I love you so much.

Your darling,
Kit

15

'Wake up,' said Jane, giving Kit a gentle shove. 'It's half past six.'

Kit groaned in the semi-darkness, emerging from a deep sleep. She'd lain awake for what seemed like hours in the middle of the night, unsettled by a dream, something about being in Paris with Frank, only it wasn't Frank, it was Nigel, and then it was London, before the war, she supposed, and they were having an ugly row...

'You'd best hurry,' said Jane, buttoning her dress in the candlelight, 'if you're planning to have tea before we report in.'

'Oh, God,' said Kit, sitting up and rubbing her eyes. 'I'm so ready for a change.'

'Well, you'll have that soon enough – lucky you.' Jane tied on her apron, pulled on her cape, and hurried out into the dark.

By the time she came off shift in the early afternoon, Kit had a feeling of impending doom, unable to shake off dark forebodings. Well, she considered, it was simply worry over what, if any, information she would learn from Violet's enquiries. She hurried along the path to the medical records hut. From the expression on Violet's face the moment Kit walked in it was obvious that the news was not good. The two women stepped outside to talk in private.

'Is he...?' said Kit, holding her hand at her mouth.

Violet nodded. 'After about the fifth call,' she said, 'my

counterpart at No. 18 confirmed that a Captain Nigel Owen, with the KRRC, had been admitted...'

'With what?'

'She couldn't say...'

'But why?' There was a desperate edge to Kit's voice.

'Please, Kit. Let me explain.'

'Sorry.'

'She couldn't say because the form had been left blank. And then it showed that he'd been discharged two days later.'

'Thank God,' said Kit with a sigh. 'Then he must be all right. But why would the form have been left blank?'

'It usually means that the admitting doctor was unable to make a diagnosis. So it's simply left blank.'

'Then perhaps he wasn't wounded after all. Perhaps he was merely ill.'

Violet nodded unconvincingly.

'What else could it be?' asked Kit.

'Well ... I shouldn't say. I mean the clerk obviously had no idea...'

'What?' persisted Kit.

'Well, here it often means that the patient's been admitted for, well, for shell shock.'

'Oh, my,' said Kit. She immediately thought back to Nigel's unravelling at the café in Boulogne. 'And that', said Kit, 'might explain why he was discharged so shortly after admission?' Violet nodded. 'Did the clerk tell you when this occurred?'

'Yes,' said Violet. 'I made a note.' She removed a folded slip of paper from her pocket. 'Admitted on November 20th,' she said. 'And discharged on the 22nd.'

'Thanks,' said Kit, rubbing her forehead. 'Thanks so much.'

'It all depends,' explained the MO who'd consented to

discuss the matter with her. 'Oftentimes these men are sent to hospital for observation. After a day or so they return to normal, fit enough to rejoin their regiment. If not, they're packed off to Britain for treatment. Frankly, it's left to the judgment of the attending physician. Some doctors are, shall we say, less charitable with these cases than others.'

'I see,' said Kit quietly.

'We're under strict orders not to keep them here,' said the MO. 'Bad for morale. No, it's a quick ticket to Blighty, unless they snap out of it.'

'Thank you for your time, Major,' said Kit, rising from her chair.

'The officer in question,' said the major, 'was he serving in the front lines?'

'Yes,' said Kit. 'He's with the KRRC. Hooge Château, the left wing of the attack at Loos.'

The doctor shook his head and frowned. 'Bloody awful,' he commented. 'Shattered the nerves of many a fine soldier.'

Walking back to her tent, thinking of Nigel in some mental ward, Kit was wracked with guilt. She couldn't help feeling that somehow it was her fault. It was one thing to turn down his marriage proposal, but to have told him about Frank ... that she was rejecting him for another man. She remembered the dazed look in his eyes, his hands trembling. Oh, God, she'd driven him to this. And yet, she reasoned, she didn't know for certain that he'd been evacuated to England. She really didn't know he was shell-shocked, though deep inside she was convinced of it.

Jane was lying on her cot, bundled up in a blanket, when Kit pushed back the tent flap. 'Well?' said Jane. 'Were you able to learn anything?'

Kit slumped down on her cot. 'Yes,' she said. 'I'm afraid so. He was admitted at No. 18, near Boulogne, and then discharged.'

'Is he all right?'

'I don't know.' Kit reached for the cigarettes on the table. 'I don't know why he was admitted, but I think it's likely because he's ... neurasthenic.' She took a box of matches from her pocket and lit the cigarette.

'Neurasthenic?' said Jane. 'How can you be sure?'

'I can't. But looking back, it all fits. God, how could I have been so thoughtless?' She took a drag and expelled a cloud of smoke, staring down at her shoes.

'I don't understand, Kit,' said Jane, swinging her legs around and sitting up. She looked like an Indian squaw, huddled under the brown army blanket. 'What does your being thoughtless have to do with it?'

'Because I told Nigel about Frank,' Kit said bitterly. 'He was devastated. And now he's been sent home to some asylum, shell-shocked.' She made a face as she uttered the word.

'But you said you can't be sure...'

'I know, I know. Perhaps he's been sent back to his regiment, or perhaps it wasn't shell shock at all.' Tapping her cigarette on the ashtray, she added, 'But I've got to find out.'

*   *   *

Frank Harrington pushed his hands deep in the pockets of his French greatcoat, strolling slowly around the colonnade that enclosed a courtyard with Henry Borden at his side. They watched the scene in the courtyard with amusement. Two groups of newly arrived volunteers, assigned to Section 1 of the AFS, were marching in their civilian clothes, including topcoats and hats. Striding along beside them was the 'colonel', a portly figure wearing the khaki tunic and trousers of an American army officer, brandishing a riding crop as he bellowed: 'Your left, left, left – right – left.'

'Look at that short fellow on the last row,' said Borden, walking with his hands clasped behind his back.

Harrington smiled. 'I have been. He just can't keep in step, and every so often he does this funny little jig to get back on the right foot. See – there he goes again.'

The colonel, a senior official with the AFS who'd appropriated the rank along with the army uniform, halted the little column and berated the poor man for his sorry marching skills. Since arriving from Neuilly, Harrington and his comrades, long accustomed to being on their own, had been sharing quarters with fifty or more Americans in an abandoned Sisters of Charity convent outside the village of Châlons-sur-Marne.

'I never thought', said Borden, 'that one day we'd be parading around some convent courtyard...'

'With an insurance man from Hartford', interrupted Harrington, 'as a drill instructor.' J. Fred McDuffie, an ample man in his late forties, had left his position with Aetna Life to sail to France and help organize the AFS, an outfit he viewed as a cross between the Boy Scouts and the National Guard.

'Instead of doing our job,' said Borden. 'We didn't realize how good we had it in Flanders.'

'You surprise me, Henry,' said Harrington, stopping to look at him. 'How good we had it? Dodging shells in Dunkirk, hiding in cellars from air raids, making those night-time pick-ups in the Salient?'

Borden smiled and said, 'Ah, those were the days.' The two started walking again.

'It's so dang quiet around here,' said Harrington. 'With so many drivers, and the lull in the fighting, we'll be lucky to be working two nights a week.'

'It's not the quiet that bothers me,' said Borden. 'It's all this damnation drill and spit and polish, instead of using the time to work on the cars and teach these boys what's expected of them in a battle.'

'And what makes you think', asked Harrington, 'that McDuffie would know how to do that?'

They halted at an archway that opened to the lawn behind the main building, where a large number of Ford ambulances were parked in a row. Several of the men, bundled up against the cold, had buckets and were washing their cars with brushes, while another group was at work painting their vehicles drab green.

'Let's have a look,' said Borden, as they passed out of the shade of the colonnade into the bright sunshine. 'And see if we can find ol' Betsy.'

Waving a friendly greeting to the men working on their ambulances, they stopped beside one of the identical Model Ts, with a fresh coat of green paint and the distinctive Indian-head insignia on its side.

'Looks as good as new,' said Borden, running a hand over the hardboard siding.

'Too bad they made you patch that,' said Harrington. The jagged hole gouged out by a piece of shrapnel on the trip to Béthune had become a badge of honour, especially in the eyes of the new men, not yet exposed to enemy fire.

Borden nodded glumly. 'Let's go inside', he said with a shiver, 'and look for the others.'

They found Talbot Pierce reclining on one of the iron beds in an upstairs room. He glanced up from the magazine in his lap and said, 'Hullo, fellas.'

'Hey, Peach,' said Harrington, slumping on the bed next to him. 'Seen Bill?'

Talbot shook his head. 'Just been reading your new issue of *Punch*. If you don't mind, Frank, there's a poem in it I'd like to cut out and send home to my mom.'

'Fine,' said Harrington. 'What is it?'

'Written by a Canadian doc with the RAMC. Called "In Flanders Fields". Want to hear it?'

'Sure,' said Harrington, leaning back on his pillow.

Talbot folded back the pages of the magazine and read: 'In Flanders fields the poppies blow between the crosses, row on row, that mark our place; and in the sky the larks, still bravely singing, fly...'

'I like that,' said Harrington with a smile. '*The larks bravely singing.*'

'Scarce heard amid the guns below,' continued Talbot. 'We are the Dead, short days ago, we lived, felt dawn, saw sunset glow ...

'Loved, and were loved, and now we lie
In Flanders fields.

'Take up our quarrel with the foe:
To you from failing hands we throw
The torch; be yours to hold it high.
If ye break faith with us who die
We shall not sleep, though poppies grow
In Flanders fields.'

The door opened and Bill Larrabee walked in, clutching a stack of letters. He was wearing a standard French Army kepi in lieu of his cowboy hat, which had been banished to a shelf over his bed. 'Loads of mail today,' said Larrabee absently.

Talbot put the magazine aside and exchanged a brief, sad look with Frank.

Larrabee examined the envelopes and tossed three to Harrington. 'One from your gal, Frank,' he said with a smile. 'Here you go, Borden. And these are for you, Peach. And this', said Larrabee with a flourish, 'is a letter from Deac.'

'I'll be...' said Borden. 'From good old Deac.'

'Deac was the fellow', Frank explained to Talbot, 'who was injured by the German shell.'

'Whose place I took,' said Talbot with a nod.

Larrabee slit open the envelope and began reading: '*St Louis, Missouri. November 26*... Hell, it took over two weeks to get here.' He continued to read the letter out loud:

> Dear Bill, Frank, and Henry.
> I hope this letter finds you in good health and good cheer, assuming it finds you at all. I'm back home at last with dad and mom and it sure feels good to be here. I spent a long spell at a navy hospital in Brooklyn when I got off the ship. They had to fix something that hadn't mended right on my broken arm...

'Gosh,' said Borden, 'did Deac break an arm, too?'

'Yes,' said Harrington impatiently. 'An arm and a leg.'

'Anyway,' Larrabee continued reading, 'they've fitted me out with an artificial limb and I'm learning to walk on it. Once I get the hang of it, nobody will know I'm crippled...' Larrabee paused, looked at the others, and said, 'Crippled. Hmm. I've made up my mind', he continued reading, 'to go to seminary as I plan to become a Presbyterian minister. I've enrolled at Princeton beginning next summer. Meanwhile I'll get by at home as best as I can...'

Larrabee finished the letter, a passage about Thanksgiving at home and questions about the Section's experiences since he left. Putting it aside, he said, 'I always reckoned Deac would be a preacher some day.'

Harrington nodded, thinking that, if it hadn't been for losing his leg, he was the sort of man who might have accomplished just about anything. But Larrabee was right – he probably would have chosen the ministry.

Frank leaned back on his pillow and studied the letter

from Kit, postmarked Camiers. Tearing it open, a smile settled on his face as he quickly read her words. The thought of spending Christmas with her in London, meeting her family, filled him with nervous excitement, an awareness that their relationship had reached a new, more serious stage. Rereading her closing words, he decided to call on the 'colonel' at once and demand at least a weekend pass.

The other letters were from home and Elsie. In addition to her usual concerns for his safety, his mother added a plea that he look after his sister, whose decision to volunteer for France worried his parents terribly. Elsie's letter was far more interesting: a fascinating description of the work of the Harvard doctors – one of whom she referred to merely as 'Bruce' – plus a clear-eyed assessment of Kit, whom she found 'strikingly pretty' and 'upper class without a whiff of snobbishness'.

'How's your gal?' asked Borden, lying on the bed next to him.

'She's going home for Christmas,' said Harrington. 'To London. And she wants me to come see her.'

'Are you going?'

'You're darn right.'

Harrington sat in an uncomfortable chair outside the colonel's office, waiting for him to conclude an interview with a contingent of local French officials. Hearing the sound of chairs scraping beyond the door, he stood up.

'All right, then,' said McDuffie as the door opened and the Frenchmen passed out into the corridor. 'I'll look into it. *Au revoir.*' He cast an irritated look at Harrington. 'What can I do for you, young man?' he asked.

'I have a request, sir.' Harrington followed the older man into his office, a spare room with a desk and two chairs in front of a window that looked out on the colonel's parade ground. An insurance company calendar was on the corner of the tidy desk, behind which an American flag hung from a stand.

'Now what is it, ... er ...?' asked McDuffie as he squeezed into his chair.

'Harrington, sir. Frank Harrington.'

'Sit down,' commanded McDuffie. 'What is it you want, Harrington?'

'A pass, sir. During the week of Christmas.'

'What for?'

'To visit ... er ... a friend. In London.'

'I assume you're aware, Harrington,' said McDuffie, 'that our men are entitled to three days' leave after completing six months' service?'

Harrington nodded. 'Yes, sir, but I ...'

'Well? Have you done your six months?'

Harrington shifted uncomfortably. 'Not quite, sir. I started at Neuilly on July the 5th, before being sent up to Dunkirk.'

'Well, sonny, I don't know what you're here to talk about. You're obviously not eligible. Now, if you don't mind ...'

'But, sir,' said Harrington, unable to conceal his anger. 'It's only a matter of a few weeks before my six months will be up. Can't you make an exception?'

'I should say not. I've got a military outfit to look after.'

Harrington stood up. 'With all due respect, sir,' he said, 'I disagree. This is *not* a military outfit. I volunteered and I paid my own way. And for what it's worth, I've spent the past five months doing some pretty rough work up in Flanders.'

'Regulations are regulations,' growled McDuffie.

Harrington considered saying that, as he was under no obligation to the AFS, what was there to stop him from simply leaving? But he knew that would mean his expulsion from the organization, something he could never countenance. 'Thank you, sir,' he said bitterly and then turned and let himself out. Too angry to discuss the matter with his comrades, he returned to their sleeping quarters just long enough to fetch his pen, writing tablet and an envelope. He sat at an empty table in the dining room with a cup of hot cocoa, thought for a moment, and then hastily wrote:

December 12, 1915
Châlons-sur-Marne

Dear Kit,
When I opened your letter today I was overcome with happiness at the thought of seeing you in London. Right away I went to see the fellow in charge of our section to ask for a pass, but the old boy turned me down cold! This martinet plays it strictly by the book, which says I'm not eligible for a pass till the first week of January. I was so mad I almost blew a gasket. I'm sick I won't be able to come. But just as soon as I get that pass I'm planning to see you, either in Camiers or Paris, or anywhere else you specify. I miss you so much and can hardly wait to be with you.
Love,
Frank
p.s. Elsie wrote to say that she loved meeting you.

*   *   *

Seated by the table at the centre of the marquee, Kit watched as Mr Maxwell carefully arranged the rolls of cotton-wool and adhesives in the sugar boxes that served as the supply cabinet for the ward. The men were still sleeping in the semi-darkness, though it was past seven thirty. She thought back to the summer mornings, arriving for the morning shift with the sun well up in a cloudless blue sky, the shorebirds wheeling over the dunes. Finished with his supplies, Mr Maxwell hefted the demijohn from the table, to replenish it with a new batch of the Carrel and Dakin solution. Though the frantic days of July were long past, the wounded were still arriving in the ward with depressing regularity, suffering from gunshot and shrapnel for the most part, though thankfully few gas cases and no more burn victims. The technique for blood transfusions developed by the Americans was now being practised with great success on the men arriving in shock; lives were being spared that only months before would have been given up as lost, consigned to 'moribund'.

Kit slipped off her stool and quietly walked over to the table where the orderly was preparing the disinfectant solution. He turned to her with a gentle smile.

'I'll miss you, Kit,' he said. 'But you deserve to be home with your family.'

'It's only for a week.' She could scarcely believe that in the morning she would be boarding a ferry at Calais, going home. To dear, old Blighty. 'Won't you be lonely here, Mr Maxwell?' she asked. 'All alone at Christmastime?'

'No,' he said with a sad shake of his head. 'You see, over here I feel I'm closer to my boy.'

Kit patted the older man's arm. His only son had been killed in the first week of the war, what seemed such a long time ago, when the British Expeditionary Force had faced the German Army at Mons. His body had never been found.

Later, after a final day in the ward helping the Sister with the dressings, and doing what little they could to ease the suffering of a young soldier slowly dying from terrible wounds, Kit returned to her tent to pack. Walking along the duckboards beneath the leaden skies, she felt an odd sadness, as though she might never see the place again. She thought about the day Frank had met her at the canteen after wandering the grounds in the hope of seeing her, and it struck her that Nigel had never been to the hospital, not once ... In fact, he never asked about her work, as though everything she'd been through over the past year had never happened. And where was he now?

With Jane still on shift, Kit had more room to lay out her things in the cramped space of the bell-tent. She decided to pack all her clothes, to allow the maids at home to give them a thorough washing and ironing, leaving out only the dress she would wear in the morning. When she was done, she picked up the envelope from the campaign table and reread Frank's note. Despite everything he'd been through, placing himself in great danger night after night, an unpaid volunteer, he wasn't permitted a weekend pass at Christmas. She felt like sending him a cable, urging him to resign from the AFS and meet her in London. She allowed herself a daydream, imagining that they were together, that she'd quit her job as a VAD, or better, that the war was over ... What would her father think of Frank? She suspected he'd like him very much. She put aside the letter with a heavy sigh. She was still eager to see her family, but, without Frank, the prospect of going home seemed strangely depressing. She glanced up at the sound of footsteps.

Jane pushed through the tent flap and looked at Kit and the suitcase on the cot beside her. 'I can't believe you're really leaving,' she said. 'I'd give anything to be going with you.'

Kit nodded. 'Just think', she said, 'how many hundreds of thousands of British men and women will be spending Christmas in France.'

'And how many', said Jane, slumping on her cot, 'will never go home again.' She reached into her pocket for an envelope. 'I stopped at the post,' she said, handing it to Kit. 'It's from your mother.'

211

Kit quickly read the letter. After confirming the day and time of her arrival, her mother promised to send the butler – 'with your father's motorcar' – to meet her at the station. She closed with wishes for Kit's safe travel and hopes for a happy reunion over the holidays, and then, almost as an afterthought, she wrote:

> Attending Sir Victor's Christmas open house last evening, we had a nice visit with the Owens. I gathered from a remark by his mother that Nigel has been sent home, though it was all a bit vague. Perhaps he can come by for tea when you're here.

Kit stared at the words. So Nigel was in London. But home? Surely he wasn't at home…

'Is something wrong?' asked Jane.

Kit looked up. 'No,' she said quietly. 'Apparently Nigel's back in London. His mother said something about him to my parents.'

'Well, then,' said Jane encouragingly, 'I suppose that means you'll be seeing him.'

'Yes,' said Kit after a moment. 'I suppose it does.'

Waiting for the others to board the bus, Kit surveyed the encampment in the faint sunlight: the neat rows of marquees, beyond them the peaked tops of the white bell-tents, and in the distance the slate-blue water of the Channel over the dunes. For the second time she felt a sharp pang of sadness, though, as she reminded herself, she would be returning in a mere seven days. Several other VADs joined her, and they waited together for two RAMC nurses to board before mounting the steps and taking their seats. Kit spent the trip to Calais lost in reflection, gazing out the window at the rolling farmland, remembering the day with Frank, the picnic on the beach and afterward on the terrace, watching the sunset, listening to the guitar...

The quay was teeming with activity: stevedores unloading heavy wooden crates; fresh-painted army lorries rolling down the ramp from the ferry; a platoon of young soldiers in new khaki greatcoats nervously waiting for orders. Following a single blast of the ferry's horn, Kit followed the other passengers across the gangway. She stood at the railing, one hand clutching her hat in the breeze, as the dark water churned and the ship slipped its moorings and gathered way with a shudder. She stayed at the railing, snug in her heavy coat in the cold sunshine, staring at the shore until it was no more than a speck on the distant horizon.

16

Seated by the window, Kit looked out as the train pulled slowly under the roof of Charing Cross Station. The first three cars were reserved for the wounded, most of them marked BL, borne on litters from the hospital ship to the train that departed from the Folkestone docks. Shortly before their arrival in London, conductors had passed through the coaches requesting the passengers to remain seated while the wounded were taken off. When her turn finally came, Kit stood at the top of the steps and searched the platform. After a moment she waved a greeting to Burton, the family's long-time butler, standing at the back of the crowd in his uniform coat and hat.

'Hullo, Miss Stanley,' he said with a slight bow as he walked up to her. 'Long day?'

'Hullo, Burton. Yes, long enough. We left Calais at nine this morning.'

After retrieving her suitcase, the butler started for the terminal with Kit at his side. 'The motorcar's parked in front,' he said. 'Welcome home.'

'Thank you, Burton. It's wonderful to be back.'

Kit surveyed the busy station, expecting to find some noticeable change in the populace after so many months of war. Instead, things appeared to be just as she remembered them: newsboys hawking their papers, flower girls at the stalls, businessmen in Derbies hurrying to their trains. The scene outside the station, however, revealed a vastly changed London, as a large crowd watched the queue of RAMC ambulances at the curb, waiting to transport the wounded

214

to St Bart's, the Royal Chelsea and the other metropolitan hospitals. Kit noticed the expression on the faces pressed against the railings; sombre, respectful, like the crowd attending the funeral of some beloved public figure. Burton seemed to avoid the ambulances in his hurry to get to the car, and it occurred to Kit that his own son, a boy several years younger than she, might well be in the service. Once they were on their way, with Kit seated in the back of the large black sedan, she leaned forward and said, 'Burton ... has Freddie enlisted?'

'Yes, ma'am.' He made eye contact in the rear-view mirror. 'He's with the army in Flanders. Near a town called Popper-ringy.'

Poperinge, thought Kit. The supply depot outside Ypres. She could visualize the name on Nigel's letters from last summer. She gazed out the windows at the streets and pavements of central London, scarcely able to believe that she was back after fourteen months away. Her heart skipped a beat when Burton turned onto the Old Brompton Road and drove past the South Kensington station. Home. She was almost home.

Burton brought the car to a stop in front of a fashionable, four-storey townhouse – No. 50 Onslow Gardens – midway down a long row of identical residences. He quickly climbed out and walked around to open the door for Kit. By the time she reached the front entrance, with Burton walking behind with her luggage, two women in matching black uniforms with white aprons and caps were standing in the threshold.

'Oh, Miss Stanley,' said Maggie, the housekeeper, with a wide smile, clapping her hands together. 'Home at last.'

'Maggie,' said Kit, leaning over to give her an embrace.

Kit could see her younger sisters waiting expectantly in the front hall. She stepped inside and gave each of them a hug. 'Hullo, Bess,' said Kit to her nineteen-year-old sister, a tall girl with dark-brown hair. 'You're looking well. And my goodness, Annie,' she said, turning to her youngest sister, a girl of sixteen, 'you've grown a foot.'

'Yes, I suppose,' said the girl awkwardly, turning to Bess with a nervous giggle.

'Let's get you upstairs, Miss Stanley,' said Maggie. 'Tea's being served. Brenda,' she added to the parlour-maid, 'help with the missus' coat.

'Let's have tea,' said Kit to her sisters. 'I'm famished.'

She started up the stairs, the banister of which was decorated with Christmas garlands. At the top of the stairs, entering the spacious living room, Kit was conscious of the familiar smells of home, as well as the pine scent of the Christmas tree in the corner and the inviting aroma of freshly baked shortbread. As she entered the room, her father appeared from the hallway, smiled broadly, and hurried over to embrace her.

'Darling daughter,' he said, holding her shoulders and looking in her eyes. 'I can't believe you're really home.'

'Yes, Daddy. I'm so thankful.' Kit turned to see her mother standing in the arched entrance to the dining room. 'Hullo, Mother,' she said with a smile.

Mrs Stanley, a petite woman in her forties whose hair had gone completely grey, stood with her hands folded in front of her, fighting back tears.

'Kit,' she managed to say at last. 'Thank God.'

The efficient Maggie appeared from the kitchen with a tea service, which she carefully placed on the sideboard. The parlour-maid, Brenda, followed with a platter of shortbread, scones, butter and jam.

'Anything else, ma'am?' asked Maggie.

'No, that will be all,' replied Mrs Stanley, recovering her composure in front of the servants.

'Let's take our tea by the fire,' suggested Kit's father.

*

216

Seated in a wingchair with her second cup of tea, and a plate of cakes on the table beside her, Kit gazed at the tall Christmas tree in the corner, decorated with strands of holly and her grandmother's Victorian ornaments. The light outside the windows was fading to dusk as her father poked the logs on the andirons. In their conversation they'd so far avoided mention of Kit's experiences in France, and she could almost imagine herself back in the innocent times before the war, making small talk with her parents over tea. Satisfied with the brightly burning fire, her father put aside the poker, straightened his jacket and looked at Kit.

'I promised your mother I wouldn't say it,' he said, 'but I'm afraid I can't help myself.'

'What, Father?' said Kit, putting down her teacup.

'I really wish you would stay, Kit,' he said. 'You've done your part...'

'Stay home?'

'Oh, George,' said Kit's mother. 'Must we?'

'It's all right, Mother,' said Kit. 'It's really out of the question, Daddy. It was difficult enough to arrange a week's leave.'

'But surely you could find something useful to do here.'

'You've no idea how badly needed I am in France.' Kit couldn't help thinking that no one at home seemed to understand how terrible things were on the other side of the Channel. 'The hospitals are quite overwhelmed. Ours alone has over a thousand beds, and believe me, all of them taken – the fighting in the Salient has been terrible, with poison gas, liquid fire...'

'Bess,' said Kit's mother, 'Annie. Go to your rooms and finish wrapping your presents.'

'But Mother...' said Bess.

'Go.'

Once her sisters were gone, Kit looked earnestly at her

father and said, 'I can't possibly stay, as much as I would love to be with you both, not to mention the creature comforts. I'm one of the most experienced nurses – volunteer, that is – at our hospital. And I don't mind saying that I'm rather proud of what I've learned to do.'

Her father gave Kit a loving look. 'We're proud of you too,' he said. 'Very proud. But it would mean so much to your mother...'

'Please, George,' said Mrs Stanley with a pained expression.

'All right,' he said. 'Let's not discuss it further. Another cup of tea?' he asked with a smile.

*   *   *

Frank Harrington sat on the side of his bed and bent over to tie his bootlaces. He was wearing his one good suit, a dark grey, worsted three-piece from the men's store in Cambridge, and had done his best to knot his tie without the help of a mirror – one of the oddities of being housed in a convent.

'You're sure you won't get in trouble?' asked Henry Borden, reclining on his bed.

'For what?' said Harrington. 'The colonel declared Christmas a holiday for the entire section. I'm merely taking an excursion.'

'But if he found out you'd gone to Paris...'

'Don't worry, Henry. I'll be back by the appointed hour. Besides, how's the old boy going to know?' He jumped up and grabbed his coat, hat, and a small parcel from the end of the bed. '*Au revoir,*' he said with a smile.

As it was Christmas morning, he was almost alone on the train. Harrington dozed briefly and then awoke as the train passed into the suburbs of Paris. Staring at the empty streets of the old city, he thought about his two-storey clapboard on Charles Street in Quincy and imagined his mother and father sitting down to Christmas dinner. The idea of travelling alone to Paris on Christmas morning struck him as strangely depressing. Thank goodness he had Elsie to spend the day with. He glanced up as an elderly woman, leaning heavily on her cane, made her way down the aisle, pausing to give him a look of sympathy or reproach, he couldn't say which.

His watch showed ten minutes before noon when the train slowly pulled into the rail-yard at the Gare de l'Est, almost exactly one hour after departing Rheims. When the train rumbled to a stop, he donned his coat and hat, slipped the parcel in his pocket, and hurried out onto the platform. Apart from the conductors stepping down from their cars, the platform was virtually deserted. As he started for the Métro, he thought back to the day he met Kit at the Gare du Nord amid the crush of people, all of them at home now, he supposed, enjoying Christmas with their loved ones.

The plan was to meet at one o'clock at one of Paris's grand hotels, where, they presumed, a fine repast would be available in the dining room. In a brief note to Elsie, Frank suggested the Plaza Athénée, though he knew it only by reputation. According to his pocket map, it was located in the fashionable eighth arrondissement several blocks from the Champs-Elysées. As he started down the stairs to the Métro station he noticed another of the war bond posters, the same half-crazed look in the eyes of the *poilu* shouting to his comrades.

The only other passengers in the rocking subway were two men of indeterminate age, with long matted hair and beards, reeking of alcohol, and slumped in their seats in rags. Sleeping it off, thought Frank as he impatiently waited for his stop, holding a hand to his face.

The skies were overcast, threatening snow, when he emerged from the Métro at the Champs-Elysées. With virtually no traffic, he crossed the wide boulevard without difficulty, located the avenue Montaigne and began walking toward the river. Within five minutes he entered the elaborate lobby of the newly built hotel, ablaze in light from the crystal chandeliers and, to his relief, crowded with women wearing fancy hats and silk and taffeta gowns, a festive holiday atmosphere in spite of the war.

After checking his hat and coat, he took a turn around the salon, admiring the Gobelin tapestries as he listened to a string quartet in the corner, playing Christmas carols. After a while he sat at one of the overstuffed sofas by a large ormolu clock whose minute hand showed a quarter past the hour. Just when he began to think Elsie wasn't coming, there was a slight commotion near the entrance, and the crowd parted for a tall American nurse, wearing her dark-blue uniform and cape and matching velour fedora.

Frank rose from the sofa with a smile. 'Over here, Els,' he called with a wave as she searched the crowded room. He met her halfway with a brief embrace.

'Merry Christmas,' she said with a happy smile.

'Don't you look swell,' he said, giving her a closer look.

'My,' said Elsie, looking around her, 'this is quite a place.'

'Did you have any trouble finding it?'

'No. I took a taxi from the station.'

'Ready for lunch? Let's check your coat and then see if we can get a table in the dining room.'

'*Bonjour*,' said the *maître d'* at the entrance to the large, elegant room. He smiled at Elsie and added, '*Ah, les États-Unis.*'

'Do you have a table for two?' asked Frank in French.

After a brief discussion, which Elsie was unable to follow, and a discreet exchange of franc notes, the *maître d'* said, '*Suivez-moi, Monsieur, Mademoiselle, s'il vous plaît*,' and began walking briskly toward a small table on the far side of the room. Once they were seated with complimentary champagne, Frank raised his glass and proposed a toast – to Christmas, Paris and an Allied victory.

'Do you really think the Allies are winning?' asked Elsie. Frank shook his head. 'No,' he said. 'I think both sides are losing. It's a question of who can hold out the longest.'

A waiter appeared at the table and explained the elaborate menu and less expensive fixed price option. 'What do you think?' said Frank to Elsie. 'The fixed price?' He turned to the waiter and said, '*Le prix fixe, pour deux. Et nous voudrions une bouteille de vin rouge, du Bourgogne.*'

On her first visit to Paris, and with a limited knowledge of French, Elsie was content to rely on her older brother. After the soup was served and the wine poured, Frank produced his parcel and handed it across the table. 'Merry Christmas, sis,' he said.

'You shouldn't have.' She tore off the gift wrap and held up a small velvet case. Opening it, she removed a hand-painted Limoges pillbox. 'It's beautiful,' she said with obvious pleasure. 'Thank you, Frank. I feel rotten for not getting you something.'

'You haven't exactly had time for shopping. Anyhow, I'm glad you like it.'

By the time dessert was served, cherries jubilee with rich vanilla ice cream, Frank had entertained Elsie with an rambling account of his section's chafing under the rigid authority of 'Colonel' McDuffie, and both shared reminiscences of Christmases past that verged on the maudlin.

'What you haven't told me,' said Elsie as she sipped her

demitasse of coffee, 'is how things are between you and your girl.'

'Did you like her?'

'Very much.' Elsie hesitated and then said, 'I think she's in love with you, Frank.'

'She invited me to visit her in London, to meet her folks, but I couldn't get a pass. I'm afraid I've fallen for her, Els. Head over heels.'

'I wonder what Mom and Dad will think.'

'I can't worry about that now. With the war, who knows what crazy things can happen? Just look at us, Els ... Christmas lunch at the Plaza Athénée.'

Elsie nodded. 'There's something else I should tell you,' she said, leaning toward him. Frank rested his chin on his hands and looked at her expectantly. 'You remember meeting Dr Carey?' she said. 'At the hospital?'

'Yes. One of the Harvard fellows.'

'Bruce Carey,' said Elsie. 'He's a wonderful doctor and, to be honest, I've been seeing him.'

'Seeing him?' repeated Frank. 'You mean...'

'Yes, going out. A lot. I like him very much.'

'Well, well,' said Frank with a smile. 'The Harrington kids go to France, and the next thing you know...'

Elsie blushed. 'I'd like you to get to know him, Frank,' she said.

He glanced at his watch and then gestured to a nearby waiter for the check. 'In time,' he said, 'I'm sure I will. But we'd better be on our way, or we're liable to miss our trains.'

*   *   *

Looking forward to being home, Kit had imagined sleeping late, luxuriating on linen under a down comforter, waited on hand and foot by the domestic staff, who would draw her bath, wash and iron her clothes ... But now, lying

222

awake on Christmas morning before sunrise, she reflected that she was distinctly uncomfortable. After months of rising before dawn, she couldn't sleep in, and she could show the upstairs maid a thing or two about cleaning floors and making up beds.

She'd spent Christmas Eve shopping for gifts in Knightsbridge, attending a party and, afterward, church services with her family. The mood in the packed Holy Trinity Church was sorrowful, notwithstanding the pine and holly garlands and Christmas anthems, with so many in the congregation separated from sons in France; some of them, clad in black, separated forever.

On the pavements, despite the young men in uniform, life in London seemed to Kit strangely unaltered, the same holiday decorations in the shop windows and houses, advertisements on the sides of the buses for the same soaps and tooth powder, the same sooty fog in the dank air ... Curled up in a chair in her flannel robe, she admitted that she longed to be back in France, where she was needed, where hopefully she could be with Frank.

Seated at her usual place at the table, Kit observed that the family adhered to the Christmas Day rituals she remembered from her earliest childhood: the opening of gifts by the tree followed by a sumptuous dinner, her father, at the head of the table, carving the roast goose, while her mother sat stiffly opposite him. Maggie, in a black silk dress trimmed in lace, supervised the serving of the soup as Burton stood to the side, ready to pour the claret from a crystal decanter. Making the atmosphere even less festive was the annoyance Bess displayed toward Annie, the result of some perceived slight while opening the gifts. Requiring Burton and Maggie and the other servants to work on Christmas Day struck Kit as cruel, though she'd probably never given it a thought in years past. She dutifully bowed for her father's mumbled blessing and then started on the lobster bisque.

Waiting for the servants to clear the table in advance of the traditional dessert – plum pudding with hard sauce – Mrs Stanley dabbed at her lips with her napkin and then said, 'Kit ... where do things stand between you and Nigel?'

Her relationship with Nigel had only been casually mentioned during the visit, and Kit had avoided asking about him, unsure how she would answer the inevitable probing questions.

'Why,' said Kit, noticing that her sisters were watching her with intense interest, 'I'm not sure what you mean. I've seen Nigel, of course, from time to time...'

'Your mother is asking,' said Kit's father with a pleasant smile, 'whether you and Nigel have made any plans?'

Kit looked down, knotting her napkin in her lap, aware that Maggie had paused at the entrance to the dining room. 'We've decided *not* to make plans,' Kit said after a moment, looking from her mother to her father. 'That is, I've decided. Nigel proposed marriage, and I, well ... I told him no.' This elicited a small gasp from Annie.

'But, Kit,' said Mrs Stanley, 'I don't understand. I thought that you and Nigel were, well...'

'I'm not in love with him, Mother. After being in France all this time, I've come to see things more clearly. Nigel's not right for me. And besides, there's someone else.'

'Someone else?' said Kit's father with a perplexed expression.

'Yes. I invited him to come for a visit over Christmas but he wasn't able to arrange leave.'

'To visit?' said Mrs Stanley incredulously. 'Visit *here*?'

'He's not coming, Mother,' said Kit with growing asperity. 'Not now, at any rate.'

'And who is this person?' asked Kit's father.

'His name is Frank Harrington.' She looked again from her mother to her father. 'And I care for him very much. He's an American, from Massachusetts. And he's a volunteer ambulance driver.'

'Good heavens,' muttered Kit's father.

'Maggie!' said Mrs Stanley sharply. 'You may instruct Louisa to serve the pudding.'

Kit picked at her dessert, conscious of the relentless stares of her family. After a while, she put down her fork and turned to her mother. 'I'm worried about Nigel,' she said. 'I fear he's not well.'

Mrs Stanley's eyebrows rose imperceptibly. 'I understood his mother to say', she said, 'that he's home. I presumed on leave. She said nothing about him being unwell.'

'I shall call on her tomorrow,' said Kit. 'To enquire after him.'

Mrs Stanley sighed. 'Fine,' she said. 'You should do just that.'

Kit stood under an umbrella in the pouring rain outside the elegant redbrick townhouse. She struggled with the impulse to turn away and walk the few blocks back to her home. What if he was there, perfectly well, merely home on leave as her mother believed? It would be terribly awkward ... But she couldn't believe that Nigel would have returned home without at least sending her a cable. She'd considered telephoning, but decided it would be easier simply to drop in. Taking a deep breath, she rang the doorbell.

After a few moments a maid appeared at the door, a girl of her own age in a black dress and snug-fitting cap. 'May I help you?' she asked in an East End accent.

'Yes,' said Kit. 'I'm Kit Stanley. Is Mrs Owen in?'

'One moment.' She partially closed the door, leaving Kit standing in the rain. The maid returned shortly and held the door open. 'Mrs Owen says to join her in the drawing room,' she said. 'I'll take your things.'

Mrs Owen greeted Kit with a wan smile, standing with her hands on the back of a chair. 'Hullo, dear,' she said. 'How nice of you to come. May I offer you tea?'

'No, thanks, Mrs Owen. I can stay only a few minutes.'

'Your mother was so pleased you were coming home; she was hoping you might avoid going back.'

'Yes, well, I'm here another day or so. Then it's back to the hospital in France.'

'Won't you sit?'

Kit awkwardly glanced around the cluttered room and selected a place on the sofa next to a sleeping cat. Mrs Owen drew up a chair beside her.

'I've come to ask about Nigel,' Kit began. Mrs Owen's face was a blank mask. 'I understand he's ... here, in London.'

'Yes,' said Mrs Owen after a slight pause. 'Yes, that's right.'

'Well, I've been worried about him as he hadn't responded to my last letter. And when I learned he was admitted to hospital...'

All at once the older woman's face crumpled, and she sat holding her forehead in one hand, eyes shut tight. 'Oh my dear child,' she murmured. 'I'm so sorry.'

'But, Mrs Owen,' said Kit. 'Why should you be sorry?'

Looking up, Nigel's mother wiped away her tears and hoarsely said, 'I should have called, or at least written, but I couldn't bring myself to do it. I didn't know what to say?'

'What is it? What's wrong?'

'He's very ill ... not physically. But very ill.'

'I understand.' Kit made eye contact.

Despite her tears, Mrs Owen seemed to brighten. 'Do you suppose', asked Kit, 'that I could see him? Perhaps it would help.'

Mrs Owen nodded. 'He's at Queen's Square clinic, in Bloomsbury. I don't know if they'll let you see him. Ask for Dr Robertson. Dr David Robertson.'

'I can remember,' said Kit. 'I'll go in the morning.'

'Oh, dear, thank you. Anything you could do would mean so much.'

17

Dr David Robertson stood at the window in his small, fourth-floor office, watching the cold rain beading the glass. An image of snow-clad highlands beneath a bowl of blue sky came to mind, compounding his melancholy, with his wife and two young children away for the Christmas holiday with family in Scotland. Robertson, a neurologist in his mid-thirties, had only been at the London clinic for a short while, having transferred from an asylum outside Edinburgh where a large number of shell-shock cases were being treated. He turned at the sound of a tap on the door and slipped a slender gold watch from his fob pocket.

'Yes,' he said. 'Come in.'

A thin young man, wearing a rumpled sweater over his khakis, opened the door and peered in. 'Good morning, Doctor,' he said with a diffident smile. 'Am I early?'

'Right on time,' said Robertson. He briefly studied Nigel Owen's appearance, noting the day's growth of beard and his carelessly combed hair. 'Please, sit down, Owen,' said Robertson as he slumped into his chair. 'Would you care for tea?'

Nigel merely shook his head and lowered himself into one of the armchairs facing the desk. Robertson flipped through the pages of Owen's file. It was only their third interview. Before Robertson's arrival, Owen had been undergoing treatment by another RAMC physician whose experimental methods Robertson regarded as barbaric.

'Now, then,' said Robertson, 'let's go over this from the beginning, shall we?' Owen nodded, avoiding eye contact. 'You were brought into the Clearing Station,' said Robertson, 'on the afternoon of November 19th.' Owen shrugged. 'And admitted at No. 18 General Hospital on the 20th.' Robertson leaned back and steepled his fingertips. 'What can you recall of the events leading up to your ... er ... episode?'

Nigel stared at the carpet, rubbing his hands together. Looking up, he said, 'May I smoke?' Robertson slid an ashtray across the desk and watched as Nigel lit a cigarette with trembling hands. Inhaling deeply, Nigel said, 'I was in the dugout. It w-was a quiet afternoon. I-I was r-reading ... yes, that's it.' He hesitated, and Robertson gave him an encouraging look. 'The l-lieutenant reported,' Nigel continued, 'we were being r-relieved. Sixteen hundred hours,' he said in almost a whisper.

'What did you say?' said Robertson, leaning forward.

'The time,' said Nigel apologetically. He swallowed and took another drag. 'I d-don't recall anything b-beyond that.' He looked at Robertson, who was smoothing the front of his heather-mixture jacket.

'Still having trouble sleeping?' asked the doctor.

Nigel nodded and then said, 'It w-would help if M-McDonald were moved. He makes a frightful lot of n-noise.'

'Yes, well, and he says the same of you, Owen. I'm afraid you'll have to make the best of it.' They sat in silence for a few moments and then Robertson said, 'I want you to keep that notebook at your bedside. And when these ... bad dreams occur, record the details as soon as you wake. Just switch on the lamp and write them down, while they're fresh on your mind. Will you do that for me, Owen?' asked Robertson, adopting a paternal tone.

Nigel nodded, staring at his lap.

'And then we'll talk about them,' said Robertson. He abruptly rose. 'That's all for now, Captain. Try to rest.'

Half an hour after seeing Owen, Robertson was interrupted by the telephone. He answered it and listened with curiosity to the receptionist's explanation. 'Yes,' he said, 'send her up.'

After a few minutes, the knob turned and Kit, wearing a dark-green dress and matching hat, stood in the doorway. 'Dr Robertson?' she said.

Robertson stood up. 'Yes, ah, Miss Stanley. Please come in.' He motioned to one of the chairs.

Kit sat down and smiled pleasantly. She was surprised to find the doctor in civilian clothes, as he held the rank of major in the RAMC. 'Thank you for seeing me,' she said.

'It's Kit, isn't it?'

'Why, yes.'

'Not Kitty?'

'No.'

'It's in Owen's file,' he explained, tapping the folder on his desk. He extracted a report and read aloud: 'Patient often refers to "Kit" during nocturnal outcries. Apparent reference to former fiancée.' Kit winced slightly, causing Robertson to ask, 'Were you engaged to Owen?'

'No,' she quickly replied. 'Though we were very close. *Are*, I should say.'

'I see. Is there some reason, Miss Stanley, why you haven't been by to visit Captain Owen before now?'

'I only learned yesterday that he was here. I've just returned from France.'

'And what...'

'I'm a VAD. At No. 4 General Hospital, outside Camiers. I've been trying to find out what happened to Nigel since my letters went unanswered.' Robertson nodded but remained silent. 'Well, Doctor,' she said, leaning forward in her chair. 'How is he?'

'Miss Stanley,' said Robertson, 'as you're a VAD, serving in France, you may have had some experience with neurasthenia...'

'Shell shock,' she interrupted. 'How bad is it?'

'He was admitted following a delusional episode. The event itself is buried deeply in his unconscious. He suffers from recurring nightmares and general nervous collapse.'

'Is he making progress?'

'Very little, I'm afraid, thus far. I've only recently begun seeing him.'

'May I? See him, that is?'

'I wonder whether your seeing him might do more harm than good. It seems that his recollection of you, even in his dreams, is very troubling to him.'

Kit considered this for a moment. 'I think it might be helpful,' she said, 'if I were able to tell him that ... that I still care about him very much.'

'Perhaps.'

'And as I have only a few days before returning to France...'

'All right,' said Robertson. 'But only for a brief visit. If it appears to be too painful for him, then...'

'I understand. Thank you, Doctor.'

Kit accompanied an RAMC nurse down a brightly lit corridor. 'Captain Owen is in the library,' said the nurse. 'I'll let him know you're here.'

'Thank you.' They stopped outside double doors.

'He may not wish to see you,' cautioned the nurse. 'And if he does, the doctor instructed me to remain nearby.' She left Kit in the corridor, but shortly returned and beckoned to Kit as she held open the door. 'He seemed embarrassed to see you,' she said quietly, 'as he hasn't washed this morning, but I assured him it's all right.' Kit followed the Sister inside the small, windowless library, where several men were seated at tables among the bookshelves. 'There's an alcove at the back,' said the nurse, pointing. 'Where you'll have some privacy.'

Nigel stood by a table, his fingertips lightly touching its surface, in a corner room with a window overlooking a courtyard. The first thing Kit noticed was the grid of steel bars over the window. Nigel stared at her with a nervous expression, like a guilty child awaiting punishment. With his pale complexion and hollow cheeks, he seemed inches shorter and many pounds lighter than when she'd last seen him.

'Oh, Nigel,' she said, rushing up to embrace him. Before she could do so, he took her hand and briefly shook it.

'Hullo,' he said. 'I-I wasn't expecting you.' They stood awkwardly facing each other.

'I came as soon as I learned you were here. I've been desperate to find out what happened.'

'Yes, well,' he said, running a hand through his unkempt hair, 'it's a b-bit of a muddle.' He abruptly sat down, and she pulled up a chair next to him. The nurse was watching them from a discreet distance. 'How h-have you been?' he asked.

She bit her lower lip, aware that he was avoiding her eyes. 'I'm fine,' she said. 'I've just now come home, on leave for Christmas.'

'Christmas? Oh, yes ... Christmas.'

'Nigel,' said Kit softly, leaning toward him, 'are they treating you well here? You've lost weight.'

He furrowed his brow and rubbed the stubble of beard on his chin, seeming to weigh his response. 'All right, I s-suppose,' he said after a moment.

232

'I feel terrible about what happened,' she said, impulsively taking his hand and giving it a gentle squeeze. 'I'm so sorry.'

For the first time he raised his eyes to hers and gave her an inquisitive look. 'W-Why should y-you feel sorry?' he asked, releasing her hand.

Kit looked away, shocked by the change in his appearance, his voice, his demeanour. Fighting back tears, she said, 'Because of that day in Boulogne, what I said.'

He blinked. 'Boulogne,' he repeated. 'Sorry, I...'

'Oh, Nigel, I've been so worried. I want you to know...' She paused and looked him in the eyes. 'I want you to know that I care a great deal about you.'

He nodded, a vacant look in his eyes. The nurse stepped forward and said, 'I'm sorry, Miss Stanley, but I'm afraid it's time.'

'All right,' she said, rising from her chair. 'Goodbye, Nigel,' she murmured. 'Please get well, darling. I'll write.'

He looked from the unsmiling Sister to Kit. 'Thank y-you for c-coming,' he said. 'W-Will you be b-back?'

Kit forced herself to smile, holding back her tears. She nodded and said, 'Of course.'

A young lieutenant in a new uniform surrendered his seat in the crowded subway to Kit. Something about his confident smile made her think of Nigel as she'd seen him last summer; the sharp crease of his trousers, his neatly trimmed moustache, and the swagger in his step in his finely polished boots. She compared the image to the broken man in the grim room with bars across the window, unshaven, hands trembling, stammering, unable to look at her. She'd witnessed what war could do to men's bodies, the gaping, suppurating shrapnel wounds, the swollen, livid faces of the chlorine victims, but my God, what it could do to a man's mind – his soul! She hung her head, overwhelmed with the feeling that somehow it was her fault.

The familiar sights of South Kensington helped to restore order and calm to her jumbled thoughts. Obviously, Nigel had experienced some devastating trauma in the trenches, something that unhinged his mind, having nothing to do with her decision to decline his marriage proposal. What had the doctor called it? A delusional episode, buried in his unconscious ... Exiting the Tube station, she opened her umbrella, crossed the busy street and started down the pavement in the steady rain. Though it wasn't her fault, she reasoned, surely there was something she could do to help him. And yet the Scottish doctor seemed to think that seeing her might actually be harmful to his recovery. By the time she reached the front steps of the townhouse, the rain had soaked her boots and her hands were stinging from the cold.

After a long soak in the claw-foot tub, Kit dressed and went down to tea. Her mother was standing by the tall drawing-room windows, looking down on the rectangle of dark green bordered by graceful elms and oaks, whose bare boughs were black with rain.

'There you are darling,' said Mrs Stanley, turning around. 'Just in time for tea.' She picked up a small silver bell and gave it a ring.

The upstairs maid entered with a large tray, which she lowered onto a butler's table before the sofa.

'Shall I pour, ma'am?' she asked.

'Of course.'

Kit took her tea and walked over to the lumps of glowing coal hissing on the grate, radiating warmth.

'In the morning,' said Mrs Stanley, seated on the sofa, 'you could go with me to the dressmaker's. You've such a

good eye for colour, and you've seen the latest Paris fashions.'
Kit nodded absently, sipping her tea. 'And then we'll go
together to the luncheon,' her mother continued cheerfully.
'You recall the luncheon honouring Emily Stanhope on her
engagement? At the Savoy. Perhaps Nigel would care to
come with us. You have seen Nigel, haven't you, my dear?'
'Nigel?' Kit put her cup aside. 'Yes, well, I . . .' She paused
at the sound of the telephone in the hall. They listened
as Burton answered it and then appeared in the doorway.
'Yes, who is it?' asked Mrs Stanley.
'A Dr Robertson, at Queen's Square clinic,' replied
Burton. 'He wishes to speak with Miss Kit.'
'How peculiar,' commented Mrs Stanley as Kit followed
the butler from the room.

'Hullo, Miss Stanley,' said Dr Robertson in a far friendlier
tone than earlier. He leaned back in his chair and visualized
her pretty face. 'I was wondering whether you might drop
by in the morning. Are you in London a bit longer?'
'I'm returning to France on the 29th,' she said.'
'I see. I'd like to talk with you about Captain Owen.
Could you be here at ten?'
'Yes,' she replied without hesitation. Hanging up, she
returned to the drawing room, wondering how the doctor
knew where to telephone her and why his tone had abruptly
changed.
'What it is, darling?' asked Mrs Stanley with a troubled
expression.
Kit walked over and placed a hand on her mother's arm.
'It's about Nigel,' she said. 'That was the doctor who's
seeing him.'
'Nigel? The doctor . . .'
'Yes, mother, he's at a clinic in Bloomsbury, undergoing
treatment.'

'Oh, my. Why wouldn't his mother have said something . . .'

'He's not wounded. Mother – let's sit.' Once they were next to one another on the sofa, Kit said, 'Nigel is not . . . well, he's not right in his mind. He's suffering from what's called neurasthenia, or nervous collapse. The more common term is shell shock.'

'How dreadful,' said Mrs Stanley. 'His poor parents.'

'It's a growing problem among our troops,' said Kit. 'It has nothing to do with bravery or cowardice. It's just that they've endured so many horrors in the trenches.' She thought back to the MO's explanation. 'At any rate, Nigel's been sent here for treatment. I saw him this morning, Mother. He's, well . . .' She fought back tears, unable to go on.

'Dear me,' said Mrs Stanley.

'The doctor telephoned to ask me to come by in the morning. I won't be able to go with you to the dressmaker.'

'Fine, darling,' said Mrs Stanley, patting Kit's arm. 'Do what you must to help poor Nigel.'

'Good of you to come, Miss Stanley.' Dr Robertson smiled pleasantly.

Kit noticed that he'd traded his heather-mixture for a Shetland tweed and school tie, which gave him an informal, almost sporting, appearance, foreign to all her experience with the RAMC.

'I'm afraid I misjudged you,' he continued. Robertson paused and reached into his pocket for a tobacco pouch and began filling his pipe. 'You were correct in thinking that seeing Owen might be helpful. He seemed to take comfort from your assurance that you still care for him.' He struck a match and cupped it over the bowl of his pipe. 'You *do* still care for him?' he asked.

Over a year in an RAMC hospital had taught Kit what

to expect from certain MOs. 'I do,' she replied, 'though frankly, Doctor, my feelings are not your concern.'

'At any rate, he seemed quite relieved. And by your promise to come back.'

'I intend to, before leaving. With your permission.'

'Owen actually passed a quiet night last evening.' Robertson sucked on the pipe and exhaled a cloud of aromatic smoke.

'I'm pleased to hear it,' said Kit, 'but I wonder what it is you wished to see me about?'

Robertson gave her another pleasant smile. 'Miss Stanley,' he said. 'I believe it would benefit Captain Owen greatly if he could continue seeing you. Your home is here, in London, is it not?'

'Why, yes. But I'm leaving on Saturday.'

'Would you be willing to consider ... extending your stay?'

'I'm needed badly at my hospital in France...'

'You may not appreciate it, but we're facing quite a nursing shortage of our own. You're aware, of course, that the most seriously wounded men are sent here for treatment, in our London hospitals.'

'Of course.'

'An old colleague of mine happens to be Chief of Surgery at Brompton Hospital.'

'Just round the corner from my home in South Kensington,' said Kit. 'Doctor ... what are you suggesting?'

'I'm sure they'd be pleased to take on a VAD with over a year's experience in France. As you say, it's convenient, and you would have time to see Captain Owen on a regular basis. I have a hunch it might be just the thing to get him on the road to recovery.'

Kit shook her head. 'I don't know,' she said. 'I'll have to think about it.'

'Fine,' said Robertson. 'I'll call my colleague at Brompton

and confirm they have a place. You have my number. I'll await your answer.'

By the time she reached home, Kit had made up her mind to tell Dr Robertson no. As sorry as she felt for Nigel, she couldn't see how his recovery depended on her remaining in London, sacrificing everything she had in France. What he needed was professional attention and rest. Arriving at the townhouse, she promptly went upstairs and placed the telephone call.

'I see,' said Dr Robertson. 'I wish you'd reconsider. I spoke with Dr Haselton at Brompton, who expressed great interest in having you join his staff.'

'I'm sorry,' said Kit. 'I appreciate the offer, but I believe I'm needed more in France. I do plan on seeing Nigel, of course, before leaving.'

'That would be fine. Mornings are best. Goodbye, Miss Stanley.'

Kit studied the array of garments neatly laid out on the counterpane. Her clothing, washed, ironed and folded, ready to be packed for the return journey. The week of indulgence had been welcome, but she was ready to return to the spartan lifestyle at No. 4 General Hospital. And, she considered with nervous excitement, in a matter of days it would be January, and Frank would have his three-day pass. The Channel coast was so dreary in winter, but she doubted the Sisters would grant her permission to meet him in Paris. As she began carefully placing her things in her suitcase, she was conscious of someone behind her and looked up to see her mother standing in the doorway. Kit could see that her rouged cheeks were streaked with tears.

'Oh, Kit,' said Mrs Stanley. 'I can't believe you're leaving so soon.'

'I haven't any choice.'

'Yes, dear, I know.' Mrs Stanley walked in and sat on the end of the bed. 'I've just been on the telephone with Clementine,' she said with a sigh. 'She's beside herself with worry about Winston. They've taken away his brigade and given him an infantry battalion. He's being sent into the trenches,' she added melodramatically.

'I'm afraid,' said Kit, 'the war is going to last a long time. That's why we all must put our duty ahead of personal considerations.' Kit thought about seeing Frank and wondered whether she was being honest with her mother, let alone herself. She glanced at the clock on the dresser and said, 'I'd better be off. I'll finish packing when I return.'

It was her third trip to Bloomsbury in as many days, riding on the overcrowded Underground, walking along the pavements in the cold rain past depressing shop fronts still displaying their Christmas decorations. At least in the morning, she consoled herself, she'd be on the ferry to Calais. The same RAMC nurse who'd escorted her to the library met her on the third floor of the redbrick-and-limestone building.

'We've been expecting you,' said the nurse in a somewhat friendlier tone. 'Captain Owen is in his room.' She stopped outside a door midway down the corridor. There was a small glass window, through which Kit could see Nigel reclining on his bed, smoking. The nurse reached for the handle and opened the door.

'Good morning, Nigel,' said Kit as the door closed behind her, surprised that she was permitted to see him in private. 'Did you sleep well last night?'

Nigel's hair was neatly combed and, freshly shaved, he

looked much more like his old self. 'B-better,' he said, avoiding her eyes. He took a deep drag on his cigarette.

Kit looked around the small, bare room with two iron beds painted white. She sat down in the single chair at the foot of Nigel's bed. 'Well,' she said, folding her hands in her lap, 'how long do you think you'll be staying here?'

'You can't leave without ap-pearing before the Board. The Board must declare you fit for d-duty.'

'I see,' said Kit with a slight smile. 'I'm sure you need rest.'

'Rest?' he said with something like a laugh. 'You don't g-get much rest around here what w-with all the loonies. This fellow' – he pointed to the empty bed – 'is up screaming h-half the night.'

Kit couldn't think what to say. Her training taught her to trust in the judgement of the MOs, but her instincts told her that something was wrong with this place. 'Dr Robertson seems a nice enough man,' she suggested, deciding to steer the conversation toward Nigel's treatment. 'I gather he's recently come here from Edinburgh.'

'B-bloody Jock,' said Nigel with an unexpected smile.

'Yes,' said Kit. 'Yes, he is...'

'H-he's been n-nice to me, s-so far, that is.' He reached over to the bedside table and put out his cigarette in a cheap ashtray filled with butts.

'Have they treated you decently here?'

For the first time Nigel raised his eyes to look at her. They immediately brimmed with tears. He seemed incapable of speech, sitting dumbly while tears streamed down his cheeks.

'Oh, Nigel,' said Kit. 'What is it?'

'T-they ... they sh-sh-shocked m-me.' He spoke in a voice so low she could barely make it out.

'Shocked you?'

'Y-yes. Electrical sh-shock.'

'My God,' she said, rising from her chair. 'What on earth for?'

'To m-make me remember what h-happened.' His shoulders jerked with his sobs, and he made no effort to wipe away his tears. 'B-but I c-couldn't.'

'Have you told your parents about this?' He shook his head.

Kit sat down beside him and put her arm around his shoulder. 'Shh,' she murmured. 'It's all right.' She gently brushed away his tears.

He looked at her and attempted a smile. 'Dr Robertson', he said, 'd-doesn't approve of the sh-shock treatments.' She held him like a child, gently rocking until the sobs abated. After a few moments, Nigel said, 'He told me that p-perhaps you'll b-be coming round to see me. I'd l-like that v-very much.'

She stared at him, aware that he was too humiliated even to confide in his parents, and that besides her, there was really no one to care for him. After a moment, she took a deep breath and said, 'I'll see what I can do.'

18

Four abreast, the column of Americans marched the length of the snow-covered courtyard, arms swinging and breath clouding, turned about-face, and began marching back again. They'd been at it for hours in the freezing cold, punishment for having joined a group of French officers in an impromptu New Year's Eve celebration. Fuelled by copious quantities of 'French 75s', an explosive blend of champagne and cognac named for the famous artillery piece first used to defend Paris in the War of 1870, they'd made the mistake of stopping on their way back to the barracks to serenade the 'Colonel' with a drunken rendition of 'Waltzing Matilda'.

When the clock on the convent bell-tower struck noon, McDuffie emerged from the vantage point of his office and gave a blast on his whistle. At the signal to fall out, the orderly column quickly dissolved, one exhausted man slumping down on the snow where he stood as the others trudged toward the colonnade. Henry Borden and Bill Larrabee walked slowly toward the corner Frank Harrington had chosen to watch the parade.

'Get the lead out, boys,' Harrington called out with a smile. It had been his good fortune to miss the party, staying behind with Talbot Pierce, a teetotaller.

Borden and Larrabee walked up and stamped their boots on the flagstones, rubbing their gloved hands together. 'Sonofabitch,' muttered Larrabee.

'Bastard,' added Borden.

'I'll treat you fellas to a cup of hot cocoa,' said Harrington, 'at the café across the road.'

Seated at a round table by the fire, the three Americans were joined by two new members of the AFS, recently arrived in France.

'The trick,' said Borden, letting the vapours from the mug of cocoa warm his face, 'is learning to drive these country roads in the dark.'

'No lights?' asked one of the new men.

'That red cross painted on the side of your Ford', said Larrabee, 'makes a nice target for the German gunners. It's bad enough when they send up a flare.'

'Anyway,' said Borden, 'there's not much goin' on in this sector. Y'all should have been with us last summer, dodgin' whiz-bangs on the Menin Road.' The new men listened in reverential silence to Borden's casual description of their night-time ordeals in the Ypres Salient.

'Where do we stay,' asked one of them, a recent graduate of Brown University, 'when we're out in the field?'

'An abandoned farmhouse or barn. Usually with the roof blown in. You'll find out soon enough.'

'If we ever get done with drilling,' said Harrington with disgust. He finished what was left of his cocoa and glanced at his watch. 'Let's head back,' he suggested. 'It's about time for the mail.'

Thirty or forty men gathered in the convent drive around a delivery truck from AFS headquarters at Neuilly. With the holiday, three days had passed without mail. Standing on the running board, the driver reached into a large leather pouch and began calling out names. After a while he shouted, 'Harrington!'

'Here,' said Frank, raising his hand. The driver tossed him an envelope. Frank's heart pounded as he studied the neat handwriting and London postmark and then noticed that a postcard was stuck to the letter. He slipped them in his pocket and hurried to their upstairs room. Thankfully, the others were out. Stripping off his coat, he sat on the bed and peeled the postcard from the envelope. He smiled at the stylized scene, a sepia photo of No. 22 General Hospital, bordered in holly, with the inscription 'Season's Greetings, Christmas 1915' on a red ribbon. On the back, Elsie had penned a brief thank-you for the trip to Paris and the porcelain pillbox.

Putting the postcard aside, he re-examined the envelope. He could just make out the smeared postmark, dated December 29th, when Kit was scheduled to return to France. He slit the envelope, extracted several sheets of pale blue bond and read:

29 Dec. '15
London

Dearest Frank,

When the train left this morning for Folkestone and the ferry across the Channel, I was lying in my bed in tears. I've only now summoned the courage to dress and write to you...

Harrington put the letter aside and looked up at the bare ceiling. So she wasn't coming back ... He continued reading:

This was the most difficult choice I've ever faced, and I beg you to understand. Knowing the man you are, I believe you will. On the day after Christmas I called on Nigel's mother, who lives nearby, and discovered that he's undergoing treatment for shell shock at a

244

London clinic. The next day I saw him, and his condition was appalling. His nerves are simply shattered. The doctor thought it would do him good if I continued to see him and asked me to consider staying in London. I told him no and my suitcase was packed, but when I went to tell Nigel goodbye, I made the most terrible discovery. He confided that they've been treating him with electric shock and pleaded with me to stay. Oh, Frank, I didn't have the heart to say no.

Dropping the letter in his lap, Harrington stared out the grimy window, trying to make sense out of it. Treating him with electric shock? What could that mean?

I've secured a nursing position at Brompton Hospital, which is quite close. Hopefully I'll be permitted to return to No. 4 GH as soon as I'm able to leave here, perhaps within weeks. In the meanwhile I'll miss you terribly. I was so looking forward to your leave. I pray you'll understand my reasons, out of a desire to help an old friend, nothing more. I long for the day we're together. Please keep away from danger.

Your loving,
Kit

He tossed the letter on the blanket with a sigh. Despite her assurances that she cared for him, there was no getting around the fact that she was staying in London to be with Nigel, a man who was in love with her, who was from her class, her neighbourhood even, and who'd asked her to marry him...

Talbot Pierce burst into the room. 'Hey, Frank,' he said breathlessly. 'Have you heard the news? We're moving out.' He studied Harrington's pained expression. 'Are you all right?' he asked.

Henry Borden and Bill Larrabee tramped in behind him. 'That's right,' said Larrabee. 'McDuffie's sending us up into the line with a bunch of the new boys. Figured we could show 'em the ropes.'

'Wants us on our way before dark,' said Borden. 'All leave's cancelled.'

'Great,' said Harrington, running his hand through his thick hair. 'This has been just my day.'

Borden exchanged a puzzled look with Larrabee, who grabbed his cowboy hat from the shelf. Slipping it on, he said, 'I can't wait to get going.'

His duffle bag packed and bed stripped, Harrington sat in a chair with his writing tablet on his knee and a pencil in his teeth. After a few moments he wrote:

> January 2, 1916
> Châlons-sur-Marne
> France
>
> Dear Kit,
> I have to say I was mighty disappointed to read you aren't coming back. With my six months up in a couple of days, I had it all worked out to take a train to Boulogne and spend a weekend together...

He paused to consider that, with all leave cancelled and the order to go into the field, he wouldn't have been able to see her even if she had come back. Well, he thought perversely, let her think otherwise; it might make her feel guilty. *'I'm sorry about your friend,'* he continued, though the word 'friend' made him grimace.

> We've seen a fair number of these shell-shock cases, though of course we don't know what's done with

them after we get them to the CCS. But I can't imagine why they would use electric shock on a man. I hope his condition improves, and selfishly hope you're back on this side of the Channel as soon as possible.

Things are generally quiet around here, on the far right of the French line. Both sides are dug in for the winter, and the general opinion is that not much will happen before spring and the Big Push we all hear Kitchener is planning. Nevertheless we're being sent out for another spell, picking up the French blessés for a change. I've been bored sick at this convent, so I'm looking forward to it.

Kit, I confess I feel pretty jealous when I think about you with someone else. I want you back for my own and sure hope that there's nothing more to your staying than wanting to help him get well. I can't wait for the day we're together again. I'll be thinking of you night and day.

> Love,
>
> Frank

'OK, Harrington,' Bill Larrabee called out from the doorway. 'Time to saddle up. And Peach is driving his own car. McDuffie's orders.'

* * *

Kit hurried along, taking a deep breath of the cold, dry air and enjoying the bright sun on her face, the first day without rain and low clouds in weeks. Brompton Hospital was within blocks of Onslow Gardens, allowing time to breakfast with her parents before heading out the door. Her mother was delighted by the turn of events, her eldest daughter unexpectedly staying home, working in the neighbourhood, and, of course, seeing Nigel again. Crossing the street, Kit looked up at the handsome brick façade of the nineteenth-century building, converted to an RAMC hospital for the most seriously wounded men evacuated from France. She passed through the main entrance into a crowded entry hall, left her coat and gloves in the closet reserved for VADs, and started up the stairs for the fourth-floor surgical ward.

'Good morning, Sister,' she said with something like a curtsey to the senior nurse on duty behind the counter, who responded with a cold stare. When Kit first arrived at Brompton, she'd been shocked by the difference from the field hospitals in France. There was little chance of a VAD being mistaken for a real 'Sister'. The unfortunate girls with the red cross on their bibs were treated with condescension that bordered on rudeness, seldom permitted contact with the patients and assigned the lowliest tasks: sweeping and mopping the floors, emptying bedpans, and replenishing supplies in the neat-as-a-pin cabinets and closets.

For Kit, however, the situation abruptly changed when, after the first week, one of the senior MOs discovered that she had extensive experience assisting in surgery at the Casualty Clearing Station and consequently was untroubled by the sight of blood. For more than three weeks, she'd been assigned to the operating theatre, assisting the RAMC surgeons and nurses with delicate, reconstructive surgery that often lasted for hours. When she wasn't in the OT, she was permitted to assist with changing the men's dressings, a difficult task she was well trained to perform by her experience in France. Kit was regarded with great respect by the other VADs, who never grew tired of her stories of life at No. 4 GH or the CCS at Bailleul.

At the end of long days, two or three times a week Kit would walk to the South Kensington station and take the Tube across central London to visit Nigel. Though he was making gradual improvement under Dr Robertson's patient methods – the stammer was almost completely gone – it was apparent that he was far from well. He still suffered from terrible nightmares and, as he reluctantly confided to Kit, from occasional 'visions', ghost-like images that intruded on his consciousness. The doctor was convinced that in order to conquer these problems he must first bring to conscious recollection the traumatic event that had triggered his sudden breakdown. This he hoped to facilitate by a careful examination of Nigel's dreams. Thus far, the approach had yielded only modest results, a vague description of a dark cloud of some kind moving across No Man's Land. Kit was certain that her visits were a comfort to Nigel, but it was unclear whether she was helping him to make progress, and she questioned how long she would remain in London.

Often returning home too late for dinner, Kit would have a bowl of soup at the table in the kitchen, chatting with Maggie, whom she'd known since childhood, before retiring to her bedroom on the fourth floor. She tried to read, but most nights she found herself unhappily dwelling on her separation from Frank. Looking back, she realized that the times they were together at the end of the summer were the happiest in her life, despite the horrors of the war. And she couldn't think about Paris without her eyes growing moist. In his latest letters Frank seemed distant somehow, almost resigned to their separation, though he would never say it. Kit filled her letters with forced optimism, confidently assuring him that she'd be returning soon, telling him how much she cared about him. She found comfort in the fact that the fighting on the Western Front had settled into a midwinter lull. At least he should be out of harm's way until they were together again.

Kit wearily emerged from the operating theatre following two-hours of reconstructive surgery on a man whose face had been largely shot away. In the small washroom reserved for VADs, she slipped her bloodied bib over her head and tossed it in the hamper, rolled up her sleeves and began scrubbing her hands at the basin.

'How do you stand it?'

Kit turned to look at Sarah Wilson, another London girl assigned to the fourth floor at Brompton. 'The blood, you mean?' she said. Sarah nodded. 'You get used to it,' said Kit. 'Let's go down to the canteen,' she suggested, 'for a cup of coffee and a smoke. I'm due for a break.'

The sun was shining through a thin layer of horsetail clouds on the midwinter day, warming the temperature to the point that the two young women were comfortable in the hospital courtyard. They sat together in their capes on a wrought-iron bench, discreetly sharing a cigarette. 'Is your ... er ... friend Nigel getting better?' asked Sarah as she passed the fag to Kit and expelled a puff of smoke.

'A bit,' said Kit, keeping an eye on the door to the canteen in case a Sister or MO should venture outside. She took a drag and looked at her companion. 'Are you familiar with neurasthenia?' she asked. Sarah shook her head. 'In France they call it shell shock. Men who suffer nervous collapse after being too long in the trenches.'

'Oh,' said Sarah. 'Is that what Nigel...'

'Yes,' said Kit. She felt oddly relieved at sharing her secret. 'He's tormented by some horrible memory – real or imaginary – buried in his unconscious. The doctor says he won't get well unless he can dig it out.'

'I have an aunt,' said Sarah, taking the cigarette for a final drag, 'my mother's younger sister, who was treated for hysteria. She spent several months at Colney Hatch. Same sort of thing, as I understood it. Some horror she couldn't call to mind.'

'What did they do?' asked Kit, raising her mug of coffee to her lips.

'She painted.'

'Painted?'

'Yes. My mother visited her at the asylum and told me the doctors had all the ladies out on the veranda with their paints and easels. Watercolours, I believe it was.'

'But why?'

'The notion was that they should paint, or try to, whatever it was they found so disturbing to think about. And gradually they would be able to see it on the canvas. A queer idea, it seemed to me.'

'Did it work?'

'Evidently so. When Aunt Martha returned home she was as normal as you or I.'

'We'd better get back to the ward,' said Kit, abruptly standing up. 'Or Miss Prescott will have us on our hands and knees cleaning the loo.'

As it was Sunday, her one day off, Kit arrived at the clinic in the early afternoon. She was a familiar figure to the nursing staff, who greeted her pleasantly and informed her that Nigel could be found reading on the garden terrace, an area reserved for patients who'd progressed beyond uncontrollable outbursts or imaginary physical disabilities. Leaving her hat and coat in a closet, Kit took the lift to the top floor, holding a parcel at her side. The area was designed as an open-air terrace, with a roof overhead, but was now enclosed with wire mesh. The terrace was warmed by coal braziers and crowded with potted plants and a miscellany of dilapidated garden furniture. She found Nigel by the railing, bundled up in an army greatcoat with a thick book in his lap. 'Why, hullo, Kit,' he said with a smile as she walked up. 'What's that you've brought with you?'

She smiled at him, thinking that with each visit some small part of the old Nigel was gradually returning, but with a subtle, yet profound, difference. She unwrapped the parcel and removed a sketchpad and a several sticks of charcoal. 'I thought you might like to draw,' she said. 'So I've brought these along.' She handed them to him. 'And a set of paints and brushes,' she added. 'Watercolours.'

Nigel accepted the pad and charcoals with a look of surprise mixed with pleasure. He opened the pad and examined a blank sheet. 'I haven't drawn,' he said, 'since I was a schoolboy. But actually I was rather good.'

'You'll need an easel for the paints,' said Kit. 'I spoke with Dr Robertson, who told me they have several here at the clinic.'

'Sit down,' said Nigel, nodding toward a nearby chair, 'and I'll do your face.'

Fifteen minutes later, the heels of his hands black with charcoal, Nigel looked up from the sketchpad with a satisfied smile. 'Here,' he said, reaching over to Kit. 'Have a look.'

She studied the portrait. He'd captured the shading of her cheekbone, her delicate mouth and her eyes with surprising accuracy and near-expert touch. 'Good heavens,' she said. 'I had no idea you had such talent.'

'I'm decent at sketching. But I don't know a thing about watercolours.'

Kit handed him the sketchpad and stood up. 'Nigel,' she said. 'There's something I'd like you to try. After I'm gone, when you're alone, fix a blank sheet of canvas on the easel, get your paints and brushes in order, and then...' She hesitated.

'Yes?' said Nigel.

'And then look at the canvas and try to visualize the view from the trenches. Looking across No Man's Land.'

A troubled look crossed Nigel's face. He knitted his brow and said, 'But why?'

'I want you to paint it,' said Kit. 'Paint what you see with your mind's eye.'

'But you don't understand,' he objected. 'One doesn't look across No Man's Land, at least not during daylight. Except, that is,' he added after a moment's pause, 'with a periscope.'

'There's something you saw,' suggested Kit casually. 'Perhaps you *were* looking through a periscope. Try to recall it, and then paint it for me.'

Nigel rubbed his chin and nodded. 'All right,' he said. 'I'll see what I can do.'

'Good. I have to go now, but I'll be back Tuesday evening. I'll be interested to see what you've done.'

Nigel rose from his chair. He tore a sheet from the pad. 'Take this,' he said, handing her the charcoal sketch. 'Thanks for coming. I-I'll see you soon.'

Kit studied her portrait. 'Goodbye, Nigel,' she said with a smile. 'And good luck.'

It was long past dark on Tuesday evening when Kit boarded the Tube for the trip to Queen's Park clinic. Walking along the almost empty pavements in the bitterly cold rain, she considered the poor men sheltering in the trenches from the Channel coast all the way to the Swiss frontier. The talk in London was all about the new conscription bill and the expectation that, with the coming of spring, Kitchener's fine New Army would launch the 'Big Push' that would shatter the German line. Kit doubted it.

She entered the foyer of the clinic, bone tired from a long day assisting in the operating theatre and uncomfortably cold and damp. Shrugging off her sodden coat, she asked the young nurse on duty to let Captain Owen know she was there. Several minutes later, Kit walked up the familiar stairs to the small waiting room on the third floor, where most of the patients' rooms were located. Finding it empty, she sat in one of the chairs and absently turned the pages of a magazine that featured English country estates.

'Hullo, Miss Stanley.'

She looked up to see Dr Robertson, looking his usual sporting self in a hounds-tooth jacket and dark twill trousers with his pipe in one hand. 'Why, hullo,' she said. 'I didn't expect to find you here this late in the day.'

'You'd be surprised. At any rate, I wanted to thank you.' She responded with a puzzled look. '. . . For your suggestion that Owen try painting,' he explained. 'I'd read something about the approach, but never seen it in practice.'

'I hope it's been helpful to him,' she said, rising from her chair.

'I've got several of my patients with their paints and brushes now,' said the doctor with a puff on his pipe. 'As for Captain Owen, I'll let you judge for yourself.'

Nigel was sitting in a green leather armchair in a quiet room usually reserved for off-duty MOs. When he stood up, Kit was surprised to see that he was wearing a neatly pressed uniform complete with Sam Browne belt and his tie knotted at the collar. 'Nigel,' she said, walking up and giving him a light kiss on the cheek. 'You're looking well.'

He nodded. 'Thank you, darling,' he replied. 'I'm feeling better. But I must say, you look exhausted.'

'It's been a long day. Dr Robertson tells me you've been painting.'

Nigel responded by walking over to a table by the window and switching on a lamp. Kit could now see an easel against the wall with a blank canvas. 'I did as you suggested,' he said. 'And this was the result.' He carefully turned over the canvas, illuminated by the lamplight.

The scene was starkly realistic, the sky the same shade of grey as the ground, shattered tree stumps in the foreground just beyond coils of barbed wire, water standing in the shell craters, and, incongruously, several blackbirds overhead. In the distance, at the dim horizon, there was a dark shape, indistinct, almost like a cloud, and somehow there was the impression it was moving. 'It's beautiful,' said Kit, walking closer. 'Terrible, but beautiful all the same.' She smiled at Nigel. 'You're such a fine artist.'

'It t-took a bit of getting used to. Until I got the feel for the different brushes.'

Kit approached the easel and bent over to examine the painting. She concentrated on the dark mass, which now looked merely like an abstract splotch of colour. Somehow, from the distance, Nigel had created the impression of movement. She turned to him and asked, 'What is it?'

Nigel walked over and peered at the canvas. 'I don't know,' he said. 'At first I couldn't see it. But gradually I did. It frightened me.' He looked at Kit. 'Dr Robertson took one look at it and said, "It's what you've been dreaming about."'

'Oh, Nigel,' said Kit, impulsively giving his hand a squeeze. 'I'm so glad you're getting better. You'll have to try another.' She glanced at her watch. 'It's late, and I should be on my way. But I'll be back on Thursday.'

Returning to Onslow Gardens, Kit found her parents preparing for bed and a cold supper waiting for her on the kitchen table. Alone at last in her room following a soak in the tub, Kit sat in her robe at her writing desk and unscrewed the cap of her fountain pen. Suppressing a yawn, she wrote:

16 Feb. 1916
London

Dearest Frank,

It's been another cold, dreary day, and I imagine you sleeping in some farmer's hayloft exposed to the elements. I only pray that you're safely removed from the guns and bombs. When I made the decision to stay here, I never imagined it would last so long. But finally, tonight, I saw real progress in Nigel's recovery. He truly seems almost his old self, yet in a strange way, transformed for the better. It means I'll be coming back soon. Thankfully Maj. Evans wrote to say that I'm welcome to return to No. 4. I feel that it's only a matter of another week, two at most, before Nigel's well enough for me to leave.

Frank, I've missed you terribly. Please don't mistake my sympathy for Nigel as anything romantic. When I go to sleep at night, exhausted after a long day at Brompton, I dream of you. I dream of Paris, walking the embankment by the Seine, holding you in my arms. Will you meet me there? I can't think of anything that would make me happier than arriving at the station with you standing on the platform. That's the image I'm taking tonight to my pillow. Goodnight, sweetheart, and please be safe. I love you,

Kit

19

The snow-blanketed fields sparkled in the light of the half-moon. Harrington eased back in the seat and relaxed his grip on the wheel. The engine stuttered, and he quickly clutched and pumped the gas. A clog in the fuel line, he supposed, that would need attention in the morning. He checked the mirror to make sure Talbot was still behind him. A quiet night in a quiet sector, until the knock on the farmhouse door and the summons to pick up two *blessés* at the aid station, one of them *très mauvais*, according to the runner. It's was Harrington's turn to go, and he would have gone alone but thought it might boost Talbot's confidence to take out his own car on the tranquil night. Harrington thought he could see the orange tip of a cigarette glowing in the distance, and then dimly saw two French sentries at the roadside. He slowly brought the Model T to a halt.

'*À droit*,' said one of the *poilus* casually, clearly familiar with the distinctive AFS ambulances. '*Peut-être une kilometre à la poste de secours.*' He tossed his cigarette into the snow.

Harrington thanked the soldier and turned onto a narrow track, with Pierce following a few yards behind. There was an occasional flash on the horizon, followed by a dull *whump*, nothing like the duelling artillery at night in the Salient. After several minutes Harrington drove up to a crude sign with the letters 'P de S' – for first aid station – pointing to the left. Occasional rifle fire echoed in the still air. He slowly made his way along the track between tall, snow-clad evergreens, undisturbed by shellfire, staring ahead in the faint moonlight, until he could see the remains of a stone barn and a group of soldiers bending over two forms on the ground. He set the handbrake, leaving the engine running, and jumped out to tell Talbot to do the same. Sliding a stretcher from the back, Harrington walked quickly over to the men.

'*Vite, vite,*' said one of them in a low voice. Harrington made eye contact with the man under the rim of his helmet, a grizzled, older sergeant with a heavy growth of beard. '*Rien qu'un garçon,*' he muttered as he pointed to the soldier lying in the snow. A mere boy.

Harrington knelt down to examine the wounded soldier. Eighteen at most, his face was ghostly white. Gently pulling open his greatcoat, Harrington glanced at the blood-soaked dressing covering his chest and listened to his laboured breathing.

'*Un éclat,*' whispered one of the other *poilus*. There was a splinter, in his heart.

The boy cried softly: '*Maman ... Chère maman.*'

Harrington was aware of someone leaning over his shoulder. Talbot Pierce dropped down on his knees and bent close to the young soldier, whispering something to him as he gently stroked his forehead. As the soldiers watched, Talbot bowed his head and murmured a prayer, asking for the blessing of Jesus and the Virgin, and then crossed himself. Harrington and Pierce gently covered the boy with a blanket, carefully lifted him onto the stretcher, and carried him to Harrington's ambulance. After sliding the stretcher onto the rack, they returned for the other *blessé*, who was suffering from a superficial gunshot wound to his shoulder.

'*Merci, mes amis,*' said the sergeant as Frank climbed behind the wheel and released the brake. The *poilus* silently watched the two Model Ts disappear into the darkness. Anxious to get back to the highway, Harrington sped up, keeping an eye on Talbot in the mirror. Once on the tarmac, he drove uncomfortably fast, able to discern the verge of the road with almost a sixth sense. When he downshifted to enter a curve, the engine coughed, backfired and then died. Harrington coasted to a stop.

'Damn,' he said softly as he threw open the door.

Talbot pulled up beside him, his engine idling smoothly. 'What is it?' he asked, leaning out the side.

'Fuel line's clogged,' said Harrington, walking up to Talbot's door. 'We'll have to leave it. Let's transfer the *blessés* to your vehicle.' He turned the handle and opened the double doors at the rear. Talbot helped him slide out the stretcher with the badly wounded soldier. In the pale light of the setting moon, they could clearly see the boy's face, his eyes open wide, staring up toward heaven as though in supplication. They listened for the sound of breathing.

'He's gone,' said Harrington after a moment.

They gently laid the dead boy on the snow and pulled the blanket up over his face. After transferring the other man to Talbot's ambulance, they returned for the body, carefully securing it in the back. Closing the doors, Harrington climbed in on the passenger side and watched as Talbot shifted, released the clutch and slowly drove forward.

'What you did back there at the aid station', said Harrington after several minutes, 'meant a lot to those men.'

'You think so?' said Talbot, giving Harrington a quick sideways glance before turning to the darkened roadway.

'They obviously cared a lot for that boy, and they knew he was dying. Most fellows couldn't have done what you did under the circumstances.'

Talbot nodded, staring straight ahead, but Frank could see the tears streaking his cheek.

* * *

Hours later, after delivering the *blessé* and his dead comrade to the French field hospital at Épernay, Pierce and Harrington found their way back along the country roads to the place they'd left the Model T. The cold air pouring through the open cab kept them from dozing. When at last Talbot made a tight turn and came to a stop by the abandoned Ford the clouds in the eastern sky were streaked purplish orange.

Harrington climbed out, stretched and said, 'Beautiful, isn't it?' The rising sun bathed the snow-covered fields in soft orange light. Pierce nodded, keeping his thoughts to himself. 'It's so quiet here,' said Harrington, 'you might almost forget there's a war going on.'

'Almost,' said Talbot.

'Anyhow, you did fine last night. You've got the knack of it now.'

'It helps to have someone to follow. Can you get it started?'

'Oh, sure,' said Harrington. 'It's just the fuel line. Think you can find your way back?'

'I'll be OK. And Frank ... Thanks for letting me go with you.'

* * *

Having reported before daylight, Kit's duties at the hospital were finished by three, and she was anxious to get home in time for tea with her mother. As she crossed the street and started down the busy pavement, a guilty feeling crept into her thoughts, debating whether she should forget tea and make the cross-town trip to pay a call on Nigel. Her last visit to the clinic had been depressingly unrewarding. He'd painted a rather pleasant still life and another watercolour of No Man's Land, but it was only a poor copy of the first. And he'd reacted with annoyance and stubborn resistance when first she and then Dr Robertson had gently tried to plumb the meaning of the mysterious dark cloud at the centre of his paintings. It was as if, having cracked open the door to this hidden room, he couldn't bring himself to look inside. No, with both sisters away at boarding school, Kit made up her mind to seize the rare opportunity for an afternoon at home with her mother.

Lost in these ruminations as she hurried past the shop fronts, Kit almost collided with a tall army officer.

'Sorry,' she murmured, and then halted at the sound of her name. She turned to look back at the officer, who was standing on the pavement with his hands on his hips.

'Kit?' he repeated. 'Miss Stanley?'

'Oh, my,' she said with a smile, recognizing the familiar features below the bill of his hat. 'It's Lieutenant Barnes.'

'What a surprise,' he said, walking up to her. 'I didn't expect to cross paths with you in South Kensington, though I see you're still working.'

'Well, yes,' she said. 'I'm at Brompton. For the time being, that is. And you're looking well, fully recovered.'

Barnes nodded. 'Yes, thanks in no small part to you and the doctors at No. 4. And I'm finally on my way back to the old regiment.'

'Are you really? To France?'

'That's right. Back to the KRRC. I leave at the end of the week.'

'I should have thought, after all you've been through, the army would allow you to remain here...'

Barnes shook his head. 'I'm ready to go,' he said. 'Back to the real army. By the way, how is Captain Owen? Have you heard from him?'

Kit bit her lip. 'Well,' she said, 'actually he's here, in London ... recuperating.'

Barnes was conscious of the reluctance in her voice, the brief look of shame on her face. Quickly looking around, he said, 'There's a tearoom in the next street. We could talk over a cup.'

Seated at a table in the corner, Barnes politely poured Kit's tea before filling his own cup and stirring in sugar and milk. He took a sip and gave her an encouraging smile.

'Captain Owen', she began, 'was in some of the worst of the fighting at Loos.'

'Yes, the battalion suffered terrible losses.'

'I saw Nigel not long afterward, and, well, he wasn't his old self. He was having a difficult time. And then he was sent back into the line, and something happened. I'm not sure what. Nervous collapse you might call it.'

'Shell shock?' said Barnes softly.

Kit nodded. 'There's a clinic in Bloomsbury where the RAMC are treating many of these cases, though I'm not sure "treatment" is an apt term.'

'I understand,' said Barnes. 'Owen is a very fine officer, quite fearless under fire. But, believe me, Kit, I've seen what the stress of battle can do, even to the strongest men.'

'Thank you,' she said with a weak smile. 'There's a fine doctor here who's working with Nigel now, and he's making progress, but very slowly.'

'I wonder,' said Barnes, 'if I could see him? He might be glad to have a visit from one of his old comrades.'

Kit considered. 'I believe you're right. Could you come with me in the morning? Tomorrow I'm working the late shift.'

Nigel was reclining on his bed, his back against the headboard, in shirtsleeves with his collar open, his tunic draped over the back of a chair. When Kit entered the room he expelled a cloud of cigarette smoke and looked up at her. He'd been studying the painting, which was resting on an easel in the corner.

'Hullo,' he said as he stubbed out the cigarette. 'Do you realize I haven't had a drink in months?'

Kit chose to sit on the other bed, which was unoccupied now that Nigel had finally succeeded in having his voluble roommate evicted. 'I'm sure it's done you good,' she said.

'I'm not. As soon as I get out of this loony house I intend to pop into the nearest pub for a double whisky.'

Kit smiled. It was the first time she'd heard him declare his intention of leaving the clinic. 'I have a surprise for you,' she said. Nigel arched his eyebrows. 'You have a visitor,' she explained.

'Visitor? Surely not one of our old friends. I don't want to see them...'

'No, Nigel. A comrade of yours. From C Company.'

Nigel drew in a deep breath and slowly exhaled. 'C Company,' he repeated with a faraway look.

'Will you see him?'

Nigel nodded.

Kit rose from the bed and went to the door. She opened it and Lieutenant Barnes stepped inside. 'Hullo, Captain,' he said cheerfully. 'It's dashed good to see you again.'

Nigel stared at Barnes with his mouth partly open. He blinked and finally managed to say, 'Barnes. Good God.' The lieutenant stood awkwardly at the foot of Nigel's bed.

'We ran into one another in South Kensington,' said Kit. 'What a coincidence.'

'Yes,' said Nigel softly, still staring in an odd way at Barnes. 'Yes ... I should say so.'

'You're looking well, Captain,' said Barnes. 'Rested.'

Nigel's eyes shifted from Barnes to the painting in the corner. Barnes turned to look at it. He walked over and silently studied it. 'It's remarkable,' he said, turning back to Nigel and Kit. 'Whoever painted it captured No Man's Land perfectly.'

'Nigel painted it,' said Kit proudly.

'Did you?' said Barnes. 'I say, Captain, it's excellent.'

Looking from the painting to Barnes, Nigel swallowed

hard and his eyes filled with tears. 'Th-thank you,' he murmured.

'Are you all right?' asked Kit, sitting down on the bed beside him.

Nigel nodded. 'Yes,' he said in stronger voice, wiping his eyes. 'Yes, I'll be fine.' He looked back at Barnes. 'Sit down, Lieutenant,' he said. 'We were amazed to discover that you'd survived the attack at the crater. I can still remember...' Nigel paused to brush another tear from the corner of his eye. 'The sight of you leading the men over the top, plunging into that hellfire.'

Barnes lowered himself into the single chair. 'I don't remember much,' he said. 'Other than the smell. I'll never forget the smell. When I awoke I was at the hospital, with Kit standing over me.'

'We were together a long, long time,' she said with a smile, conscious of a subtle change in Nigel. The tension seemed to have gone out of him. 'I thought you'd never make it out of hospital.'

'I should be going,' said Barnes, rising from the chair. 'I'm on my way back to the regiment, Captain.'

Nigel gave him an admiring look. 'Good, Barnes,' he said. 'I'm glad to hear it.' He stood up and warmly shook the lieutenant's hand. 'Please give my regards to the colonel, and to Parker and the sergeant-major, of course.'

'Yes, sir,' said Barnes. 'I will. And Captain ... Stick with it, and you'll be out of here in no time.'

*　　*　　*

Harrington slid his glass across the scarred surface of the table and gestured to Henry Borden to pour him more wine. The estaminet was packed with American drivers and a handful of the more adventuresome girls from the village near their farmhouse billets. Passing the glass to Harrington, Borden resumed his game of acey-deucey with Bill Larrabee. Harrington took a sip and watched as one of the French girls, a rather homely lass, crawled into the lap of a tall, raw-boned fellow at the next table and draped her pudgy arm around his neck. A farm boy from somewhere in the Great Plains, Harrington speculated. Liable to get into trouble. He sipped his wine with a sigh.

'You all right?' asked Talbot Pierce, sitting beside him with a glass of cider.

'Just feeling a little blue,' admitted Harrington.

The scene at the next table grew more raucous, with another of the local beauties climbing into the lap of a somewhat embarrassed young man, who lost his cap in the process.

'Homesick?' said Pierce.

Harrington nodded and said, 'Yeah, I guess so.' The truth was he was feeling bitterly sorry for himself, thinking about Kit with Nigel.

'Me too,' said Pierce. 'Hard to be so far from home.'

After watching the horseplay at the next table for a few more minutes, Harrington noticed that one of the men from the corner table, the group of volunteers from the West Coast, had taken a seat at the upright piano. 'Play us something, Charlie,' called one of his comrades. '"Tipperary" or something.'

The handsome young man removed a song sheet from his tunic and placed it on the piano. 'It's the latest tune from the home front,' he said with a smile. He studied the music and then effortlessly played the introduction, a sweet, lilting melody, at once silencing the din in the crowded tavern. '*There's a Rose that grows in No Man's Land,*' he sang in a clear tenor voice, '*and it's wonderful to see.*'

Harrington took a swallow of wine, conscious of a strange sensation in his chest at the unfamiliar melody.

'*Though it's sprayed with tears, it will live for years,*' the young man sang to a rich accompaniment of chords, '*in my garden of memory...*'

'*It's the one red rose the soldier knows, it's the work of the Master's hand...*'

Harrington swallowed hard, fighting a tightness in his throat.

'*In the war's great curse, stood the Red Cross Nurse...*' The singer slowed the tempo. '*She's the Rose of No Man's Land.*'

The room erupted in a chorus of cheers and applause. Harrington quickly brushed his eye and pushed back from the table. 'C'mon, fellas,' he said to the others. 'We better get some sleep while we've got a chance.'

'What's that?'

Harrington rolled over in the darkness with a groan. He'd lain awake for hours, unable to go back to sleep after waking from a dream – he'd been in Paris with Kit when suddenly she'd announced she was leaving him to marry Nigel – so vivid that several moments passed before, to his great relief, he realized it was only a dream.

'What *is* that?' repeated Talbot Pierce.

'Quiet,' mumbled Bill Larrabee from somewhere in the pitch-black room.

Harrington propped himself up on an elbow and rubbed his eyes. Then he heard it, a deep, reverberating rumble, like rolling thunder or a passing freight train, but unrelenting. He threw off the bedroll and sat up. 'What the heck...?' he said.

Talbot struck a match and lit a candle, casting a circle of yellow light across the bare floor where the four men were sleeping. Larrabee poked his head out of his bedroll and blinked his eyes at the light. Suddenly he sat bolt upright. While Henry Borden slept on, the others silently stared at the darkness outside the windows, trying to identify the strange sound.

'It's coming from the east,' said Harrington.

He got up and quickly pulled on a pair of pants. Shrugging on his coat, he opened the door and stepped outside. The thunder was much louder, like the grumbling of angry gods. The house was on a slight rise, affording a view of the rolling farmland. The eastern sky was filled with flashing light, a constant flickering chiaroscuro, illuminating the undersides of a thick mass of clouds. After a few moments Harrington was joined by Larrabee and Pierce. They silently watched and listened for a full minute, awed by the display of sound and light.

'Must be thirty miles away,' said Larrabee at last.

'I've never seen anything like it,' said Harrington to Pierce. 'Not even in the Salient.'

Henry Borden stumbled out the door and said, 'Jiminy ... must be firin' every damn gun in the German Army.'

'We'd better dress and get everything packed and loaded,' said Harrington, shivering in the cold. 'And send for those boys in the barn. I've got a feeling they're gonna need every driver they can lay their hands on.'

By first light, the squad of new AFS volunteers billeted in a nearby barn had loaded their ambulances and driven with Frank Harrington back to the farmhouse. They were Californians, part of the Leland Stanford Section, with its distinctive insignia on their ambulances, the badge of the Friends of France emblazoned over the Stanford tall pine on a scarlet field. Though the flashes could no longer be seen on the horizon, the thundering cannonade continued without let-up, more than three hours since it had awakened them.

Bill Larrabee emerged from the farmhouse with a duffle

bag over his shoulder, a comic sight in his cowboy hat and French Army greatcoat.

'Coffee's on the grate,' he said as he passed by the new men, jerking a thumb back toward the house. 'Help yourself.'

The men thankfully went in from the bitter cold. Harrington and Borden sat on the floor with their backs against the wall, sharing a mug of coffee while Pierce knelt over his bag, packing his things. The last of the room's furniture was burning in the fireplace along with several logs scavenged from the nearby woods.

'There's a couple more mugs on the mantel,' said Borden.

One of the Stanford men poured coffee and passed the mugs to his comrades. 'Why do you think they'll be sending for us?' he asked Harrington.

'We've never seen anything even half this big,' replied Harrington. 'Not at Ypres or the Battle of Loos. The Boche must have launched a massive attack.'

'What makes you think it's the Boche?' asked another.

'It's the Boche,' said Borden flatly. 'The French are dug in for the winter. How many cars you boys drivin'?'

'Four,' said a third. He took a sip of coffee and passed the mug to the next man.

'Just remember,' said Harrington, 'if we come under fire, keep moving. As fast as you can till we're out of sight of the gunners.'

'You mean to say they'll be *aiming* at us?'

Borden nodded. 'And chances are we'll be drivin' in daylight.'

'All set, Frank,' said Pierce, hefting his bag. He turned at the sound of an automobile's exhaust outside the farmhouse.

'Sounds like company,' said Harrington. He stood up and dusted off his pants. The men filed out the door as two French Medical Corps officers emerged from a sky-blue Renault with a tricolour flag mounted on the hood.

Larrabee latched the rear doors of his ambulance and walked over to join the others in a semicircle around the French officers.

'*Écoutez, écoutez,*' said one of the officers, a captain. 'I have very little time, so pay close attention.' The Americans were barely able to follow his rapid-fire French. 'You must pack your things immediately,' he continued, 'and get on the road. All ambulances, French and American, are ordered to report without delay to the military hospital at Bar-le-Duc. You will find it on your maps.'

'Driving in daylight?' asked Larrabee.

'We have no choice,' replied the officer. 'You should be far enough to the rear to escape the guns. The Germans have launched a massive bombardment at Verdun. No doubt they mean to overrun the forts. General Joffre has issued an order to hold at all costs and is ordering up the Fifth Corps.'

'What do we do when we reach Bar-le-Duc?' asked Harrington.

'I'm told the casualties are staggering,' said the officer. 'We'll need every car and driver to go up into the line and get them out. Other questions? Very well.' He touched the bill of his cap and started for his car.

*   *   *

Kit stood with her back to the fire before her father, who was in his favourite armchair in the drawing room for the hour before dinner. The butler appeared with a salver and placed a crystal tumbler on the table at her father's elbow.

'Thank you, Burton,' said Mr Stanley. 'Will you have anything, Kit?'

'I don't believe so. Then again, I'll have a glass of sherry.'

Mr Stanley sipped his whisky and soda and gazed admiringly at his oldest daughter. 'It's been wonderful having you at home.' He often considered how he would

269

endure sending a son to France. So many friends and work colleagues had already lost sons in the war, which was clearly far from over.

'Well, Daddy,' said Kit, 'I've loved having this time with you and Mother, but you know I'll be leaving soon…'

The butler reappeared and served Kit her sherry. She was careful not to broach the subject of her return to France when her mother was present. 'You see, Nigel at last is making real progress.'

Mr Stanley nodded sadly. He knew his daughter too well to think he could dictate her plans. 'Yes,' he said. 'I understand.'

The telephone in the pantry rang, and after a moment Maggie appeared. 'It's for you, Miss Kit,' she said. 'It's the doctor at the clinic.'

Kit assumed it was one of the MOs at Brompton and so was surprised to hear Dr Robertson's Scottish burr. 'Would it be possible for you to come by my office in the morning?' he asked. 'I'd like to thank you personally.'

'Thank *me*?' Kit thought for a moment. 'Yes, I suppose so,' she said.

'And, of course, there will be time for you to see Owen. I'll be in by nine.'

Having arranged to report for the afternoon shift at Brompton, Kit boarded the early Tube train and arrived at Queen's Park clinic at ten minutes before the hour. She went directly to Robertson's office on the fourth floor and chatted with his nurse about conditions in the RAMC field hospitals as she waited for him to arrive.

'Good morning,' Robertson said breezily as he walked in, placing his hat and coat on the stand. 'Come in, Miss Stanley. Will you have tea?'

'No thanks.' She followed the doctor into his office and sat in a chair facing his desk.

'Well,' he said, sitting down and resting his elbows on the tidy desk. 'Your method has produced exceptional results. So exceptional, in fact, I intend to publish a paper on it in the *Journal of Neurology*.'

'How do you mean?' asked Kit.

'After you left the other day,' he explained, 'with the lieutenant, Owen returned to his easel. And this was the result.' Robertson reached for a painting lying on the table behind him and held it up for Kit to see. It was Nigel's first effort, the chilling view from the trenches looking across No Man's Land, but now, in place of the dark cloud on the horizon, he had painted a small body of men, dressed in dark suits, and beside them a single British officer.

Kit peered at the painting. 'I'm afraid I don't understand,' she said, looking up at the doctor. 'What does it mean?'

'It's what Owen saw that caused him to snap. He was finally able to recollect it. He says he saw the lieutenant, er...'

'Barnes?'

'Yes, Barnes, leading these strange-looking chaps.'

'But why? Why would it have caused him to snap?'

'Here's the interesting part,' said Robertson, putting the painting aside. 'Once he was able to visualize this, it all came back to him. At the time he thought it was *real*, of course. And so he ordered a sentry up on the parapet to have a look, and the poor man was shot dead. *That's* what caused Owen to snap. The vision of that dead man and the guilt it caused Owen.'

'Is ... is he all right now?'

'Yes. He broke down, naturally, wept for some time. But he's got it all out now and feels enormously relieved. A great burden has been lifted from him.'

* * *

271

Nigel was standing by the railing on the rooftop terrace, gazing out through the wire mesh. He was wearing his uniform, his hair neatly parted, and smiled at Kit as she walked up to him.

'Nigel,' she said, taking his hand. 'I've seen your painting.'

'What a bizarre hallucination,' he said. 'Too much time in the trenches and one starts seeing things.'

The old Nigel, she realized, was fully restored, only without the swagger. 'I'm so proud of you,' she said. 'I can't imagine how difficult this must have been.'

'I could never have done it without you. Thanks to you, I've found my way back.'

She allowed him to take her in his arms and hold her tight, running a hand through her hair. Pulling away, he looked in her eyes and said, 'Darling ... how can I ever thank you?'

Kit closed her eyes, expecting him to kiss her, but he merely touched his lips to her forehead and then released her.

'I've got to go,' she said, 'or I'll be late to work. But I'll be back tomorrow.'

'Goodbye, darling.'

Waiting on the platform for the train, Kit was aware of the cries of a newsboy, hawking a special edition of the morning paper, and a crowd peering at the bold headline. With the sound of the approaching train echoing through the Underground, she reached into her pocket for a coin and quickly purchased a copy. Boarding the car amid the crush of passengers, she found an empty seat and spread open the paper in her lap: 'GERMANS LAUNCH MASSIVE OFFENSIVE ON FRENCH RIGHT WING' blared the headline. 'Fortress at Verdun is Threatened.'

20

Harrington chose a chair next to Henry Borden on the back row of the officers' mess at the hospital at Bar-le-Duc. American drivers were filing in, nervously joking around, scraping chairs on the hardwood as they assembled for the briefing. Over the commotion, Harrington could hear the deep rumbling of diesel engines. In a desperate attempt to reinforce the beleaguered garrison, supply trucks were rolling day and night on the single road to Verdun, destined for immortality as *la voie sacrée*, the 'Sacred Way'. Harrington looked up as a tall French officer strode to the front of the room and stood with a hand on his hip by a large map on an easel.

'As you can see,' he said as the room quieted, speaking in heavily accented English, 'the Verdun garrison consists of fortresses erected on the heights to the east of the Meuse – Douaumont, here,' – he tapped the map with his pointer – 'and Fort Vaux, here. Fortresses, I might add, which never fell in the War of 1870.' From his tone, Harrington could tell the French Army was in no mood to surrender them in 1916. He studied the eager faces of the AFS drivers, with few exceptions men who'd never been under fire and who would be driving the narrow highway at night under heavy German bombardment.

'The Boche are threatening to overrun Douaumont,' said the officer, 'using poison gas and liquid fire on our troops. Already, our casualties number in the tens of thousands. Every available ambulance is needed.'

Harrington looked down at the writing pad on his lap.

He'd hastily pencilled a note to Elsie, explaining that their section was being sent to Verdun, and he was determined to post a letter to Kit before they were sent on their way. *'The Germans have launched a massive attack,'* he wrote,

> on the old fortresses ringing the town of Verdun. The French mean to hold the garrison and we've been ordered up to help evacuate the wounded. We're going in this afternoon and I fear it's going to be plenty rough. As I don't know how long we'll be needed, it may be a while before I can write again...

'All right, then,' concluded the officer in a loud voice. 'The convoy departs promptly at 3:00 p.m. Dismissed.'

'No matter what happens,' Harrington hurriedly wrote, 'always remember how much I love you.'

He folded the note in an envelope and quickly addressed it. As he stood up and turned to go, he noticed a group of young French soldiers in wheelchairs, all missing limbs, parked at the back of the room. As the Americans filed past them, one smiled and said, *'Merci, mes amis,'* and another called out, *'On les aura!'* with a thumbs-up gesture.

After dropping his letters in a mailbox, Harrington joined the rest of the men on the gravel drive in front of the hospital. Twenty drab-green Model Ts were parked behind a long line of French Army ambulances. The road by the hospital was jammed with slow-moving munitions trucks, the cold air thick with exhaust.

'Ready, Frank?' said Bill Larrabee, standing at the door of his Ford.

Harrington paused to listen to the distant thunder of the guns, mingling with the roar of the trucks. 'Yeah,' he said with a frown, 'Ready as I'll ever be.'

'Where's Peach?' asked Larrabee.

Talbot Pierce crawled out from under his ambulance.

'Down here,' he said as he hauled himself up. 'Checking the oil pan.'

An open-air staff car pulled up and screeched to a halt beside the convoy. An officer climbed up on the seat and shouted the command: start the engines and move out, the French ambulances first, followed by the Americans. Report to the aid stations at the village of Dugny, seven kilometres from Verdun.

Harrington took the crank from the toolbox and knelt by the radiator.

'Frank...'

Harrington looked up to see Pierce standing over the hood. His boyish face was pale with worry.

'Hey, Talbot,' said Harrington. 'What is it?'

'Can I follow you, Frank?'

'Sure. Just stay close. Keep your eyes on my fender, OK?'

'OK.'

Harrington gave the crank a hard turn. Nothing. He cranked it again, harder, and with an angry backfire the tool flew out of his hand.

'Damn,' muttered Harrington.

His thumb felt like it'd been torn from its socket. Faint from the pain, he cradled his throbbing hand and climbed behind the wheel. With a grimace, he reached for the gear-lever and pulled out on the highway behind the line of Renaults, glancing back to make certain Pierce was there.

Leaving the village, the convoy passed slowly through the open fields with the blue outline of the steep Ardennes hills visible to the east. After a while the pain in his right hand abated, so long as he avoided gripping the wheel. They crept forward, following behind the heavy army *camions*, overtaking a column of French infantry that reached all the way to the horizon. The *poilus* seemed indifferent to the thunder of the guns, marching in their greatcoats and steel helmets, rifles on their shoulders. Harrington

275

checked his watch, calculating that it would be well after dark when they reached their destination. As daylight faded, he struggled to avoid the ambulance in front of him and to keep from drifting off the road. The sky flickered constantly in a strange version of the Northern Lights. He was dimly aware of men along the side of the road, the jangling of their gear drowned out by the guns. A road sign pointed to Verdun, fourteen kilometres. Though night had fallen, he could easily see the line of ambulances in front in the glow of the bombardment. If *he* could see them, reasoned Harrington...

An ear-splitting concussion coincided with a blinding flash. Instinctively jerking the wheel, Harrington almost lost control but recovered, just avoiding the car in front of him. He checked his mirror to make sure Talbot was there, certain that the high-explosive round had landed within fifty yards of the convoy. A French battery on the hillside answered with a volley, tongues of orange erupting in the darkness from the muzzles of the 75s.

Breasting a hill, the line of vehicles stretched for miles, bumper to bumper, straight into the cauldron of Verdun, glowing lurid red from the fires burning in the city and the surrounding forts. The convoy slowed to a crawl, halted and then inched forward, moving at most at five miles an hour. The pounding of the guns was constant, shaking the ground, the air blowing through the cab pungent with cordite and drifting smoke. Harrington glanced in the mirror, trying to make out Talbot's face but unable to identify the driver. Finally, after what seemed an eternity, the convoy halted at a crossroads, where an MP directed them to turn left. Harrington followed the French ambulances along a badly rutted road for another few minutes until a sign announced their arrival at the tiny village of Dugny.

A sentry appeared from the shadows and raised a gloved

hand. '*Il y a deux postes*,' he said. Two aid stations. The sentry leaned over the passenger door of Harrington's Model T. '*À droit*,' he said, '*la Cabaret Rouge*', pointing to a dirt track. 'Take your men there.'

Harrington leaned out the door and waved to the others to follow him. Free from the French ambulances, he was able to drive faster now. Cabaret Rouge, he considered. A strange name for an aid station. They found it a half-mile down the track, a large stone barn eerily illuminated by oil-burning torches, in whose flickering shadows dozens of men were milling about a courtyard, with many more lying on stretchers. An officer directed the Americans to park by the barn's entrance. As Harrington climbed out, an incoming round shrieked overhead, exploding with a deafening crash several hundred yards to their rear.

'That was close,' said Talbot Pierce, standing beside the door of his car.

'Talbot,' said Frank. 'I was worried I'd lost you.'

'It wasn't too bad,' said Pierce, 'except for that one shell.'

'C'mon, boys!' called Bill Larrabee in a loud voice. 'Let's get these stretchers unloaded.'

As they slid the canvas stretchers from the racks, French *brancardiers* emerged from the shadows, stooped and too exhausted to look up. Amid the boom of the guns, Harrington was conscious of the groans and cries of the wounded lying in the courtyard. He approached a nearby officer and in French said, 'Why don't we load these men first, while your men are putting the others on the stretchers?'

With a quick shake of his head, the officer replied, '*Non*. We've triaged these men,' gesturing to the courtyard. 'They can wait. The serious cases are inside.'

Harrington followed the *brancardiers* into the stone building, lit by more torches, where at least fifty badly wounded men were lying on the straw-covered ground. Doctors in blood-stained gowns moved among them, inspecting dressings, instructing the orderlies to dispense morphine.

'*Vite!*' commanded a doctor to the stretcher-bearers. 'Get these men out, to make room for the others.' The building shook with an explosion.

Harrington bent down to help a soldier lift an unconscious man onto a stretcher, wincing at the sharp pain in his injured thumb. They grasped the handles and started for Harrington's car. In the chaos of the barn, he was vaguely aware of other drivers doing the same. As they loaded the stretcher in the back, Harrington listened to the sputtering and wheezing of a man on the upper rack, the telltale signs of poison gas. Within minutes the ambulances were loaded, the severely wounded *couchés* lying in the back, and the *assis* crammed into the seats with the drivers.

Climbing behind the wheel, Harrington called to a nearby officer: 'Now where to?'

'The field hospital at Véel. It's on your map.'

Harrington briefly studied the map under the beam of his flashlight. 'Henry!' he yelled to Borden. 'Let's go! Tell the others to follow me.'

*   *   *

Kit held Nigel's hand as they walked up the wide staircase in the foyer of the National Gallery. For the past several days, he'd been free to come and go from the clinic as he pleased, and Kit had suggested an outing to the museum.

When they reached the top of the stairs, Nigel glanced around and said, 'Let's start with the Renaissance Italians.'

There were few visitors to the museum on the weekday morning in midwinter, apart from several parties of schoolchildren with their mistresses. Nigel paused at the entrance to the long gallery, staring at the large painting at the far end. He released Kit's hand and began strolling through the spacious rooms, occasionally stopping to study a particular painting. In the quiet, Kit's thoughts turned to Frank. She'd been sick with worry since she received his brief note, unable to sleep at night for more than a few hours at a time, listless and preoccupied in her duties at the hospital. The newspapers were filled with accounts of the battle raging at Verdun, the heaviest fighting of the war.

She'd fallen several yards behind Nigel, who was gazing at a Titian with his hands clasped behind his back. Standing ramrod-straight in his khakis with Sam Browne belt, his hair neatly combed and moustache trimmed, he might have been the old Nigel, of the acid tongue and condescending eye. But those were gone. Though almost completely well, there was still a certain vulnerability about him. Having been utterly broken, Kit considered, he'd never be quite the same again.

'Remarkable, isn't it?' he said as she walked up beside him. 'The use of shadow and light to achieve such realism.'

'You should keep painting,' said Kit. 'You have real talent.' He acknowledged the compliment with a modest smile and then moved to the next painting.

When they reached the end of the gallery, Nigel turned to her and said, 'What next?' Kit shrugged and started into the adjoining gallery, an exhibit of seventeenth-century Dutch and Flemish masters. As Nigel stopped to admire a Vermeer, Kit noticed a banner for a travelling exhibition of French Impressionists.

'Nigel,' she said. 'I'm going to have a look at the Monets. Take your time here, and I'll be back to find you.'

He responded with a smile and a nod.

Kit made her way through the labyrinthine galleries to the exhibition of French paintings. She had the room to herself except for an art student, a young man in his early twenties, working on a copy of a Renoir. She wondered how he'd avoided the army until she saw the crutch resting against the bench and his missing leg.

279

Impatient to find the Monets, she was drawn to a painting of lilies in bright shades of blue and green. From a distance it was remarkably lifelike, but as she walked closer the lines and edges grew indistinct. With a smile, she slowly made her way around the gallery. Kit couldn't understand what the older generation had found so objectionable about these marvellous paintings. Nearing the end, she stopped to admire a small canvas, a graceful stone bridge spanning a river. Conscious of a powerful feeling of déjà vu, she carefully examined the scene, blue water sparkling gold and white in the sunlight, puffy white clouds in the blue sky. In the foreground a sailboat with a boy at the tiller ... She stared, her heart pounding. And then it struck her – the day on the riverbank, lying with Frank on the soft grass by the towpath. She closed her eyes, remembering the sensation of lying in his arms, kissing him in the warm sunshine. Opening her eyes, she stared at the painting until her eyes blurred with tears.

'Kit?' said Nigel softly.

Startled, she turned to look at him.

'Are you all right?' he asked. She nodded, but her lips trembled and she couldn't stop the tears. Nigel glanced from Kit to the painting. 'I suspect I understand,' he said, taking a step closer to her. 'How much you must miss him!' Kit held a hand to her mouth, fighting to regain her composure. 'If you love him,' Nigel continued in a steady voice, 'you should go back to him.'

'But Nigel,' she managed to say, 'what about...?'

'If it's me you're thinking of, you shouldn't. I've made my decision.'

'Your decision?'

'Yes. I'm going before the Medical Board next week. I intend to ask them to return me to the regiment.'

'But, Nigel, surely you could stay here...'

'No. I'm fine now, perfectly fit. And with so many men lost, God knows they'll need every experienced officer, especially with the big push that's coming.'

Kit threw her arms around him and held him tight. 'Oh, Nigel,' she murmured.

* * *

'*Encore un verre de vin?*' Bill Larrabee asked Henry Borden, holding out a bottle.

'Sure,' said Borden sleepily. He lifted up a battered tin cup, which Larrabee refilled with red wine. Bundled up in greatcoats, the four men were squatting on the floor in a tight semicircle around the hearth of an abandoned farmhouse. Part of the roof had been blown in by a *loupé*, an unexploded shell.

Harrington leaned forward to stir the fire. 'You know,' he said, 'after a while you forget about the shelling. It's just background noise.' He paused to listen to the rumbling in the distance and then took a sip of wine. When they arrived at the billet they were surprised to discover several cases of decent claret in the cellar.

'Yep,' said Larrabee, 'like the warbling of the songbirds on a spring morning.'

Borden chuckled. 'You can sleep through just about anything after drivin' all night.' He noticed that Talbot's eyes were closed, dozing where he was sitting. Fat snowflakes drifted through the hole in the roof.

'And you can bet we'll be out again tonight,' said Harrington. 'It's what we deserve for complaining about not having enough to do.'

'Wonder where the colonel is now?' asked Larrabee.

'One thing's for sure,' said Borden, tossing back the rest of his wine. 'He ain't within fifty miles of this hellhole. Frank – your turn to go out and get another log.'

After a few minutes Harrington returned with an armload

of firewood, stamped his boots and tossed several logs on the fire.

'You reckon the Frogs can hold?' asked Borden.

'They'll hold, all right,' said Larrabee. He emptied the wine bottle into his cup. 'With the number of fresh troops they keep bringing up that road? Playing right into Fritz's hand.'

Harrington slumped on the floor. 'How do you mean, Bill?' he asked.

'Listen,' said Larrabee, 'the Germans don't mean to break through the French line. They know Joffre will fight to the last man to hold those forts. *Pour gloire! Pour la Patrie!*' Larrabee thrust out a hand as if waving a sabre. 'So the Germans will just pour it on, kill as many men as possible and bleed the French white.' He gulped down the last of his wine and jumped up. 'Talbot's got it right,' he snapped, eyes blazing. Pierce looked up at the sound of his name.

'That's right,' said Larrabee hotly. 'It's like Talbot says. War's wrong – it's stupid. And if I live through this thing, I'm planning to quit and go home. And tell anyone who'll listen that we should stay out of this lousy war.'

'Get some sleep, Bill,' said Harrington. 'You're gonna need it tonight.'

They were awakened by the honk of a Renault and a voice calling, *'Allons! C'est l'heure.'* Harrington rolled over and looked at the glowing embers on the grate. Snow fell steadily through the roof, accumulating in a pile on the floor. He lit a candle and then pulled on his boots and went outside to confer with the French driver.

'Time to make a pot of coffee?' asked Larrabee with a yawn when Harrington returned.

''Fraid not, Bill. With this weather, we'd better get started.'

'Where to?' asked Borden.

'Same drill,' said Harrington. 'Back to the Cabaret Rouge, and then the hospital at Véel.' He looked at the other men's faces, the dark shadows under their eyes and three days' growth of beard. 'Ready?'

Slipping on his gloves and cap, he walked outside to start his Ford. The night was eerily quiet, with all noise, even the heavy guns, muffled by the thickly falling snow, and so dark he was unable to see the trees by the farmhouse.

'We're gonna have one hell of a time finding our way,' said Larrabee.

'Yep,' said Harrington. 'We'll just take it nice and slow. Can you handle it, Talbot?'

Pierce nodded and adjusted his glasses. 'I'll follow you, Frank.'

Harrington bent over and cranked the engine, careful to let go of the tool just as the pistons kicked in. He lowered the canvas covers on the sides of the cab, swept the snow from the seat and climbed in. With a glance in the mirror at Talbot, he shifted into gear and eased down the accelerator. With the snow swirling through the open cab it was almost impossible to see; the flashes of the guns that blossomed in the dense clouds provided just enough illumination to make out the trees lining the road. The convoy passed out of the woods to an open field, where Harrington stopped to get his bearings. Eyes adjusted to the darkness, he could barely see the ruts in the snow that marked the road to Verdun. After a quick look back at the others, Harrington started slowly forward again.

After half an hour they drove past the sign for Dugny, crossed the bridge over the Meuse and finally came to a stop at a roadblock. Checking the lettering on the side of the ambulance, the French sentry gestured to Harrington to proceed. By now the Americans were accustomed to the procedure at the aid station and the misery they would find there. Harrington drove slowly into the courtyard, just able to discern the outline of the barn's roof against the pale-orange sky. The German advance had reached within a mile, and the only lights were the oil torches burning inside the stone building.

Leaving the engines running, the men quickly unloaded the stretchers and started for the barn, picking their way among the men lying on the ground. Out of the shadows more wounded arrived on stretchers, the *brancardiers* stumbling through the thick snow, muttering curses. The Americans hurried inside, shivering as the French doctors selected the men for evacuation. The building shook from the constant shelling and reeked of chloroform and filth. The dishevelled *brancardiers* grasped the handles of the stretchers and hauled the gasping, groaning men to the ambulances, sliding them onto the racks with a final curse.

Another scene from the Inferno thought Harrington as he swung the doors shut and turned the latch. He climbed behind the wheel and looked back to make sure the others were ready. A French medical officer walked up and in English said, 'Are you sure you can find your way?'

Harrington nodded and said, 'I think so.'

'Another convoy of your men left a short while ago,' said the officer. 'Be careful to make the left turn after the bridge. You don't want to miss it.'

'*Merci*,' said Harrington with a grim smile. He pumped the gas and started forward, aware of the groans of the men in the compartment behind him. Actuated by an unconscious impulse to get away from the danger, Harrington sped up, tightly gripping the wheel and concentrating on the ruts in the snow. Crossing over the bridge, he searched for the turn. 'Where the hell is it,' he muttered, struggling to see through the thick curtain of snow and wincing as a shell whistled overhead and burst in an orange flash. He drove for another hundred yards and then slowed to a stop. He climbed out and walked back to Pierce's car.

'I think we missed the turn,' said Harrington. 'I can't see a thing.'

'But look,' said Talbot, pointing ahead, 'aren't those fresh tyre tracks?'

Harrington walked past his Model T and knelt down to examine the ruts in the snow.

'What is it?' asked Bill Larrabee, holding his arms around himself in the cold.

'Must be the tracks of the group that left ahead of us,' replied Harrington. 'I don't know if we're on the right road.' One of the men in his ambulance was calling for water.

'Well,' said Larrabee, 'let's keep going and see if we find them.'

'OK,' said Harrington, 'but look for a turn to the left.'

They drove a short distance further down the road, vaguely aware they were climbing a gentle slope. Just as they breasted the hill, a rocket shot into the sky, bursting into a star-shell that glimmered in the low clouds.

'Jeez!' exclaimed Harrington, slamming on the brakes and skidding in the snow. The road disappeared into an open field. In the pale light of the star-shell he could clearly see three AFS ambulances moving slowly, blindly, across the open ground. Pierce pulled up beside Harrington, with Larrabee and Borden in line behind him. As they watched, the lead ambulance traversing the field suddenly exploded in an orange fireball, a direct hit, causing the cars following behind to overturn.

'Oh, my God!' cried Talbot.

'Let's get the hell out of here!' yelled Larrabee. 'We're sitting ducks!' He shifted into reverse and hit the gas, smashing into Borden's ambulance.

'We can't leave them!' cried Talbot, appealing to Harrington with a look of disbelief in his eyes. Harrington thought he could see several men stumbling out of the flaming wreckage.

'C'mon, Frank!' shouted Larrabee. 'We'll just get ourselves killed...'

Pierce suddenly gunned his engine and started forward. 'Talbot!' called Harrington. 'Stop!'

He realized in an instant it was too late, popped the clutch and jammed his boot on the accelerator. The Fords ploughed through the thick powder, sliding and slewing down the gentle slope. Harrington could clearly see the men silhouetted against the burning ambulance, waving their arms. As the star-shell thankfully winked out, Harrington sped up, closing the gap with Talbot. Almost there, he thought .... *C'mon now...*

He was dimly conscious of a tremendous concussion, a brilliant flash of crimson-orange, the image of Talbot's car hurtling into the air ... and then all was blackness.

21

Kit stood at the gate, admiring the long row of identical townhouses. The quiet elegance of Onslow Gardens, the perfect symmetry of the architecture, struck her as the essence of the ordered, tranquil world she remembered before the war, before Europe had gone mad. She doubted things would ever be the same, and she wasn't sure how much longer she could bear it, reading of the horrors day after day, and still no word from Frank.

Maggie greeted her at the door with a grim, funereal expression. They might as well have hung crepe, thought Kit, after she announced that she was returning to France.

'You're too late for tea,' said Maggie.

'I know,' said Kit with a wan smile. 'But I'd wager the cook saved me a piece of shortbread.'

Kit sat at the kitchen table waiting for the teakettle to whistle, watching the housekeeper who'd supervised the family's servants since Kit was a child. There were strands of grey in her tight bun now and a slight stoop to her shoulders. Lifting the kettle from the stove, Maggie poured and waited for the leaves to steep.

'Your poor mother,' she said as she handed Kit a small plate of shortbread. 'She breaks into tears when she thinks no one's watching.'

'Well,' said Kit after taking a nibble, 'Mother shouldn't worry. I'll be fine. But I understand it's difficult for her.'

Maggie poured a cup from the pot and placed it before Kit. 'You could stay, of course,' she said, 'working at Brompton...'

'Maggie...'

'It's not so much your *duty* to go back, is it, but more that you want...' She stopped and looked at Kit with her sad, grey eyes.

What, Maggie? thought Kit. Want what?

'To be with *him*. With the ... the other gentleman.' Never married, she found it difficult to discuss matters of the heart. 'The American,' she added quietly.

Kit nodded and said, 'Yes. It's true. I can say it to you,' she confessed. 'If it weren't for Frank, I wouldn't be leaving.'

'And Captain Owen?'

'Captain Owen and I are, well, friends. And besides, he's returning to his regiment.'

'I see. You've scarcely touched your shortbread.'

'You don't mind if I smoke?' said Kit as she reached into her purse for a cigarette and box of matches. Ignoring Maggie's exaggerated look of disapproval, she lit it and blew out the match. 'You see,' she said, taking a drag and expelling a cloud of smoke, 'I'm in love with Frank. And he loves me. I'd never been in love before.' The declaration caused the housekeeper to blush. 'There's more to my wanting to go back, of course,' insisted Kit. 'I'm needed badly at the hospital. But I'm desperate to be with him.' She heard the doorbell chime.

Maggie looked up, listening for the butler's tread on the stairs and the sound of the door opening. 'Too early for your father,' she commented.

Moments later Burton entered the kitchen, holding an envelope. 'It's a telegram,' he said with a worried expression. 'For Miss Stanley .' He handed it to her.

Kit briefly studied the envelope, immediately perceiving it was from France. Her heart pounding, she stubbed out the cigarette on her plate and quickly stood up. 'I'll be in my room,' she said as she hurried to the stairs.

Kit tossed the yellow sheet onto the counterpane, stood up and walked over to the basin on the dressing table. Bending over, she repeatedly splashed water on her face, thinking it might help stop the tears. *Gravely injured*, she thought – a term that Elsie, with her training, had chosen advisedly. No doubt it meant he was clinging to his life. Towelling off her face, she knew precisely what she must do. She would take the first train in the morning to Dover, cross the Channel and board the express to Paris. Pulling open the drawer, she began laying out her things on the bed, packing enough clothes for an extended stay.

After several minutes there was a gentle tap on the door. 'Yes,' said Kit hoarsely. 'What is it?'

The door opened to reveal her mother. 'Kit?' she said, taking a step into the room. 'All you all right?'

Kit nodded, rubbing her eyes.

'What's this?' said Mrs Stanley, pointing to the bed. 'Kit – you've been crying.'

'Yes,' Kit mumbled, suppressing a sob. 'Here,' she said, picking up the telegram. 'Read this.' She handed it to her mother.

Mrs Stanley held a hand to her mouth as she quickly scanned the message. Glancing from the clothes on the bed to her daughter, she said, 'You're going?'

'Yes, Mother, on the first train in the morning.'

'But where is this ... Neuilly?'

'It's a suburb of Paris, and there's a fine American hospital there.' Kit walked over and placed a hand on her mother's shoulder. 'Frank's badly wounded,' she said. 'I've got to see him.'

* * *

'Still sleeping?' the doctor quietly asked the nurse standing at the foot-rail of the bed. The patient was obscured by a cloth-covered partition separating his bed from the next in the long, high-ceilinged ward.

'Yes, Doctor,' replied the nurse. 'When he began to stir, we gave him more of the analgesic.'

'When was the last injection?'

The nurse consulted the patient's chart. 'Two o'clock,' she said. 'It should be wearing off.'

'Let's have a look,' said the doctor. Pulling the screen aside, he studied the tall, young man in the weak light shining through the high windows. Most of his face was covered by a bandage, though one bruised and swollen eye was exposed, and his left leg, from the thigh to the ankle, was encased in plaster of Paris. Though sleeping, he grimaced and partly opened his mouth.

'Ohh,' he moaned. As the doctor watched, the young man opened his badly swollen eye. At first he registered no recognition, but then swallowed and managed to say, 'Could I have a drink ... of water?'

The nursed poured a glass from a carafe and held it to his lips. 'Thank you,' he murmured. Looking from the nurse to the doctor, he said, 'Where am I?'

'In Neuilly,' said the doctor. 'At the American Hospital.'

'Neuilly,' said Frank Harrington, wincing in pain. 'How did I get here?'

'You were evacuated by train from the field hospital at Lemmes. The French owe a great debt of gratitude to the AFS, and so they saw to it you were returned to our care.'

Harrington nodded and another groan escaped his lips.

'Are you in much pain?' asked the doctor. 'You can have another injection.'

'I'll be OK,' said Harrington. 'How bad is it?'

The doctor glanced at the nurse, who bit her lower lip. 'You were seriously injured,' he replied. 'Concussion, internal injuries, as well as a badly broken leg. The main thing now, young man, is to try to rest.'

Harrington closed his eye and took a deep breath. As the doctor was turning to go, Harrington said, 'Have the others been by? The other drivers from my section?'

'Why, yes,' said the nurse. 'Several of your friends were here yesterday to ask about you. We couldn't allow them to see you, of course.' Turning to the doctor, she said, 'These were the two I mentioned, Major, who were responsible for rescuing him and the others under German fire.'

'I see,' said the doctor. 'It seems that you owe your life to your friends.'

'And your sister was by to see you as well,' said the nurse. 'A lieutenant in the nursing corps,' she explained to the doctor.

'Elsie?' said Frank, opening his eye. 'Elsie was here?'

The nurse nodded. 'She was here last evening, when you came out of surgery. She spoke directly to the surgeons.'

The muscles of Harrington's face seemed to relax, and he drew in a deep breath. Closing his eye, he said, 'I think I'll try to sleep now.'

*　　*　　*

Kit chose to dress in her VAD uniform for the long day's journey. After bidding her mother and father a tearful goodbye at Charing Cross, she boarded the train. Staring out the window, she thought back to the day she arrived in London before Christmas; the months she'd lingered, the operating theatre at Brompton, the long Tube journeys across town to the clinic, Nigel standing before her at the museum...

The ferry departed Dover in a driving rain, the crossing so rough that many of the young soldiers preferred the open deck to the crowded lounges, filled with seasick passengers. Unconcerned about expense, Kit bought a ticket on the express from Calais to Paris, arriving at the Gare St-Lazare by late afternoon, where she hired a taxi for the drive to Neuilly. Daylight was fading when she arrived at the impressive Victorian-style structure, formerly known as the Clinique Louis Pasteur, but now rechristened the Ambulance Américaine.

Staring up at the high ceiling, Harrington examined his dressing with his uninjured right hand. The thick bandage covered his belly and most of his chest, radiating pain if he tried turning over on his side. The serious pain, though, that took his breath away came from his leg, above and below the knee, eliciting a gasp at the slightest movement. With a sigh, he looked across the ward where a VAD was folding bandages in the supply cabinet. Gazing at her long, blue–grey dress, the apron tied at her waist and the white scarf covering her hair, he imagined that she was Kit.

'Sister,' he weakly called.

Glancing over her shoulder, the VAD put down the bandages she was folding and walked over to his bedside. 'Yes,' she said. 'Are you hurting?'

'Of course I'm hurting. But I have a question.'

'All right,' she said with a polite smile.

'It's about my leg,' he said. 'The doc didn't say it had gone septic, did he?'

'Septic?' she repeated. 'Why, no.' She lifted the covers and examined the exposed skin of his ankle. 'It looks fine,' she said. 'No sign of infection.'

'Thanks,' he said with a sigh. 'Now you can give me that shot.'

When Harrington awoke, the ward was dark, dimly illuminated by the gaslights at the door and a lamp at the nursing station midway down the long room. The windows were black and he had no idea of the hour. For the first time, however, he was not only thirsty but anxious for something to eat. The man in the bed next to him, whose leg was in traction, groaned loudly. Harrington could hear the sound of footsteps on the bare floor as well as voices, but was unable to see around the cloth partition. He was determined to get the nurse's attention and ask for a cup of broth and some toast. In the dim light he saw her walking slowly from bed to bed, almost as if she was counting the patients.

'Nurse,' he called softly, raising his good hand. He could tell she was one of the VADs, who hopefully would be more likely to grant his request than the stern American nurse. She slowly walked to the end of his bed, her face obscured by the shadows.

'Nurse,' he said, trying to sit up a little. 'I was wondering whether...'

'Frank?' she said. 'Frank?'

When she took a step closer he could see her face beneath the scarf. Tears welled in his eyes. 'Oh, Kit,' he murmured. 'Oh, my God.'

She gently took his uninjured hand and bent down to kiss him. She looked at his face, bravely fighting back tears. 'Oh, Frank,' she said. 'Thank God you're alive.'

'I ... I didn't know if you...' He swallowed hard, unable to go on.

'Shh,' she said. 'Don't try to talk. It's going to be all right now. Everything's going to be all right.'

JOHN C. KERR

In Memoriam

Robert Talbot Pierce. Killed at Verdun,
25 February 1916

Lieutenant Albert S. Barnes. Killed in action,
Thiepval, the Somme, 21 July 1916

Major Nigel Owen. Killed in action, Passchendaele,
Flanders, 18 August 1917